ON A DARKLING PLAIN
BY RICHARD LEE BYERS

A novel based on the Vampire: The Eternal Struggle™

Collectible Card Game from Wizards of the Coast™

White Wolf
Publishing

Cover Illustration: Drew Tucker
Art Direction and Cover Design: Michelle Prahler

Printed in Canada

For Debra

And we are here as on a darkling plain
Swept with confused alarms of struggle and flight,
Where ignorant armies clash by night.
— Matthew Arnold, "Dover Beach"

PROLOGUE: CALAMITIES

When sorrows come, they come not single spies,
But in battalions.
— William Shakespeare, *Hamlet*

The marble facade of the Sarasota Performing Arts Center shone ghostly white in the starlight. Above the main entrance, sixty-foot composite columns rose to an entablature carved with scenes from American history, where a knowledgeable vampire could pick out the portraits of the undead lords who had steered the course of the republic. The structure's attic story was a fantastic wedding cake of lanterns, pediments and balustrades.

As he climbed out of his vintage Jaguar into the balmy night air, Elliott Sinclair remembered how, arriving on other nights, he'd been transfixed by the building's beauty. Or amused by its pretentiousness. And in either case, eager to sample the evening's entertainment. Now he vaguely dreaded walking into it. But he had nowhere else he'd rather be, nothing to do that would please him better, so he glumly supposed he might as well honor his social obligations.

Elliott surrendered the car to a liveried mortal valet, then set to work on his appearance. He no longer truly cared how he looked, but a habit cultivated over centuries died hard. He combed his long gray hair and smoothed down his eyebrows. Wiped his mouth to remove any lingering trace of blood. Made sure his elegant black tuxedo draped his tall, gaunt frame properly and that his patent-leather shoes still gleamed. When satisfied, he composed his aquiline features into an amiable smile and sauntered into the foyer.

No one was there but a pair of servants. No doubt the prince's guests, Kindred elders from all over the South, were gossiping and sipping blood from crystal glasses in the grand saloon. Elliott gave the attendants an affable nod, then climbed the stairs to join his peers. He passed one gorgeous Impressionist painting after another without sparing any of them a glance.

Upon entering the grand saloon, he saw that nearly everyone on the guest list had chosen to attend. He wasn't surprised. Kindred of Clan Toreador, his bloodline, were the unchallenged arbiters of taste and style in vampire society, and thus their soirées were the high points of the social calendar. Even undead too gauche to appreciate the entertainment turned out to hear news, conspire in shadowy corners, and demonstrate that they were of sufficient consequence to receive an invitation.

Working his way around the edge of the room toward the polished ebony bar, Elliott passed an exquisite Chinese porcelain vase full of lavender orchids. Like many Toreador, he possessed preternaturally keen senses, and to him the flowers' fragrance was almost unpleasantly heady.

Emerging from the cloud of scent, he brushed past two elders with whom he was acquainted. One was Catherine Cobb, a blond, Junoesque Ventrue. Like many members of her backward-looking clan she wore antique clothing: in her case an elaborate powdered wig and a rose-colored gown appropriate for the court of Louis XIV. The other vampire was Otis McNamara, a short Brujah with a coppery handlebar mustache and an iron ring in his septum. Kindred of Otis' bloodline revelled in their reputation as the rebels of the Camarilla, the sect that united and governed, however haphazardly, the seven principal vampire clans; Elliott wasn't surprised to see that the redhead had eschewed formal wear for scuffed, steel-toed boots, torn jeans and a motorcycle jacket.

For some reason Elliott had never fathomed, Catherine and Otis were deadly enemies. Had they met in another setting, they probably would have tried to destroy one another. But the Performing Arts Center was an Elysium, a sanctum where violence between Kindred was forbidden, and here the two rivals stood chatting with every appearance of amiability. The display of suavity was no doubt winning high marks from their peers, for whom poise was virtually a religion.

Though Elliott had felt obliged to put in an appearance at the soirée, he didn't want to talk to anyone. He tried to slip past Catherine and Otis quickly, before they noticed him. But the Brujah turned, grinned, and gripped his forearm.

"El!" Otis boomed. "How ya doin'?" The vitae in his half-empty glass smelled rich and appetizing.

Sighing inwardly, Elliott gave his fellow undead a cordial smile. "I'm well, old friend. How are both of you?"

"I'm very well," said Catherine. She offered her beringed, satin-gloved hand and Elliott bowed over it and kissed it. "Despite a certain unfulfilled longing for intelligent conversation." She gave Otis a malicious smile. "When I arrived and didn't see you, Elliott darling, I hoped it was because you were preparing to perform."

"Alas, tonight's play didn't have an appropriate part for me," Elliott lied.

"Fiddlesticks," said Catherine, pouting. "No part for an actor who can play *any* role superbly?"

"You're too kind," said Elliott. "But I'm sure that with Prince Roger playing the lead, you won't miss me."

"I was hoping it would turn out that you'd written the damn show," Otis said. "*Your* stuff doesn't put me to sleep. But I guess you didn't, did you, or you'd be backstage."

"No," Elliott said. "One of Roger's mortal protégés did the honors. It's a wonderful piece." At least Elliott assumed it was. Despite Roger's urging, he hadn't read it.

Otis grimaced. A fleeting, unaccustomed gentleness came into his jade-green eyes. "Do you think you'll ever act or write anything again?" he asked.

"Of course," Elliott said, annoyed at the Brujah's prying but holding his smile in place. "I'm just taking some time off. Recharging my batteries."

Clearly undeceived, Catherine said, "Do you intend to mourn *forever*, chèri? I can't believe that Mary would have wanted that."

For some reason the mention of his late wife's name infuriated Elliott. Who the devil was Catherine to tell him how to grieve? He opened his mouth to say as much, then heard the rapid thump of a heartbeat, and pattering footsteps scurrying up behind him.

Kindred hearts didn't beat; obviously, one of the mortal servants was approaching. Grateful for the interruption which had prevented him from indulging in a shamefully unseemly outburst, Elliott turned and saw Lazlo, Roger's personal dresser and valet. "Did you want me?" the Toreador asked.

Lazlo was a stooped, balding man with horn-rimmed glasses. As usual, he had a sewing kit clipped to his belt. "I'm sorry to interrupt," he said breathlessly, "but Mr. Sinclair, can you come? There's" — he hesitated — "a little problem."

Thank God, Elliott thought. Here was his chance to extricate himself from his fellow vampires' clutches. "Of course," he said. "If I'm needed." He smiled at Catherine and Otis. "Please excuse me."

Lazlo led Elliott out of the grand saloon, then shut the

ornate art deco door. "I'm so glad you're here," the dresser half-whispered. "The prince didn't think you were going to come."

"Well, I did," Elliott said, unconsciously adjusting his cuffs. "But frankly, that doesn't mean I want to sort out whatever opening-night snafu may have arisen backstage. Where's the stage manager? Go tell him."

"You don't understand," Lazlo said, his voice still lowered. He glanced around as if worried that someone might be lurking at his elbow, eavesdropping. "It's not the show. Something's wrong with the prince himself!"

Elliott frowned. "What do you mean?"

"I don't want to say," Lazlo replied. "Not here." Elliott supposed that, considering the hyperacute hearing of some vampires and the powers of invisibility possessed by others, the dresser's caution was appropriate. "Just come and see."

"All right," Elliott agreed reluctantly.

Lazlo ushered him back to the ground floor and then through the maze of rooms and twisting corridors beneath the stage. Elliott, who possessed the vampire power of superhuman speed, kept drawing ahead of his scurrying human companion. He guessed that he'd caught Lazlo's sense of urgency, the weariness and ennui that had dogged him these last few years notwithstanding. As they neared the dressing rooms, the Toreador heard voices murmuring back and forth.

As befitted his status as Prince of Sarasota and star of the production, Roger occupied a well-appointed suite consisting of a dressing room and a sitting room. Entering, Elliott found his lord and sire sprawled on a red leather couch in the latter chamber, with fully fifteen of his lean, pallid, bright-eyed followers hovering anxiously around him. Relying on a constant influx of tourists to replenish the blood supply, and on the Kindred of his domain to hunt unobtrusively, Roger had permitted his vassals to beget more childer than were generally found in cities of comparable size.

Roger Phillips was a tall, broad-shouldered man with a strong, deeply cleft chin and a curly mane of lustrous chestnut hair. He was already in costume — an outfit incorporating a grimy, many-pocketed photojournalist's vest with a press badge clipped to it — and a layer of makeup stained his alabaster face. Elliott was shocked to see that the prince was trembling and his wide, expressive mouth was twitching. His blue eyes were glazed.

Pushing through the crowd, Elliott made his way to Roger. Dropping to one knee so they could talk face to face, he said, "Sire! What's wrong?"

"Nothing," Roger croaked. Elliott was horrified by the labored rasp of his sire's voice. "I'm just a little under the weather."

"Do you mean you're ill?" Elliott asked, praying the answer was no. Kindred diseases, contracted by imbibing tainted blood, were always serious and frequently fatal.

"No," Roger growled. He tried to stand up, lost his balance, and sprawled back on the couch.

"Just rest," said Elliott. "We'll help you."

"No!" said Roger. He lurched up again, this time making it to his feet. "We have a performance. I've never missed one, and I'm not about to start now."

"I don't think you have a choice," Elliott said. Roger swayed, and the younger vampire took his arm to support him. "It's obvious something's happening to you, something serious. For all we know, your life could be in danger."

"Mr. Sinclair is right," said Lazlo firmly, edging through the mass of vampires. Amid a crowd of Toreador, many of whom had been inducted into the clan for their beauty and grace, the aging mortal looked homely, flabby and decrepit. "I think we should call your doc—"

"Damn you!" Roger screamed. He tore his arm out of Elliott's grasp, stumbling and nearly dumping himself back on the sofa in the process. "I'm fine! Why do you keep insisting otherwise?" He peered at Elliott, squinting as if he were having trouble seeing him. "Are you trying to make me look weak? Undermine my authority?"

"No!" said Elliott, astonished.

"Sneaky little rat," said Roger. His gleaming fangs lengthened, garbling his speech. "Creeping around behind my back, plotting and spreading rumors about me! Want to be prince yourself, don't you?"

"No!" Elliott repeated. He couldn't imagine how anyone could suspect he wanted to seize the throne, not when he'd spent the years since Mary's death shirking his less-demanding duties as a member of the primogen, Roger's council of lieutenants. Nor could he fathom how the man who'd made him a vampire could suspect him of *any* treachery. Through their four centuries of constant association, acting, sharing the joys and pains of vampire existence and guarding one another's backs, Roger had always treated his childe like a favorite son, and Elliott had responded with uncompromising devotion. "I assure you—"

Roger rounded drunkenly on the other Toreador. "How about the rest of you?" he said. Despite his manifest irrationality and the slurring of his speech, in his fury he began to radiate a palpable force of personality. Like many of his bloodline had a preternatural ability to influence an audience, and even though Elliott knew his sire was exerting the talent, even though he possessed the same power himself, he felt a wave of shame and fear wash through him, making his knees wobbly. "Do you want to pull me down? Would you rather see this gutless fop in my place?"

"No!" cried Amanda, a willowy young neonate only recently released from her maker's care. "We love you, Roger!"

"Then take your damn places!" snarled the prince. The other members of the cast and crew exited the suite, some scuttling, anxious to get away from him, and others dragging their feet, looking helplessly at one another.

Exerting his will, Elliott managed to cast off the unnatural fear with which Roger's voice had filled him. "Please," he said to the prince, "don't endanger yourself needlessly. You don't have to go on. We'll think of an excuse to cancel the performance, something that won't alert our guests that anything's wrong with you." Kindred society was rife with both hypocrisy and murderous intrigue. Though every elder in the grand saloon professed to be Roger's friend, it would be foolhardy to let them know he'd fallen ill. Someone might decide to strike at him in his hour of weakness.

Roger smiled and squeezed Elliott's shoulder, just as if he hadn't accused his offspring of treachery only a moment before. "Good old El, always looking out for me. But you worry too much." He staggered out the door and vanished in the direction of the stage.

Lazlo was cowering in the corner, where the force of Roger's rage had driven him. Panting, his face beaded with sweat, he said, "You see what he's like? Completely irrational! How can we help him?"

"I don't know," Elliott said, frowning. "One thing's obvious. He'll go on unless we physically restrain him. And I doubt anyone's willing to go that far. He might *really* decide that we were traitors. Indeed, he might destroy us on the spot." Older vampires were almost invariably more powerful than younger ones, and thus Roger, even in a debilitated condition, might well prove more formidable than any of his brood.

"But he'll disgrace himself!" said Lazlo, his wrinkled face a mask of anguish.

The mortal was in so much distress that Elliott felt an urge to reassure him. "Perhaps not," he said, exerting his own unnatural powers of persuasion. "Perhaps his problem is that he drank from someone intoxicated. If so, he may be himself again by the time the curtain goes up."

Lazlo peered at Elliott dubiously. "Do you really think that's what's wrong? He's usually so careful about his vitae."

Elliott shrugged. "That's a matter of opinion. He usually drinks from actors or other artists. You know what we're like. Always putting something down our throats, in our arms, or up our noses. I'll tell you what. Speak to the stage manager. Ask him to find an excuse to hold the curtain for a few minutes, to give Roger that much more time to recover." He gave the dresser an encouraging smile.

"Good idea!" cried Lazlo, abruptly succumbing to the vampire's influence. The mortal scurried out of the room.

Wishing that he had some method of easing his own fretful mind, Elliott made his way back upstairs and took a seat in one of the shadowy boxes overlooking the stage. The rest of the audience would no doubt choose to sit in the orchestra, where the view was better, and now that he was worried about Roger he was even less inclined to socialize with them than he'd been before.

He wondered if Roger really *had* drunk blood laced with alcohol or drugs. Lazlo was right; given the prince's habits, it seemed unlikely. But Elliott *hoped* it was true, because all the other possibilities were worse.

He prayed that, whatever was wrong, Roger would give a creditable performance. It wasn't impossible. During his centuries as an actor, Elliott had seen his fellow artists work drunk, starving, and afflicted with influenza and pneumonia. The attention of an audience enabled them to tap into some mysterious reserve of inner strength.

Except, of course, when it didn't, and the poor wretches wound up collapsing or babbling lines from the wrong play.

Elliott wished he could just get up and leave. Whatever was wrong, let someone else put it right. His labors, his days of troubleshooting problems, were supposed to be over. But he couldn't go. However joyless his current existence was, he'd been happy once, and he owed that happiness to Roger. If the Toreador prince hadn't made him a vampire, extending his life beyond any mortal's natural span, Elliott would never have met Mary. Roger had even introduced him to her at the riotous party following the opening of *The Old Bachelor* at Drury Lane.

After a few minutes, the house lights dimmed and brightened. Elliott knew they were doing so throughout the building, signalling the imminent beginning of the play. Shortly thereafter, the guests filed into the cavernous auditorium and selected seats in the first few rows. Gazing down at them, Elliott noticed that Otis and Catherine had chosen to sit together. He wondered absently if they'd decided to make peace. That too seemed unlikely. It was a rare vampire indeed who ever forgot a grudge.

The hall darkened, and the crowd fell silent. With a whisper of ropes and pulleys, the golden curtain rose toward the masks of comedy and tragedy carved on the proscenium arch. The spotlight picked out two Toreador standing center stage. Both were costumed and made up as Vietnamese peasants.

As the scene unfolded, they did their best to give a good performance. Still, Elliott could see that they were carrying themselves a little stiffly, and hear a subtle undercurrent of tension in their voices. Obviously they were anticipating Roger's entrance as nervously as he was.

Eventually one of the peasants said, "The village has to eat. We can always make more children." Then the two actors fell silent, as if awaiting some event, but nothing happened.

"We can always make more children," the actor repeated after a moment. Elliott surmised that someone, probably Roger, had missed his cue.

Sure enough, wiping his face with a red bandanna, a camera hanging around his neck, the Toreador prince strode in from stage right. He was moving with his customary grace, and Elliott felt a pang of hope. Whatever his mysterious malady had been, maybe Roger had recovered.

"How can you people live in this heat?" Roger said peevishly. "Where am I, anyway?"

"Ten miles outside An Tuc," said one of the other actors.

Roger frowned as though perplexed and then, suddenly, sneered. His fangs began to lengthen.

With his hypersensitive hearing, Elliott heard the prompter stationed in the prompt box at the front of the stage whisper Roger's next line: "Shit. No way am I walking that far. Where can I hire a car?"

With one violent motion, Roger tore the camera from around his neck, breaking the sturdy leather strap in the process, and hurled it into the concealed opening of the prompt box. Elliott heard the device shatter and the prompter's body thump to the floor.

Roger's fellow actors goggled at him in horror. The audience sat in stunned silence for a moment. Then they murmured and leaned forward, peering with heightened interest, as if they'd decided that Roger's behavior, however aberrant it seemed, must be a part of the show.

"Bastards," the prince snarled to the peasants. "Trying to upstage me. Trying to ruin my reputation."

One of the actors pivoted toward stage left and gestured frantically. Elliott assumed that the performer was signalling to someone to lower the curtain. It didn't come down. Perhaps the stagehands were frozen in dismay.

"And you," slurred Roger as, swaying, he rounded on the audience. "You think you're bloodsucking little gods, don't you? The lords of creation. Well, I say you're corpses. Vermin. A pack of mosquitoes and fleas."

Shocked, the thin, white faces of the spectators gaped up at him. Such insults were egregiously offensive and a gross breach of the etiquette proper to any Elysium whether a part of the script or not, although, somewhere in the darkened hall, a single thick-skinned Kindred was chuckling appreciatively.

"Want some vitae, little fleas?" Roger mumbled, his long ivory fangs extending fully. "Of course you do." Lifting his bare right forearm to his mouth, he scored his flesh from elbow to knuckles. The coppery aroma of Kindred vitae, even sweeter and more enticing than that of mortals, suffused the air. Red drops, shining like rubies in the spotlight, pattered onto the stage. The prince started to tear open his left arm.

"No, sire, please!" cried one of the actors. The two faux Vietnamese grabbed their leader, trying to wrestle his muscular arm away from his bloodstained lips.

Roger knocked one peasant on his butt with an elbow to the belly, then hurled the other crashing into the orchestra pit. As the first actor tried to scramble to his feet, the prince whirled and kicked him in the jaw. Bone snapped, and the performer slumped back down.

Intending to help restrain Roger, Elliott surged to his feet. Some of the audience did the same. Voices babbled backstage.

Turning, suddenly looking as formidable as a crazed, maimed god, Roger stared at his would-be rescuers. A spasm of unreasoning dread locked Elliott in place. Below him, vampires recoiled back down into their plushly upholstered seats.

The Toreador prince tore open his other arm, thrust his fingers into the gaping gashes, and flicked spatters of vitae into the orchestra pit. "Go on!" he cried. "Soup's on! Get down on your knees and lick it up!"

No one moved.

After a moment, Roger said, "Well, perhaps I've misjudged you. Maybe you're not fleas, but maggots. In that case, have some carrion!" He put his index finger between his teeth and bit down hard, evidently intending to sever it and throw it to the crowd as well.

Elliott wondered sickly if Roger meant to dismember or even destroy himself completely. His horror at the prospect drove the paralyzing awe out of his mind. Moving faster and more nimbly than any human acrobat, he scrambled onto the gilded, rococo balustrade of his box and leaped down toward the stage.

He slammed down on the edge of the platform. The impact jolted pain through his joints and threw him to one knee, but he was all right; the fall hadn't torn any ligaments or broken any bones. Roger spun around, snatching his bloody hand away from his mouth.

Elliott tried to project his own unnatural charisma. "Please, take it easy," he crooned soothingly. "I'm your friend. Your faithful childe. I want to help you."

Roger snarled and lunged at him.

Elliott twisted aside, slamming his fist into Roger's kidney as the prince blundered past. But, unlike certain other Kindred, the younger vampire only possessed the strength of an ordinary human. In his delirium, Roger didn't even seem to feel the blow.

Spinning, Roger kicked at Elliott's head. Elliott ducked, then sprang forward, right into a second kick to the solar plexus. The impact threw him halfway across the stage and down onto his back. Black spots swam before his eyes.

Christ, he thought, dazed, trying desperately to clamber to his feet, *how can he move like a drunk one second and Bruce Lee the next?*

Addled with pain, Elliott never even sensed Roger approaching. But without warning, another kick smashed against the younger vampire's temple, hurling him back down onto the stage. Roger dove on top of him and pinned him.

Elliott struggled, but couldn't break free. The punishment he'd taken had stolen his strength. Roger opened his jaws and lowered his head toward his opponent's throat. Elliott realized that, despite the presence of nearly one hundred witnesses, despite the fact that diablerie, the practice of preying on one's fellow vampires, was perhaps the most heinous crime an undead could commit, Roger meant to drink his blood.

"No," Elliott gasped, gazing imploringly into Roger's maddened eyes. "Please. If the other elders see you do this, they won't rest until they've destroyed you."

"To hell with them and to hell with you," Roger replied. Overcoming Elliott's last feeble attempt to fend him off, he plunged his canines into his childe's neck.

Elliott felt a stab of pain, then a wave of numbness. One part of his mind gibbered in terror, even while another part opened itself willingly to the final death, to an end to futility and sorrow. He prayed that he was about to see Mary again.

Then several of his fellow Toreador charged onto the stage. Apparently they too had finally managed to break through the artificial cowardice Roger had implanted in their minds. They grabbed the prince and pulled him off his victim. As Roger's fangs tore free, they ripped ragged gashes in Elliott's throat.

Roger struggled in the grasp of his childer for another moment, then went limp. His eyes rolled back in his head as the younger Kindred began to haul him offstage.

Amanda, the same slender, fresh-faced cheerleader of a neonate who had assured Roger earlier that his offspring loved him, knelt beside Elliott. "Are you all right?" she asked, her eyes wide with concern.

Feeling addled and slow, Elliott gingerly touched his wounded neck. The gashes were closing, though more slowly than if they'd been inflicted by a blade or the teeth of a natural creature. "I'll be all right," he managed. "Just help me up. Get me offstage." It wasn't prudent for *him* to look weak and helpless in front of his peers, either. In any case, a pride he'd half-forgotten he possessed rebelled at the prospect of further humiliation.

The neonate lifted him to his feet and draped his arm around her shoulders, helping him toward the wings. His head swam; the theater seemed to spin around him. The audience, now convinced that what they'd witnessed had been real, maliciously rejoicing in the disaster that had overtaken the Kindred of Sarasota, began to applaud.

◆

The aquarium was a four-story box of a building standing beside the Gulf of Mexico. A huge, wraparound mural of whales and porpoises, only vaguely visible in the darkness, decorated the exterior. By the time Forbes and his partner Ryan pulled up in front of the staff entrance, one of the facility employees was waiting under the light on the stoop to let them in. She was a dumpy, middle-aged woman dressed in a baggy gray sweat suit. With her short, gray-brown hair disheveled, she looked as if she'd been dragged out of bed. Given the lateness of the hour, that was no doubt precisely the case.

The two policemen, clad in green uniforms with orange trim, climbed out of the prowl car. Forbes, a lanky man with a straw-colored crewcut, paused for just a second to savor the cool sea breeze and the murmur of the ghost-white breakers. Ryan, a burly African-American with a neatly trimmed mustache and a broken nose, hitched up his gun belt, trying to position it comfortably over the beer gut he'd been growing for the past two years.

"Let's take care of this nonsense as fast as possible," Ryan said. "We've had to stay past end-of-shift the last two nights. I'll be damned if I'm going to do it again this morning."

"I'm with you," Forbes said. "I'd like to get home in time to see the wife before she goes off to work. Maybe even catch her still in bed, if you get my drift." God knew, he and Julie didn't get nearly enough quality time together. He loved being a cop, but working his current hours was playing hell with his home life.

The two men hurried up the sidewalk that led to the entrance. "Thank goodness you're here," the dumpy woman said. "I'm sure there's nothing to this, but I was getting nervous, waiting here by myself."

"It would have been safer to wait in your car with the windows up and the doors locked," Forbes said reflexively. Then, realizing that this little safety tip might spook the woman even more, he gave her a reassuring smile. "But you're okay, so what the heck. I'm Sergeant Forbes and this is Officer Ryan."

"I'm Mattie Purvis," she replied. "Mr. Bronson's assistant. Of course I was glad to come when the police called, but I can't imagine how there could be a dead body inside the building. How could anybody *get* it inside without setting off the alarms?"

"Beats us," said Ryan wryly. "All we know is that an anonymous caller phoned 911 and said you had a corpse on the premises. Ninety-nine chances out of a hundred it was a crank call, but we've got to check it out anyway. So if you could please let us in?"

"All right," said Mattie, lifting the jingling key ring in her hand. She unlocked three locks, then ushered the policemen through the door and into the hallway beyond.

The corridor was far darker than the moonlit night outside. Though Forbes was as sure as Ryan that this call was bogus, for some reason a chill oozed up his spine. For a moment he nearly believed that something terrible might be waiting in the lightless rooms and passages ahead. Then Mattie threw a wall switch. Down the length of the hall, fluorescent lights pinged and flickered on, and his momentary trepidation dissolved.

Forbes grinned sheepishly. He was a day person. He'd always hated the graveyard shift, even before he had a relationship for it to disrupt, and he guessed it was getting on his nerves again. He was glad Ryan apparently hadn't noticed his jitters. His partner would have kidded him mercilessly.

"Let's get to it," Ryan said.

They worked their way through a series of hallways, checking cramped offices and storerooms full of janitorial supplies, bundles of promotional brochures and barrels of fish food. They didn't find a body.

"Let's move on to the part of the building where the public goes," said Forbes at length.

Mattie conducted the cops to the atrium inside the main entrance. When she turned on the lights, Forbes saw that the floor was decorated with a tile mosaic of teeming undersea life. Similar frescoes adorned the walls. Beside the exterior door was a kiosk with books on ichthyology and bright cloisonné jewelry fashioned to resemble tropical fish on display. A map and directory had been mounted on the wall to guide patrons to the various exhibits, including *Florida's Rivers*, *Wonders of the Reef*, and *Manatee Encounter*.

Mattie pointed to one of the arches along the wall. "This way?" she suggested, the statement garbled by a gaping yawn.

Ryan shrugged. "Whatever. We're going to have to check out every inch of the place before we're through."

Mattie led them through another series of chambers. Whenever she switched the lights on, driving the darkness deeper into the building, the illumination revealed countless amberjacks, skates, eels, groupers, clowns, angels and gars, swimming sullenly back and forth in the blue-green world beyond the plate-glass walls.

To his disgust, Forbes felt his jitters creeping back. His mouth was dry and his stomach, queasy. Even though he knew how stupid it was, he couldn't shake the feeling that the fish behind the glass were staring at him. Or perhaps it was some presence lurking in the shadows that always hovered ahead of the searchers, no matter how many lights Mattie turned on.

Snap out of it! he silently ordered himself. But the uneasiness didn't go away.

He and his companions entered yet another room. It was no different from the one they'd just exited — merely an octagonal space with windows for walls and two long, backless wooden benches set in the otherwise bare linoleum floor — and yet his anxiety intensified.

Finally yielding to the feeling, he said, "Call me crazy, but I think there *might* be a body around here somewhere. Or some kind or problem, anyway."

Mattie gaped at him. Ryan's eyes narrowed quizzically. "Why?" he asked.

Forbes shrugged helplessly. "Intuition. Something in the air. Can't you feel it?"

Ryan grimaced. "Frankly, no. You sure you didn't just get a bad burrito at Pablo's?"

"No," Forbes admitted. "I'm not sure of anything. But my instincts are telling me that something's wrong *here*. Right in front of us."

Ryan gestured at the largely empty space around them. "If there is, you'll have to show me, because I sure don't see it."

Squinting, stooping low, Forbes scrutinized the surfaces of the benches and the floor. Behind the walls sea creatures drifted and darted, some as beautiful and delicately shaped as butterflies, and others as dark and grotesquely formed as the denizens of a nightmare.

Forbes didn't find any bloodstains, or anything else suspicious. In the face of Ryan's skepticism he was feeling increasingly like a fool, yet his nervousness still wouldn't go away.

"Well?" said Ryan. "Ready to move on? I'm sure Ms. Purvis would appreciate it. If we hurry, she might have time to go home and catch another hour or two of sleep."

"Okay," said Forbes reluctantly. He straightened up and trudged toward the entrance to the next room in the chain.

But as he did, he glimpsed another peculiar form floating behind the glass. He couldn't make it out clearly, not from the corner of his eye, but he sensed a wrongness about it. His heart jolting, he turned.

The shape was the nude body of a little girl. Her wide brown eyes peered sightlessly through the glass, and her mouth gaped in a silent scream. An octopus had wrapped itself around her ankle, the ceaseless writhing of its tentacles mimicked by the stirring of her floating black pigtails. A cloud of small orange fish flickered around her, nibbling her flesh.

Forbes gasped and lurched backward. Sick with horror, he wondered vaguely why he and his companions hadn't seen the corpse right away. He supposed they'd been too intent on checking the rooms to pay much attention to what was on the other side of the glass. Or perhaps they'd unconsciously resisted the sight of anything so ghastly.

Mattie and Ryan turned. "What's wrong?" the black officer asked. His throat still clogged with revulsion, Forbes pointed at the little girl. Ryan cursed, and the woman squealed and wrenched her gaze away.

Ryan swallowed audibly. "Chalk one up for intuition," he said, moving closer to the window. Straining to reestablish a cop's properly stoic demeanor, Forbes followed him. The little girl's white hand brushed against the glass as if she were feebly knocking on a door.

"Do you think she drowned?" Ryan asked. "Hm, maybe not." He pointed. "Check out her throat."

Peering, Forbes saw that the child had twin punctures in the side of her neck. The marks looked like a vampire bite in a movie. In another situation such a ridiculous notion might have amused him, but now it only served to make his discovery seem even grislier.

"Let's call this in and seal the building," Forbes said grimly, reaching for the radio clipped to his belt. He turned. "Ms. Purvis, you might want to phone your boss—"

He faltered in bewilderment. The woman had disappeared.

Forbes guessed he must look as shaken as he felt, because Ryan gave his shoulder a reassuring squeeze. "Don't get rattled," he said. "I'm sure she just left the room while our backs were turned, so she wouldn't have to look at the kid. Can't say as I blame her." He raised his voice. "Ms. Purvis! Are you there? Answer me, please!"

The shout echoed hollowly down the lighted chain of rooms through which they'd come. No one answered. Forbes couldn't help feeling that his companion had bellowed in the wrong direction, that someone or something had dragged the plump woman into the stygian chambers ahead.

"I guess she panicked," said Ryan, a subtle tremor in his voice. "Ran all the way out of the building."

"Or the guy who killed the girl is still here," said Forbes. He could feel his pulse beating in his neck. "And he grabbed her."

"Without making enough noise for us to hear it six feet away?" Ryan asked.

"Yeah," said Forbes tensely. He knew the idea didn't make sense, but his instincts were shrieking that it was true — they hadn't been wrong so far.

Ryan grimaced. "I guess it could happen. So we'd better go look for her."

Forbes radioed the dispatcher to describe their situation and request backup. Then he and Ryan drew their .38 automatics. Since they no longer had Mattie, who knew where all the wall fixtures were, to guide them, they took their pencil flashlights out of their belts. Thus equipped, they crept warily into the dark.

The flashlight beams slid back and forth, illuminating a nurse shark and a starfish behind the glass. Forbes could hear Ryan's quick, shallow respiration and smell the sweat that had begun to soak his partner's shirt.

The policemen slunk around a corner, moving from one exhibition area to another. Now the massive gray forms of manatees, their backs grooved with white propeller scars, floated beyond the glass. Forbes' flashlight beam picked out another light switch. He moved toward it, and then a nearly inaudible tapping ticked through the blackness.

Forbes froze, reflexively holding his breath, waiting for the sound to reoccur. It didn't. "Did you hear that?" he whispered.

"I thought I heard *something*," Ryan answered. "I'm not sure."

Forbes abruptly realized what the noise had sounded like. "I think it was water dripping," he said.

"Maybe the killer got wet when he threw the body in the tank," said Ryan, sweeping his flashlight around the room. The beam revealed only the placidly drifting sea cows and empty space.

"If we are hearing him, he must be close," said Forbes. "Let's be really caref—"

Ryan's gun boomed. The roar was deafening in the enclosed space. The bullet cracked into the linoleum.

Yelping, Forbes spun around. His hand shaking, he shone his light on his partner. Ryan stared back at him with wide, stricken eyes. The black officer dropped his pistol and flashlight, then made a gurgling sound and clutched the side of his neck. His knees buckled, and he fell face down on the floor.

Forbes felt as if he were trapped in a nightmare. It wasn't possible that Ryan had been attacked. He'd swung his light around the room only a moment before and, except for the cops themselves, there hadn't been anyone there.

But possible or not, it had happened, and now, Forbes suddenly realized, the assailant might be creeping up on him. His heart hammering, he frantically swept his own light around until it flew across a round, inhuman face. He almost snapped off a shot before he realized that he was looking at one of the manatees.

The light didn't reveal the attacker.

Forbes flipped the wall switch and felt a wave of relief when the fluorescent tubes on the ceiling flickered on. Surely, if he watched his back, no one could sneak up on him now!

His own safety presumably secured, it was time to assist his partner. Forbes knelt beside the injured man. His knee landed in a spreading pool of blood. The coppery scent of the liquid rose to mingle with the tang of gun smoke drifting in the air. Ryan's breathing was a labored wheeze.

Forbes winced. It was obvious that his partner needed immediate first aid. With a pang of renewed trepidation, he set his .38 on the floor and took a folded white handkerchief out of his pocket. He pressed it against the twin punctures in Ryan's neck, wounds like the dead girl's, struggling to stanch the bleeding. In half a minute, the makeshift compress was red and sodden. The flow of blood wouldn't slow.

Forbes awkwardly used his left hand to switch on his radio. Static crackled. "This is Forbes," he said. "I have an officer down. Repeat, Officer Ryan is down. We're in the manatee exhibit. Get an ambulance."

"Understood," the tinny voice of the dispatcher replied. "Help is on the way."

After that, the minutes crawled by. Despite Forbes' best efforts, Ryan kept bleeding. Every few seconds, Forbes looked over his shoulder or glanced at his pistol to make sure it was still lying where he'd put it.

The murderer heard me radio for help, Forbes told himself. *So he must have run away by now. I'm not in danger anymore.* But he was having trouble believing it. Perhaps the phantom he'd been chasing wasn't afraid of a new contingent of cops. After all, the bastard hadn't had any trouble neutralizing the first wave.

Forbes looked around again. No one was behind him. Panting as if he'd run a marathon, his eyes stinging with unshed tears, he returned his attention to the dying Ryan. When he lifted his gaze again, only a moment later, he saw a smear of reflection on the aquarium window before him. It was barely visible, but seemed to possess a human shape.

Terrified, Forbes snatched for his gun. At the same instant, powerful hands grabbed him, jerked him to his feet, and thrust him toward the glass. With a burst of pain, his forehead slammed against the window. His shooting hand clenched convulsively, and the automatic blazed. Somewhere in the room, glass shattered and water gushed.

Forbes' assailant yanked him back from the window and pulled him against his body. A powerful arm wrapped itself around the policeman's chest and fresh pain ripped into his throat. His wife's face shone before Forbes' inner eye; then the world went black.

◆

Pallid and slender, her waist-length raven hair seeming to shine even now that the moon had set, the vampire paced along the eight-foot stucco wall, psychically sensing what lay on the other side. Her diaphanous white gown, her only garment, rippled in the night breeze, and the cool, dewy grass kissed her feet.

After a minute an image of guard dogs, stocky black animals with cropped tails and ears, entered her mind. Despite her anxieties, she smiled for an instant. She'd always found animals even easier to manage than she did humans. She stepped away from the wall and then bounded over it, noticing as she did so the alarm strip embedded in the top of the barrier.

She landed lightly, her lovely, inhumanly powerful legs soaking up the shock of impact. Before her extended a broad expanse of exquisitely manicured lawn, its flower beds planted with red and yellow roses and orange hibiscus with magenta eyes. To her sight, the colors shone as brightly by night as they would by daylight, and she could smell the sweet scent of the rose petals from fifty feet away.

Her sense of urgency notwithstanding, the loveliness of the grounds tugged at her, tempting her to linger. She no longer thought of herself as a Toreador. She'd long ago grown beyond such categorizations to become a singular entity. But she'd been reborn into undeath a Toreador, and her identity was still defined by the bloodline's fascination with art and beauty.

Shaking off the bewitching spell of the verdure, she walked toward the darkened mansion standing at the center of the grounds. A horned owl, a fellow night hunter, swooped over her head. Then three snarling hounds slunk out of the shadows.

She smiled at them and spread her arms. *I love you*, she thought, *and I want you to love me too.*

The animals stopped growling. One of them whined, as if ashamed of its truculent behavior. Their tails began to wag. She knelt and they ran to her, nuzzling, licking, lolling on their backs so she could tickle their stomachs. Their wet tongues laved her skin. She gave them all a good petting, crooning "Good boy," "What a pretty dog," and similar comments. For a moment, she felt a pang of nostalgia for her mortal childhood in Athens, when she'd romped with her father's hunting hounds.

After a minute she clambered to her feet. "Go away," she said, making shooing motions with her hands. "You're good dogs, but I can't take you in the house with me." The adoring canines permitted her to depart alone, but watched her mournfully as she walked away.

Nearing the house, she saw that it was a hideously botched attempt at a grand home in the neoclassical style, with an incongruous string of leering gargoyles running along the roof line. Obviously her unwitting host had been more fortunate in his landscaper than in his architect.

She climbed the circular steps to the twin-paneled front door. Instead of a keyhole, it had a keypad mounted on the jamb. She laid her hand lightly on the buttons. After a moment, the numbers eight, four and three came into her mind. She punched in the combination and the door clicked softly open.

She stepped into the vestibule. The smells of furniture polish, pipe tobacco and dry white wine hung in the air. Above her, on the second floor, the hearts of four humans slowly thumped while their breath sighed in and out. By the sound of it the mortals were all fast asleep. Easy prey, but not for her. Vampires as ancient as she could only be nourished by the blood of their fellow undead.

Her intuition urged her toward the arch directly opposite the front door. She stepped through it into the house's central hall, then gasped with delight.

A treasure trove of paintings hung along the walls. There was no rhyme or reason to the way the owner of the house had assembled his collection, or to the manner in which he'd chosen to display it. An early self-portrait by Picasso hung beside a gorgeously illuminated page from a medieval Bible, which in turn bordered a voluptuous nude by Rubens. But the disorder, the jarring clash of cultures and periods, didn't matter in the least, because every piece was magnificent. The vampire could have lost herself in any one of them for hours.

And they were *safe*. Intact. Perhaps the dream that had roused her from her year-long trance had been only a nightmare. Perhaps the masterpiece for which she feared was safe as well. Except for the warning embodied in her vision, she could think of no reason why it shouldn't be.

Encouraged, she paced on into what in the eighteenth century would have been the withdrawing room. Here it was an extension of the householder's art gallery; he'd eliminated the windows in the bowed back wall to provide more hanging space. The pictures here, a Wyeth and a Mondrian among them, were as exquisite as the ones in the central room. All except one: a portrait of an Elizabethan lady. The lady's shoulders, eggshell-colored ruff, long white neck and dark brown hair were as the vampire remembered them, but her face was only a muddy blur.

Aghast, moving as fast as a cheetah, the vampire rushed to the painting. A sharp, astringent smell stung her nostrils. Someone had employed a solvent to scour away the pigment of the Elizabethan lady's features, destroying the portrait beyond any hope of restoration.

The vampire lifted the picture gently off the wall. Holding it to her bosom as if it were her dead child, she dropped to her knees on the polished oak floor and rocked slowly back and forth.

John Kincaid had painted this portrait: grinning, mercurial John. She'd never even spoken to him — by Elizabeth's time, she'd already withdrawn from both mortal and undead society — but she'd been fond of him nonetheless, ensuring that he found generous patrons, savoring his triumphs and endearing quirks as one might the antics of a character in a play. And, of course, marvelling at the passion and technical proficiency of his art on those rare occasions when he could be lured away from his amusements and his myriad lovers long enough to paint. She'd intended to arrange for his induction into the ranks of the Toreador, but he'd perished, knifed in a senseless tavern brawl, before she'd gotten around to it.

He'd left only a handful of canvases behind, and now one of the finest was lost forever. Anguished and outraged, keening softly, the vampire wept tears of blood.

ONE: THE PARIAH

*Loneliness and the feeling of being unwanted
is the most terrible poverty.*
— Mother Teresa

Dan Murdock was trolling one of the beach bars, a crowded, raucous place decorated with circus photos and memorabilia, when he spotted the other vampire.

One moment, everything was fine. Pretending to sip a Heineken, he was jammed in with the youthful, sun-bronzed mortals watching the limbo contest. The blood thirst beginning to burn in his throat, he was peering about, looking for a drunken girl to seduce. Drunks were easier. He didn't have to be particularly charming to convince them. His tall, athletic build, arresting gray eyes, shock of blond hair and what one would-be lover had called his "cruel, chiseled good looks" generally did the trick all by themselves. Even more importantly, the drunks rarely understood or remembered what he'd done to them. And he liked the buzz their alcohol-laced vitae gave him.

Then the hairs on the back of his neck had stood on end. Turning, he had spied the other undead standing across the room, between the door and a calliope, glaring at him. He'd seen her around town before, though he didn't know her name. She was a big-boned, butch-looking woman as tall as he was, with short, dark hair cut in bangs, and a pug nose. She had a sloppily hand-rolled cigarette smoldering in the corner of her mouth and was dressed in a stained Tampa Bay Lightning sweatshirt, denim walking shorts and flip-flops. Judging from her homeliness and lack of any vestige of sartorial elegance or style, Dan surmised that she wasn't one of the Toreador who comprised the majority of Sarasota's vampire population, but rather a Kindred of some other bloodline.

She arrogantly jerked her head, summoning him outside. He supposed that she wanted to tell him to keep away from prime hunting ranges like the strip of bars opposite the public beach, which "Prince" Roger's subjects wished to reserve for their own use. Some of her peers had tried to deliver the same message on previous occasions.

He mouthed the words, "Fuck you," and began to turn away.

The female vampire stared at him even more intently. Without meaning to, he took a shuffling step toward her, jostling a young man's elbow, sloshing beer over the rim of his stein. On the dance floor, the MC lowered the limbo bar another notch. Reggae music tinkled from the speakers set around the concrete-block walls.

Despite his thirty years of vampiric existence, Dan still considered himself woefully ignorant of the world of the undead. Clanless, transformed and summarily abandoned by his anonymous sire, he hadn't had anyone to teach him about it; what little he had learned he'd discovered through observation and experiment. But he knew enough to recognize that the woman by the door was mesmerizing him. Exerting every iota of his willpower, he managed to wrench his head to the side, breaking eye contact. His rebellious feet stopped trudging forward.

Hoping that he'd shaken her confidence sufficiently to convince her to leave him alone, he turned away and moved toward the chiming, chirping pinball machines and the pool tables at the rear of the bar. After a moment, he glanced stealthily back and then scowled in annoyance. The woman was pushing through the crowd. Coming after him.

He turned and waited for her, trying to look tough and forbidding without quite reestablishing eye contact. Perhaps because of the crowding in the bar, she wound up standing just inches away from him. They could have put their arms around one another and waltzed.

"I gave you an order, Caitiff," she told him.

"I don't take orders," he replied. "If you're smart, you'll go hassle somebody else."

"I guess I'm not smart," she said, sneering. Something hard pressed against his navel.

He looked down. She was holding a snub-nosed revolver against his belly. All around them mortals drank and chattered, joked and flirted, oblivious to the battle of wills being waged in their midst.

Dan was puzzled. Though he'd had his share of altercations with Prince Roger's flunkies, they didn't defend their "domain" from outsiders nearly as zealously as other vampires he'd encountered; that, together with the fact that he'd been born in the area, was why he'd settled here. In fact, none of them had ever pulled a gun on him before, even when he'd provided considerably greater provocation. "Would you really shoot me in the middle of this mob?" he asked calmly.

"Believe it," she replied. "I could be gone before any of the kine realized what happened. And even if they did notice, they couldn't stop me. Now, are you coming, or what?"

"I'm thinking it over," he said. It was almost inconceivable that a bullet in the guts would kill him. He was even more resistant to harm than the average vampire; that, and prodigious strength, were the powers his unknown creator had passed on to him. But the wound would be painful and inconvenient — too high a price to pay for the pleasure he'd derive from frustrating his would-be abductor's desires. Besides, he was curious to discover what she wanted. "Oh, hell, why not?"

She edged around him and jabbed the revolver into the small of his back. Setting his green beer bottle on a table, he led her toward the door, past a tiny yellow clown car and a plastic statue of a rearing elephant, twisting and sidestepping as he worked his way through the crowd. He realized that it would be child's play to interpose one of the mortals suddenly between himself and the gun, thus frustrating her rather pitiful attempt to coerce him. But then he wouldn't find out what was going on.

They emerged from the stuffy, smoky atmosphere of the bar into the cool, sea-scented air. To the south, over the black waters of the Gulf, lightning flickered. "Let's take a walk on the beach," the female vampire said.

They crossed the street and the largely empty parking lot on the other side, then walked onto the soft white sand. The waves murmured. A few other people, mere shadows in the dark, were strolling on the shore, while a handful of anglers fished off the concrete pier.

In a minute Dan and the woman were well away from the lights shining in the parking area. He stopped walking and turned to face her. "I assume this is isolated enough for you," he said.

"It'll do," she replied grimly.

"Then tell me what you want. If it's a sex thing, I have to warn you, beefy, ugly women aren't my type." The remark was a joke, if not a very witty one. Vampires had no more sex drive than any other dead thing. When they were transformed, the desire to make love warped into the insatiable craving for blood. It was one of the many aspects of his condition that he didn't like.

"I want to know what you were doing last night, and three nights before that."

He raised his eyebrows in surprise. "What a weird question. I wasn't thirsty" — his stomach churned, reminding him that he was now — "and didn't need to go out, so I stayed in, playing a computer game and slogging my way through *The Complete Works of Dickens*. Why?"

She ignored his question. "Was anyone with you?"

"Yes," he said sarcastically, "my hundreds of Kindred buddies. No, no one was there. And now, if you want any more answers, you're going to have to tell me what this is all about."

She lifted the little revolver, reminding him of its existence. Moonlight rippled down the barrel. "You aren't in any position to make demands."

"Because of that popgun?" He snorted in derision.

She stared at him. After a moment, he sensed that she was trying to take control of him again, but this time the magic didn't work at all.

Abruptly feeling bored with the situation, perhaps even a little sorry for this woman who wanted so badly to be tough and wasn't especially good at it, he said, "Can't we just talk like a couple of reasonable people? What will it hurt? If you'll fill me in on what's bothering you, maybe I can even help you." He smiled sardonically. Right, help the prince's people, who shunned him. They'd certainly given him a lot of incentive to do that!

The woman grimaced. "All right. We — the clans — need to get to the bottom of these murders. I saw you in the bar and decided to see if you knew anything about them."

He held up his hand. "Whoa. You lost me. What murders?"

She blinked in surprise. "The triple murder at the aquarium, and then the double one on Siesta Key. You *must* have heard about them on the news."

He shrugged. "Afraid not. I don't pay much attention to the news." Why should he? The stories were about the living, not creatures like himself; although, come to think of it, tidings about the doings of other undead wouldn't have been all that relevant to his solitary existence either.

"Well, the killings were… strange," she said, "for all kinds or reasons. The police obviously don't understand how the murderer could have done the things he did and gotten away clean. And each of the victims had twin puncture wounds in the jugular vein or the carotid artery."

Dan frowned. "Like the bite of a vampire." A *careless* vampire, or one unconcerned with secrecy, to be precise. Ordinarily Kindred licked the wounds they had inflicted when they finished drinking, which caused the fang marks to close instantly. "And you're worried that whoever it is will give away the Masquerade."

"You got it," she said. A pickup truck, its radio blaring a satanic anthem by Cannibal Corpse, its cargo bay full of whooping teenage boys waving beer bottles, hurtled down the street separating the beach and the bars.

"Not entirely," Dan said dryly. "What made you think I might be involved? You know I've been living quietly in this town for years now, hunting about as discreetly as anybody else."

"But there's something different about you," she said contemptuously, "something cold and nasty. People say you're crazy, maybe crazy enough to unmask us to the kine without caring that you're jeopardizing your own safety as well."

Dan had heard this kind of disparagement of his character, or at any rate his demeanor, before, but had never had any idea what the Kindred who offered it were talking about. Probably nothing real. Generally speaking, vampires were no less self-righteous and self-deluded than humans, and perhaps it was only to be expected that they rationalized their snobbery by convincing themselves that he was some sort of freak. "Well, whatever you think of me, my mother loved me," he said ironically. "And you're barking up the wrong tree, so why don't we break this off. I don't want to delay your little manhunt." He began to turn away.

"Hold it!" she barked.

Sighing, he pivoted back to face her. "What now?" he demanded.

"You admitted that no one can vouch for your whereabouts at the time of the killings," she said.

"And you," he replied, "have pretty much admitted that you don't have a shred of evidence to implicate me. You just suspect me because I'm not one of your sissy prince's snotty little bunch of ass-kissers."

To his surprise, she snarled like an angry dog, her lengthening fangs gleaming even in the darkness. His intuition told him that, for some reason, his slighting reference to her leader had really gotten under her skin. "I don't need evidence," she said, articulating the words with difficulty. "*All* Kindred in a prince's domain exist there at his sufferance and are subject to his commands. And in his name, I *order* you to accompany me to his haven for further questioning. Maybe I can't tell if you're telling the truth, but the psychics will be able to."

For the first time since sighting the other vampire, Dan felt a pang of genuine anxiety. If his would-be captor actually meant to drag him off to the vampire equivalent of the slam, this nonsensical situation was more serious than he'd thought. Granted the prince and many of his followers were Toreador, a clan widely considered to have a softer disposition than the others, but Dan was still unwilling to trust them to treat him with justice or compassion. *Every* vampire, even the most seemingly human, occasionally fell under the sway of the Beast lurking inside.

Indeed, Dan felt his own Beast awakening even now, roused by the female vampire's obdurate hostility. His own fangs lengthened, indenting his lower lip. His fists closed and his knees flexed to hurl him at his captor.

He'd hoped to take her by surprise, but she sensed his

hostile intentions. Her revolver blazed, and searing pain stabbed into his gut.

Grunting, he lunged at her and threw a punch at her jaw. She hopped frantically backward, and the blow missed. Her gun barked, sending its next bullet into his right forearm, shattering the bone. The limb flopped down to dangle uselessly at his side.

Focusing beyond the agony of his wounds, Dan sprang at the female vampire again. This time she shot him in the forehead.

The head wound didn't inflict any more pain, but he instantly acquired double vision and his body began to shake. Hoping that neither problem would ruin his aim, he pivoted, lashing out with a low roundhouse kick. His foot crunched into her knee, snapping bone, tearing her leg out from underneath her. She fell on her back and he dove down at her.

Her revolver fired once more while he was in flight. It seemed impossible that the shot could miss at point-blank range, but he didn't feel it hit him. Perhaps his other pains masked the shock of impact.

He slammed down on top of her and, using his uninjured arm, grabbed the wrist of her shooting hand, squeezing and wrenching, trying to make her drop the gun. She clawed and snapped at him like a rabid animal. Thrashing, locked together, they rolled across the ground, his blood staining the pale sand black.

He felt the bones in her wrist begin to give. He gave her arm a final violent jerk and they shattered. A jagged splinter of bone lanced through her skin and scraped the palm of his hand. She cried out, her fingers spasmed, and the revolver tumbled out of her grip.

The fury in her face gave way to astonishment, as if she were amazed that, even with a bullet in his head, he was stronger than she was. Abruptly releasing her broken wrist, he began to batter her face.

The female vampire jerked both arms, injured and sound, up in front of her features, trying to deflect his hammering fist, but her efforts were to no avail. His blows smashed through her guard as if her limbs were made of paper, flattening her nose, snapping her fangs and pounding her skull out of shape. Finally she shuddered like a mortal in her death throes and passed out.

Still trembling himself, Dan crouched over her. The thirst he'd been experiencing even before she had accosted him burned like a bonfire in his throat, intensified by both his anger and the massive blood loss from his system. He wanted to sink his fangs into the unconscious vampire's throat more than he'd ever yearned for food, drink, or sex when he still breathed.

But, much as he generally tried to pretend to himself that he was inured to his lonely existence, deep down he knew it wasn't so. He still yearned for the acceptance of his fellow undead. If he began breaking their most sacred laws, he wasn't likely to win it.

The memories of countless insults and rebuffs rose in his mind, and he wondered who he was kidding. His fellow Kindred would never accept him in any case. For whatever reason, they'd always loathed him, and no doubt they always would. And perhaps it was time to start avenging the mistreatment he'd suffered at their hands.

Making himself move slowly, savoring the moment, he lowered his head toward the female vampire's throat. A bullet fell out of his breast as his regenerating flesh ejected it. Just as his fangs pricked his victim's skin, a lovely contralto voice behind him said, "Wait."

TWO: THE PROGNOSIS

*If I am a great man, then a good many of the great men
of history are frauds.*
— Bonar Law

By the time he reached the top of the wide oak stairs,
Elliott knew there hadn't been any improvement in Roger's
condition. The Toreador prince's voice echoed hoarsely
through his four-story beachfront Victorian house, ranting
threats, accusations of treason, and obscenities.
Nevertheless, cringing at the prospect, the younger vampire
felt honor-bound to look in on his sire.

Straightening his green silk tie, Elliott paced down the
softly lit, luxuriously carpeted hallway. Baroque paintings
depicting the world of the undead — macabre masterpieces
unknown to the art historians of the mortal world — hung
along the walls. For a moment one of the pictures glimpsed
from the corner of his eye, a depiction of a pretty young
vampire spying on her own funeral, tugged at him in the
old familiar way. But even as he turned to gaze at it, his
sense of incipient rapture died unborn.

Sighing, he moved on and tapped on the door to Roger's
bedroom. His knock triggered a renewed outburst of his sire's

cursing. Simultaneously, a solemn baritone voice said, "Come in."

Elliott entered the chamber. Roger lay, not in his ornate canopy bed, but on the hospital gurney his subjects had procured the night he'd fallen ill. Leather restraints bounds his arms and legs to the steel rails to keep him from hurting himself or someone else. Even those hadn't prevented him from gnawing his lips bloody. The scent of the vitae tinged the air.

Lazlo perched miserably on a Queen Anne chair in the corner, looking as if he'd aged ten years. A tall, black, shaven-headed vampire with a square, oversized head and narrow maroon eyes, his skin as dark as it had been in life but with an underlying grayness, stood beside the ailing prince's resting place. Several gold studs gleamed in his left ear, in striking contrast to his conservative attire. The front of his three-piece pinstriped suit was stained with blood. Roger had probably spat it at him.

Seeing the Kindred, Elliott felt a faint stirring of hope: the man was Lionel Potter, come at last. When mortal, Potter had been a brilliant physician; in the century since his induction into the ranks of the undead, he'd become the closest thing there was to an expert on vampiric physiology and disease. Thanks to his invaluable knowledge, skills and discretion, he'd transcended his humble Caitiff origins to become one of the most respected young Cainites in the Camarilla.

Elliott gave Roger a respectful, affectionate smile. "Good evening," he said. "How do you feel?"

Roger's lip curled. "Well, the leader of the rats, come to gloat. If you have a shred of courage or honor, you'll let me up from here so we can settle our vendetta in a fair fight."

Elliott's head swam. For a moment he felt a burst at rage at his sire for impugning his bravery, and yearned to give the older vampire the duel he was demanding. Stepping forward, he reached to unfasten the restraints. Then his mind cleared, and he realized that Roger was using his charismatic powers to manipulate him. Feeling foolish, Elliott lowered his hand, and the prince of Sarasota burst into peals of mocking laughter.

Elliott turned to Potter. "Thank you for coming," the one-time actor said. "I'm Elliott Sinclair. We met in Paris two years ago."

"Of course," the physician said with a cursory smile, "at the party in the Louvre. I remember."

"How is the prince?" Elliott asked.

Potter frowned. "Let's talk outside."

"That's right, get out of my sight!" Roger raved. "Plot against me behind my back! It doesn't matter — I'll get free and kill you all!"

His heart heavy, Elliott escorted Potter out of the room and down the painting-lined corridor far enough that, if they spoke softly, even Roger's hypersensitive hearing shouldn't be able to eavesdrop on their conversation. Lazlo trailed along behind them. Potter stared at the dresser coldly for a moment, as if displeased that the human had followed them unbidden.

"All right," said Elliott to Potter, "what's wrong with him?"

"He's paranoid, agitated, delusional, hostile, assaultive, and has a compulsion to engage in self-mutilatory behavior." To Elliott's annoyance, Potter's sing-song delivery sounded as if he were reading from a psychiatric textbook, not describing a patient about whom he was supposed to be deeply concerned.

"Yes," the Toreador said, "but *why?*"

"I don't know," the physician said, frowning. "It's a pity I couldn't have seen him closer to the onset of the illness."

"We called you the night he got sick!" Lazlo exclaimed.

Potter glared at Lazlo. For an instant, Elliott was afraid that the vampire physician would strike the human down for what he manifestly considered an insolent outburst. The

Toreador had observed that Caitiff often lorded it over mortal servants in the most arrogant manner imaginable. Perhaps it was the clanless vampires' way of compensating for feelings of inferiority.

Elliott reflexively lifted his hand to restrain his fellow undead. But Potter seemed to recall that he wasn't standing in his own home, about to chastise one of his personal flunkies. Some of the fury fading from his eyes, he pivoted pointedly away from Lazlo and back toward Elliott. "It's true what they say," he remarked. "You Toreador permit your slaves too many liberties."

"Perhaps that is true of some Toreador," Elliott said evenly, "but the ones in Sarasota don't *have* slaves. Lazlo here is the prince's faithful friend, and as such did not, I'm sure, intend any offense to you. He's just profoundly worried, like the rest of us." He made his voice steely: "I might observe in passing that I too was disappointed at how long it took you to arrive."

Potter frowned uneasily. He was prudent enough to understand the danger of offending Elliott, a respected and powerful clan elder. "I came as soon as I could," the doctor said. "I was treating another gravely ill patient in Venice. Surely you understand, I couldn't just walk out on him."

"Of course," said Elliott in a slightly more conciliatory tone. "Now, about the prince. We conjectured that he might have drunk tainted vitae."

"It's possible," Potter admitted. "I won't know for certain whether there are toxins or disease organisms in his blood until I run a battery of tests. But judging from his physical symptoms, or rather, lack of them, I very much doubt it. Has he been in a fight lately? Has he been bitten by another Kindred, perhaps, or a Lupine?"

Elliott didn't think so, but he glanced enquiringly at Lazlo, who, as Roger's valet, knew the prince's movements and activities even better than himself. Wisely reluctant to speak and risk provoking Potter anew, Lazlo simply shook his head.

"No and no," Elliott said to the physician. "Roger's subjects all love him, and we don't even *have* werewolves hereabouts, although I hear there's a pack in Tampa." In fact, thanks to Roger's skill as a ruler and diplomat, Sarasota had been at peace for decades, an oasis of calm in a savage, conspiracy-ridden world.

"Well," said Potter glumly, "that would seem to rule certain possibilities out. In all candor, you ought to prepare yourselves for the possibility that his condition doesn't *have* a physiological basis, in which case there will be little I can do."

Lazlo shook his head, mutely denying that what Potter had said could be true.

"I'm not following you," Elliott said. "When someone is ill, there *must* be a reason for it."

"But the cause could be psychological," Potter replied, "or spiritual. You know as well as I do, it's a traumatic thing to be one of the Kindred. One struggles constantly to hold the Beast in check. Sometimes it slips its reins anyway, and then the vampire must cope with the guilt its subsequent atrocities inspire. And at the same time he must deal with all the negative aspects of immortality. Boredom. Watching everything and everyone you love pass away."

You don't know the half of it, Elliott thought, remembering Mary's severed head and mangled body. A pang of anguish wrang his heart, and his eyes stung with unshed tears.

"Many Kindred can't handle the strain," Potter droned on, oblivious to Elliott's distress. "They go insane, like your prince, capitulating to the Beast and becoming sociopathic, or committing suicide. The pathology frequently manifests itself as they approach their thousandth year, and I understand that Prince Roger was born around the time of the First Crusade."

The way Potter was talking, it sounded as if he'd already written off Roger. Lazlo shot Elliott an imploring look.

The Toreador struggled to cast off the paralyzing pall of melancholy that had fallen over him. "I *do* know all that," he said to Potter. "Your medical credentials notwithstanding, I daresay that at my age, I comprehend the vicissitudes of Kindred existence rather better than you. And I can assure you that if there was ever a man capable of transcending them, it's Roger Phillips. I've never known an elder with so much humanitas, who adapted so readily to changes in the world around him, or who so rejoiced in each new night."

For a moment, as Elliott spoke, he felt a fierce surge of pride and affection for Roger, an emotion he hadn't experienced for a long time. He had always been devoted to his sire, but he usually couldn't *experience* the devotion except in an abstract and superficial way. His love for Roger lay buried, cold and inert, beneath his grief for Mary.

"Perhaps you're right," said Potter. "But on the other hand, perhaps the prince is a private person, who up to now has been hiding his growing depression. In which case—"

Remembering the manner in which he'd portrayed Henry V, that indomitable, commanding warrior-king, Elliott gave Potter an intimidating stare. "I think," he said, "that it would be best to proceed on the assumption that there *is* a physical cause for Roger's malady. You will remain here until you discover the cause and bring about his full recovery. Needless to say, your success will be well rewarded, just as — and here I'm speaking purely hypothetically, of course — your premature departure would earn you the enmity of every Kindred in this domain."

Potter tried to match Elliott stare for stare, but after a moment he was forced to lower his eyes. "Of course," he mumbled. "With your permission, I'd better get back to my patient."

Elliott gave him a regal nod. Potter turned and strode back down the corridor.

Lazlo sighed. His shoulders slumped as the tension went out of his body. "I had the same feeling you did," the dresser said. "He wasn't going to try to help Roger if he could get out of it."

"Because he's baffled," said Elliott somberly. He felt the momentary passion that his clash of wills with Potter had engendered ebbing, and the accustomed deadness stealing back into his soul. "And it won't do his reputation any good if he actually tries to cure Roger and fails."

"If he doesn't know what to do," said Lazlo, "maybe we should get somebody else."

"There scarcely is anyone else," Elliott replied. "And even if we could find another qualified doctor, the chances of him knowing any tricks that Potter doesn't are remote. The problem is that, until very recently, nobody was even trying to use modern science to study vampire physiology. Now that they are, their efforts are hampered by the fact that the Kindred are supernatural entities, whose very existence violates natural law. The upshot is that even the most knowledgeable of us, like Potter, comprehends the disease process in vampires about as well as Galen understood the analogous phenomenon in his fellow humans."

Lazlo nodded, though Elliott could see that some of what he'd said had gone over the human's head. But the aging valet understood the essential point: "You're saying there isn't any hope, aren't you?"

"No," said Elliott quickly, although that was precisely what he feared. "Potter has cured *some* Kindred. He saved Pierre Delacroix in Marseilles six years ago, when everyone else had given the old monster up for dead. And you know how resilient Roger is. He might shake off the madness all by himself. So promise me you won't despair."

Lazlo nodded, encouraged either by Elliott's arguments or by the unnatural force of personality which, the vampire now realized, he'd just exerted without even intending to. "I won't," the dresser said.

"Good man." Elliott squeezed the mortal's shoulder. "I'm going home. Call me if there are any developments." He began to turn away.

"Wait!" Lazlo cried. Elliott turned back around. "You can't go! They need you downstairs!"

Like the residences of most monarchs, vampire or mortal, throughout history, Roger's haven was more or less a public place, where affairs of state were conducted and some of his subjects could be found hanging about at any given hour of any night. At the moment Elliott could hear at least two dozen of them, babbling and pacing anxiously.

"Are the rest of the primogen here?" the actor asked.

Lazlo grimaced. "Yes."

"Then you don't need me," Elliott said reasonably, striving to project the power of his charisma again.

But this time, for some reason, Lazlo was scarcely affected. He gave his head a shake as if to clear it, then said, "We do! You haven't listened to them. I have. They're afraid, and they can't agree on anything. But they'll listen to you."

Elliott sighed. "You don't know that."

"I do," said the human, scowling stubbornly. "You're the oldest, and the one Roger valued" — his mouth twisted — "*values* most."

"Once," said Elliott, "that may have been true, but I'm sure that if Roger were in his right mind he'd tell you that it isn't anymore."

"That's bullshit!" Lazlo said.

Elliott felt a flash of anger, a shameful, unaccustomed desire to strike the impudent, importunate human down. Instead, turning away, he said, "Watch this."

Two paces farther down the hallway sat a small, round, cherrywood William Morris table and, atop it, a beautiful twelve-inch marble statue of a nude woman. Elliott recalled Roger telling him that the sculpture had been unearthed by archaeologists digging in Pompeii.

The gray-haired Toreador picked up the statue by its

head, swung it into the air and slammed it down against the edge of the table. The blow splintered the wood and echoed down the corridor, but it didn't break the stone figure. He had to smash it against its stand again before it shattered.

He set the base back down and then, dusting marble dust off his hands, turned back around. Lazlo was goggling at him in horror. "Do you understand now?" the vampire asked, feeling vaguely ashamed. "No Toreador should be able to desecrate a beautiful work of art. But I can do it easily, because I'm broken inside. I can't feel the things I used to feel, or care about the things I once cared about. Now do you understand why I'm unfit even to sit among the primogen?"

"No," Lazlo said. "You're an actor, aren't you? If you don't feel confident and ready to lead, fake it! Snap the other Kindred out of their funk and get them organized. Don't you think your wife would want you to?"

Elliott realized that she would indeed. He shrugged uncomfortably.

"Don't you think you owe it to Roger to support him in his hour of need?" Lazlo continued relentlessly. "Come to think of it, don't you think you owe it to me? Or are you going to urge me to hang in here with the prince come hell or high water — using your damn powers on me too, I'll bet — and then run out on us yourself?"

Elliott held up his hand. "*Enough!*" he said, scowling. Then, to his surprise, the situation began to seem obscurely funny, and his frown quirked into a wry smile. "Didn't anyone ever tell you that the Kindred are savage, amoral predators, utterly incapable of guilt?"

"Are you going to help?" Lazlo persisted.

"You can't push me into standing in for Roger," said Elliott. "I'm truly not up to the job. I'd make a botch of it. But I will meet with the others now and try to help them pull themselves together. Will that satisfy you?"

"It'll do for a start," Lazlo said.

THREE: THE METHUSELAH

The chess-board is the world; the pieces are the phenomena of the universe; the rules of the game are what we call the laws of Nature. The player on the other side is hidden from us.

— T. H. Huxley, "A Liberal Education"

Startled, Dan turned. Behind him, her form blurred by the darkness and his still-impaired vision, stood a pale, slender woman. Her white, gauzy gown and long black hair stirred in the sea breeze.

A kind of confused awe flowered inside him, supplanting the blood lust that had filled him only a moment before. Some instinct insisted that the newcomer was a ghost, or an angel, even though she was manifestly as solid as he was; a patina of sand clung to her dainty, naked feet, and she'd left a trail of tracks in her silent progress across the beach.

"Please stand away from her," said the stranger, nodding at the motionless form of the vampire Dan had battered unconscious. "I need her more than you do, and I promise to provide you with something else to drink."

Dan rose and stepped away from his erstwhile attacker. It was only when the stranger broke eye contact, knelt over the defeated Kindred and sank her own fangs into the woman's neck that the feeling of awe began to fade and he realized that he'd had a choice about whether to obey her command.

The newcomer, evidently another undead and a diabolist to boot, sucked her victim's vitae for what seemed a long while. Meanwhile, torn between anxiety, annoyance and curiosity, his body throbbing as broken bones mended and shredded flesh repaired itself, Dan peered up and down the beach. He was concerned that someone might have heard the shots and called the police, but there was no sign that the cops were on their way. Perhaps, as was more and more frequently the case in these final, decadent years of the twentieth century, no one who had heard the commotion had cared enough that some poor soul might be in trouble to pick up a phone.

Finally the vampire in the white gown flowed to her feet. Licking herself as unselfconsciously as a cat, she ran her pale tongue over her lips, cleaning the residue of vitae off them. Dan realized that if he'd still been mortal he would have found the sight erotic.

Determined not to allow the newcomer to cow him again, he glowered at her. "It's dangerous for one animal to try to steal another animal's kill," he said.

The newcomer smiled at him. "I see the intimidation has worn off already. Good. That, no less than your victory a minute ago, is a mark of strength. I'm called Melpomene, after the muse of tragedy." She sighed. "A name of good or evil omen, depending on how you look at it."

"I'm Dan Murdock," he said.

"I know. I've been looking for you."

He frowned, his emotions still an untidy jumble of interest and apprehension. "I guess it's finally my night to be popular. What do *you* want with me?"

"Let's talk as we stroll by the water. It's been too long since I visited the sea."

He looked down at Prince Roger's unconscious flunky.

Blood was still oozing sluggishly from the twin punctures in her neck. "Is she dead?"

"No," Melpomene replied.

"You didn't lick the bite closed," he observed. "Are you the murderer she was worried about?" He paused, groping in his memory for the details. "The one who killed the mortals at the aquarium?"

"No," Melpomene said. "The humans have been safe from me for a long time." She held out her white hand. "Come."

Either because of her palpable charisma or his own loneliness, he wanted to take her hand, but caution held him back. Nodding at Prince Roger's subject, he said, "This bitch never even saw you, did she? If she wakes up a quart low, she'll blame me."

"I know," said Melpomene. "We want her to. Trust me, and everything will be all right."

Dan *didn't* trust her. Over the last thirty years, he'd learned the hard way not to trust anyone. But he yearned for her to prove herself a friend. And he didn't care all *that* much if Prince Roger's vassal crawled back to her master believing the worst of him. He hadn't exactly been chummy with the other undead denizens of Sarasota as it was. If their ruler declared a Blood Hunt against him, he'd simply run away to some other town. The perpetually feuding lords of the Camarilla were unlikely to exert themselves unduly to help one of their peers track down a fugitive.

And so, gingerly, irrationally half-afraid that his touch would disgust her, Dan took Melpomene's hand. Her grip was firm yet gentle, her skin cool, smooth and soft. The contact reminded him yet again of the days when he'd burned for the embrace of lovely women.

They strolled toward the susurrant surf. She took a deep breath, perhaps savoring the salty tang in the air. "Well?" Dan said.

Melpomene shook her head. "The impatience of youth.

But in this case, justified. My capacity for urgency dwindled away a long time ago. Now I have to revivify it."

They reached the water's edge. When the first sheet of cool white foam washed over her feet, Melpomene quivered as if a lover had caressed her. The two undead turned and headed south, away from the site of Dan's battle.

As his vision finally sharpened into perfect focus, Dan said, "Okay, then get urgent. Tell me what you want with me."

"Very well," Melpomene said. For a moment, her eyes strayed to an elaborate sand castle, its turrets and crenellated battlements now crumbling in the incoming tide. "Do you know what a Methuselah is?"

"A very old vampire," he said, "living in hiding or sleeping the centuries away. Or at least that's what the legends say." He peered at her skeptically. "Are you telling me that you are one?"

"Yes," she answered. "Do you believe me?"

He felt another twinge of the instinctive awe that had overwhelmed him when he'd first turned and beheld her. "Maybe," he said, although suddenly he was sure she was speaking the truth.

Seemingly satisfied with his answer, she said, "We live apart from you, our descendants, for two good reasons. One is that we require vampire vitae to survive." He tensed, and she gave him a reassuring smile. "I promise I'm not after yours. Remember, I just fed."

The blood thirst smoldered in his throat, reminding him that he had yet to do likewise. The craving was so inexorable that not even the fascination of an encounter with a virtual demigoddess of the undead could take his mind off it for long. "Okay," he said, "I believe that. If you wanted more vitae, you could have sucked Butch back there dry. Or jumped me before my wounds healed, when I was easier pickings."

"Exactly," Melpomene said. "As I was saying, we hide

from you because, comprehending our need to prey on you as you batten on mortals, you'd destroy us if you could. But even more importantly, we hide from one another. Do the legends with which you are familiar speak of the Jyhad?"

He frowned, not quite sure what she was getting at. "A jyhad is a war among Kindred, isn't it?" He'd fought in one such conflict as a kind of mercenary when some of the elders of Baton Rouge had rebelled against their prince. He'd hoped that his efforts on their behalf would win him a place in the new social order they established; but after their victory they'd paid him off and made it clear they'd prefer he leave the city.

"Is that how the term is used these days?" she asked wryly. "The *true* Jyhad is the war among us ancients. It's been going on for thousands of years, and for all I know, it will continue until there's only one of us left. Or until the Antediluvians, *our* sires, awaken from their sleep of millennia and destroy all younger vampires to satisfy their hunger."

A chill crept up Dan's spine. *What a cheery prospect,* he thought. "What are you guys fighting about?" he asked.

"Everything and nothing," Melpomene said wearily. "Some of us want to rule the world. Others, to stave off boredom. Still others, to pursue ancient quarrels." Her lovely mouth twisted. "We are, after all, not only killers by nature but also children of the earth's savage dawn, when vengefulness was a virtue and forgiveness, contemptible weakness. Still other Methuselahs have surrendered to the Beast or gone mad, their reason crumbling under the weight of ages of loss and remorse, and they lash out at those who were once closest to them as the murderously insane so often do."

Suddenly she seemed so full of bitterness and self-loathing that, to his surprise, Dan felt an urge to comfort her. "You don't seem vicious or crazy to me," he said.

She arched an eyebrow. "Don't I? Look deeper. But thank you for your kind words."

The Hunger seared Dan's mouth again. His stomach ached. If he didn't hunt soon he was likely to fly into a frenzy when he did find prey, and drink so deeply that he left the unfortunate mortal dead. "You still haven't told you what you want with me," he said. He heard a soft splash: a fish had jumped.

"First I have to explain more about the Jyhad, and my position within it," she said. "Because we spend our lives in hiding, we Methuselahs are rarely afforded the opportunity to strike at one another directly. But each of us controls, by various means, certain factions in vampire society, just as Kindred elders direct the destinies of the mortals dwelling in their domains. And we mobilize our minions to strike at our enemies' chattels. When victorious, we impair a foe's ability to exert power, and injure his pride. If we succeed in destroying some servant or possession he truly cherishes, we can cause him actual pain. And once in a great while, our efforts are so successful that we force him into the open, at which point we can attempt to annihilate him."

"Are you telling me," said Dan, frowning, "that whenever the Kindred plot and fight against each other, it's because you old vamps are pulling our strings?"

"Not always," Melpomene replied, "but frequently. Rebuke me if you like. I know it's cruel of us to manipulate you into strife and risk of ruin. That's why I tried to opt out of the game." The black, angular form of a half-constructed condominium loomed out of the darkness ahead.

"You can do that?" asked Dan.

The woman in the white gown sighed. "I thought I could. One night about four hundred years ago, after the Armada but before the founding of Jamestown, I slew the last of my special enemies, by which I mean the last of the Methuselahs who were actively striving against me. I was weary and heartsick from centuries of bloodshed and intrigue, and it occurred to me that if I hid myself even more thoroughly than before, if I refrained from making any moves against the remainder of my peers, they might leave me alone to live in peace. After all, each of them had rivals who were actual threats to worry about.

"And for a while my plan seemed to work. As my confidence grew, I let some of my minions pass from my control altogether and loosened the reins on the rest. When my Toreador, my descendants, contrived to live in peace here in Sarasota, I permitted it gladly. I was no longer sufficiently wary to worry that a placid existence would blunt their fighting edge, or that their refusal to join in military alliances might leave them friendless in some future hour of need."

As they neared the unfinished condominium, the breeze sighed through the empty windows. Noticing the absence of any construction equipment, and the obscene graffiti on the concrete-block walls, Dan realized that the project had been abandoned. Perhaps the builder had run out of money. "And now it is their 'hour of need,'" he guessed.

"Yes," said Melpomene somberly. Her head turned as if she were tracking the motion of something through the air. Dan squinted, but he still couldn't see whatever it was that she was looking at. "I spent most of the last century asleep. It's something we ancients do to refresh ourselves when existence begins to seem too burdensome. But my dreams provided a window on the waking world, and in one of them I saw that a wonderful painting, a work by an artist my Toreador and I had nurtured and cherished, had been destroyed. I roused myself and found that the vision was true."

"And you figure that was the opening shot in a new war," said Dan.

"It was," Melpomene replied. "I felt it instantly, and subsequent events have proved me right. Other works in whose creation I played some role have been destroyed — you would have seen the reports if you followed the news

— and, though they may not fully realize it themselves as yet, the Kindred of this domain are under siege."

Gosh, Dan thought sardonically, *and I didn't even know anything was wrong.* Maybe there were advantages to being an outcast, if it kept you out of the line of fire. "You know," he said, "just because somebody's calling you out, that doesn't mean you have to go out in the alley and fight. You could just keep lying low."

"No," Melpomene said grimly, "my opponent knows how to compel me. Even if I could bear to abandon those of my own lineage, the art must not be lost! It's my legacy to the world!" Her voice grew softer. "Perhaps it's my atonement for all the evil I've done."

"So what are you going to do?" asked Dan. Sand crunched beneath his sneakers. "March into Prince Roger's stronghold and take charge?"

"No," the ancient vampire said. "That's what the enemy would like, to flush me into the open."

In other words, Dan thought, *the art is precious, but not precious enough for you actually to risk your own neck.* To his surprise, he felt a little disappointed in her.

"By and large," Melpomene continued, "I'll have to trust my Toreador to direct the defense themselves. What I am going to do is plant a spy in the enemy camp."

Cocking his head, Dan gave her an incredulous smile. "Me?" he asked.

She nodded. "I've been out of touch too long. I have no idea which of my peers is assailing me, nor even who his principal minions are. Some occult force is shielding them from my psychic abilities. However, I have managed to sense one small contingent, no doubt the most ignorant and least significant, of my enemy's forces. But it's a place to begin. A clever agent could infiltrate them and begin working his way up the ladder of command, amassing intelligence as he went."

"Swell, but why me?" Dan said.

"I saw you in my dreams, too," she said, "before I even realized what bond would bring us together. Despite your youth, you're strong. You've proved it many times in the course of your wanderings. And you're a Caitiff, with no ties to Prince Roger, the Toreador of Sarasota, those elders kindly disposed toward them, or anyone else I might be thought to control. Indeed, in the wake of your altercation tonight, the Kindred of the domain should soon be crying for your head. That should keep anyone from suspecting you when you join the other side."

A pang of self-pity stabbed through his chest. Struggling to quash the feeling, he said, "I wouldn't count on them letting me join, even so. If your dreams showed you very much of my life, you know that I'm not exactly good at winning friends and influencing people, not when the people in question are vampires."

"Don't worry about that," she said. "The enemy will encounter you in circumstances that will make your acceptance inevitable."

"If you say so," he said dubiously. "Now for the big question: Considering that Prince Roger and his gang are no friends of mine, why should I risk my neck to help you? What's in it for me?"

"Power," she said. "If you agree to help me, I'll enhance your abilities."

His eyes narrowed in consideration. Many vampires aspired to improve their existing supernatural talents or to master the exotic arts practiced by Kindred of other bloodlines, and he was no exception. "It's a tempting offer," he said slowly. "I just don't know if it's tempting enough for me to take on what could turn out to be a suicide mission. After all, you're asking me to snoop into the secrets of a bad-ass just as powerful as you."

"But you haven't heard my *complete* offer," she said. The cool breeze gusted, pasting her thin dress to her slender body. Even in the darkness he could see her nipples through the gauze. "After the war is over, I'll exert whatever influence is required to gain you the acceptance of your fellow Kindred. You'll finally have a place in the world. Isn't that what you've always wanted?"

"Yes," he admitted, pondering the deal. He supposed that a lot of people would think he was crazy even to consider jumping into a deadly feud that was really none of his business. But Melpomene was right, he *was* tough: in the perilous years since he'd submitted to his unknown sire's Embrace, delirious on the hallucinogen someone had slipped into his drink, he'd learned to trust in both his strength and his ingenuity. And if they proved inadequate to the challenge this time, well, he didn't have to be as old as Melpomene and her rivals to feel that his current existence was becoming wearisome. "Okay, what the hell. I'll do it."

"Excellent," the ancient vampire said, her dark eyes shining.

"What do we do first?" Dan asked.

"You do what you've been wanting to do," she answered softly, releasing his hand and raising her own. He hadn't seen her cut herself, but blood began to flow from a gash in the fleshy base of her palm. "You quench your thirst."

A feeling of awe came over him again. Hesitantly, half-suspecting that this was a test of his respect and good judgment and that she'd strike him down for his temerity, he took hold of her wrist and pressed his mouth against the cut.

At his first taste of her vitae, a lightning bolt of pleasure blazed through his body. Drinking blood had never filled him with such euphoria, not even when he'd been starving or berserk. The sensation transcended the ecstasy he normally felt when feeding as far as that exhilaration surpassed human orgasm. He lifted his becrimsoned face and howled with delight, then frantically kissed the cut again.

The rapture of guzzling her life so possessed him that he was nearly incapable of sensing anything else. Yet, dimly, his eyes closed, he felt a cool fingertip tracing a design on his forehead. The touch left a tingling trail on his skin. Then Melpomene laid her free hand on his brow and shoved him suddenly and hard, like a faith healer thrusting the power of God into one of his flock.

Another blast of energy crashed through Dan's body. This one *was* painful, but he was so lost in the bliss of consuming Melpomene's vitae that the hurt didn't matter. The world began to spin, and his knees buckled. Still clinging to the ancient's arm, he collapsed onto the sand. She flowed down to the ground with him and covered his shuddering form with her own.

FOUR: DELIBERATIONS

You may take the most gallant sailor, the most
intrepid airman, or the most audacious soldier,
put them at a table together — what do you get?
The sum of their fears.
— Winston Churchill, *The Blast of War*

Elliott paused at the foot of the stairs to run a comb
through his hair, straighten his tie and vest, adjust his cuffs
and make sure his handkerchief was protruding from his
breast pocket properly. At the same time, he reflected again
on Henry V, Shakespeare's most heroic and charismatic king,
trying to cloak his own despondent apathy in the role's
dynamism. Gradually his back straightened, and his jaw set
in bogus resolution. When he felt as ready as he imagined
he could be for the ordeal to come, he strode on into the
room that Roger humorously referred to as the arena.

With its vast expanse of gleaming hardwood floor, its
high ceiling and its glittering crystal chandelier, the arena
would have made a satisfactory ballroom. Indeed, on
occasion Roger had moved the furniture out and used it for
precisely that purpose. Currently, however, the chamber was
full of comfortable antique sofas and easy chairs grouped into
conversation pits in a manner that reminded Elliott of a posh
hotel lobby or a gentlemen's private club. Holbein's portrait

of Roger hung above the ornately carved fireplace where someone, heedless of the warmth of the evening, had kindled a crackling yellow blaze.

Many of the Kindred of Sarasota had assembled in the room. Some were lounging with an enviable display of poise, but others were sitting on the edges of their seats or nervously prowling about. A pungent blue haze of tobacco smoke hung in the air.

To better assess the mood of the crowd, Elliott invoked a perceptual power he hadn't bothered to use in a long time. The pale auras of his fellow vampires shimmered into view. As he'd suspected, most of the envelopes of light were tinged with orange, the color of fear.

Judith Morgan, a Brujah elder, was sitting on a maroon leather sofa talking to the rest of the primogen. Judy was as tall and thin as a fashion model, with skin the color of café au lait. She was dressed in ragged jeans, a black leather halter, a choke-chain necklace and a blue Union infantry soldier's cap. Long scars crisscrossed her naked shoulders and back. When breathing, Judy had been a slave. She'd been transformed into a vampire in the early 1830s and released from her sire's supervision in 1861, just in time to help the North win the Civil War. Sensing Elliott's presence, she turned and beckoned to him urgently.

As Elliott started toward her, his remaining peers twisted in their seats to look at him. Schuyller Madison, a fellow Toreador, gave him a welcoming smile. Sky was a poet and a patron of human poets whose delicate-looking frame, soulful, wounded eyes and languid, abstracted demeanor made him a caricature of the dreamy, oh-so-sensitive aesthete. Even Elliott, who'd grappled with more than one crisis at the versifier's side, had difficulty remembering just how misleading this appearance could sometimes be.

Gunter Schmidt, the remaining elder, gave Elliott a hostile glower. The actor had never understood why the burly, piggy-eyed Malkavian, whose face was always as strangely ruddy as if he were constantly sipping blood to replenish the glow, disliked him so. Perhaps it was a part of his insanity. Supposedly all members of the Malkavian clan were mad in one way or another, although Gunter never displayed any obvious signs of derangement.

"How kind of you to honor us with your presence," Gunter said snidely. "How fortunate that the petty problems of the domain have finally kindled your interest."

Elliott supposed that, since he was here to urge everyone to stay calm and work together, he ought to adopt a conciliatory tone. "I have been dilatory," he admitted. "I apologize." Gunter's beady, bright-blue eyes blinked in surprise. "What have the three of you decided?"

"Nothing yet," said Sky with a fluttering, helpless gesture of his long-fingered hand. "We're just going back and forth."

In the midst of the youngsters, Elliott thought sourly, *allowing them to eavesdrop on your uncertainty. Feeding their fear.* It was the worst possible way for the elders to palaver. Judy, Sky and Gunter must be far more shaken than they appeared; otherwise, they would never have forgotten such an elementary principle of leadership.

"Then let's turn this into a proper meeting," Elliott said briskly, "and include everyone in the discussion." He nodded toward the rest of the Kindred in the room.

Gunter's mouth twisted. "What insights can these childer offer *us?*" he demanded.

"Conceivably some very useful ones," Elliott replied. "That they can't match our level of power doesn't mean they aren't bright. I would hope that their sires chose them to Embrace partly because they *are* intelligent. And in any case, they're in a funk. If we talk with them, perhaps we can calm them down."

"A true elder doesn't care how his brood *feels,*" said Gunter contemptuously, "only that they obey." He looked to Judy and Sky for support and then, discerning from their faces that they agreed with Elliott, made a spitting sound.

"But all right. Invite them all to jabber if you think it will do any good."

"Thank you," Elliott said, hoping he didn't sound sarcastic.

He walked to the midpoint of one of the walls — one of the natural visual focal points of the parlor — where a semicircle of four straight-backed chairs and music stands, set up, perhaps, for some string quartet, sat beside a harpsichord that had once belonged to Bach. He clapped his hands together.

The drone of conversation ebbed. Everyone turned to peer at him. For an instant his stomach felt queasy, just as it always did when he first confronted an audience, even after all these centuries.

Drawing on his charismatic powers, reminding himself to be the magnificent King Henry and not a useless, disconsolate widower, he said, "May I have your attention, please? We all know the domain is facing a crisis. I think we should discuss the situation and decide on the appropriate measures to set things right. Make yourselves comfortable and we'll begin."

Wood squealed on wood as the vampires shifted their seats around to face him.

"Thank you," Elliott said. "As I see it, we have four problems." He raised his hand to count them off on his fingers. "One: Our prince has mysteriously fallen ill. Two: our financial holdings are under attack. Suddenly people are launching hostile takeovers against our companies, filing suits and seeking injunctions against them, and manipulating stock and bond markets to our detriment. Three: we have a rogue Kindred stalking our territory, feeding wantonly and jeopardizing the Masquerade. And four: someone is roaming the world systematically vandalizing works of art which we created, or which were created by mortals under our patronage."

Judy raised her hand. Elliott acknowledged her with a

nod. "It can't be a coincidence that all these things are happening at once," she said. "Somebody's pursuing a comprehensive strategy to destroy us."

"I agree," said Elliott. Many of the onlookers began to babble. The actor raised his hand and the noise subsided. "Does anyone have any idea who the enemy might be?"

The assembled Kindred looked at each other uncertainly. Apparently no one had any specific candidate. In point of fact it could be anyone, any powerful vampire seeking to extend his power, to settle an old score that the offending party had forgotten all about, or to relieve the boredom of centuries by playing a vicious game. Insulated in their pleasant little kingdom, some of the undead of Sarasota had probably forgotten the ruthless machinations in which many of their fellows delighted; but they were remembering now.

"I can't think of a candidate either," said Elliott wryly. "So we'll have to maintain a defensive posture until we can ferret out more information. Now, why don't we discuss the four aspects of our problem in turn and determine what to do about each one. First, of course, and very dear to all our hearts, is Roger."

"How is he?" a male voice cried from the back of the room.

"Not good," Elliott admitted. "But at least, though his reason is impaired, his body is still strong. It's not as if he were dying. We've brought in Lionel Potter to attend him, so he's getting the best care possible. We have every reason for hope, and we can do two things to help him: we can stand guard over this haven, so no enemy can attack him in his hour of weakness; and, much as I know you want to visit him, those of you who don't belong to the primogen can stay away from him. Don't give him a chance to trick you into releasing him from his restraints."

Gunter rose from his couch. "At the moment, Roger can't lead," he said flatly. "Who will?"

Not you, Elliott thought, *not if I have anything to say about it*. Gunter was powerful enough to dominate most assemblages of Kindred, but in the Toreador's opinion, the perpetually flushed, flaxen-haired Malkavian was neither concerned with anything beyond self-aggrandizement nor particularly bright.

"I trust that for the time being we can make decisions by consensus, with the primogen providing direction as needed," Elliott replied smoothly.

Gunter stared into Elliott's eyes. The Toreador felt he was receiving a message as clearly as if his fellow lieutenant were speaking it aloud: *If anyone succeeds Prince Roger, it will be me. If you try to steal the throne, I'll kill you.*

"All right," Gunter said. "We'll do it that way for the time being."

Elliott turned, reestablishing eye contact with the rest of the crowd, or at least giving them the impression that he'd done so. "Now, about our finances," he said. "We employ some of the best executives, financial planners and lawyers in the world. I'm confident that with their assistance our little investment cartel will weather the present storm. As a matter of fact, I'm glad our enemy has made this move. By investigating *his* front men, his puppet investors and litigators, we may be able to determine his identity."

"Oh, God," moaned Karen, a pretty brunette vampire in amber-tinted glasses. "I can't believe this. Every penny I have is in that fund." Some of the other Kindred muttered similar sentiments.

"Fools!" Judy cried in a voice like the crack of a whip. Many of the audience flinched.

The Brujah sprang out of her seat and stalked to Elliott's position center stage. "Do you think money is important?" she asked the crowd. "Money is nothing! You can wring it out of the kine whenever you choose. Strength and courage are what matter! If you've grown so soft that you've forgotten that, perhaps you deserve to be destroyed!"

"Damn straight!" one of her clanmates cried. Throughout

the audience, people, shamed by her scorn, were visibly trying to conceal their trepidation. Judy quirked an eyebrow at Elliott and he gave her an infinitesimal nod, complimenting her on her performance.

"Are we agreed on the proper way to handle our financial difficulties?" Elliott asked. Members of the audience nodded or mumbled in affirmation. "Good. Then let's talk about the killer. Does anyone have any idea who *that* might be?"

"There are one or two Kindred in town who never swore allegiance to the prince," Gunter said. "I always said they should be destroyed or driven out, but certain others" — he glowered at his fellow members of the primogen — "felt differently."

"You may be on to something," Elliott said, thinking of one outsider in particular: a sullen blond man named Murdock. There was something subtly disquieting, even repellent, about him, though the Toreador had never quite been able to put his finger on what it was. "We should certainly look into their recent activities."

Dmitri, a handsome, muscular ballet dancer Roger had Embraced twenty-five years ago, raised his hand. "Yes?"

"What does killer matter?" asked Dmitri in his faltering, heavily accented English. "No matter what he does, humans will not believe in us. They will think he is just crazy man who believes he is Count Dracula."

"I hope you're right," Elliott said, "but we don't dare depend on it. On occasion, in other domains, the Masquerade *has* been breached, and only reestablished by the most desperate, ruthless measures imaginable."

"Maybe the killer *is* just a mortal psycho," said Scott, one of Gunter's brood, a baby-faced vampire as blond and Nordic as his sire.

"I've read the police reports," Judy said, which meant that she'd broken into police headquarters, or into their computer system. Unlike the Kindred of some cities, the vampires of Sarasota didn't actually control the municipal government. Roger had preferred to guide the affairs of the mortal community by subtler means. "And I wouldn't bet the rent on the guy being human. There are indications that the murderer can turn invisible, melt through locked doors and do other tricks that no kine can manage. Which means that the cops couldn't catch him even if we wanted them to. We have to nail him, and we will. By patrolling the city and conducting our own investigation." She grinned at the audience. "Who's up for a little game of hide-and-seek?"

A number of vampires, many of them her fellow Brujah, yelled that they were.

"Fine," Elliott said, "we know what we're doing about the killer. The remaining problem is the preservation of our art."

"You're speaking incorrectly," Gunter said.

Turning toward him, Elliott arched an eyebrow. "I beg your pardon?"

"It isn't *our* art," Gunter said. "It's *your* art. The *Toreador's* art."

No, it isn't mine, Elliott thought, *not anymore.* He felt a pang of grief, and asserted his will to keep the emotion out of his expression. "You're splitting hairs," he said. "It's an irreplaceable treasure created by members of our community. Somehow our enemy has identified all the masterpieces which have passed from our possession, and now they're under attack. I suggest that we retrieve them for safekeeping."

The Toreador in the audience babbled in agreement.

"Your paintings and statues may be irreplaceable," Gunter said, rising to address the crowd better, "but in a time of war they're not *essential.* I oppose diverting manpower from critical tasks to collect a set of trinkets."

The Malkavian's brood clamored in support of his position.

Judy grimaced. "I know the art is more than trinkets," she said to Elliott, "but I have to admit Gunter's got a point."

Sky flowed to his feet. "You don't understand," he said to the Brujah and Malkavians in the room. "A Toreador's art *defines* him. He invests his soul in it. We could no more turn our back on the beauty we've brought into the world than you Brujah could renounce the wild, free spirit that makes you what you are, or than a Malkavian could restrict himself to" — he paused, obviously trying to think of a tactful way to express himself — "conventional modes of thought." A crimson tear slid down his cheek.

"Maybe," said Philo, a Brujah slouched in an easy chair, his cowboy hat tilted down over his eyes, "but you can't expect the rest of us to give a damn about your personal problems."

Alice, a stunning redheaded Toreador in a blue silk minidress glared at the Brujah. She'd been brought into the clan because she *was* beautiful, not because she could create beauty, but she professed her bloodline's aesthetic ideals as ardently as any of her fellows. "You'll care if we tell you to," she said. "This is *our* domain. The prince is a Toreador, and there are more of us than the rest of you put together, so you'd better do as we say if you want to live here."

Philo surged to his feet. His hand, tattooed with a picture of a hornet, shot inside his voluminous black leather coat, obviously reaching for a weapon. Baring her fangs, Alice leaped up from her seat and crouched to spring at him.

Moving at superhuman speed, Elliott lunged between the would-be combatants. "No!" he cried. "This is a conference, not a brawl. Save your aggression for our foes!"

Angry as she was, but accustomed to obeying her clan elders, Alice backed down at once. Shuddering on the brink of a true frenzy, Philo glared at Elliott, willing him to stand aside. Elliott could feel the other vampire's coercive power pounding at his mind like a hammer.

Straining to resist the domination and to project his own subtler influence, Elliott gave the Brujah an amused, confident smile. After a few seconds, the younger Kindred began to feel what the Toreador elder wanted him to feel: namely, that Elliott was manifestly far more formidable than he was. Retracting his fangs, Philo averted his gaze.

The Brujah were a proud warrior clan. Elliott didn't want any of them to go away from the meeting feeling that they'd been humiliated, particularly now that the domain needed their loyal support so desperately. He gripped the younger vampire's shoulder. "Thank you," he said warmly. "Thank you for your forbearance." He turned to Alice. "Please apologize at once."

She stared at him, flabbergasted. "What? Why?"

"Because you insulted him and all the rest of our friends who don't share our lineage. Sarasota is *not* a Toreador domain. It belongs in equal measure to every Kindred whose fealty our prince has chosen to accept. If your sire never taught you as much, I'm certain Roger did."

The redhead made a face. "All right," she muttered, "I'm sorry."

Philo shrugged contemptuously and dropped back into his chair.

Elliott felt himself relax. If he hadn't defused the situation, in another moment the entire room might have been fighting. Vampires were like that; frenzy could leap from one to the next like wildfire, and the Brujah in particular were notorious for their hair-triggers.

The actor returned to the front of the room and surveyed his audience. "All right," he said, "I understand that those of you belonging to other clans don't see the urgency of protecting the art. I hope that you in turn comprehend that the matter is of compelling importance to us. Accordingly, I propose that we Toreador will retrieve the art ourselves, without anyone else's help, while also assisting in the resolution of the domain's common problems. Is that acceptable to everyone?"

Judy sighed. "We'd rather have you guys working on the other issues full-time," she said, "but yeah, I guess that's a reasonable compromise."

Elliott turned to Gunter. "Do you agree?" he asked.

Gunter shrugged. "I suppose. I doubt that your people would be much use on the front lines anyway. Especially if you were pining for your baubles."

"Do you actually know where all the art is?" Judy said to Elliott.

"We know where a lot of it is," the actor replied, "and we can find the rest. Sky wasn't speaking figuratively: a portion of our collective soul *does* reside in it, and it calls to us. A couple of us can find it psychically. A more interesting question is, how are our enemies striking at the art so unerringly? How do *they* know what we created, and where it wound up?"

"Someone has been watching us and preparing this strike for a long time," Sky said soberly, his silvery, vitae-stained handkerchief dangling from his hand.

"I think so, too," Elliott replied with a grim smile. "Imagine how upset they're going to be when we make the plan blow up in their faces."

"Here's a tactical question for you," Judy said. "You can't retrieve the art without visiting other domains. Are you going to ask the permission of their princes?"

"I suppose we must," said Sky. "The Fifth Tradition requires it." Some of the assembled Brujah hooted derisively. The Toreador poet blinked as if puzzled by their reaction, or as if he were in danger of weeping again.

"The problem is," Elliott said, "that we don't know who the enemy is. Any prince we contact could be an adversary who'll use his knowledge of our movements against us."

"On the other hand," said Judy, scratching absently at one of the long-healed welts on her shoulder, "if they catch you guys on their turf without permission, there could be hell to pay."

"Unless someone objects" — Elliott glanced around the room, but none of his fellow Toreador called out or raised a hand — "I think we'll risk it. It's a big world, and Kindred are thin on the ground. We really should be able to sneak in and out of the average city without being noticed."

Judy nodded approvingly. "That's what a Brujah would do." She turned toward the crowd. "Okay, kids, it all sounds like a plan to me. Let's figure out who's going to tackle what job. Why don't the Toreador go off in a corner and decide how to get the art, and the rest of us will start working out everything else."

"That sounds all right," said Elliott. He and his clanmates gathered at one end of the chamber, beside a display case full of gray stone and gleaming gold artifacts plundered from a pharaoh's tomb.

"I've never done anything like this before," said Karen nervously. "I hope I do all right."

"Sure you will," said Glenn, a sculptor with a salt-and-pepper beard and red clay under his fingernails. "If you can steal a mortal's blood, you can certainly steal an object from his house. It'll be fun!"

Rosalita, one of Roger's brood, a short, bosomy, curly-haired Hispanic singer wearing a necklace of tiny jade skulls, gave Elliott a diffident tap on the shoulder. "If we're going in teams," she murmured, "I'd like to go with you."

Elliott opened his mouth to explain that that wouldn't be possible, then realized that he did indeed have to go.

When he'd entered the room, his fellow undead had been on the brink of panic. Through common sense, oratorical technique and a dash of his preternatural stage presence, he'd calmed them down and gotten them organized. So far, so good, but now they needed him to lead by example. If he withdrew into his accustomed seclusion instead of helping to further the strategy that he himself had advocated, everyone else was likely to lose faith in it.

One mission, he thought grimly. *I'll run one errand, to get them started, but then somebody else will have to run the show. God damn you, Lazlo.*

FIVE: FIRST BLOOD

To save your world you asked this man to die:
Would this man, could he see you now, ask why?
— W. H. Auden, "Epitaph for an Unknown
Soldier"

A cold winter wind moaned through the streets of downtown Columbus, Ohio, where, according to a Toreador sensitive, one of the clan treasures awaited. The chill didn't bother Elliott but, remembering how uncomfortable it might have made him when he was mortal, he had to repress a reflexive shiver anyway. Striding along at his side with a rolled-up piece of canvas under her arm, shooting nervous glances in all directions, Rosalita clutched the collar of her lightweight topcoat shut.

The homeless were everywhere, wrapped in blankets of newspaper, huddled twitching, moaning and shivering in doorways, on grates, or inside cardboard boxes, but at three in the morning no one else was about. No one but the ranks of sooty gargoyles peering down from the upper stories of all the office buildings.

For a moment, Elliott felt a thrill of excitement. It had been a long time since he'd embarked on a clandestine, potentially dangerous errand. Once upon a time he would have relished the challenge.

Then he remembered that on his previous adventures it had been willowy, blond, blue-eyed Mary pacing at his side, and his instant of pleasure died in a spasm of grief.

Rosalita clutched his arm. "I think that man is staring at us," she murmured.

Striving to shrug off his misery, Elliott looked where his companion was looking, at a hulking man with a long, tangled beard sitting with his back against a graffiti-scarred brick wall. Sharpening his senses, the Toreador elder heard the thump of the mortal's heart and the rasp of his breathing, smelled his fetid body odor and saw the red, brown and silver aura flickering around him.

"He may be watching us," Elliott conceded, "and if so, judging from the crimson in his aura, he doesn't like us very much. But he's human, and by all indications a genuine homeless person, so I doubt that he poses any threat."

"Then maybe it *wasn't* him that I sensed," Rosalita said, peering about again.

Elliott felt impatient with her, yet sympathetic as well. She was young and had never done this kind of thing before. Sheltered in Roger's hitherto placid domain, she'd probably thought that being a vampire was *easy*, a never-ending round of feeding on unwitting or even acquiescent mortals, making music, and attending parties. She had no real concept of the perils that stalked her world of perpetual night, of the ordeals a Kindred must sometimes endure to preserve his endless life.

"Please," he told her, smiling confidently, exerting his charismatic powers, "calm down. I've done this kind of thing many times before. I promise you that we'll get through it."

Rosalita smiled ruefully. "I know we will, with you calling the shots. I'm sorry I'm so jumpy."

"It's all right," Elliott said. "You should have seen how timid I was the first time I got caught up in a struggle among Kindred." The two undead walked past a bookstore and what, before it went out of business, had been a boutique. Perhaps Elliott had caught a mild case of his companion's jitters, because he imagined that one of the bald, naked mannequins in the window turned its head slightly when they went by. He repressed the impulse to look back and see if it really had.

"Here we are," Rosalita said.

The door of the office building they intended to enter had an electronic lock requiring both a magnetized plastic key card and the proper combination to open. Earlier that night Elliott had intercepted a secretary who'd been working late as she exited the place. He'd charmed her, spirited her away to a nearby bar for a drink, teased the combination out of her without her quite realizing that he'd done so, and stolen the key from her handbag. Now he inserted the card in the proper slot and entered the numbers she'd given him on the keypad. One of the four heavy plate-glass doors clicked open, and he and Rosalita slipped into the lobby.

In the middle of the marble foyer was a semicircular desk with a rack of black-and-white video monitors linked to the building's security cameras situated behind it. Elliott had expected a guard to be stationed here, watching the screens and signing after-hours visitors in and out. He'd been prepared to talk his way past the mortal or subdue him if necessary. But, though the monitors were live, no one was on duty.

"Nobody home," Rosalita said, frowning. "That's funny."

"Perhaps the guard's patrolling," Elliott said, "or using the restroom, or catching a nap somewhere. In any case, it's one fewer obstacle for us to worry about, provided we can make it in and out before he comes back."

As they hurried to the elevators, their footsteps tapping on the slick, newly polished floor, Elliott studied the images on the monitors. All they showed him were vacant expanses of dimly lit corridor.

The bronze-colored elevator door opened as soon as Rosalita pushed the call button, and the two vampires stepped aboard. The Latin singer flinched when the panels rumbled shut again. Elliott suspected that, edgy as she was, being inside the car made her feel trapped.

The elevator stopped on the fourteenth floor. The doors opened. Emerging, Elliott smelled a hint of rot in the air. Frowning, he sniffed, but the odor was gone. Probably he'd caught the stink of someone's unwanted lunch rotting in a wastebasket.

The two Kindred skulked down the shadowy hall to one of the doors. The gilt lettering on the frosted-glass window read NICOLL, HAWKE, SOMMERS & ANTCZAK, ATTORNEYS AT LAW. According to Elliott's information, the firm was one of the most prosperous law partnerships in the Midwest, and Nicoll, the senior partner, had a painting by Thomas Fouquet, a brilliant nineteenth-century landscape artist and a Toreador protégé, hanging on his office wall to prove it.

The door had a mechanical lock. "Now," said Elliott, removing a black leather satchel of locksmith's tools from the pocket of his long cashmere overcoat, "we'll find out if I still remember what my burglar tutors taught me." He selected a gleaming pick, inserted it in the keyhole, and set to work.

He found that he hadn't lost the knack. His keen sense of touch still made opening the average lock a snap. He defeated this one so quickly that an observer watching from a distance might well have believed that he'd opened it with a key. He twisted the brass knob and swung the door open, revealing a receptionist's desk and a waiting room. A vase of roses, ghostly white in the gloom, sat on a table, suffusing the air with their perfume.

"Come on," he said, entering. Rosalita took a last wary look up and down the corridor, then followed him.

He led her on into the interior of the building, past an open area occupied by file cabinets, desks with computers on them, a photocopier, piled boxes of office supplies, and a kitchenette. "Do you know where you're going?" Rosalita whispered.

"I think so," Elliott replied. "I'd give twenty-to-one that Nicoll has the corner office, and, unless my sense of direction is on the fritz, that's this one." He twisted a doorknob; this time the door was unlocked. Beyond it was a large room with a row of windows running along the back and right-hand walls. A handful of the slumbering city's lights glowed in the darkness beyond the glass. On the left-hand wall, behind Nicoll's drawerless, glass-topped table of a desk and between floor-to-ceiling shelves of leather-bound law books, hung Fouquet's painting. The canvas depicted a view of a weathered covered bridge spanning a peaceful river, with oaks and maples, their leaves ablaze with autumn, growing all around. Rosalita, who, like Elliott, could see the picture clearly despite the dimness, gasped at its beauty.

Momentarily jealous of her rapture, Elliott moved to the painting and lifted it off the wall. "Don't just stand there," he said gruffly, "give me the cover."

Blinking, Rosalita gave her head a shake and unrolled her piece of canvas. The two vampires wrapped it around Fouquet's picture and tied it in place with a length of rope.

Elliott tucked the landscape under his arm and turned toward the door. Then he caught a whiff of the foul odor he had smelled before, and heard a faint, scuffing sound. "Hold it," he whispered, raising his hand. "Did you hear that? Or smell it?"

"No," she replied uncertainly. He grimaced. It would have been nice to have confirmation, but the fact that she hadn't sensed what he had didn't necessarily mean he'd been imagining things. Her perceptions, though more acute than any mortal's, weren't as sharp as his.

"I think somebody's out there," he said, nodding to the rest of the suite and other rooms and corridors beyond.

"Do you think they followed us?" she asked.

He shrugged. "I would have sworn that nobody was tailing us out on the street. I wonder if it could be the vandal, come to destroy the Fouquet. It would be a hell of a coincidence if we all went after the same picture at the same time, but stranger things have happened." Almost despite himself, exhilaration like that he'd experienced on the street began to infuse his spirit. His errand had just become considerably more interesting. "If it *is* our culprit, we're going to catch him. Wait here while I scout around."

Elliott leaned the Fouquet against the wall, drew his Beretta 92F automatic from its shoulder holster and then, crouching, stalked silently out the door. His senses probed the gloom, seeking a flicker of motion or aura, noise, or the stink of decay.

After several seconds, darkness stirred at the periphery of his vision. Whirling, he aimed the gun, then saw that he had no target. Outside the window at the end of the corridor a cloud had swallowed the moon, dimming the wan light seeping through the glass.

Before long, he was convinced that no one but himself and Rosalita was lurking in the office. That left the hallway outside. He prowled to the exterior door, started to twist the knob, then froze.

Frequently his enhanced perception enabled him to detect sights, sounds and aromas that another person would have missed. More rarely, it kindled his intuition, as it did now. Though he didn't actually see or hear anything to indicate he was in danger, he *felt* that it could be fatal to stick his head outside.

Hoping the bolt wouldn't make an audible click, he locked the door, then braced one of the waiting-room chairs under the knob. Such a flimsy barrier wouldn't hold back vampires for long, but it might buy him and Rosalita a vital second. Pointing the Beretta at the door, he backed out of the waiting room and on through the suite.

When he reached Nicoll's office, Rosalita said, "Did you find anything?"

"There's an ambush waiting for us in the hall," he said. "As soon as we step outside, they'll catch us in a crossfire."

Her lustrous brown eyes focused on him in shock. "Are you sure?"

Actually, he wasn't. The trouble with relying on his hunches was that even a Toreador elder's intuition occasionally played him false. But it would be a mistake to betray any uncertainty to a nervous subordinate. "Yes," he said.

Rosalita gave a jerky nod, reached inside her own coat, and brought out her Sig Sauer Pistole 75. "Then I guess we'll have to shoot our way out," she said.

Elliott felt proud of her. She might be jittery, but she was game. Roger had made a good choice when he'd Embraced her; better, perhaps, than when he'd transformed Elliott himself. "No," the actor said.

She frowned. "But if it's just one or two guys, or if they're human, they shouldn't pose all that much of a threat."

"But I don't think that's how it is," Elliott replied. "I think that up until now your instincts have been sharper than mine. The enemy has been lying in wait for us here. We were in trouble from the moment we climbed out of the car. Perhaps from the moment we arrived in town. And I think our best hope is to find another way out of the building." He strode past her into Nicoll's office. Crossing to the windows, he raised one and looked down.

Below him was an expanse of grimy, weathered stone wall riddled with cracks and pockmarks, decorated with gargoyles and other bits of decorative carving, and transected by the occasional narrow ledge. Along the bottom ran a narrow side street, where bits of windblown trash scudded along the broken pavement. More of the homeless were huddled in the shadows, but Elliott didn't see anyone who looked like a sentry; not that that meant much, peering from such a distance. Even his vision had its limits.

He was willing to bet his life that he could climb down the outside of the building. He was, after all, more agile than any human, and his enhanced perception gave him an exquisite sense of balance. Rosalita possessed the same abilities, though to a lesser degree. He gave her a smile. "Not afraid of heights, are you?" he asked.

She stared at him. "You're kidding, right?"

"I'm afraid not. It's our best option."

"Can we just go a little ways and then climb back through another window?"

"We *could*," Elliott said, "but then we'd still be stuck inside the building, and I suspect that by now there are people watching the exits. I'd rather climb all the way to the ground if you think you can make it."

"All right," she said, returning her pistol to the holster on her belt, "I can do it if I have to."

"Good girl." He put away his own gun, discarded his topcoat, suit coat and vest, and tied the rope securing the Fouquet to the back of his belt. The painting bumped against his butt and legs whenever he moved. "Have you ever done any climbing?" he asked.

She shook her head.

"Take your time," he said, "and think before you move. Test your handholds before you trust your weight to them. Don't hug the wall and don't look down. I'm going to go out first and stay right underneath you, so I'll be there to help if you get into trouble. You close the window when you get outside. Are you ready?"

"As ready as I'm going to get," she said.

He eased himself out into the darkness. The cold wind gusted, riffling his hair and clothing, batting at the painting dangling from his waist. Quickly but methodically testing the hand- and toeholds afforded by the cavities in the eroding stone, he descended ten feet to a gargoyle with the fangs of a sabertooth tiger and the curling horns of a ram. He peered up at Rosalita's pretty, heart-shaped face. "Come on," he said.

The younger Kindred lowered herself from the window and pulled it shut, hanging from the sill for a moment. Then she started down. Almost at once, stone cracked. She yelped and began to drop. Elliott stretched out his arm to catch her, but she grabbed a handhold and arrested her fall. Bits of rock clattered down the wall to smash on the sidewalk below.

"I thought I put my hands exactly where you did," Rosalita said, a tremor in her voice.

"You have to test the stone for yourself," Elliott said. "But that's all right, no harm done. Climb on down."

For a moment she didn't move. He was afraid that she was too rattled to continue, but then she resumed her descent. Releasing the wall, balancing as confidently as a tightrope walker, he backed a step away from the side of the building on the gargoyle's narrow granite spine, making room for his companion to alight.

When she did, he asked, "Are you all right?"

"I think so," she said. "Let's keep moving. I don't want just to hang here in midair and think about what comes next."

He studied her aura. It was tinged with the orange of fear, but not ablaze with it. He didn't think that she was in any danger of panicking. Satisfied, he said, "All right," and lowered himself from the stone monster. Hanging by one hand, he grabbed a jagged crack in the wall with the other, then continued his descent. Rosalita followed him.

To his relief she didn't slip again, though occasionally she couldn't find a place to put her groping feet and he had to climb back up and guide them for her. After a few minutes she said, "I wouldn't have believed it, but this is starting to be fun."

He decided that she was right. Long ago, he'd enjoyed climbing, swimming, riding, fencing and the martial arts, but in recent years he'd nearly forgotten the pleasure of pitting himself against a physical challenge. Or the joy of outwitting a band of enemies, leaving them bewildered and humiliated.

He began to smile, then heard a muffled crash overhead. The would-be ambushers had gotten tired of waiting for the Toreador to emerge from the office and had broken in to find them. Hoping that, with all the windows closed, the enemy wouldn't realize where he and Rosalita had gone, Elliott said, "If you're getting the hang of mountaineering, now would be a good time to pick up the pace."

"I'll try," Rosalita said grimly. She began to move faster. Then one of Nicoll's office windows opened. A creature stuck its head out.

The newcomer's countenance was as hideous and asymmetrical as a visage encountered in a nightmare. Framed by oversized, pointed ears, the face had two eyes, positioned one above the other, on the right side, and one, milky as if sealed with a cataract, on the left. Half its scalp was bald, while the other half sprouted stiff gray spines resembling a porcupine's quills. Its broad, flat nose had three nostrils, and crooked tusks jutted from its diagonal slash of a mouth. Trails of dark drool streaked its chin.

When Elliott saw it he realized why he hadn't detected the enemy sooner. The thing was surely a Nosferatu, a member of the loathsome Camarilla clan whose members were monstrously deformed. Many of the bloodline possessed powers of invisibility so effective that even a Kindred with heightened senses had difficulty penetrating them.

For one more instant, Elliott dared to hope that the Nosferatu wouldn't see him or Rosalita in the gloom. Then, its three eyes widening, the freakish Kindred screamed, "They're down here!" in a high, female voice.

Several other windows shattered as the hideous vampire's companions smashed them. Shards of glass showered on

Rosalita and Elliott, nearly knocking them from their perches, and crashed on the street below. Other Nosferatu, their features altogether different but just as misshapen as those of the first one, leaned out into the night and aimed their guns at the Toreador. The weapons flashed, barked and chattered, and bullets ricocheted whining off the wall.

Elliott looked down. He and Rosalita were still about forty feet above the street. A fall that far onto hard pavement would kill or at least cripple a mortal, but two preternaturally agile vampires might survive it intact. Certainly it seemed preferable to leap now, of their own volition, rather than wait a moment for the enemy to shoot them off the wall. Clambering out from under Rosalita to keep her from landing on top of him, he yelled, "Jump!" and thrust himself into space.

Though he knew the fall could only be taking a second, he seemed to plummet for a long time. Then, abruptly, his feet slammed down on the sidewalk midway between an overturned trash barrel and a graffiti-covered newspaper box. He tumbled into a roll to soak up the shock of impact, and emerged from it scraped and bleeding but essentially unharmed. Ragged, grubby mortals, already in the process of fleeing the barrage of gunfire hammering the street, gaped at him in amazement.

A split second later, Rosalita smashed down on the pavement. Elliott heard a sharp crack, and then she pitched forward on her face.

"Are you all right?" he asked, crouching over her.

"My leg's broken," she whimpered, breathless with pain. "Something's hurting in my chest and back, too."

Since she'd survived the moment of impact, her injuries couldn't kill or permanently incapacitate her. She'd recuperate in a matter of minutes or hours. But for the moment she wouldn't be able to run fast enough to get away. Stifling a curse, moving with superhuman speed, he tore the Fouquet off his belt. The canvas bundle was now shapeless rather than rectangular, since the fall had smashed the frame. For once thankful that art and beauty no longer captivated him as they once had, he chucked the package into the street.

"No!" Rosalita croaked. "The frame broke, but the *picture* may still be all right!"

"I can't carry it and you both," Elliott replied. He picked her up, draped her over her shoulders in a fireman's carry, and ran. Bullets pounded the sidewalk like hail.

Zigzagging, he made it across the street and around the corner without getting shot. Now the gunmen in Nicoll's office could no longer see him, but he didn't dare slow down. He was certain that they had comrades stationed on the ground.

He sprinted on toward his rented LeSabre. He and Rosalita had left it three blocks away, in the nearest legal parking space; they hadn't wanted to return to it only to find it that it had been towed away, or immobilized with a boot. It had seemed like an intelligent decision at the time, but now it could cost them their lives.

Elliott began to feel the strain of sprinting at superhuman speed while carrying a hundred-pound woman. He wasn't growing tired or winded in the way a mortal would, but the exertion was burning the vitae in his system like flame consuming gasoline.

Something whispered through the air above his head.

He frantically peered upward. For a moment he couldn't see anything, but then he glimpsed the three-eyed Kindred who'd spotted him and Rosalita when they were clinging to the wall. Naked, her white, chancrous breasts and crooked legs as ugly as the rest of her, the Nosferatu was riding the night wind on winglike flaps of skin extending from her wrists to her knees. Evidently, when the Toreador had run out of gunshot range, she'd swooped from Nicoll's office in pursuit.

Unlike the shapeshifters of the Gangrel clan, who could assume the forms of huge bats, the Nosferatu was gliding precariously, not flying. She couldn't have aimed a gun and remained aloft. But she could, and did, drop the small, round object in her right hand.

Elliott dove to one side. He lost his grip on Rosalita and she tumbled off his shoulders. The grenade exploded as soon as it hit the street, peppering the Toreador elder with shrapnel. The boom spiked pain through his hypersensitive ears.

Staggering to his feet, grateful that the blast hadn't crippled him, Elliott snatched out his Beretta and aimed it at his attacker. The Nosferatu snarled and hurtled down at him.

Elliott squeezed off three shots. Two hit the Nosferatu in the chest and one in the cheek, but the hideous undead kept coming. He spun out of her way.

Or at least he tried. Perhaps his wounds were slowing him down, or perhaps she possessed a touch of the supernatural quickness that only those of Toreador or Brujah blood ordinarily possessed. In any case, her gnarled, taloned hand shot out and grabbed his forearm, and her momentum jerked him off balance.

The two combatants tumbled to the ground and rolled over and over, grappling. The Nosferatu's fetid body odor, the same stink Elliott had smelled in the office building, filled his nostrils as she clawed and bit at him. He could feel that she was far stronger than he was, strong enough to tear him apart. Butting and gouging, using every infighting trick he knew, he barely managed to fend her off until he could point the Beretta at her midsection and fire two more shots.

The Nosferatu convulsed. Blood, black in the moonlight, gushed from her misshapen mouth. Elliott scrambled out from underneath her and pointed the automatic at her head.

"Who's attacking my people?" he demanded. "What's it all about? Talk, or I'll kill you."

The Nosferatu's arm flopped like a fish lying in the bottom of a boat. Elliott suspected that she'd tried to claw him, but presently lacked the strength. "Go fuck yourself," she moaned.

Elliott opened his mouth to press the issue, and then automatic-weapons fire crackled through the night.

The actor spun around. Three more Nosferatu stood a few yards down the street. He suspected they'd been stationed on the ground floor of the office building and had chased him when he ran away. With his supernatural speed, he'd outdistanced them, but their winged comrade's attack had delayed him long enough for them to catch up. Now, seemingly indifferent to the fact that she was in the field of fire, they were blasting at their quarry with Uzis.

Elliott flung himself to the ground as bullets hurtled through the space he'd vacated. Moving with blinding speed, he rolled and fired, rolled and fired, snap-shooting, relying on his inhuman coordination and eyesight to place the bullets.

One of the Nosferatu's shots slammed into his left shoulder, shattering bone. Ignoring the resultant burst of agony, he kept his own gun blazing. One of the hideous Kindred, then another, and finally the last crumpled to the ground, felled by repeated shots to the head.

Elliott watched them for a moment, making sure they weren't going to jump back up any time soon. Finally satisfied, the elation of victory counterbalancing his Hunger and the pain of his wounds, he remembered Rosalita. Smiling, he turned to check on her.

His companion lay motionless in a pool of her own fragrant vitae. When she'd fallen from his shoulders, she must have wound up closer to the grenade than he'd realized. The explosion had obliterated her features and virtually severed her head.

Elliott wailed. Suddenly he felt that he was living not merely in the present but simultaneously fifteen years in the past. That the Toreador woman lying on the broken asphalt, her gory, outflung hand dangling in a pothole, was not only Rosalita but Mary, butchered by the mortal vampire hunters who'd attacked her so mysteriously.

Squinching his eyes shut, he tried to push the grisly memory aside. He mustn't cave in to his grief over Mary's death, not now, or he wouldn't escape this killing ground. God knew, the horror of what had happened to Rosalita was nearly overwhelming by itself.

When he felt that he had control of himself, he opened his eyes, ran to Rosalita and knelt beside her. Perhaps she was still alive. In the course of his centuries of existence, he'd seen one or two members of his resilient species recover from injuries nearly as severe. But no matter how closely he scrutinized her, he couldn't see any signs of incipient tissue regeneration, nor the slightest flicker of aura. After a few seconds, her flesh began to rot.

The three-eyed Nosferatu chuckled, a broken hiccup of a sound, as if she were choking on the blood still flowing from her mouth. "We got one of you," she croaked. "The night wasn't a total loss."

Furious, Elliott thought, *You won't think it's so funny when I torture your secrets out of you.* Then, somewhere in the night, out of sight but not far away and drawing nearer, he heard tense voices muttering and hurrying feet pattering along the pavement.

More of his enemies were approaching. But if he couldn't take the time to interrogate the Nosferatu, he could at least avenge Rosalita's murder. He dashed to one of the three-eyed Kindred's downed companions, grabbed the deformed vampire's Uzi, and ran back to the object of his wrath.

Cowering, the Nosferatu tried to lift her arms, probably hoping to wrap them around her head for protection, but she was still effectively paralyzed. Elliott pointed the machine gun at her neck and fired every bullet in the clip, decapitating her.

Hearing the reports, his oncoming enemies quickened their pace. Elliott wheeled and sprinted for the car, past dozens more homeless mortals. He half-expected that one of them would prove to be another of his foes and leap into his path brandishing a weapon, but everyone cringed from the racing man with the raw face and shredded, bloody clothes.

He rounded another corner and the LeSabre swam out of the murk ahead. His first impulse was to return to the hotel room he'd rented, but then he realized that the enemy might have a lookout posted there. It would be safer to drive out of town.

He unlocked the car door, scrambled inside and twisted the key in the ignition. The engine roared to life. As he threw the LeSabre into gear, scarlet tears of rage and regret began to seep from his eyes.

SIX: THE WARNING

Every good gift, and every perfect gift, is from above.
— James 1:17

As Judy rode her Harley through the gate in the coquina wall encircling Roger's estate, a spectacular fork of lightning flamed over the expanse of ocean behind the imposing house. A stray drop of water, harbinger of the downpour to come, smacked against the motorcycle's bug-splattered windshield.

Ordinarily the Brujah elder relished storms, just as she delighted in riding her hog as fast as it would go, slam-dancing to death metal, or any other spectacle or pastime that somehow mirrored the savage spirit of her bloodline. But tonight she scowled at the prospect of violent weather. A storm would further hamper the search for the rogue vampire who threatened the Masquerade, a search which seemed to be getting nowhere as it was. They hadn't even found any trace of that diabolist bastard Murdock.

She hurtled up a brick drive lined with towering royal palms, parked her Harley under the porte-cochère, and marched up the front steps and through the front door into the foyer. The handcuffs suspended from her studded belt clinked.

Visible through arched doorways, the spacious interior of the house looked as lovely and well-tended as ever. Every object was a work of art, and the contents of every room had been meticulously arranged into a pleasing gestalt. But nevertheless, a lonely, desolate feeling hung in the air, an atmosphere she'd never encountered here before. She remembered how, on her first meeting with Roger Phillips in the 1880s, she'd scorned his haven as evidence of his fundamental Toreador effeteness, just as she'd chafed at the notion of conceding him any measure of authority over herself and her brood.

The two of them had come a long way since then, facing a number of crises shoulder to shoulder, and gradually, against all expectation and contrary to the prejudices common to those of her lineage, Roger and his Toreador lieutenants had won her respect. Today even the most fractious of her independent childer were willing to abide the prince's governance, at least while he ruled as lightly as he had hitherto. Judy would be saddened if he never recovered his sanity and his progeny were exterminated or driven from their domain.

The Brujah scowled at herself. Such defeatist thoughts were unworthy of the warrior who'd engineered Stonewall Jackson's demise. Striving to shove her forebodings aside, she bellowed, "Lazlo!" The shout echoed through the house.

After a moment, a door on the second floor clicked open and shut. Floorboards creaked and Roger's mortal confidant, looking haggard and careworn, started down the majestic oak staircase. He was wearing a ratty, stretched-out sweater, incongruous in such elegant surroundings, with a bone-white cellular phone protruding from one of the pockets. "Good evening, Judy," he said. "I wish you wouldn't yell. You might have gotten Roger agitated again."

The former slave shrugged. She liked Lazlo, and knew he was right to scold her, but she had her limits: it wasn't in her nature to admit error to a human, particularly a white male human. "I don't hear him hollering," she replied, "so obviously, I didn't. How is he?"

Shaking his head, Lazlo alit from the bottom stair. "Unresponsive," he said. "He's started having what Dr. Potter calls 'episodes of catatonia.' I don't think he knows why."

"What a surprise," Judy said dryly. As far as she'd been able to determine, the celebrated Dr. Potter hadn't managed to learn *anything* about Roger's condition. "I didn't see any guards when I came in."

"They're some of Gunter's Malkavians," Lazlo said. Some members of the lunatic clan, like many Kindred of the deformed Nosferatu bloodline, possessed uncanny powers of concealment. "You're not *supposed* to see them." He gestured toward one of the doorways, inviting her to step into a darkened room which, she knew from past experience, was a cozy parlor. "Would you like to sit down? And is there something I can help you with?"

She walked into the parlor and dropped heavily into a red, velvet-covered armchair. She assumed that it was some priceless antique and that Lazlo, who was almost as much of an aesthete as his master, could bore her with its provenance if she were fool enough to ask about it. "I just came by to find out how Roger was," she said, "and to see which of the art thieves has checked in." And to give herself a break from the frustrating manhunt her people were conducting on the streets.

Lazlo switched on a green and gold Tiffany floor lamp, driving the shadows into the corners of the room, then slumped down on an ornately hand-tooled leather sofa. "I've heard from three of the teams," he said. "Two achieved their objective, one didn't."

Judy glanced at the ormolu pendulum clock softly ticking on the mantelpiece. It was almost four-thirty. "Shouldn't you have heard from more of them by now?" she asked, frowning.

"They were *supposed* to check in," Lazlo said, "but

perhaps they simply aren't bothering." He gave her a smile that tried and failed to mask his worry. "Toreador are sometimes as bad at following instructions as you Brujah, especially when they have some coup to celebrate."

"Maybe so," she said. One of her scars throbbed, and she twisted her arm around behind her back to rub it. She often wondered how the old welts could still ache one hundred and sixty years after she'd passed from life into undeath. People had told her that the pain was psychosomatic, but she refused to believe that her mind was masochistic or weak enough to cause her needless discomfort. "I hope so. But if they're screwing around partying when they know we're at war, I'm going to have a little talk—"

Lazlo's cellular phone buzzed.

The mortal fumbled the instrument out of his pocket. Judy watched impatiently, fighting the urge to tear it from his hand. Surely no vampire ever moved so clumsily, even when filled with anxiety.

Finally the mortal managed to bring the cordless phone to his mouth. "Phillips residence," he said.

The person on the other end of the line began to reply, but Judy, whose senses were no keener than a mortal's, couldn't make out the words. Moving as quickly and nimbly as a cat, she surged out of her chair, crouched over Lazlo and poised her ear beside his head and the phone. The aging mortal cringed slightly, probably without even realizing it — the prey instinctively shrinking from the predator.

"I'm at a gas station a few miles south of Columbus," the voice on the line continued. It was Elliott's voice, but his normally rich tones were weak and shaky. Had he been human, she would have inferred that he was out of breath.

"Is something wrong?" Lazlo asked. "You sound upset."

"I had to feed," Elliott said. "It was an emergency, and I was rough. I clubbed someone unconscious, and I drank a lot."

Judy scowled. Ordinarily, she knew, Elliott was a

sandman, one of those squeamish Kindred who fed only from sleeping vessels and, except for a touch of anemia, left them none the worse physically or psychologically for his visit. But in the past, when necessary, he'd taken down wakeful, frantically struggling kine, so she doubted that the scuffle he'd just experienced was truly what had unnerved him. Once again she fought against an impulse to snatch the phone and demand an explanation.

"Did you leave any evidence that could compromise the Masquerade?" Lazlo asked.

"No," Elliott said.

"Is the man alive?" said Lazlo.

"Yes," the Toreador elder replied.

"Then this part of the situation is under control," Lazlo said soothingly. Obviously, like Judy, he'd figured out that Elliott hadn't told him the really bad news yet. "If you want, you can call the man an ambulance just before you leave. Now, what else is wrong?"

"Rosalita and I walked into a trap," Elliott said. "A gang of Nosferatu were lying in wait for us, and they killed her. Has everyone else checked in?"

"No," Lazlo said, frowning.

"Damn!" Elliott exclaimed. "The ones who haven't must have been ambushed too!"

Judy couldn't bear to listen passively any longer. She grabbed the phone away from Lazlo. Startled, recoiling involuntarily, the dresser gaped at her. Perhaps she'd used a bit of her supernatural strength or speed without even realizing it.

"Are you wounded?" demanded the former slave, speaking into the phone.

"Not badly," Elliott replied. "Now that I've fed, I'll be all right. But poor Rosalita—"

"Forget Rosalita!" Judy snapped, wishing that they were talking face to face. If she could have made eye contact, she might have been able to use a touch of her power to

Dominate to jolt him out of his funk. "There's nothing you can do for her now. Did anyone follow you out of town?"

"I don't think so."

Judy scowled. "Did you *check?*"

"Yes."

"Then hang up the phone and keep moving," she said. "Switch cars if you can manage it. Watch the time; remember you have to find a safe refuge before the sun comes up. Catch a flight home tomorrow night. Do you understand?"

"Yes."

"Then do it! Now!"

After a moment of silence, Elliott broke the connection.

Judy handed the phone back to Lazlo. The mortal's face twisted as if he were trying not to cry. "Rosalita," he said sadly. "Roger loved her like a daughter. Before he got sick, news of her death would have broken his heart. Now, I don't suppose he'd even care."

Judy scowled. She was dismayed by the present turn of events herself, but that was no reason to blubber about it. The proper Brujah reaction was to get angry. She began to pace around the room, fighting the urge to pick up some piece of bric-a-brac and smash it, or punch a hole in the wall. "Does Roger have any Nosferatu enemies?" she asked.

Lazlo shook his head. "None that I can think of."

"I don't know of anybody either." And it was entirely possible that the Sewer Rats who'd waylaid Elliott had been acting on behalf of a non-Nosferatu master. Judy and her allies were no closer to unmasking their phantom nemesis than they'd been before. "Shit!" she snarled. "Shit, shit, shit!" She kicked the leg of a small, round, marble-topped table, snapping it. Toppling, the table spilled a green jade statuette of some Chinese goddess onto the Persian rug. Judy felt disappointed that the carving hadn't broken, but managed to refrain from stamping and grinding it under her steel-toed boots.

Rounding on Lazlo, she said, "Gunter and I both warned everyone that going after the art was a bad idea."

Lazlo sighed. "The Toreador had no choice but to go. You know that."

"What I know," she said, "is that Elliott can't cut it as a leader or a fighter anymore. You heard him just now. He sounded like he was in shock."

Lazlo stared at her reproachfully. "How can you say that, after all that he's accomplished in the past? I'm told that he once saved your life."

Judy felt a pang of guilt. It was a weak, useless, *human* emotion, unworthy of a Brujah, and, scowling, she tried unsuccessfully to quash it. "I haven't forgotten," she said, resuming her pacing. "He was a good man once. He still is, in a way, and I still consider him my friend. But something inside him died along with Mary." Remembering the mysterious tragedy, she sighed. "Did you guys ever find out any more about why it happened?"

"Not really," Lazlo said. "We tried for years, but considering that Elliott killed the murderers as soon as he caught them, and then we couldn't identify them, we really didn't have any leads. There were indications that the men belonged to the Society of Leopold." The Society was a fanatical clandestine organization cognizant of the existence of vampires and dedicated to their extermination. "But we have no idea how they discovered Mary's true nature, or why, out of all the Kindred in Sarasota, they chose to target her.

"You know," Lazlo continued, "Roger never lost faith in Elliott, and I hope you won't either. In a crisis like the one we're facing, the Toreador need a captain of their own blood to follow, and I can't imagine Sky filling the bill. He's actually brave and resourceful, but the way he flounces around, people don't take him seriously."

"You have a point," Judy conceded, straightening her Union soldier's cap. "And I don't *want* to see Elliott pushed to the sidelines. But I'm not going to let him screw up the war effort, either. We'll have to see what kind of shape he's in when he gets back into town."

Lazlo's phone buzzed. He lifted it to his ear and said, "Phillips residence." After a moment, he looked at Judy. "It's for you."

The Brujah frowned in puzzlement. She'd stopped in at the prince's haven on impulse, without telling anyone where she was going; no one should have known where to call her. She held out her slender, delicate-looking hand, and Lazlo put the phone in it. Raising the instrument to her mouth, she grunted, "Yeah?"

"Good evening," said the musical contralto voice on the other end of the line.

Judy felt a thrill sing down her nerves. Some quality in the speaker's tone was both captivating and intimidating. The Brujah had spent enough time around Toreador and Ventrue, many of whom possessed uncanny powers of personal magnetism, to recognize that she was falling under the sway of some Kindred's supernatural charisma. But such an ability, like her own talent for coercion, didn't normally work when the target couldn't see the face of the vampire employing it.

She struggled to shake off the fascination she was feeling, and was partially successful. "Who is this?" she demanded.

"A friend," the other woman said.

"That doesn't cut it," Judy said, wishing that she had the means in place to trace the call. But of course she and her allies had had no way of knowing that they might need to do such a thing. Even the Kindred, for whom a moderate level of paranoia was not a sign of derangement but of sound survival instincts, couldn't be prepared for every contingency.

"My identity isn't important," the other vampire said. "I'm calling to guide you to four of your enemies. They're in Sarasota now, prowling the streets around the Tropical Gardens."

"Why?" Judy asked.

"They're scouting. And if they happen to find one of your people alone, they'll kill him. They'll be leaving your territory soon, to beat the dawn, but if you hurry you can catch them."

"Who *are* these bastards?" Judy asked. "Why are they out to get us?"

The other vampire hung up.

Frustrated but excited as well, Judy tossed the phone onto the couch. "Our first break," she said.

"What do you mean?" Lazlo asked.

"We've got an anonymous informant, maybe a traitor in the enemy camp who just gave us a present. She told me that we can catch some of the bad guys near the Tropical Gardens."

"What if she isn't really a friend?" Lazlo asked, his forehead creased with worry. "What if she's leading you into another trap, no different from the ones the enemy set for the Toreador?"

It might have been the lingering influence of the unknown vampire's charisma, but Judy doubted that she'd been gulled; in any case, she was too eager to come to grips with the foe to worry about the possibility. "If it's a setup, we'll just have to turn the tables on them," she said. "I'll round up some of my people on my way to the party. You see who you can scare up on the phone."

Too impatient to discuss the matter further, she wheeled and marched away, her pace accelerating with every stride. By the time she reached the foyer, she was running.

SEVEN: THE RESCUE

People must help one another; it is nature's law.
— Jean de La Fontaine, "L'Âne et le Chien"

The Sarasota Tropical Gardens, a ten-acre artificial jungle housing lemurs, alligators, otters, monkeys, wallabies and numerous other animals, was a tourist attraction, and the businesses on the other side of Bayshore Road catered to vacationers and day-trippers as well. The four vampires from out of town sauntered past T-shirt shops, fast-food franchises, bars and souvenir stands, all silent and dark in the final hours before dawn.

Dan had been stalking the strangers since just after midnight, hanging about half a block back. At first it had been a nerve-wracking experience, but gradually he'd concluded that, as long as he was careful, they wouldn't spot him. One of the new talents that Melpomene's vitae had instilled in him would see to that. When he stood motionless in shadow or behind some piece of cover, no matter how inadequate it seemed, he became virtually invisible.

The Methuselah's magic had also made his muscles even stronger than before, as well as intermittently sharpening his senses. He could smell the stale odors of cooking grease, smoke and beer wafting from the establishments along the strip; the sweet perfume of flowers and the musky scent of animals drifting from the Gardens across the street; the ozone tang of the storm brewing overhead. At certain moments, when his worn, faded jeans and soft denim work shirt seemed to chafe unbearably, his newly heightened perception became a nuisance. He hoped that he'd learn to filter out the unwanted side effects in time.

To his annoyance, despite his enhanced hearing, he couldn't quite make out what the other Kindred were murmuring to each other, so he still had no idea what they were doing wandering around town. He suspected that they were on a scouting mission, not that it mattered. What was important was that Melpomene had supposedly arranged for some of Prince Roger's flunkies to attack them. When they did, Dan was going to jump into the fray and save the intruders' butts.

He just hoped that he was up to the job. Melpomene's blood had made him more powerful than before, but he knew damn well that he still wasn't Supervamp. The ancient undead had given him an ace in the hole to employ in this particular situation, but he had no way of knowing how well it was going to work. Like everything else about his new boss, he was taking it on faith.

Engines rumbled in the night. After a moment, Dan could tell that they were drawing nearer.

He assumed that the noise was the prince's troops approaching. Until recently, Sarasota had been a hedonistic artists' colony, beach resort and college town, where people partied through the night. But in the days since the mysterious killer the news media were calling Dracula had begun his reign of terror, the kine had begun cowering in their homes. After twelve, the dark streets were empty except for the undead.

Still, Dan didn't *know* that Roger's goons were on their

way. He'd better hold off using Melpomene's gift until he was sure. Once the stuff was gone, it was gone for good.

One of the foreign vampires, whom Dan had tentatively identified as the leader, was a tall, teenage-looking guy with bleached white eyebrows, mohawk and goatee. He was wearing white leather gloves with steel studs on the back, a voluminous white leather overcoat with an intricate pattern of rivets on the back and shoulders, a torn white tank top, camo-patterned parachute pants, and high-top sneakers. He spoke to his companions, and all four of them retreated into the narrow gap separating two of the shops.

Dan frowned. He hoped that the strangers wouldn't conceal themselves so well that the prince's searchers would fail to spot them. If that happened, Melpomene's scheme would fall apart. Dan guessed that, at that point, his only option would be simply to reveal himself to the intruders and try to win their trust; he knew from long and bitter experience just how well *that* ploy was likely to work.

Wearily, he wondered for the millionth time just why his fellow Kindred disliked him so. He'd always been popular when he was a kid, had always been in the thick of things, playing varsity football and basketball, organizing a school computer club, a welcome guest at everybody's parties. His fellow soldiers had liked him, too. After his transformation, the universal loathing with which even other Caitiff regarded him had come as almost as much of a shock as the Hunger itself.

Wind gusted, lightning flared, thunder boomed; the storm was drawing closer. An instant later, five motorcycles and a Mustang convertible turned onto Bayshore. Dan imagined that the bikers at least were Brujah; many of Judith Morgan's progeny shared her enthusiasm for Harleys. The headlights momentarily dazzled his newly sensitive eyes.

As he'd feared, for a moment it looked as if Prince Roger's search party would speed right past the strangers' hiding place. But then the driver of the Mustang blew a blast on his horn, and everyone braked sharply. The convertible's tires squealed, and the bikes spun in tight arcs as their riders turned them around.

Dan took the tarnished silver vial Melpomene had given him out of his pocket, hastily unscrewed the cap and tossed the contents down his throat.

The Methuselah had told him the liquid was giants' blood, the vitae of actual Jack-and-the-Beanstalk-style ogres who'd walked the earth at the dawn of history. He couldn't help doubting that such creatures had ever existed, even though his new patron swore that she'd seen them with her own eyes. At any rate, whatever the liquid was, he'd been rather hoping it would give him a flash of ecstasy comparable to what he'd experienced when drinking Melpomene's blood.

It didn't. The elixir tasted so bitter that he nearly retched it back up. An instant later, a burst of agony racked his stomach. As his knees buckled, sprawling him on the sidewalk, he wondered if Melpomene had poisoned him, betraying him for some mad, inscrutable reason. She *had* warned him that she was neither as kindly nor as sane as she appeared.

Up ahead, Judy Morgan herself, dressed provocatively as usual in her Civil War cap, a skimpy halter, skintight jeans, and boots, pulled a machine pistol from her saddlebag and gunned her Harley toward the narrow space into which the strangers had disappeared. The other bikers readied their own weapons and followed her, of necessity going single file. The convertible shot forward, its tires squealing; no doubt the driver intended to circle the block.

The cramping in Dan's gut eased, though a foul aftertaste lingered in his mouth. Heat tingled through his muscles and he imagined that he could feel his body swelling larger. Suddenly he was so full of energy that the thought of remaining still for another second was utterly intolerable. He surged to his feet, then bounded lightly onto the roof of the ice-cream shop beside which he'd been hiding.

As he raced down the strip of tourist traps, vaulting across the alleys between them when necessary, the battle ahead of him gradually came into view. At first he could only see headlights and the muzzle flashes of the guns, a diminutive counterpoint to the lightning strobing in the thunderheads above. Then, as raindrops began to patter on the shingles beneath his pounding feet, he glimpsed the shadowy forms of the hunters and their quarry.

It looked as if, when the strangers had fled into the street behind Bayshore, another contingent of the prince's flunkies had intercepted them and pinned them down in a construction site. Now the intruders were crouched down behind the scant cover afforded by the low beginnings of concrete-block walls. Motorcycles snarled, circling the makeshift fortress, and firearms chattered and banged. The smells of gun smoke and engine exhaust hung in the air.

The strangers were outnumbered three-to-one and manifestly in trouble. *Just the way I wanted it*, Dan thought sardonically. Reaching under his khaki Army surplus jacket for his Smith and Wesson Undercover .38, he leaped down into the street.

Dan shot one biker in the back of the head before the prince's troops even realized that a new opponent had materialized in their midst. The wounded Brujah tumbled from his seat. His motorcycle rolled a few more feet and overturned, striking sparks from the pavement as it skidded along on its side.

Dan heard an engine roar and glimpsed movement from the corner of his eye. He hurled himself to one side. The Mustang convertible shot past, missing him by inches, and smashed into the base of a storefront display window. The glass shattered, showering the car's newly crumpled hood with glittering shards. The vehicle's horn began to blare, adding to the cacophony of the battle.

The driver, a shaven-headed Kindred whose brow was now gashed and bleeding, scrambled out of the wreckage, fangs bared and a revolver in his hand. Dan could have tried shooting this opponent, too, but he realized that he didn't want to. With the vitality of the giants' blood roaring inside him, he wanted to use his body to the fullest, wanted to humble his foes with his bare hands. Casting his weapon aside, he lunged at the other vampire.

The driver's gun barked once, but if the shot hit Dan, he didn't even feel it. Before the shaven-headed Kindred could fire again, his assailant was on top of him. Dan hit him in the face, a punch that broke bone and sent him reeling back against his car; then he pounced on him.

The hairless Kindred struggled frantically, perhaps trying to bring his gun to bear. He was far stronger than a mortal, but nowhere near as powerful as his opponent. Dan sank his fingers into the other vampire's skull as if the bone were no more resistant than modelling clay, then, with one sudden motion, wrenched his head off.

Since undead hearts didn't beat, blood didn't spurt from the raw space between the dead vampire's shoulders; it flowed copiously enough, however, suffusing the air with its intoxicating scent. With a sudden pang of guilt, Dan remembered that he hadn't intended to destroy any of Prince Roger's vassals. Ultimately, he was on their side. But the feverish excitement induced by Melpomene's potion had opened the door for the Beast to take control.

He did his best to shrug off a spasm of self-disgust. He was still in the middle of the battle; he had no time for remorse. Still clutching the severed head in his right hand, he spun around to survey the rest of the combatants.

Another biker, a moon-faced Asian girl, was hurtling toward him, riding no-handed, firing bursts from her automatic rifle. Dan threw the head at her, but it sailed past her, bounced on the pavement and rolled away into the darkness. He pivoted back toward the convertible, ripped one of its doors off the hinges and hurled that, skimming it like a Frisbee.

The missile slammed into her, knocking her and her motorcycle over. Tumbling end over end, the rifle flew from her hands. Instantly, moving with superhuman speed, her fanged, pallid face a mask of fury, she scrambled out from under her bike, flipped open a butterfly knife, and charged him.

Seeking his .38, Dan looked around his feet, but he couldn't see where the revolver had fallen. Fists clenched, he shifted his body into a T-stance the way his unarmed-combat instructor at boot camp had taught him.

The Brujah sprinted as fast as a cheetah. It only took her a second to close to striking range. Her arm a blur, she stabbed and slashed at him repeatedly. Bursts of pain flowered in his chest.

But even if he hadn't been pumped up on giants' blood, Dan could have endured a few jabs in the torso. In any case, though the Asian girl clearly wasn't a skilled knife fighter, he wasn't sure that he could react quickly enough to parry her attacks. Better to concentrate on landing some blows of his own. He lunged at her, kicking and jabbing.

Still hacking and stabbing, her almond eyes aglitter with bloodlust, she gave ground. She ducked and slipped his first five attacks, but swung her arm up to block the sixth.

That was a mistake. With her pantherish speed and grace, she had no trouble connecting, but she simply lacked the strength to deflect the blow. His fist drove on to smash her nose flat, snap her neck and fling her eight feet backwards. She lay on the ground and thrashed.

Dan looked around. More of the prince's subjects were turning in his direction. Someone yelled, "Get the diabolist!" in a high, excited voice.

Okay, Dan thought, *let's see just how strong I really am.* He scrambled back to the convertible, dug his fingers into the body and, with a grunt of effort, heaved it over his head. The horn stopped blowing and the suspension groaned. Bits of broken glass and one of the hubcaps fell tinkling and clanking around his feet.

Dan had known other vampires who could lift a car, but they had had to do it with a certain amount of care, taking heed of the vehicle's center of gravity; they couldn't just jerk it into the air any old way. Confronted with such a spectacle, even the Brujah, whose battle rage was proverbial, faltered momentarily in their attack.

Bellowing, Dan threw the wreck at Judy Morgan, the berserker queen herself. It missed, landing short with a deafening crash, but he received the satisfaction of seeing her dark eyes widen in dismay.

Now all the prince's people were gaping or glaring at him. He beckoned to the embattled vampires in the unfinished building. *Come on!* he implored them silently. *I drew away the enemy's attention. This is your chance to break out of the circle.*

As if they'd heard him, the strangers burst out of the concrete-block enclosure, guns blazing. Some of the Brujah jerked as the bullets caught them in the back. One, his head bursting like a melon, toppled off his bike.

The foreigners drove through their would-be captors and back into the narrow, weed-infested space between the tourist joints. Dan scrambled after them.

The vampire in white had waited at the mouth of the alley. As soon as Dan rushed past him, the stranger, who must have been carrying his sawed-off shotgun inside his voluminous coat, pumped three blasts into the street, perhaps in the hope that the barrage would discourage pursuit. Then he wheeled and pounded after his fellow fugitives. Catching up with Dan, he said, "We have a car. It's about three blocks over and two blocks up."

Since Dan had been tailing the strangers, he knew where they'd parked, but he couldn't see any advantage in saying so. "Let's cut through the Gardens," he replied. "The enemy might have trouble following us through all the trees and bushes."

By the time he and the white-clad vampire caught up with the other invaders, Dan could hear Judy Morgan shouting orders. The pursuit was getting organized again and would no doubt be after them in a matter of moments. Somewhere to the north motors growled, getting louder by the second. It probably meant that enemy reinforcements were arriving.

The fleeing vampires raced across the street to the twelve-foot chain-link fence encircling the Tropical Gardens. Except for the guy in white, each was wounded and bloody. Dan didn't doubt that they could all scramble over the barrier anyway, but he didn't want to take the time. He grabbed the fence with both hands and pulled in opposite directions, ripping a hole in it, shredding the steel mesh like tissue paper. He and his companions scrambled through the gap.

Before them extended a flat expanse of land filled with palms and flowering shrubs. Night-blooming orchids glowed in the dimness, filling the air with their perfume. In the dark, the unnatural order imposed by the establishment's gardeners was scarcely evident; Dan could almost imagine that he was entering a true jungle. For a moment, the contrast between the tranquillity ahead and the carnage behind seemed nearly surreal. Then lightning blazed, thunder roared a split second after, and the rain began to fall in torrents, drenching him instantly, hammering the leaves and blossoms as if some inimical deity sought to deny the fugitives even the illusion of peace.

Dan grinned savagely — the downpour would make it harder for the Brujah to spot the fugitives. He and his companions raced on, not keeping to the paved paths but plunging through the foliage. At their backs, engines snarled and headlights slashed across the darkness as the bikers rode into the Gardens. Evidently they'd enlarged the hole in the fence.

The fugitives dashed through a sort of open-air religious exhibit, hand-carved dioramas illustrating the life of Christ; Jesus seemed to glower disapprovingly from his cross. Beyond that, the vampires found a number of steel cages with paths winding among them. The zoo. Roused by the storm, the rumble of the motorcycles, or simply sensing the presence of their supernatural visitors, the animals were awake. Some were cowering at the backs of the cages, some were pacing, and some snarled at the unliving creatures outside.

The growl of the Harleys drew closer. One of the strangers, a petite brunette with sodden bangs plastered to her forehead and a bloody hole in the bottom of her tie-dyed Grateful Dead T-shirt, turned to the Kindred in white. "I think they're going to find us again!" she said.

"What we need," said the vampire with the mohawk, "is another diversion. Something else running through the dark."

"I get your drift," said Dan. He turned to the cage on his left, gripped the door and ripped it off its hinges. The hulking black gorilla inside the enclosure glared at him and bared its teeth.

"Get back," Dan said to his fellow vampires. "It won't come out if you're standing around the door." The other Kindred obligingly spread out. Two of them, who must have had some degree of inhuman strength of their own, started breaking open a cage with a leopard in it.

Exposing his own fangs, Dan edged into the gorilla's cage and started to circle to the primate's left. He hoped if he got behind it, it would retreat in the opposite direction and out the door. Instead it lunged at him, its huge hands raised to grab and maul him.

Dodging its initial attack, Dan stepped to its side and punched it in the ribs. The ape grunted and staggered. Dan circled behind it, seized it and sank his fangs into its hairy back. The gorilla screamed.

The primate's blood was rank, not sweet like the blood of humans, but with Dan's own vitae leaking away through the knife cuts in his chest, it was enticing anyway. Repressing a witless desire to cling to the animal and feed, he released it and kicked it in the ass.

Cowed, the gorilla scrambled out of the cage and vanished into the rain. Dan followed the animal through the door, froze for a moment to let the fleeing leopard hurtle past him, then dashed to an enclosure with four bears in it.

The fugitives opened half-a-dozen cages in less than a minute. "That will have to be enough," said the vampire in white. "We need to move on."

The Kindred ran, out of the zoo and back into the greenery, weaving through the secondary trunks of a huge banyan tree. Behind them the Brujah were still too close, but now their guns began to bang and crackle, firing shots that didn't come anywhere near their quarries. Sounding startled, some of the hunters cried out.

"Yes!" said the vampire in the Grateful Dead shirt, delighted that their ploy was working.

The fugitives raced around a flamingo lagoon. The rain roiled the surface of the lake with a sound like bacon sizzling in a pan.

Beyond the lagoon was the border of the park. When he peered through the fence, Dan was pleasantly surprised to see the strangers' vehicle. The green van, nondescript except for the dark one-way glass in the windows, was parked on the street almost directly in front of him. Their headlong flight had taken them straight to it. Either they'd been lucky, or the Kindred in white, who'd more or less led his companions through the Gardens, had a keen sense of direction.

Dan ripped another hole in the fence. As the vampires

surged into the street their driver, a fleshy, middle-aged black ghoul who looked like a linebacker gone to seed, opened the sliding door in the rear of the panel truck. Dan could tell he was a ghoul because, to his newly sensitized nose, he smelled different from an ordinary human. "What's wrong?" the servant asked.

"Get behind the wheel!" snapped the Kindred in white. "We have to disappear!"

As the ghoul obeyed, the foreign vampires scrambled into the back of the van. The guy in white and the woman with the Grateful Dead shirt peered out at Dan.

And here's the kiss-off, Dan thought suddenly. *Melpomene was wrong. Even though I saved them they want to leave me behind, just like all the other bastards always have.* A wave of fury crashed through his mind.

"What are you waiting for?" said the vampire in white. "Get in!"

Dan blinked in surprise. His anger evaporating, he jumped into the van. The interior was carpeted, with a number of pillows and boxes of ammunition strewn about the floor, a small refrigerator and microwave oven on a shelf, and sundry rifles, pistols, swords and knives hanging from mounts on the walls. Rain rattled on the roof. As the Kindred in white slammed the door, the motor roared to life. The van shot forward, then turned left.

In the next three minutes the driver changed direction several times. The vampires peered out the windows until they were sure that the Brujah had lost their trail. Then one of them, a muscular Hispanic guy with a thin black mustache and several gold chains around his neck, grinned and opened the refrigerator. Taking out a bottle of blood, he put it in the microwave. "Miller time," he said, winking at Dan. "At least I *think* the guy said his name was Miller. When the stuff warms up, we'll pass it around."

"Uh, thanks," said Dan. With the excitement of the

chase and the savage exhilaration produced by the giants' blood fading, he felt absurdly awkward and shy. He wasn't *used* to other vamps being friendly.

The Kindred in white peeled off his right glove and held out his hand. "I'm Wyatt Vandercar," he said. "Welcome to the Anarch Movement."

EIGHT: THE HUNTER

*Whosoever is delighted in solitude is either a wild beast
or a god.*

— Francis Bacon, "Of Friendship"

Cloaked in the form of a huge gray wolf, his eyes glowing crimson, Angus stalked silently through the snow, sniffing the odors — gasoline, smoke, the blood of seals — that drifted on the freezing wind. At the base of the hill, lights glowed in the windows of the tiny village; beyond that, ice floes drifted in the water.

The vampire skulked closer. As far as he could tell, none of the Eskimos was out of doors. In fact, he got the impression that the settlement was locked up tight. Perhaps the mortals had even set a trap for him.

He bared his fangs in a bestial grin. This was the way he liked it. In a huge modern city full of lonely, displaced souls about whom no one cared, where mortals were always running around outdoors at any hour of the night and people didn't even credit the existence of the Kindred, seizing prey was so easy any fool could do it. But the village below him was a close-knit community of humans hardened by the daily battle for survival. And despite the evidence of technological advance — the chugging generators, the aluminum boats with outboard motors, the prefabricated buildings scattered among the traditional turf-covered log cabins, and the satellite dish — they still remembered the lore of their ancestors. Now that Angus' previous incursions had put them on their guard, stealing their blood should provide a modicum of sport even to an elder of his talents.

Already plotting tonight's raid, he began to glide down the slope; then a silvery shimmer flowered in front of him. Thinking that some unseen sentry had picked him out with a searchlight, he leaped to one side, but even as his paws touched down he realized that he'd been mistaken. No human device was projecting the glow; to all appearances it had no source of any kind. It was just a streak of phosphorescence, about as tall and as wide as a human being, seething in the air.

Now that Angus had had a better look at it, he recognized it for what it was. Regretting that he'd compromised his dignity by revealing how badly it had startled him, he glumly waited for it to finish materializing.

It was like watching an image on a movie screen swim into focus. Over the next few seconds it developed a recognizable head, then a face, clearly discernible limbs, hands and feet. Before long he was looking at Melpomene, floating three inches above the snow. She looked as solid as he was, but he knew that was an illusion. In reality, only a psychic projection hung before him.

"Hello, old friend," she said.

Angus stared at her.

The Methuselah heaved a sigh. "Is it still like that, then? I'd hoped that time would wither away your resentment. We need to talk. Please, put on your true form."

As he reluctantly did as she'd requested, Angus wondered fleetingly why Cainites who couldn't change shape as his clan did never understood that *all* of a Gangrel's bodies were his "true forms." Perhaps if they could, they'd discover the same gift in themselves. Not that that would be a good thing.

In a world where Kindred of different bloodlines often battled ruthlessly for supremacy, his people needed every edge they could get.

Angus' body took on additional mass. His bones and muscles rearranged themselves. In a moment it felt more natural to stand erect than to remain on all fours, and he surged to his feet. His muzzle shrank back into his skull and some of his fur melted away, though he remained an exceptionally hairy man. Centuries of shapechanging had left their mark on him.

When the transformation was complete, he was an ivory-skinned giant with deep-set eyes, bushy brows and a beak of a nose, whom various people had likened to a Cro-Magnon warrior, a Viking, or a mountain man. He was dressed in jeans, hiking boots, a red flannel shirt and a parka, worn open with the hood thrown back. A gold ring gleamed in his left ear and his brown beard and shaggy mane of hair blew in the frigid wind.

Melpomene smiled. "You haven't changed," she said.

Angus shrugged. "We don't change. That's the point of it all, isn't it? The point of being what we are."

"I hope not," the Methuselah said, turning her head this way and that. "I don't sense any other vampires. Did you come up here alone?"

"There isn't enough game for more than one," Angus said.

Melpomene gave him a sympathetic smile. "It all becomes tiresome eventually, doesn't it? Even your own progeny. Especially your own progeny."

Angus didn't want to share his feelings with her. She was right: he still held a grudge against her. And yet, simultaneously, he *did* want to talk. Their relationship had always been like that. She was one of the few creatures in the world old enough truly to understand his perspective, and he supposed that she had that damn Toreador charisma, that sweet, melancholy smile and those soulful, compelling eyes, prying away at his reserve. He understood the nature of her power, but it was so insidious that it was difficult to resist.

"Sometimes I do want to get away by myself," he admitted, scowling. "So what?"

"Are you tempted to go down into the ground?" she asked. "Sleep a few decades or a century away, see how the world looks when you wake up?"

He hesitated, then repeated, "Sometimes."

"When you rise from the earth," Melpomene said, "you'll be more like me." Her somber tone implied that that would be his misfortune.

The tenor of the conversation was making Angus uncomfortable. "What do you want?" he demanded. "Why have you sought me out?"

"I'm at war," the Methuselah said.

Though the statement was exactly what he'd been expecting, Angus grimaced. "Well, of course you are," he said sardonically.

Absurdly enough, given their bloody history together, she winced as if he'd wounded her feelings. "I didn't want to be," she said. "After our final struggle in England, Castile and Normandy, I tried to get out of the game, but it hasn't worked. Someone's attacking me."

"And I'm supposed to drop everything and rally to the cause," the Gangrel said. The icy wind moaned and, out over the water, the yellow-green arcs of the aurora borealis wavered across the sky. "Even though there's no sane reason for me to care who wins. Even though I've seen you send good people on suicide missions."

"Never you," she said.

"You mean, never *yet*," Angus replied. "Don't try to convince me that I'm not as expendable as the next puppet if that's what it takes for you to win."

She grimaced. "All right, I won't. You've been a warlord yourself. You know that one does what one has to."

"Well, do it to someone else."

"I need *you*, Angus. I don't have as many agents as I used to. I don't have *any* other Justicars, and this conflict is likely to be addressed in a Conclave before it's through."

"If anyone found out that I was working for a Methuselah," he said sourly, "and not just the Inner Circle of the Camarilla, you wouldn't have *any* judges in your pocket. The princes would gleefully burn me alive."

"Then I suggest that you be discreet," Melpomene said. "But I don't want you just for your political prestige. I need a master hunter and detective. A vampire in Florida is killing recklessly, flaunting his powers, jeopardizing the Masquerade. My descendants in the area have been trying to track the rogue down, to no avail. But I know you could do it."

Angus had to admit to himself that he was intrigued. Though he wasn't malevolent enough to do it simply for sport, tracking a powerful, cunning fellow undead was the grandest game of all; the mere prospect robbed his beleaguered Eskimos of their allure. Yet he was still reluctant to resume the role of a pawn in Melpomene's game. "I've hunted down Cainites before," he said. "That pastime has grown stale as well."

The ancient vampire frowned. "I didn't want to have to say this. It seems… gauche. But apparently I must remind you that I saved your life and the lives of three of your childer," she said. "When everyone else betrayed you and left you to die, I extracted you from the torture chambers of the Inquisition."

"To make me your servant," Angus said. When one Kindred did another a kindness, the latter was honor-bound to reciprocate. Huge favors demanded heroic measures in return. "And I have served. I've risked the life you saved on your behalf."

"I saved four lives," Melpomene said. "I've called you to war on three previous occasions. You owe me one more."

Angus sighed; unlike the breath of a warm-bodied mortal, his exhalation didn't steam in the frigid air. He supposed that it had been a foregone conclusion that he would wind up fighting for Melpomene one last time, but the stubborn streak in his nature had compelled him to put up at least a token resistance. "Damn your bookkeeper's soul," he said. "All right, I'll do it. Tell me everything."

NINE: THE ANARCHS

What is wrong with a revolution is that it is natural.
It is as natural as natural selection, as devastating as
natural selection, and as horrible.

— William Golding, "Sayings of the Year"

Dan awoke on the floor of the van. For a moment, befuddled, he thought he was young and mortal again, travelling cross-country to some rock concert or ball game in his best friend Billy's panel truck. Then he noticed how silent the interior of the vehicle was without the slightest hiss of respiration, how pale his slumbering companions were, the dried bloodstains around the holes in their garments. His memory came surging back.

Dawn had caught the fugitives still on the road and put them to sleep. Shortly thereafter the van had probably reached its ultimate destination — it certainly wasn't moving now — but the ghoul driver had sensibly opted to let the Kindred rest where they lay. Matters of taste and style aside, a hard bed was no different from a soft one to a vampire. All that truly mattered was that the undead was shielded from the sun.

Dan slipped his fingers through the rents in his shirt and touched his chest and stomach. As he'd expected, his wounds had finished healing while he slept. All that remained were itchy crusts of scab. Except for the blood thirst parching his throat, he was as good as new.

Or was that an overstatement? He was okay physically, but he had to assume that he'd lost his home and all his possessions but the ruined clothes on his back. Prince Roger's people wanted to kill him, and if his new companions discovered he was a spy, they would too. Hell, he didn't even know what city he was in. Giddy with blood loss and jubilation over their escape, the anarchs hadn't gotten around to telling him where they were headed, and he hadn't asked. He'd been reluctant to do anything that might jeopardize his newfound rapport with them, even though he knew he'd have to start asking questions soon.

Smiling wryly at his situation, Dan sat up and peered out of one of the van's one-way windows. The vehicle was sitting in what appeared to be one of the work bays of an abandoned auto-mechanic's shop. No tools hung from the pegboards along the walls, gray sheets of cobweb shrouded the work benches, and the girlie calendar beside the time clock was from 1991. The garage doors were all closed, blocking any view of the outside world. Seated on a metal folding chair, the burly ghoul was eating a Cuban sandwich. With his newly heightened hearing, even through the side of the van Dan could hear the crisp bread crunch.

Behind him, something brushed along the carpeted floor. As he turned the brunette in the Deadhead shirt, whose name, he had learned the previous night, was Laurie Tipton, sat up, blinking. "Hi," she said. "Welcome to our place."

Still feeling shy, as if the anarchs might turn on him if he said or did anything the least bit out of line, Dan said, "Thanks. Uh, what town are we in, anyway?"

"Tampa," Laurie said. When Dan thought about it, it made sense. Vampires liked big cities, where prey was plentiful and they could lose themselves in the crowd. If a gang of undead wanted to conduct hostilities against the prince of Sarasota, it would be smart for them to base themselves in the nearest such community outside the borders of his domain.

Laurie looked Dan up and down. "You could use a wash and some fresh clothes," she said, sliding open the door. "Come on."

As they emerged from the van the ghoul began to stand up respectfully, but she gave him a dismissive wave and he slumped back down. Dan wondered fleetingly if the man had entered the vampires' service willingly, grateful for the longevity his new condition would afford, perhaps aspiring to be undead himself one day; or if he'd been forced to drink the vitae of one of the anarchs. Not that it mattered. Either way, he was Blood Bound now, his will no longer his own.

Laurie led Dan out of the work area and into a small complex consisting of offices, storerooms, restrooms, a waiting room and a cashier's station. Someone had painted all the windows black, but a chain of small yellow lightbulbs strung along the ceiling provided dim illumination.

One of the storerooms contained cartons and heaps of clothes. Laurie nodded to the items by the right-hand wall. "That stuff's up for grabs," she said. She moved to what must have been her own personal possessions. The collection included headbands, granny glasses, a fringed buckskin jacket, bellbottoms, and T-shirts decorated with pictures of marijuana leaves, psychedelic swirls of color and the logos of bands like the Jefferson Airplane, Country Joe and the Fish, and Big Brother and the Holding Company.

Dan inferred that she'd been young and mortal in the '60s. So had he, but the hippie movement hadn't attracted him as it obviously had her. Instead, he'd wound up in the service, and shortly thereafter in Nam. Maybe he was a conformist by temperament. Maybe that was why, after his transformation at the hands of his unknown sire, he'd tried so hard to find a place for himself inside the Camarilla. It was only after repeated rejections that he'd attempted to join what amounted to the Kindred counterculture, only to discover that, at least hitherto, its adherents hadn't wanted him either.

With an utter lack of self-consciousness, Laurie peeled off her filthy, perforated clothing, revealing the trim, small-breasted ivory body underneath. Even those vampires who still behaved modestly in the presence of mortals often had no qualms about stripping in front of other Kindred; they knew their fellow undead were incapable of a sexual response.

Raking through a jumbled mass of shirts, underwear, socks and jeans, Dan asked, "How long have you been an anarch?"

"Fifteen years," Laurie replied. She selected a long muslin dress, then walked to the restroom across the hall and started filling the sink. The pipes groaned and the water hissed. "I joined after I ran away from my sire. I always knew she was crazy and mean, but eventually I found out that she'd tortured and fed on a bunch of her other childer, for no reason at all. I was sure my name was on the menu, too. Other elders knew what kind of monster she was, but nobody had ever done anything about it because she was too well-connected. That's the so-called justice of the Camarilla for you."

Dan found a large blue T-shirt that looked as if it would fit him. "But do you really think you can bring the old vamps down?" he asked.

"Sure!" she said, sounding surprised, as if it had been a silly question. She picked up a bar of soap and started to wash herself, slopping water over the edge of the basin onto the grubby linoleum floor. "Wyatt says that the old ones are powerful but stagnant. They can't adapt to modern ways of doing things, and that will give us the advantage in the end."

Remembering some of the Ventrue he'd seen clad in powdered wigs and tricorn hats like tourist guides at Williamsburg, Dan suspected that she might be right. As he pulled off his old shirt, he said, "Is Wyatt the leader?" He'd certainly gotten that impression last night.

"Anarchs don't have leaders," the female Kindred said, reaching for a Holiday Inn bath towel draped over the back of a chair, "anymore than we have princes, Justicars, or any of that. We're all equal. But he is the cell coordinator."

"I don't know what that means," said Dan.

"It means that I handle communications with our brothers and sisters around the world," said a pleasant baritone voice. Wyatt appeared in the doorway. Startled, Dan was chagrined that, his heightened hearing notwithstanding, he hadn't heard the vampire in white approaching.

"There are a lot of Kindred who believe in the anarch cause," said Laurie, emerging from the bathroom still nude. She wasn't completely dry, and water dripped from her body onto the floor. "More every day. But most of them aren't ready to devote their lives to fighting for it. I only reached that point myself a few weeks back. The Camarilla is hunting us militants, so all information is on a need-to-know basis. That way, if a member of the underground gets captured, he can't be forced to give away too much. Wyatt says it's a classic resistance tactic." She looked up at the vampire with the bleached mohawk as if for approval, and he gave her an indulgent smile.

"What were you guys doing in Sarasota last night?" Dan asked.

Wyatt lifted a milk-white eyebrow. "You do ask a lot of questions."

Inwardly, Dan winced. Wyatt was right, he was coming on too strong. He didn't have the instincts of a spy, didn't know how to elicit information unobtrusively. "Sorry. I was just wondering."

"No offense taken," said Wyatt lightly. Dan noticed that the patterns of rivets in the other Kindred's leather coat seemed to form some sort of indecipherable characters, like hieroglyphs in an extinct language. "You've wandered into a strange situation. Of course you have questions, and we'll be glad to answer most of them — after which, I'm sure, you won't mind answering a few of ours. We were checking out the lay of the land in Sarasota for future reference, and if we'd gotten a chance to pick off one of the prince's stooges, that would have been fine, too. Right now, Roger Phillips' domain is one of the Movement's special projects. We're going to bring him down and set up an Anarch Free State, just like they did in California."

"Why pick on old Roger?" Dan asked. "I mean, *I've* got reason to hate his guts, but I also know that he and his primogen have a pretty benevolent reputation as elders go." True, the prince had rebuffed *him*, but then, until last night, so had the rest of the vampire world. "Wouldn't it be better PR to knock off some Marquis de Sade type that everybody hates?"

Laurie peered at Dan quizzically. "The princes are *all* corrupt," she said. "They *all* have to go."

"She's right," Wyatt said. "Besides, we have to start someplace, and Roger Phillips and his brood are *soft* — Toreador who haven't fought a real fight in decades. The strategy is to knock over the easy targets first, increasing our strength with the plunder and new recruits we win in the process, then tackle the tough ones."

"That makes sense," Dan conceded. "When's the big push?"

"I don't know that myself," Wyatt said. "I'm waiting for my contacts to let me know. But I'm sure it's coming soon."

"Are you the guys committing those 'Dracula' murders?" Dan asked.

Wyatt shook his head. "No, but maybe some other cell is responsible. I wouldn't be surprised. It's an effective tactic; it ought to confuse, distract and demoralize the prince's people."

Effective but dangerous, Dan thought. If it worked *too* well, if it actually did blow the Masquerade to hell, then *all* Kindred, Camarilla and anarchs alike, might suffer.

"We're the guys trashing the Toreador's precious art," Wyatt continued. "Some of it, anyway. Have you heard about that?"

Dan decided to play dumb. It might seem suspicious if he was too conversant with Toreador affairs. "I heard on the news that some art had been destroyed, but I didn't know that it had anything to do with Roger and his brood."

"Well, it does," said the white-clad vampire, grinning. "It's their treasure, their heritage and obsession. Once it's lost, I bet they won't even care about defending their turf. And when they try to retrieve the art for safekeeping, it gives us a chance to ambush them."

Dan nodded. "Smart."

"Anything else you'd like to know?" Wyatt asked.

Dan shrugged. "I can't think of anything."

"Then it's my turn," said Wyatt. "I take it that you lived in Sarasota?" It was a sensible assumption since, except for members of the Gangrel and Ravnos clans, Kindred were generally loath to travel away from their well-defended havens.

"Yeah," Dan replied.

"What was your relationship with the prince and his vassals?"

"Hostile," said Dan. "When I first hit town, I presented myself to Prince Rog like the Fifth Tradition says you're supposed to. Since I was a low-life Caitiff, he made it clear that I wasn't welcome to hang around. I did anyway, for spite, and because I had nowhere else to go. Afterward, his people tried periodically to run me out of the prime hunting areas. Sometimes the confrontations got pretty nasty.

"When I saw Judy Morgan — the black woman in the cap — and her Brujah hassling you, the way they've hassled me only more so, I just felt an urge to help you. So I did."

"It must have been a *strong* urge," said Wyatt, "if it made you lay your life on the line for perfect strangers. How did you happen to be in that particular area?"

"I like to walk in the Gardens," Dan said. "It's peaceful." He wondered if Wyatt interrogated every newcomer like this. He was glad that, being undead, he couldn't sweat.

"I believe Dan's what he seems to be," Laurie said diffidently. She clearly didn't want Wyatt, her guru, to think that she was questioning his judgment. "He *did* rescue us, and I saw him kill at least one of the bikers in the process."

"You have to admit, his presence at the battle was quite a coincidence," Wyatt said reasonably. "And his aura is a confusing, constantly changing blend of colors. That suggests that he may have something to hide." Then the anarch leader smiled. "But you know what? I believe him, too. Heck, *all* Kindred have something to hide, and like you said, he did kill for us. What's more, I just made a call to find out something about him." Dan wondered *who* Wyatt had called. "Danny boy told us the truth about his life in Sarasota, except that he didn't mention how 'nasty' things really got. A few nights ago he beat one of the Brujah unconscious and diabolized her."

Dan tensed. *Now*, he thought, *now they'll send me away if they don't try to kill me outright.* Trying to move unobtrusively, he shifted his feet into a fighting stance.

Wyatt laughed, his white teeth gleaming. "*Now* I can read your aura," he said. "Scared you, didn't I? But there's no need to be afraid. To the Movement, diabolism is no crime as long as you pick the right target. In fact, it's a weapon and an objective of the revolution. We aren't just going to kill the elders, we're going to drink them. Take their power for ourselves."

Dan smiled grimly. "Now that idea, I like."

"Sorry if the third degree bugged you," Wyatt said, "but we have to maintain security. Now that we're sure you're clean, how do you feel about the idea of joining us? I understand that you didn't know we were anarchs when you helped us, but now you do, and I believe you know what the Movement stands for, too. The destruction of the Camarilla and the princes. The liberation of the young from the tyranny of the old, and the Caitiff from the domination of the clans. The right to live where and how you like, and sire as many progeny as you like, without asking anyone's permission."

Dan wondered what would happen if he declined the proposition. Would the anarchs let him walk away, now that he'd heard something of their plans and seen their lair? Fortunately, he wouldn't have to find out. Narrowing his eyes thoughtfully, he pretended to consider the invitation for a moment and then said, "Count me in."

Wyatt grinned. "All right!" he crowed, "I knew you had the right stuff!" Laurie threw her arms around Dan and hugged him, pressing her cool, bare body against his. Even though the anarchs were the enemy, even though he'd come here to betray them, for a moment the spy felt a surge of joy. No one who understood his true nature, no one of his own kind, had treated him like this since his sire had transformed and abandoned him.

"What do you like to do for fun?" Wyatt asked.

"I don't know," said Dan, surprised by the question. "Work out, swim, go to the movies, listen to music, dance—"

"Great!" Wyatt said, all boyish enthusiasm. The calculating guerrilla leader had given way to the exuberant teenager whose unaging shape he wore. "You guys finish cleaning up and then the five of us will go out, feed and celebrate having a new recruit. The revolution can spare us for one night."

TEN: QUESTIONS, SORROWS AND DOUBTS

*We have suffered the inevitable consequences of a
combination of unpreparedness and feeble counsel.*
— Julian Amery, speech before the House of
Commons

Elliott parked his Jaguar among the other cars and
motorcycles clustered in front of Roger's beach house. As
he climbed out, he caught the sound of two of his fellow
Toreador, Glenn and Karen, murmuring in the gazebo to his
right. Glenn was smoking, the red tip of his cigarette shining
in the darkness that filled the enclosure.

"I can't believe it," said Karen sadly. "So many killed in
one night. And the beautiful, beautiful art, shattered, burned
and shredded, gone forever!"

"And we don't even have any real intelligence to show
for it," said Glenn. "We still have no idea who's behind all
this. The team that went to Buenos Aires was ambushed by
Malkavians. The one we sent to Seattle ran afoul of what
seemed to be a bunch of Caitiff. The one that visited St.
Louis fought two Ravnos and their ghouls. Where's the *link?*"

"I don't know," said Karen.

"Neither do I," said her companion. The cigarette flared brighter as he inhaled. "All I know is that everything's falling apart. I nearly got shot just trying to hunt this evening. It's *hard* when the humans are on their guard." He hesitated. "You know that I think the world of Roger."

"Yes," Karen said.

"And I'm not a coward. But if he's never going to get well, if no one else can fix everything that's wrong, maybe we'd be better off in another domain. Other cities have Toreador princes. Some of them have told me they like my sculpture! I'm sure one of them would make a place for me."

Wincing, Elliott trudged up the steps to the mansion's front door. He paused reflexively to check his attire, pointless though the effort seemed to be. Instead of his usual elegantly tailored suit, he was wearing the seedy, beige polyester thrift-shop offering that had been the first fresh, unripped, unbloodied outfit that he could lay his hands on in Ohio. As he'd driven away from Sarasota-Bradenton Municipal Airport, he'd been tempted to go home and change. But he'd felt honor-bound to come directly to Roger's mansion, even though it was the last place in the world he wanted to be.

He was still fidgeting with his lapels when Lazlo threw open the door. "I saw you drive up," the mortal said. "Are you all right?"

"I suppose," Elliott said.

"Have you fed?" Lazlo asked.

"Yes," said Elliott, experiencing a pang of guilt. The sensation was becoming horribly familiar. "A young woman in Dayton. I was too brutal, but I was rushed. I had to catch my plane. How many Toreador died last night?"

The human glanced back into the foyer. Voices, some anguished, some frightened, some angry, muttered through the arch that led to the arena. "I think we should talk in private," Lazlo said.

Elliott shrugged. "If that's what you want."

Lazlo led him into Roger's office, a smallish room with French windows, where bookshelves, crammed for the most part with volumes pertaining to acting and the theater, climbed the walls. The scent of the old leather bindings tinged the air. A marble bust of Molière sat in an alcove and a model of the Globe Theatre, where both Roger and Elliott had acted, reposed under glass in the corner.

As Lazlo shut the door, the vampire repeated, "How many?"

"Including Rosalita, nine," Lazlo replied.

Elliott bowed his head and rubbed his aching eyes. He'd wept on the flight back to Florida. It was a wonder that no one had noticed the scarlet tears. "Oh, God," he said.

"It could have been worse," Lazlo said. "Considering that they walked into traps, it's amazing how many fought their way clear."

Elliott grimaced. "I suppose that's one way of looking at it."

"I need to update you," Lazlo said. "Roger's condition is no different. If Dr. Potter has any new ideas, he hasn't confided them to me. No one's made any progress with regard to catching Dracula, either. One of Judy Morgan's brood is dead, too."

For a moment at least, a twinge of curiosity pierced Elliott's pall of despondency. "How did *that* happen?"

Speaking as tersely as possible, Lazlo filled him in. "The Brujah had them surrounded," the dresser concluded, "but then that diabolist Murdock came out of nowhere and attacked our people, destroying one. Obviously he *is* working with the enemy, and evidently he's a lot more powerful than anyone realized because, thanks to him, the strangers managed to escape. We have no idea where any of them are now."

"We shouldn't have allowed the bastard to live within our borders," Elliott said. "Gunter was right." He sighed. "I never expected to hear myself say that."

"What you have to understand now" — Lazlo hesitated as if trying to decide how to phrase his statement tactfully — "is that people are frightened. You need to reassure them. Reassert your leadership."

"You mean you think that Gunter is going to try to proclaim himself the boss."

"I think it's very likely," Lazlo said. "And frankly, even Judy isn't sure she trusts your judgment anymore."

Elliott smiled bitterly. "Good for her."

Lazlo blinked. "I beg your pardon?"

"Why *should* anyone trust my generalship?" Elliott demanded. "I sent our people out to die. Hell, Rosalita was only a fledgling and her instincts were better than mine. She sensed trouble coming before I did. And then I couldn't save her!"

"Every commander occasionally finds himself outwitted or outmaneuvered," Lazlo said. "I know that from listening to Roger's war stories. I still believe that, in his absence, you're the best man to lead the defense. He certainly thought so."

"Then maybe he was always crazy!" Elliott snarled. Lazlo's eyes widened in shock, and then he scowled. The Toreador felt another rush of shame. "I'm sorry. You know I didn't mean that. It's just that I'm not up to the challenge. I can feel my inadequacy even if you can't see it."

"You couldn't help Mary, and now you're afraid that you'll fail everybody else. But no one could have prevented what happened to her."

"Don't try to be my psychiatrist or my confessor, Lazlo. No offense, but you're not qualified. No mortal is."

The dresser laid his bony hand on Elliott's shoulder. "As the years passed, some people thought your grief was excessive, even affected, but I never did. She was a wonderful person."

"Yes," Elliott said heavily, "yes, she was. I always thought that we Toreador were uniquely blessed among the clans because we could love one another as passionately as mortals do. The joys of creation and aesthetic appreciation we share take the place of sex. But now I think our nature is a curse. You can't imagine what it's like to lose someone you've adored for three hundred years!"

Lazlo shrugged. "Perhaps not. I won't argue that particular point. But I still say that Mary would want you to fulfill your responsibilities."

"You already played that card," said Elliott. "I won't succumb to the same ploy twice. She wouldn't want me to act if she knew it would lead to disaster."

"You just don't get it, do you?" Lazlo said. *"There isn't anybody else.* Judy's impulsive and reckless, Gunter's arrogant and self-serving, and most of the time Sky's too passive. None of them has both the personality to lead and the subtlety of mind to unravel the puzzles we desperately need to solve."

"The identities of our enemy and Dracula," Elliott muttered reflectively.

"Plus, who was the woman who phoned here last night?" Lazlo said. "Oh, and here's a good one. There are hundreds, maybe thousands of pieces of Toreador art out in the world, aren't there? After all, you people have been cranking them out for centuries."

"Yes."

"Do you think that the enemy has enough manpower to set up an ambush around even a quarter of them?"

Elliott frowned. "It does seem unlikely."

"Then, if he could only cover a fraction of the locations, how likely is it that, purely by the luck of the draw, his men intercepted *seven* of our teams?"

"He must have known where our people were headed."

"Yes, and somebody needs to figure out how."

For a moment Elliott felt intrigued by all the mystery. A part of him which had lain dormant for a long time itched to unravel it. Then another wave of self-loathing drowned the feeling.

He said, "You seem to be way ahead of everybody else—"

"Only because you haven't switched your brain on," Lazlo interjected.

"—maybe you should take charge."

"Oh, yes," said the stooped, aging mortal, raising his eyebrows. *"That'll* work. I can just see all those high-and-mighty Kindred taking orders from a little nebbish of a kine like me."

"Well, share your ideas with whoever does wind up in command."

"Nobody else would listen to them the way you would."

Elliott shook his head. "Lazlo, you can't talk me into it, and believe me, that's for the best. I'm going to go speak with the others because they deserve a chance to berate me for the debacle I created, but after that, I'm out of it."

Lazlo tilted back his head and spat in the vampire's face.

Elliott felt a surge of anger, a furious desire to retaliate. He trembled, fighting for self-control. "You mustn't provoke a Kindred like that," he said thickly. "Not even me. It isn't safe."

Lazlo slapped him.

Snarling, his fangs extending, Elliott grabbed the human and slammed him back against one of the bookcases. He was acutely conscious of the warmth of Lazlo's flesh, the enticing scent of the blood coursing through his body, the pounding of his heart, the carotid artery pulsing in his throat.

"Do it!" Lazlo gasped. "At least you'll be doing *something!*"

Elliott opened his jaws and leaned forward. Lazlo cringed. Then, for some reason, the vampire thought of the stricken Roger and realized that Lazlo had lashed out at him only because he was so desperately worried about the prince. Abruptly ashamed of his rage, closing his eyes to shut out the sight of the human, wishing that he could seal his other senses as well, Elliott released him and stepped back.

"I'm going to the arena," the Toreador said. "Stay away from me for the rest of the night." He turned and strode out of the room.

As he marched through the house toward the clamor of agitated voices, he tried to calm down; attempted, in essence, to exchange his anger for his familiar bleak depression. The sadness wouldn't feel any better, but it was how he *ought* to feel. How he *deserved* to feel.

But he was only partially successful. Lazlo's insults had roused his Beast, and once awakened, it wasn't easily quelled. Elliott could virtually feel his personal demon pacing back and forth inside him.

When he reached the arena he saw that the spacious, lofty-ceilinged hall was still arranged as it had been on his previous visit: all the seats faced the harpsichord and the setup for the string quartet, the portion of the room his fellow elders were currently occupying. Sky, looking morose, was slouched on what had probably been the cellist's straight-backed chair; Judy was sitting Indian-fashion atop the gleaming antique keyboard instrument; and Gunter, predictably, was on his feet haranguing the assembled Kindred of Roger Phillips' domain.

Elliott tried to slink into the room unobtrusively, but it didn't work. Pivoting dramatically in his direction, Gunter cried, "So! Back at last! What do you have to say for yourself?"

Elliott bristled at the other elder's belligerent tone. Reminding himself that his fellow undead, even the overbearing Malkavian, had a right to reproach him, he tried to answer calmly. "I understand that several of us died last night, following the course I advocated. I regret that."

"You regret it," Gunter mocked. "Well, isn't that a comfort."

The sarcasm was too much. Despite his resolve to bear

any chastisement meekly, Elliott gave Gunter a level stare. "I don't appreciate your tone, and I suspect that my fellow Toreador don't either. Perhaps you wouldn't be so flippant if it had been some of your clan who'd come to grief."

"But there was no chance of that, was there?" Judy Morgan said sourly. "I still don't understand why no Kooks showed up at the Gardens until after the invaders got away. I know Lazlo phoned you as soon as I left here."

The ruddy-faced Malkavian glowered at her. "We've already been over this. We got there as soon as we could; your skirmish just didn't take very long."

Grateful that Judy had changed the subject, Elliott headed for a vacant seat in the back. When they saw he didn't intend to join the rest of the primogen at the front of the room, some of his fellow Toreador frowned and muttered back and forth. Sky gazed at him beseechingly, Judy gave him an inscrutable, narrow-eyed stare, and Gunter leered in malevolent satisfaction.

As Elliott dropped into a chair, the Malkavian chieftain swept his eyes across the room, reestablishing contact with the audience at large. "We need to talk about one of the most important problems facing us," he said. "What we do about it will affect our ability to resolve all our other difficulties. Roger Phillips was a great prince." Elliott winced at Gunter's use of the past tense. "When we had him, a single elder, in charge, we could handle any crisis with aplomb. Now, facing a challenge, we're bereft of such leadership, and floundering."

"I do believe I see where this is going," said Judy, interrupting again. "You think we need a new prince. Even though Roger isn't dead."

"Of course not," said Gunter, scowling. "What I'm proposing is an *acting* prince, call him a warlord or a marshal, someone to command until Roger recovers."

Judy uncrossed her legs and hopped off the harpsichord.

"This is just a shot in the dark here, but are you nominating yourself?"

"In time of war," Gunter said, "I think it would be logical for it to be either you or me, rather than a Toreador." He gave Sky a condescending smile. "No offense, my friend. It's just that everyone knows your people lack the killer instinct. In a way I suppose that does you credit, but perhaps if you were as fierce as the rest of us, your art thieves wouldn't have taken such a beating last night."

Despite his long and thorny acquaintance with Gunter, Elliott could scarcely believe that the Malkavian was exploiting the Toreador tragedy in the service of a naked grab for power. The actor's muscles tensed with resentment. His fangs slid reflexively from his gums.

Sky gave Gunter a reproachful stare. "We were ambushed," he said. "I doubt that your progeny would have fared any better."

"Perhaps you're right," said Gunter soothingly. Then he gazed into the audience. "But also conceivably not. Sarasota has some magnificent fighters to call on in time of need. I can't help wondering how the battles might have gone if those had been on the front line instead of you." Many of the Malkavian and particularly the Brujah onlookers murmured and nodded in agreement.

Sky pouted but didn't say anything more. *He's going to take it,* Elliott thought. *He's going to let Gunter remove him from contention.* He remembered a time when the poet's effete appearance had cloaked a personality that could be decisive and even ruthless when circumstances demanded. Now Elliott wondered if the burden of the passing centuries or some private sorrow had sapped his clanmate's inner strength, turning him into a useless shell of a Kindred like —

Like, Elliott realized, himself. He felt another throb of guilt, but this one differed subtly from those he'd experienced earlier. Rather than causing him to slump in despair, it made him shift restlessly in his seat.

"If the boss is going to be you or me," said Judy to Gunter, "how about me?" Some of the boisterous Brujah whistled and cheered.

"We could do a lot worse," Gunter said, smiling cordially. "But may I speak frankly?"

"Could I stop you?" she asked dryly.

Gunter's smile widened. To Elliott's annoyance, at that moment an innocent onlooker might have mistaken the Brujah and the Malkavian for friends, even though she didn't like her burly, flaxen-haired fellow lieutenant much better than Elliott did. "No one could fault the skill with which you fight and lead your own brood," Gunter said. "But the domain is being attacked on a number of levels. I think our leader needs to be able to preside over every aspect of the defense, and I'm not quite as certain of your ability as an attorney or a financier. Whereas I'm quite confident of my own acumen. In the forty-eight hours since I assumed tacit, interim command of the economic front of our little war, I've slowed the precipitous decline in the value of our portfolio, averted a hostile takeover of our Pacific Rim conglomerate, and squelched a potentially ruinous lawsuit."

Judy frowned. For one of the few times in the century that Elliott had known her, she looked uncertain, and it was scarcely any wonder. She truly did lack any interest or expertise in the fields of law or business. She was wealthy, but only because she'd blindly followed the investment advice of Roger, Gunter and himself. "I think I could manage," she said.

"But would you even want to?" the Malkavian asked, gazing into Judy's eyes. Elliott wondered if Gunter was trying to control her mind. Since she possessed the same talent, Judy should be able to detect and resist such an attempt, and yet, if the Malkavian was wielding his power with sufficient finesse, it was possible that she wouldn't. "Wouldn't you rather leave the bean-counting and the paperwork to somebody with the knowledge and the patience to deal with it, just as you always have?"

The ex-slave shrugged. "I don't know. Maybe. But here's the thing. The Brujah are a free people." Some of her progeny began to cheer again. She silenced them with an irritable wave of her slender hand. "We don't *owe* anybody our allegiance. We *chose* to give it to Roger Phillips, and we would have yanked it away in a second if he'd ever abused our trust."

"I understand that," Gunter said, "and if you give me any authority, I'll do my best to use it as wisely and respectfully as he did." He grinned. "What do you think, I want you people wearing uniforms and goose-stepping? Come on, Judith, this is *me*! A Malkavian! A lunatic, according to common prejudice! How could my clan walk the path we tread without cherishing freedom and nonconformity as much as those of your blood do?"

Judy stared at him. "I just want it understood that my people and I expect to participate in any decision-making that affects us."

"And you would be," Gunter said. He turned to face the audience. "You *all* would be. It's just that we need to have someone empowered to break ties, set priorities and keep things organized."

Elliott glanced around the room at the tense, frightened faces of the other Kindred and thought, *The bastard's going to get away with it*. In their currently distressed and demoralized condition, the undead of Sarasota yearned for the same kind of effective leadership that Roger Phillips had provided; Gunter had convinced them that he could deliver it. Even the normally independent Judy, perhaps rattled by her failure to capture Murdock and the intruders last night, seemed ready to go along.

An irresistible impulse carried Elliott to his feet. He wanted to charge Gunter, attack him, batter him into submission — that was the influence of the Beast, still seething inside him — but he knew that that tactic couldn't win this particular conflict. Regretting fleetingly that he wasn't wearing his own handsome clothing, he drew upon his charismatic powers and composed his face into an ironic smile.

Gunter swung around to face him. The ruddy-cheeked Malkavian looked surprised that his seemingly humbled rival would dare to rejoin the discussion. "Yes?" he said, an edge in his deep, faintly accented voice.

"Before this gathering grants you your field marshal's baton," Elliott drawled, "perhaps you'd like to tell us what plans you've pondered for the common defense. After all, I believe you did just promise us an open government."

It seemed an obvious question to the Toreador, but, his piggy blue eyes narrowing, Gunter hesitated as if he were uncertain how to answer. Elliott had noticed that the Malkavian, while cunning, occasionally failed to plan for contingencies that any sensible person should have been able to anticipate. Perhaps it was a manifestation of his underlying madness.

"Redouble our efforts to patrol and fortify the domain, catch the Dracula murderer, determine our enemies' identities, and protect our holdings," said Gunter at last.

"That's brilliant," said Elliott, and was gratified when a few of the audience laughed. Gunter's heavy jaw clenched in anger. "With all due respect, my worthy colleague, we scarcely need a deputy prince to exhort us to pursue plans we've already initiated."

"I suppose you have some more 'brilliant' ideas of your own," Gunter replied, his voice dripping scorn.

"I'm not running for warlord," Elliott replied. In a sense, that was a lie. He was fairly certain that either he or Gunter would emerge from his meeting as *de facto* if not official commander of the defense. "So I didn't prepare a formal platform. Fortunately, given the, shall we say, lack of progression in your own thinking, that doesn't place me at any sort of disadvantage." Once again some of the assembled Kindred laughed. "As it happens, I do have an idea or two." In point of fact, he didn't have a clue what he was going to say next, but he felt what had become an unfamiliar confidence that he could improvise something appropriate.

The actor strode toward the front of the room, establishing eye contact with the audience in the process, trying to cast the spell of his personality over them. "First off, it should be obvious to anyone with good sense" — he shot Gunter a mocking glance — "that we have a security leak. The enemy intercepted too many Toreador; they knew where we were going." The crowd babbled. Elliott quirked the corners of his mouth down in the hint of a frown, and the assembled Kindred obediently fell silent again. "Until we find out how they knew, I'm afraid that we need the opposite of an open government. Our leaders, whoever they are, should weave certain plans in secret, only informing those agents responsible for carrying them out."

Elliott reached the front of the arena. "The recovery of the art," he said, "will continue."

The audience clamored again. Gunter guffawed. "And people call the Malkavians mad!" he said. "Didn't you kill enough of us last night?"

"I regret that the first sortie came to grief," Elliott said. "For what it's worth, I accept the responsibility for not organizing it properly. But one tragedy doesn't alter the fact that our creations must be protected. There are ways to reduce the risk. The secrecy I just mentioned should do it. And we'll go after them in force. If our enemies somehow intercept us again, we'll make them sorry."

"You just don't understand, do you?" Gunter said. "Nobody else thinks the damn art is important anymore, not even your own kind."

Elliott regarded the other Toreador, some strikingly beautiful, others makers of beauty as he himself had once been, assembled in the room. They peered back at him uncertainly. In some of their faces he saw doubt, in some fear, and in some a glimmer of hope, but in few the loathing and bitter reproach his guilt had led him to expect.

"I wonder if he's right," said Elliott, gesturing to Gunter without taking his eyes off the crowd. He summoned all his powers of persuasion, the natural ones honed through centuries of acting and the inhuman ones derived from his undead nature. "Perhaps he is, and perhaps the rest of you are wiser than I am. After all, you're immortal. Why should you risk your lives for any cause when you can be young and strong forever? And let's be honest. If our mysterious foe knows where all the art is, and if he continues to attack it as aggressively as he has hitherto, we can only hope to save a fraction of it, no matter how zealously and fearlessly we proceed. So why bother?

"Well, here's one reason. How do you feel every time you read a newspaper or turn on CNN and learn that a work has been vandalized? It's like a piece of your soul has been ripped to pieces, isn't it?" Once again, Elliott was briefly conscious of the irony that he himself could no longer experience the emotion he was describing, but he was less aware of the discrepancy than he'd been two nights previously. He'd been a method actor for hundreds of years before the term was coined, and, now thoroughly immersed in the role of an exemplar of the Toreador ethos, he *did* feel an essentially bogus but convincing counterfeit of his clanmates' grief, just as he'd once felt the infatuation of Romeo and the jealousy of Othello.

Toby, a grizzled Toreador seated just in front of the harpsichord, a glassblower whose exquisite creations had been smashed in the first wave of destruction, began to sob.

"I want you to imagine," Elliott continued, "how we'll feel if the destruction goes on night after night and we don't lift a finger to stop it. When our heritage, the justification for our very existence, is lost forever. I believe we'll find that we've died inside. That our powers of creation have deserted us. And that our endless existence has become an intolerable burden!"

"Tell it," Judy murmured.

"We Toreador have heard our bloodline disparaged here tonight," Elliott continued. "I won't respond in kind. I admire the Brujah and the Malkavians." He glanced at Gunter. "Most of them, anyway." This time, his quip got a bigger laugh, a sign that more of the audience had fallen under his spell. "But I don't esteem any clan more than my own. History from the Greece of Homer on down to the present day demonstrates than no bloodline is worthier, or, if challenged, braver and deadlier than ours. Some of you youngsters have hitherto lived in peace. Fate has never afforded you the opportunity to discover just how formidable you are. I promise you that the talents which are our birthright make us a match for any opponent. Let's use them to save our heritage and lay our enemy low!"

For a moment the room was silent, and Elliott wondered if his eloquence had failed him. Then someone began to applaud enthusiastically, and a woman cried, "I'm with you! Save the art!" Other hands joined in the clapping —

A crash resounded through the arena. Startled, Elliott whirled to see that Gunter had interrupted the Toreador's demonstration of support by lifting a chair and dashing it to the floor.

"I don't blame you for getting sucked in by his nonsense," the Malkavian said to the crowd. "It's that voice of his. It bewitches even Kindred who possess the same power. But for your own sakes, *think!* Everyone here knows that Elliott Sinclair has been useless for years. He's done his level best to avoid being saddled with even the simplest responsibilities. Now, suddenly, some feckless whim has prompted him to want to lead us. But do you really want to trust him with your lives?"

"You're essentially right about me," Elliott said. Gunter's beady blue eyes narrowed in wary confusion. "Everyone knows the flaws in my character and the stains on my record. But if indeed someone else must lead while Roger lies stricken, perhaps the domain would be better off with a reluctant caretaker like me than an ambitious schemer like you. I doubt that I'm the only one who would fear for the prince's safety if you ever managed to ensconce yourself as his logical successor."

Gunter's fangs slid over his lower lip. Articulating with difficulty, he said, "There's only one answer to that. You claimed that the Toreador are mighty fighters. Here's your chance to prove it."

Despite his own anger, Elliott didn't want to brawl. He was now fairly certain he could win a duel of words; he was far less sure of his ability to prevail in physical combat. Drawing on his charismatic powers, trying to strike awe and uncertainty into the Malkavian's heart, he stared him coldly in the eye. "You forget yourself," the actor said. "Violence is forbidden in a meeting such as this. Roger decreed as much long ago."

This time his talent didn't work. "I knew you were a coward," Gunter said. Some of his brood laughed, shouted their agreement, or made clucking-chicken noises.

"It doesn't matter what rules Roger laid down," Judy murmured to Elliott. "Not now. The confrontation got too nasty; you guys threw too many insults back and forth. Now your honor's on the line. You either have to fight the son of a bitch or step aside and let him be boss."

"Then I'll fight him," Elliott said, his own fangs slipping from their sockets. Despite his reluctance, now that he'd committed himself to battle he couldn't help sharing the Beast's excitement at the prospect of spilling an enemy's blood. Judy and Sky retreated a few paces down the back wall, giving the combatants a little more room to battle.

Gunter stuck his hand inside his tan safari jacket. When he pulled it out again, it was armored in brass knuckles with protruding spikes. His body faded from view like frost melting off a windowpane.

Drawing on his superhuman speed, Elliott leaped and thrust out his leg in a side kick. His heel brushed Gunter's now-invisible body, but didn't connect solidly. As the Toreador landed, he heard a blow whizzing at his head. He swept up his arm with a circular motion and barely managed to block the attack.

Elliott instantly counterattacked, snapping kicks and punches at the space where he judged Gunter had just been standing. But he didn't connect. Somehow, despite the actor's superior quickness, his opponent had slipped aside.

Elliott slowly turned, hands poised to strike or parry. His senses probed the space around him, seeking a flicker of aura or a blur of movement, the rustle of a canvas jacket or the creak of shoe leather, or the scent of the stolen vitae in Gunter's system. It was no use; he couldn't zero in on his opponent. The Malkavian elder's powers of concealment seemed capable of thwarting even his own heightened perception, at least now that the excited members of the audience were shouting cheers, advice and catcalls.

The Toreador wondered if he could goad Gunter into revealing his whereabouts. Drawing once more on his charisma, he cried, "Now who's the coward? Show yourself! Fight like a man!"

"But I'm not a man," Gunter replied. His voice seemed to come from everywhere at once. Elliott couldn't home in on it. "I'm a Cainite, a real one, not a spineless, whining mockery like you."

Elliott sensed a blow streaking at his back. Raising his arm to block, he spun, a split second too slowly. Cold metal points tore into his shoulder. He stumbled, and the audience cried out.

Recovering his balance, the actor pounced, grabbing for his unseen opponent. His fingers only closed on air. Another blow slammed pain into his ribs and flung him staggering sideways. He almost fell on some of the spectators before he recovered his equilibrium.

"Give up," Gunter said, "before I *really* hurt you. Go home and resume your sulking, and leave war to the warriors."

Struggling to block out the pain of his wounds and the scent of his own blood, Elliott tried to sense the Malkavian's location. It was still impossible.

The Toreador wondered if he should stand with his back against the wall to keep Gunter from creeping up behind him. After a second, he rejected the idea. Such a purely defensive posture would limit his ability to maneuver, partially cancelling out whatever advantage his supernatural agility gave him. It might also persuade the onlookers, whom this spectacle must ultimately impress, that he was afraid. Instead he edged toward the string quartet's music stands and chairs.

Then at last he glimpsed an evanescent smear of motion behind the harpsichord. He suspected that Gunter had permitted him to spot it, to lead him in that direction and set him up for another attack. Pretending that he'd seen nothing, he halted and said, "Come on. Let's move this along before the audience gets bored."

After a moment, he thought he heard a footfall beside the harpsichord. He was tempted to charge at the noise, but he was still afraid that Gunter was setting him up, or that the Malkavian would be able to get out of the way. Better to stick to the plan, force his opponent to initiate the next flurry of action, even if it cost him another wound.

For a few more seconds nothing happened. Then, suddenly, he sensed a punch speeding at the side of his head, a blow that could fracture his skull or rip out an eye. Frantically, he sidestepped and blocked. The parry lashed through the air without catching Gunter's arm, but the Malkavian's spiked fist didn't connect, either.

This time Elliott didn't attempt to strike back with his

bare hands. He grabbed one of the musicians' chairs and, spinning, swept it around in a circle, as if it were his partner in some madly athletic dance.

Gunter was a good fighter, skillful at making the most of his invisibility. Ordinarily he could sneak up, attack and retreat back out of striking range before even an inhumanly agile opponent like Elliott could get a fix on him and retaliate. But the chair extended the Toreador's reach. Gunter didn't move far enough fast enough.

The chair crashed into an unseen obstacle; the impact stung Elliott's hands. Becoming gray and translucent, half-visible, Gunter reeled against the harpsichord. Elliott sprang after him and battered him about the head and shoulders with the remains of the shattered seat.

Becoming completely visible, Gunter tried to shield himself with his arms, but to little avail. He couldn't block as quickly as Elliott could swing. After a few moments, his scalp streaming fragrant vitae, he collapsed to one knee.

Elliott yearned to throw himself on the Malkavian and sink his fangs into his throat. Repressing the impulse, he snapped a rod out of what was left of the back of the chair, grabbed Gunter, jerked him to his feet, and pressed the jagged point of the makeshift wooden stake against his adversary's chest. "Do you surrender?" he said.

Gunter's furious blue eyes bored into his. "Back off!" the blond vampire said. "Back, back, back!"

For a second, Elliott's head swam and his knees felt rubbery, but Gunter's hypnotic powers failed to overcome his will. Perhaps his near-frenzy rendered him less susceptible. In any event, he yanked the Malkavian up on tiptoe and jabbed the stake an inch into his chest. "Surrender! Do you think I won't ram this through your heart and take your head? You've been asking for it for more than a century!"

The threat was a bluff. Furious as he was, Elliott still had sufficient presence of mind to grasp that he mustn't risk alienating the Malkavians by slaughtering their leader, not when every hand was needed for the common defense. But, perhaps influenced by the actor's charismatic talents, or simply cowed by the beating he'd received, Gunter evidently didn't realize it. For an instant his angry glower slipped, and he looked afraid.

"All right," the flaxen-haired elder said, retracting his fangs. "I surrender. I withdraw my suggestion that we appoint a deputy prince. And despite your previous lapses, I concede your right to participate in all deliberations of the primogen."

"Thank you," Elliott said dryly. He let Gunter go and stepped away from him. The audience whistled, clapped and cheered. Some of them surged out of their seats and clustered around the victor, babbling congratulations.

"I didn't think you still had it in you," Judy said. "Welcome back, El. You've been gone too long."

Elliott's anger faded, supplanted by a feeling of unreality. How, he wondered, could he have entered this chamber intent on disengaging himself from the present crisis and ended up fighting for the right to command the defense? But of course he knew the answer; the Beast was to blame. Once roused, it wasn't inclined to suffer slights from anyone. Perhaps Lazlo had been counting on that when he spat in his face and slapped him.

All right, mortal, Elliott thought grimly, *you've finally got me where you wanted me. I just hope I don't give you cause to regret it.*

From across the room, the gashes in his scalp and forehead already healing, Gunter glared at him. His expression promised Elliott that, no matter what public concessions the Toreador had wrung out of him, the conflict between them wasn't over.

ELEVEN: THE HUNT BEGINS

Happy is the hare at morning, for she cannot read
The Hunter's waking thoughts.
— W. H. Auden and Christopher Isherwood
Dog Beneath the Skin

As he pushed through the door that separated the lobby of the old hotel from the dark, narrow side street beyond, Angus took a moment to savor the evening air, balmy and warm even in the dead of winter. Though largely immune to the cold, he still had to admit that, after the subzero temperatures at the Arctic circle, the Florida climate made for a pleasant change.

He was less enamored of his new gray suit, white dress shirt, maroon tie and black oxfords. He knew it was just his imagination — purchased at a big-and-tall-men's shop, the clothes fit well enough — but the outfit made him feel constricted. The older he grew, the more he hated all but the loosest and most comfortable garments. It was as if, though he still felt thoroughly at home in human shape, he were losing patience with the senseless constraints and inconveniences of human civilization.

But if he was going to track a quarry through Sarasota, conventional white-collar attire would open more doors than his stained, ratty wilderness clothes. He was tempted to cut his long mane of hair and shave his beard as well, except that, due to his powers of regeneration, they'd regrow so quickly that it scarcely seemed worth the trouble. A vampire's form clung to the appearance it had worn in life, even in trivial respects.

Angus glanced up and down the sidewalk, checking to see if any mortals were watching him. None were. Downtown Sarasota seemed all but deserted, as if the kine, terrified of Dracula, had barricaded themselves in their homes.

Patience, the Gangrel told them silently. *Deliverance is at hand*. Then he grinned at his own cockiness. *I hope so, anyway*.

He spread his arms and invoked the unique gift of his people. Instantly he felt his irksome new clothing melt away and silky fur sprouting to take its place. His huge frame shrank. His legs shortened drastically in proportion to his torso, while his ears expanded and moved to the top of his head. Extending, his arms grew membranes which linked them to his sides.

In the blink of an eye, he'd become a large black bat. A beat of his wings sent him spiraling upward toward the crescent moon.

As usual, for a moment he couldn't resist surrendering himself to the delights of his new body, the exhilaration of riding the sea breeze and the wonder of his altered perception. As a bat, he could detect a universe of sounds beyond the range of human hearing. When his own high-pitched cries echoed back to him, he could hear *shapes*.

Angus wasn't thirsty. He'd fed last night. And thus he felt a familiar urge to forsake both Kindred and kine, to live the primal existence of an animal until the imminence of dawn sent him retreating to his lair. Resisting the impulse, reminding himself that he'd promised to catch Melpomene's rogue vampire and that, with any luck, the undertaking might actually be fun, he began to fly back and forth over the streets and rooftops, crisscrossing the city. Above him shone the stars. It pleased him that they burned brighter here than in many other, more smog-ridden cities. He wondered if it was the influence of the now-stricken Roger Phillips and his beauty-loving Toreador that had kept Sarasota from becoming as polluted, filthy and decayed as many other urban centers of the modern world.

After a few minutes he sighted a pale, slender, freckle-faced young woman, dressed in sandals, jeans and a black Metallica T-shirt with the sleeves chopped off, slinking through a seedy apartment complex. Though the world abounded in thin, fair-complexioned kine, he was instantly all but certain that the stranger was undead. Over the course of centuries, he had developed an instinct for recognizing his own kind. He wheeled above her unnoticed, studying her, ears straining. Sure enough, she wasn't breathing, nor was her heart beating.

Angus wondered if, by some incredible stroke of luck, he'd stumbled on Dracula minutes after beginning the hunt. He watched the other Kindred for a while to see if she was looking for prey, and if she'd take it in a way that left it dead and drained with holes in its throat, or otherwise endanger the Masquerade. Before long, noting the manner in which she crept along, scrutinizing every shadow, ignoring the noises of human occupancy, the murmur of conversation and the jangle of TV and stereos that sounded from the apartments, he decided that, far from being Dracula, she might well be hunting the outlaw herself. Melpomene had informed him that the Toreador and their allies were conducting their own frantic search.

Angus had considered revealing his presence to the local vampires and taking charge of their manhunt, but had decided against it. It was entirely possible that Dracula was some trusted member of their own community. If so, the Gangrel might have to shadow the indigenous Kindred to unmask him, and it would be easier to do that if the rest of Sarasota's undead didn't know of his existence. Besides, there were others to whom he could turn for aid.

He decided that he'd flown around enough to orient himself to the city. Wheeling, he headed west. In a minute, unaffected by the baseless superstitions that forbade his kind passage across open water, he was winging his way over the placid black waters of Sarasota Bay toward the narrow island called Longboat Key.

The aquarium, a four-story slab of a building, loomed out of the night just where Angus' tourist map had said it would be. The Gangrel dived toward the ground. With the ease of long practice, and confident that his vampire body's resilience would protect him from any injury, he began to change shape even before he touched down in the middle of a cluster of sheltering palm trees. His powerful human legs soaked up the impact.

Angus peered through the trees. As far as he could tell, no one else was around. Utterly silent despite his height and bulk, he slunk to what appeared to be the aquarium's staff entrance.

Someone had installed two shiny new stainless-steel locks in the door, a perfect example of closing up the barn after the horse was gone. Lacking the proper tools, Angus doubted that he could pick them, but fortunately, he didn't need to. He began to change form again.

His body and clothes turned pearly gray and then began to steam. Over the course of fifteen seconds, he melted into a roiling mass of faintly phosphorescent vapor.

In one respect, turning one's body to mist was rather the opposite of becoming a bat or a wolf. When he put on the guise of a beast, his senses grew sharper, but when he was fog, he had no eyes, ears, or nose, and his perceptions dimmed to a murky psychic awareness of shape and position.

That, however, was sufficient to guide him to the crack beneath the bottom of the door. He flowed through it and reverted to human shape in the dark hallway on the other side.

Angus honed his vision, and the shapes of the doors lining the corridor swam out of the dimness. His eyes now shining with a spectral crimson light, he headed for the exhibits.

He had little doubt that some of the fish had seen Dracula. According to the accounts in the media, the murderer had dumped a little girl's corpse in one of their tanks. But such creatures were nearly mindless. They couldn't possibly remember the encounter days later.

Warm-blooded animals, on the other hand, conceivably might, and so Angus made his way to the manatee exhibition where the two police officers had died.

Inside their tank, the massive, neckless, slate-colored animals floated, some motionless, possibly sleeping, and others swimming, their flukes sweeping smoothly up and down. Their forms reminded Angus of the seals and walruses he'd seen in the frozen north. He positioned himself in front of one of the observation windows, stared into it, and willed the manatees to commune with him. Two points of red light, the reflections of his eyes, gleamed on the surface of the glass.

One by one the six sea cows swam to the window. Their round, placid faces gazed out at him. Now linked to their minds, he could feel their friendly curiosity.

As was proper, he introduced himself, not giving his name, which would have been meaningless to them, but radiating a sense of his identity. No one, kine or Kindred, who lacked the power to converse with beasts could have understood the process, because no human language possessed the words to describe it. The manatees answered in kind, and then he asked them about the murders.

At first the animals conveyed incomprehension. They saw the two-legged shapes that moved beyond the windows, but ordinarily they didn't pay any attention to them. There was no reason to.

With a patience that sometimes eluded him in his dealings with humans and vampires, Angus kept talking, trying to stimulate the manatees' memories. Though the animals had little concept of either time or number, he managed to communicate that the killings had happened several nights ago. One of the men who'd died had accidentally broken a window.

The smallest manatee, an immature female with the indented white groove of a propeller scar on top of her head, exclaimed in recognition. The hole! They didn't know anything about any killing, but of course they remembered the hole.

The animals projected a jumble of remembered impressions so intense that for a moment Angus nearly believed that he was one of them, his heavy, rounded body suspended in cool, soothing water. It had been a night like any other, and then, suddenly, they'd heard a sharp crack and felt a shock. An instant later they'd sensed a new current in the tank, flowing not to the drains but somewhere else. Following it, they'd discovered the hole in the window.

At first they'd been merely curious and then, as the water level dropped, somewhat alarmed. But eventually the humans who fed them had come and moved them to another tank, one without windows in the walls. When their keepers had moved them back again, the water had been at its accustomed level, and the breach in the glass was gone.

When you first peered at the hole, Angus asked, what did you see beyond it on the other side of the window? You must have noticed *something*.

For a moment the manatees regarded him blankly, and he decided that, in fact, they *couldn't* help him. Then the same female who'd recalled the bullet hole projected the image of a woman crouching over two motionless bodies. The picture was murky and distorted, but Angus could make out a tall, slender form, a pale, oval face, short raven hair capped with a sort of beret, and a long black coat with the collar turned up.

He was somewhat surprised. He realized that, though he'd encountered plenty of depraved and dangerous female Kindred in the course of his long existence, he'd been unconsciously assuming that Dracula was male. He supposed it was a carryover from his youth, when, by and large, the men had done the raiding, feuding and killing while the women stayed home to bury them and teach the bairns to hate the enemies of their clan.

Pleased if not jubilant — it would have taken a clear view of Dracula's face to make him truly rejoice — he thanked the manatees for their help, bade them good-bye, and retraced his steps.

Once outside he moved away from the building and back into the palms. Then he tilted back his head and began to call with an inhuman, ultrasonic cry.

A shape like a ragged scrap of shadow swooped out of the night and wheeled around his head. Then another. Before long, he was standing at the center of a whirling, squealing cloud of bats. Smiling, he hailed them, introduced himself, and then began to give them their instructions.

TWELVE: THE NEXT MOVE

All wars are planned by old men
In council rooms apart.
> — Grantland Rice, "Two Sides of War"

Elliott prowled restlessly around Roger's cramped little study, which he'd decided to usurp as his own office for the duration of the crisis. Though twenty-four hours had passed, the feeling of unreality that had overwhelmed him at the conclusion of his combat with Gunter had yet to release its grip. He wondered morosely just what course of action the unofficial warlord of Sarasota ought to be pursuing, what cunning strategies ought to be springing to his mind. He felt as if he'd been forced to perform an utterly unfamiliar play, one in which he didn't even know the story, let alone any of his lines.

He contemplated the model of the Globe Theatre, wondering if he and all his associates wouldn't have been better off if he'd never been Embraced. If he'd lived a normal mortal lifespan in good Queen Bess' London, then died when his allotted years were through.

Someone tapped on the door. Inhaling, he caught Lazlo's clean but slightly musty scent — he smell of a human who attended to his personal hygiene, but whose body had begun to deteriorate with age. "Come in," the vampire said.

Lazlo shuffled into the room. His aura, more vividly colored than any undead's, was shot through with orange and gray, hues suggestive of worry and sadness respectively. "Judy said you wanted to see me," the mortal remarked.

Elliott nodded. "Please sit down," he said, waving his hand at one of the antique green leather chairs. He, however, remained on his feet to tower ominously over his companion.

The Toreador also kept silent for a few seconds, hoping the tactic would rattle Lazlo's nerves. Finally the mortal said, "Well? What is it? What's happened this time?"

"Nothing," Elliott said. Drawing on his charismatic abilities, he tried to project a subtle vibe of menace. "I just need some information."

Lazlo's eyes narrowed in seeming puzzlement — or suspicion. "All right. Ask away."

"Does Roger have a master inventory of all the Toreador art?"

"Well, not as such," Lazlo replied. "But if somebody went through his journals and other papers, he could identify a lot of it."

"Who knows about those documents?" Elliott demanded.

Lazlo shrugged. "I don't know. I don't think their existence is any big secret."

"But it might be difficult for most people to get at them," Elliott said. "I imagine it would help considerably if one lived here in the house and could move around by daylight, when Roger was certain to be asleep."

Lazlo gaped at him. "What are you saying?"

"It also occurs to me," Elliott continued remorselessly, "that Roger may have been rendered ill by some exotic, undetectable poison placed in his clothing or on his intimate effects. If so, who would have as good an opportunity to commit the act as his mortal secretary and valet?"

"That's insane!" Lazlo cried. "There are other ways that the enemy could have found the art. And anybody could have crept up behind Roger and brushed poison on his clothes, assuming that's even what happened in the first place. And — and — damn it, I'm *loyal*, and everybody knows it!"

Elliott scrutinized the human's aura anew. The envelope of light blazed the fiery red of outrage, without a hint of the shifting patterns of orange and sienna which might have indicated guilt and the fear of discovery. Nodding, the Toreador said, "Yes, I do know it, but I had to be sure. Please forgive me."

Not entirely mollified, Lazlo scowled. "How could you even imagine that I was a spy?" he grumbled.

"Well, given the security leak, I have to look into the possibility that somebody is," Elliott replied reasonably. He'd also arranged for Roger's house to be swept for bugs.

"Yes, but how could you think it was *me?*" Lazlo persisted. "What possible motive could I have?"

"Speaking hypothetically, how about your age?" Elliott said.

Lazlo blinked. "I'm not following you."

"You've served Roger long and faithfully," Elliott said, moving behind the desk and dropping into the comfortable, high-backed executive chair behind it, the only piece of furniture in the room that wasn't an antique. The notes he'd scribbled pertaining to the defense of the domain lay strewn across the blotter. "And yet, for whatever reason, he hasn't made you immortal, hasn't given you the Embrace or even made you a ghoul. In your position, many people would resent that."

Lazlo snorted. "It's a cute theory, except for one thing. Roger did offer me the Embrace. Many times. I always turned it down."

Intrigued, Elliott cocked his head. "Why?"

"I grew up around here," Lazlo said, "only out in the

country, in a subdivision where a lot of circus people and carnies spend the winter. D. L. Hicks, the lion and tiger trainer, owned the property next to my family's. He let me come over and watch him rehearse the act, and I got to know him pretty well. And you know what? The big cats fascinated him. I think he even loved them. But I'm damn sure that he never wanted to *be* one. He understood them too well for that."

Elliott laughed. The sensation felt odd, and he wondered fleetingly just how long it had been since he'd given vent to mirth. "Is that how you see us?" he asked. "As your own personal menagerie, performing stunts for your entertainment?" The concept was so at variance with the lofty opinion most Kindred held of themselves that, for a moment, it seemed irresistibly comic.

"Obviously not in the sense that I control you," Lazlo said.

You've done a pretty good job of pulling my strings, Elliott thought wryly.

"But in the sense that you're beautiful and captivating, dangerous and alien, yes," the mortal continued. "I've never regretted that I fell in with Roger. I can't imagine a more interesting life than to exist in your world. But as myself, not a Kindred. If I thought that one of you were going to force me to accept the Embrace, I'd run screaming into the night and never look back, because I see you more clearly than you can see yourselves. I can tell how the Hunger and the long years of preying on men and women corrode the soul. I see which human qualities even you Toreador, the gentlest vampires, inevitably lose."

Elliott felt uneasy, because Lazlo's words had the ring of truth. The vampire wondered in what respects he himself had changed without even realizing it, yet, if the process was inexorable, perhaps he was better off not knowing. Suddenly eager to change the subject, he said, "Be that as it may, I'm glad you're not a traitor. Because that would have meant that you only pushed me to take charge because you expected me to make some catastrophic error."

Lazlo gestured irritably, flicking the notion away as if it were a gnat. "I assume that you've been interrogating other people too," the dresser said. "Otherwise, I'm *really* going to feel offended. Have you found any good suspects?"

Elliott sighed. "Except for you and some of our other mortal associates, I've scarcely found anything else. I'd give odds that every Kindred I've spoken to, even the brashest, youngest member of Judy Morgan's brood, is hiding some sort of secret. Not necessarily one that pertains to the present situation, but *something*. I suppose the Masquerade is to blame. It turns us all into inveterate deceivers. And it isn't easy to pick one particular liar out from all the others."

"My money's on Gunter," Lazlo said. "He wants to be prince, so he stirs up a crisis that will let him take Roger's place. If you hadn't stopped him, he'd already have done it, more or less."

"There's no doubt that Gunter wants to exploit the present situation," Elliott replied. "That doesn't necessarily mean that he helped create it. Have our other enemies promised him Roger's throne in payment for his treachery? If so, then what do *they* stand to gain from their victory? From their perspective, what makes the war worthwhile?"

Lazlo frowned, pondering Elliott's point. "Just off the top of my head," the mortal said, "maybe Gunter is *paying* the outsiders. Maybe they have a grudge against Roger and the rest of you, though I can't imagine what it could be. Or perhaps they want a Prince of Sarasota who'll back their proposals in the councils of the Camarilla."

"Those are all possibilities," Elliott conceded. "But it's also possible that Gunter is innocent. We know too little to assume anyth—"

The green phone on the desk chimed softly.

Inwardly wincing at the prospect of more bad news, Elliott picked the receiver up. "Elliott Sinclair," he said.

"I've seen Dracula," said a deep, gravelly voice.

Elliott felt a pang of excitement. "Who is this?" he asked.

"She's tall, thin, young-looking and long-legged, with a white, oval face," the caller continued, ignoring the question. "She has black hair cut in what people used to call a pageboy. On the night she visited the aquarium, she was wearing a long black coat and a beret."

"Who are you?" Elliott said.

The line went dead.

Elliott punched the intercom button on the phone and dialed a two-digit number. As soon as the ghoul assigned to trace calls picked up the receiver, the Toreador said, "Did you get that?"

"Yes," the servant replied in a reedy tenor voice. Elliott felt a thrill of hope, which the other man instantly dashed. "He called from a pay phone near the planetarium."

"Dispatch somebody to investigate right away," Elliott said. "Whoever's out there patrolling the area. Thanks." Breaking the connection, he turned back toward Lazlo. "But they won't find anything. Damn it!"

"Was that the woman who spoke to Judy and me?" the dresser asked.

"No," Elliott said, "that was a man, calling to provide a description of Dracula."

"Did he say who he was, or how he knew to call here?"

Elliott grimaced. "Of course not," he said ironically. "You wouldn't want anyone to tell us the complete and unembellished truth, would you? What fun would that be?"

"I wish we did know who you were talking to," Lazlo said, "but still, if he told you what Dracula looks like, that's good, isn't it?"

"Assuming that we can believe him," Elliott said, "I suppose so." Suddenly edgy, he rose and began to stalk around the study, past the bookshelves and some of Roger's mementos: a poster from *Man and Superman*, a program from *Mother Courage*, a prop dagger from *Julius Caesar* and a crystal unicorn from *The Glass Menagerie*. "Still, you have to wonder how many players are involved in this game, how many sides, how many agendas. How can I make decisions when I don't understand a fraction of what's going on? I don't know if even Roger could have coped with a mess like this."

"Our people are recovering some of the art," Lazlo said, "without getting attacked. You're looking for the leak. All the other defensive operations are proceeding as planned. I'd say that you're on top of the situation."

Elliott shook his head. "When the enemy does something, we react. You can't win a war that way. You have to anticipate at least your foe's next move, and preferably his next several moves." He sighed. "I used to be reasonably good at it, but I feel as if that part of my mental machinery has rusted solid."

"Let's hope not," Lazlo said.

"Let me tell you how I see the situation," Elliott said, continuing to pace. "Maybe you can point out something I'm missing. The enemy poisons or otherwise incapacitates our prince. He sends a rogue Kindred into our domain, forcing us to divert manpower and resources to the defense of the Masquerade. He assails our financial holdings. He vandalizes our art, and when we send out troops to protect it, he ambushes them.

"Evidently his strategy is to attack us on all levels, in every way he can, and I have a hunch that he hasn't run out of ideas yet. That being the case, where's the *next* blow going to fall?"

"Maybe the next assault is a full-scale invasion of the city," Lazlo said.

"I doubt it," Elliott said. "Many of his opening moves were intended to frazzle and humiliate us, and, considering that none of our people has fled the domain for greener pastures, I don't think we're demoralized and disorganized enough to suit him yet. I imagine he'll keep trying to soften us up. I just wish I knew —" The vampire's gaze fell on a framed photo of Roger with one of Hollywood's hottest new directors and he froze, his words catching in his throat.

"What is it?" Lazlo asked.

"God help us all, I *do* know," Elliott replied. He turned and lunged for the phone.

THIRTEEN: COMRADES

Only solitary men know the full joys of friendship.
— Willa Cather, *Shadows on the Rock*.

The narrow streets of the Little Havana district of Miami were crowded, even at two in the morning. Groups of teenagers, many wearing gang colors, strutted along the sidewalks while others, packed into cars whose stereos blared heavy metal or Latin music, cruised slowly up and down. Drug dealers and heavily made-up hookers in miniskirts loitered in shadowy doorways. Open-air stalls and push carts sold crab rolls, hot dogs, paper plates of black beans and rice, beer, Cuban coffee and shoddy plastic toys and trinkets. The warm night air smelled of exhaust, tobacco, alcohol, marijuana and human sweat. Surveying the scene though one of the windows in the rear of the van, Dan said, "This place reminds me of Saigon."

"You were in Vietnam?" Laurie asked. He nodded. "Were you in combat?"

Dan nodded. In fact, he'd seen a lot of action. Looking back, it was strange to remember just how much it had bothered him to watch people die.

"Of course he was," said Wyatt, tucking his battery-powered electric razor, with which he'd just removed the stubble sprouting around his mohawk, back in the pocket of his white leather coat. Given the peculiarities of vampire physiology, he probably had to shave the sides of his head at least once a night. "Where do you think he learned to fight like Superman?" He gave Dan a friendly wink.

Dan hadn't explained to the anarchs that when he'd saved them from the Brujah he'd had an infusion of giants' blood enhancing his strength. Hoping they wouldn't expect him to toss around any cars in the future, he turned toward the driver. "Hey, Cassius," he said, "how are we doing?"

"The traffic is hell," the heavyset black ghoul replied. "Most of the streets keep twisting or dead-ending, or else they're one-way going the wrong way, and a lot of the signs are either missing or in Spanish. But don't worry, I *will* find the place."

"You're having trouble with the Spanish?" said Felipe, the Hispanic vampire with the weight-lifter physique and a liking for gold chains. "You should have said something before." He rose from the floor of the van and squirmed into the bucket seat beside the Blood-Bound servant.

"Was Vietnam as terrible and as stupid as people say?" Laurie asked, pushing her rose-colored granny glasses back up to the bridge of her nose. "My friends and I protested it." She blinked. "Oh, jeez, I hope that isn't going to be a problem between you and me."

"Of course not," said Dan. It still felt odd to chat with his own kind companionably, to perceive that another vampire cared whether he liked her. Odd, but nice. "It's ancient history now. Looking back, I guess the whole thing *was* stupid. It sure didn't accomplish anything, did it?"

"No," Wyatt said. "It was just another Camarilla fiasco."

Dan cocked his head. "How do you mean?"

"Why do you think you were sent over there?" replied the vampire in white. "The elders of the West have been fighting a slow-motion war with the clans of the Orient for a long time, and you poor bastards were the foot soldiers.

I'm no great bleeding-heart protector of the kine — I'll worry about my species and let them worry about theirs — but my God, what a pointless waste of human life! It illustrates why the old order has to go."

Laurie nodded solemnly, the way she so often did when Wyatt preached the anarch gospel.

"So how old are *you*, Wyatt?" Dan asked curiously. "What was going on in the world when you were human?"

"The Revolutionary War," said the anarch chieftain, a spark of pride glowing in his eyes. "I was one of Francis Marion's guerrillas. Did you ever hear of him?"

Dan nodded. "The Swamp Fox."

"Right," Wyatt said. "I really believed in the ideals of the Revolution. I had the Declaration of Independence and *Common Sense* down by heart. I thought that after we ran off the redcoats and the Hessians we could turn the colonies into a utopia.

"Then a Ventrue elder seduced me into accepting the Embrace. I guess she saw something in me that convinced her I'd make a useful addition to her brood, and frankly, it wasn't that hard to sell me on the idea of obtaining immortality." He smiled wryly. "I wasn't *entirely* idealistic, you see.

"Anyway, the world of the Kindred took me completely by surprise. Dreamer that I was, I'd believed that vampires, virtual demigods with centuries of accumulated wisdom, must have created a perfect society, an even grander and nobler version of the nation my fellow rebels and I had been striving to build. You can imagine my disgust when I discovered the tyranny and cruelty with which the old dominated the young. The never-ending violence and intrigue. The unquestioning acceptance of institutions like torture, the duel, and trial by ordeal, which mortals were coming to abhor as barbaric even in the eighteenth century.

"I never regretted becoming a Kindred — eternal youth is nothing to sneeze at, even in a fascist oligarchy — but I rapidly began to despise my fellow Ventrue. How could I not, considering that they'd *created* the Camarilla and were its most fervent supporters? When Salvador Garcia founded the Movement, I ran away to join, and I've been fighting for it ever since."

Wyatt grinned. Once again his revolutionary ardor seemed to give way to a more boyish, even mischievous, zest. "And it's a pretty cool life! It's exciting, and you make true friends." He beamed at the other vampires. Laurie took his hand and squeezed it. Somewhat to his dismay, Dan felt a twinge of affection himself for the youth with the mohawk. "In my sire's brood, I never had that. Everybody was always stabbing everybody else in the back, jockeying for the old gorgon's favor."

"I think we might be getting somewhere," the driver said.

All the vampires in the back of the van tried to rear up and look out the windshield at the same time, a maneuver which crowded them together. Dan noticed that no one pulled away from him with a reflexive wince or shudder of distaste.

Craning to peer over Laurie's brunette head, he saw that the character of the streets the van was traversing had changed. Now the narrow, twisting avenues, scarcely more than alleys, really, were empty, their gutters choked with trash. There were few lights burning, and many of the shops were vacant, with whitewashed or boarded windows. Little Haiti, assuming that the Kindred had indeed reached their destination, was manifestly far less lively and considerably more impoverished than the Cuban immigrant quarter it abutted.

"Can anybody see any house numbers?" the driver asked.

Turning, Dan peered through the window closest to him. A few of the doorways they were passing had had numbers once, but time had largely worn away the paint. In the dark and at a distance, even his newly enhanced vision couldn't make the numerals out. "Sorry," he said, "not from here."

Rounding a bend, the van encountered the blackened shell of a burned-out convertible which completely blocked the way. The ghoul stamped on the brakes and the panel truck lurched to a stop. "Shit," he said.

"Don't worry about it," Wyatt said, reaching for the handle of the door. "We can hoof it from here. I'm tired of being cooped up, and I think that we might find the place we're looking for faster that way. You just turn the car around and be ready for a fast getaway."

"You got it," Cassius replied.

As the vampires climbed out of the van, Dan smelled a strong odor of combustion. The car obstructing the road had burned only hours ago, and it stank of charred meat as well as singed metal and paint. Moving closer, he felt the heat still radiating from it and saw the two black husks sitting in the front seat. Each had been dusted with pale yellow flower petals and a sprinkling of crimson powder.

"I wonder," said Dan, "whether these stiffs are still here because nobody called the cops, or because the police won't come into Little Haiti after dark. Either way, I'm guessing that this isn't a great neighborhood."

"I think you've got a point," Laurie said. Peering warily about at the dark alleys and doorways, the heaps of rotting, stinking garbage that shifted and rustled as rats burrowed through them, and the claustrophobic passages that ran between the buildings into impenetrable shadow, she looked more like a timid mortal girl than a predator on humankind. "They say Miami is contested territory. The Camarilla and the Black Hand both claim it. I wonder if these deaths have something to do with that. The petals and the powder make them look like some kind of ritual murders."

Wyatt put his hand on her shoulder. "Hey," he said gently, "whatever happened here, it's got nothing to do with us. We're going to be fine. We'll nail the target and be out of town before anybody even knows we've been here. I mean, who's slicker than we are?"

She gave him a game smile. "Nobody."

"Damn straight." He brushed a stray strand of her brown hair off her glasses. "So let's get to it."

Circling the burned car and its grisly contents, the vampires set off down the street. Everyone, watching not only for street signs and house numbers but any sign of trouble, peered about in a manner that reminded Dan of his old platoon making its way through the jungle.

His fellow GIs had been his last real friends — until the anarchs had made him welcome. Though he'd only known them for a couple of nights, he already felt close to them. Perhaps it was because they'd faced death together. In any case he was becoming increasingly uncomfortable with the notion of selling them out.

The Kindred neared an intersection where a street sign, which some vehicle had apparently jumped the curb and run into, leaned drunkenly. Squinting at it, Wyatt read, "Southwest Thirtieth Street. All right, we're nearly there!" Heading right, the vampires turned the corner. The cross street was as black and empty as the last one.

Why, Dan wondered, *should* he betray his friends? In recent years, he'd become a little too cynical to believe now that the anarch cause would ever actually improve the lot of the common vampire; but on the other hand, he didn't have anything against it, either. Certainly its dogma was more congenial than the authoritarian strictures of the Camarilla. Nor did he have any particular desire to aid Roger Phillips and his vassals against their enemies. The bastards had certainly never done anything for him!

A chalk drawing, a double circle quadrisected by a cross, with cryptic symbols incised in the four sections, gleamed on a crumbling brick wall ahead. Jimmy Ray, an anarch with a hillbilly twang in his voice and an Elvis haircut, whom Dan had yet to see without his black wraparound sunglasses, muttered uneasily: "More voodoo stuff."

Dan reflected that he'd undertaken this mission because

Melpomene had promised him a place in vampire society. But now he already had one. Why, then, should he follow through?

Ultimately, he could only think of one reason. He'd given the Methuselah his word. But his infiltration of the anarch cell had required him to pledge his loyalty to them as well. Therefore, he was going to be a liar and a traitor no matter what he did.

He was still mulling over his dilemma when he and his companions came to a doorway sealed with a wrought-iron gate. Beyond the bars was a sort of tunnel that led to a small courtyard with a dry, fungus-spotted fountain in the center. The air inside smelled of cooking, of roast chicken and goat, conch chowder and fried plantains.

Wyatt pointed at the numerals someone had crudely scratched on the wall beside the gate. "Seven ninety-five," he said. "We're in business." He smiled at Dan. "Would you care to open this?"

"Sure," said Dan. He gripped the gate and pulled. After a moment the lock broke, and the barrier lurched open.

When the vampires skulked into the courtyard, it became apparent that they'd found an apartment complex. Clotheslines ran back and forth between windows and rickety balconies, slicing the square patch of sky at the top of the enclosure into sections. Dan could hear people snoring, and a rhythmic squeak of bedsprings that indicated that somewhere a pair of insomniacs were making love.

"This way, I think," murmured Wyatt. He led his companions toward a shadowy doorway on the left. Dan wondered if the anarch leader was responding to a bit of psychic inspiration or a more mundane source of information.

The doorway opened on a staircase. As the vampires climbed, the risers flexed beneath their feet. Now the air smelled of dry rot and mice. Dan could hear the rodents and other vermin skittering through hollows in the walls.

At the top of the stairs was a single door. Wyatt stepped up to it, touched his fingertip to the keyhole, closed his eyes, and froze. After a moment, Dan whispered, "What are you doing?"

For another second Wyatt didn't answer. Then, blinking like a mortal awakening from slumber, he said, "Just trying to see if one of my skeleton keys will fit this. I think it will." He put his hand in the pocket of his white leather coat, paused again and then brought out, not the ring of keys that Dan had been expecting, but a single brass one. He eased it into the lock and twisted it. The bolt disengaged with a click.

"Why didn't you try a skeleton key on the gate downstairs?" asked Dan.

"Outdoors, I wasn't as worried about being quiet," replied Wyatt, grinning, "and hey, with a moose like you around, why should I do all the work? Shall we?" He pushed open the door.

Beyond the threshold was a spacious loft, an artist's studio redolent with the sharp smell of turpentine, illuminated by the silvery moonlight cascading through the skylight. Canvases stood on easels or, completed, leaned against the walls. Inside another doorway along the left-hand wall, hearts thumped slowly and breath hissed softly in and out of mortal lungs.

"Let's trash us some art," said Jimmy Ray, pulling a plastic spray bottle out of his pocket. He sauntered to one of the easels and spritzed down the canvas it held. The harsh tang of the solvent stung Dan's nose. The paint steamed, bubbled and ran, reducing the picture to a meaningless smudge.

The remaining anarchs sauntered into the loft and began to ruin other paintings. Removing his own container of solvent from inside his jacket, Dan moved to do the same. He felt a twinge of shame. Since becoming a vampire, he'd done a lot of things he wasn't proud of, things that, by any sensible standard, were worse than vandalizing a bunch of pictures; yet something about this particular act made him feel petty and mean. But he guessed that if he wanted to remain in his companions' good graces, he had no choice.

As he twisted open the nozzle of the bottle, he casually scrutinized the painting before him, a vision of yellow lions and blue parrots in a tropical forest, rendered in what he thought was a rather childlike style of simple shapes and primary colors. For a moment it merely seemed kind of pretty and kind of strange, and then it seemed to change before his eyes.

Even as he froze in awe, he realized that the picture hadn't truly altered. Instead, he was perceiving it with a depth of appreciation of which he'd previously been incapable. He saw how the seemingly rudimentary forms and garish hues combined to form a single gorgeous, exquisite gestalt. How the meticulous brushwork created the illusion of depth and texture. He felt as if he'd glimpsed a different world, one infinitely richer and more beautiful than the quotidian reality in which he'd always dwelled.

Something touched him on the arm. Startled, he jerked around so violently that Laurie recoiled a step.

"Are you okay?" the petite former hippie asked. "You were just staring at that picture and then, when I spoke to you, you didn't hear me."

Dan *hoped* he was all right; he was damned if he knew. "Sure," he said. "I was just, you know, checking it out for a second."

Laurie turned to look at the canvas. Warily, Dan followed suit. He felt relieved when, though it still looked more beautiful than he could have imagined a minute ago, it failed to hypnotize him as it had before.

"It's a shame to ruin them, isn't it?" Laurie said wistfully. "But Wyatt says that if it makes the Toreador stupid with rage, or destroys their will to fight, it will be worth it."

"Makes sense to me," Dan said. "What the hell, there are plenty of pictures in the world." Laurie gave him an affectionate pat on the arm, then advanced on a painting of a dilapidated wooden sailboat.

Steeling himself, Dan aimed his bottle at the canvas before him, then faltered again. Finally, squinching his eyes shut, he convulsively clenched his finger on the trigger. When the painting sizzled, he had to strain to hold in a sob.

Fortunately, the act of desecration became a little easier with repetition, though it always felt as if a piece of himself were dying along with the work he was destroying. By the time all the art had been ruined, he was desperate to flee the scene, frantic to escape the sight of the ravaged masterpieces. Fighting to keep his voice steady, he said, "I guess we can go."

Wyatt shook his head. "Not quite yet."

"Why not?" Dan said. "Are there more pictures in another room?" He didn't think he could stand it if there were.

"Nope," said Wyatt, "or at least, not as far as I know. But can you hear the painter and his family, snorting and wheezing away?" He nodded at the doorway in the left-hand wall. "I've been instructed that tonight the war is entering a new phase. It's time to start killing the Toreador's pet kine." He smiled at Dan.

He's watching me, Dan realized, *waiting to see my reaction.* Wyatt might *believe* that his newest recruit was a genuine convert to the anarch cause — Dan was almost certain that he did — but that didn't mean that he was ready to stop testing him. The cell leader was too wary a conspirator for that.

Thirty years of deceiving and preying on humans, of watching them age while he remained young, had hardened Dan, attenuating his emotional bond to what had once been his own kind. Still, the thought of slaughtering helpless innocents sickened him, and the notion that one of the prospective victims had created the beauty the vampires had just finished ravaging made the prospect even more loathsome. But once again, whether he wound up staying with the anarchs or betraying them, it wouldn't do to reveal his revulsion.

"Good thinking," he said, smiling back at Wyatt. "After all, what's the point of destroying the paintings if you leave the artist alive to make more?"

"Exactly," Wyatt said. He beckoned, and the Kindred stalked toward the doorway. Jimmy Ray's fangs slid over his lower lip.

As the would-be murderers slipped into the artist's living area, Dan positioned himself at the back of the procession in the hope that it would keep him from actually having to commit any of the violence. He wound up gliding along beside Laurie. Her expression seemed resolute but somber, and he wondered if she found the business at hand as distasteful as he did.

The vampires passed through a sparsely, shabbily furnished living room, dining area and kitchen, and then into what must have been the bedroom hall. The hiss of respiration and the muffled thud of heartbeats grew louder. Dan smelled the pungent tang of sweat.

Suddenly Jimmy Ray lunged through a doorway. Dan heard bedsprings squeal, and a brief thrashing sound. When his companion reemerged into the hall, he was holding a skinny, naked black boy in each hand, clutching them by their throats. Half-strangled already, the children squirmed feebly.

Wyatt and Felipe darted into a room farther down the passage. The other vampires followed them. By the time Dan made it through the door, the duo in the lead had dragged a black man and woman, nude also, out of their battered, sagging, four-poster bed. Felipe was restraining the man, a middle-aged, partially bald, paunchy guy with paint-stained fingers, by dint of his superior strength. Wyatt was gazing into the slender, trembling, long-necked young woman's eyes, paralyzing her by force of will.

"No!" cried the artist, mad with fear. "No! No!"

"Sorry, amigo," said Felipe. "This is what you get for running with the Camarilla."

"No!" said the painter. "You're making a mistake! I don't even know what that is!"

"That's too bad," said Felipe. "They should have told you what you were getting into." He buried his fangs in the immigrant's neck. The human wailed.

The black woman shuddered more violently and moaned. Her heartbeat raced. "It's all right," said Wyatt soothingly. "It will all be over very soon." He took her in his arms and bit her.

Jimmy Ray handed one of the now-unconscious children to Laurie and ripped out the throat of the other, savagely, wastefully, spattering blood on himself and the floor. The intoxicating scent of the vitae suffused the air.

Laurie shivered and squinched her eyes shut. "Oh, Christ," she whispered, as if she were mortal and a lover had caressed her. She dropped to her knees, clutched the other boy to her bosom, and began to feed.

Nor was Dan immune to the effects of the spectacle before him. Hard as he tried to stay calm, to cling to his inner disgust, the smell of the blood and the slurping, gurgling sounds his companions made as they sucked it from their prey were kindling his own Hunger. By the time Wyatt offered him the woman, he was eager to finish draining her.

He pressed his mouth to the twin punctures that his companion had made, and the world dissolved into pleasure. Finally he noticed that the woman's heart had stopped, and her vitae had begun to cool and lose its savor.

As Dan lifted his head, Felipe licked the artist's wounds closed and carried him to the window. "Take this, Sarasota!" he said, his voice giddy with high spirits, and hurled the body through the glass. The resultant crash hurt Dan's ears.

No doubt curious to see where and how the body had

landed, Felipe stuck his head out into the night. His body tensed. "Oh, shit," he said.

Dan dropped the woman's corpse on the floor, strode to the window and looked down. The painter lay facedown on the crumpled roof of a black limousine. Eight men — vampires, judging from the pallor each displayed — who'd evidently just gotten out of the limo and the sedan parked behind it, stared up at Felipe and Dan for another moment, and then reached inside their coats.

FOURTEEN:THE SAMEDI

He who pretends to look on death without fear lies.
— Jean-Jacques Rousseau, *La Nouvelle Héloïse*

Dan recoiled, then saw that Felipe had yet to do likewise. He grabbed the anarch's arm and yanked him back inside. An instant later, a hail of gunfire blazed upward through the window.

"What the hell's going on?" Wyatt cried. For once the vampire in white looked rattled.

"There are Kindred out there," said Dan. "Since they seem to be pissed at us for killing the artist, I guess they're Prince Roger's people."

"They must have figured out that we meant to start killing their protégés, and come to take the kine and his family to safety," Wyatt said. "Not that that matters now, God damn it." He pulled his shotgun out of his coat. "How many are there?"

"Eight that I saw," Dan replied, drawing from the back of his jeans the stainless-steel Smith and Wesson Model 669 that he'd commandeered from the anarchs' armory.

"We could make a stand here," said Jimmy Ray, peering nervously about.

"We could try," Dan said, "but we don't know how many guys there are, or what kind of weapons they have to use against us. You get a dozen vamps dropping through that skylight at once, or the enemy blasting this dump apart with explosives, or setting it on fire, and we could be pretty well screwed. I think we ought to try to get away."

"If that's what we're doing, we need to go now, before they box us in," Wyatt said. He pivoted, scatter-gun leveled in one hand, the tail of his white coat sweeping out behind him, and strode toward the exit of the apartment. The other Kindred trotted after him.

Reaching the door, Wyatt cracked it open and peeked out onto the landing. Dan tensed, half-expecting another barrage of shots to smash through the panels. Then Wyatt pulled the door all the way open. "So far so good," he said. "Come on."

Running with the quiet, sure-footed grace of the undead, the Kindred bounded down three flights of steps without incident. Dan could hear rapid heartbeats and quick, fearful breathing behind the closed doors on the landings. Evidently the gunfire had awakened the residents of the other apartments. He wondered if anyone had called the cops, or if everybody was simply lying low, hoping that whatever trouble was happening, it wouldn't happen to them.

The vampires plunged onto the second-floor landing. Wyatt grabbed the wooden knob at the top of the newel post and swung himself onto the final flight of stairs. Guns barked and rattled up at him. He grunted, and his feet flew out from under him.

Jimmy Ray and Felipe snapped off shots at the gunmen massed at the foot of the steps. Laurie grabbed Wyatt and hauled him up. Dan spun and kicked one of the doors on the landing. It flew open, crashing against the wall. "This way!" he cried.

As he scrambled into the apartment, he noticed that it

was cramped and essentially unfurnished, with ancient, dingy paper peeling off the walls. Mortals lay everywhere, a few on stained, dilapidated mattresses, others on piles of rags or newspaper, and some on the bare linoleum. Most of the humans were content to cower and avert their gazes, but one chunky woman, the scleras of her wide, dark eyes the yellow of a stained tooth, reared up and babbled in what Dan assumed was Creole.

Whatever she was saying, he had no time for her. He brandished his pistol and bared his fangs, and she shrank back from him. Momentarily uncertain of his directions, scrambling over several of her fellow tenants, he made his way to a window. Then he saw that it overlooked the courtyard, and that a pair of sentries were stationed there. Hoping to find a better way out, acutely aware that the gunmen they'd encountered on the stairs were only seconds behind them, he wheeled and led his companions on into a tiny room at the rear of the apartment.

Here the residents were packed in like sardines. He stepped on some of them as he made his way to the window. Peering out, he saw a narrow street which forked into two even narrower ones at the end of the block. As far as he could discern, no one was standing watch on the pavement below.

"Come on!" he said, and hurled himself at the window pane. The glass shattered, and he plummeted toward the sidewalk below, falling in a rain of glittering shards. He landed awkwardly; the impact slammed him down on one knee, tearing his jeans and the skin beneath. He leaped up and spun around —

To see that none of his comrades had followed him into the open. Guns banged, the muzzle flashes lighting up the darkened window, as the anarchs fired at the pursuers swarming after them. For one terrible moment Dan was afraid that his new friends wouldn't make it out, that he was alone again, alone forever. Then, the white tanktop inside

173

his coat now dark with blood, Wyatt leaped. His friends began to scramble after him.

Dan ran to Wyatt's side. Up close, the vampire with the mohawk smelled of vitae and gun smoke. "Are you all right?" Dan asked.

"The bullets... hit my lungs," said Wyatt, smiling, his voice a ghastly whisper. "Good thing Kindred... only use them to talk." Pivoting abruptly, he raised his gun and fired.

Dan turned to see that Felipe, Jimmy Ray, and now Laurie had jumped to the pavement. Wyatt was shooting through the window to discourage anyone from leaping after them. After pumping off a couple of rounds, he wheezed, "Now... back to the van. We'll try... to lose the bastards."

Laurie peered up and down the unfamiliar street. "Do you know which way it is?" she asked fearfully. Wyatt pointed and they started running, turning periodically to fire behind them. Guns barked back from the window, but none of Prince Roger's people had dared to follow their quarry into the open yet. Dan was sure that would change in the next few seconds.

Wyatt began to stagger. His wounds couldn't threaten his existence as they might a human's, but the blood loss and trauma could certainly weaken him. Laurie put her arm around him, but she lacked both the strength and the stature to help him along at anything like the necessary speed.

"Let me," said Dan. He shoved the Smith and Wesson back in his waistband, took Wyatt from her, and lifted the anarch leader in his arms. She gave him a grateful smile, the vitae smeared around her mouth making the expression look peculiar.

They ran on, through the intersection and down the right-hand fork of the Y. Wyatt kept grunting and going stiff as Dan's stride jarred him. Then, behind them, bursts of automatic-weapons fire rattled. Felipe stumbled and nearly fell.

Awkwardly shifting Wyatt to one arm and grabbing the

Model 669 with the other, Dan spun around. Two vampires were running at them as fast as swooping hawks, fangs bared, blasting away with assault rifles

Dan and the anarchs returned fire. One of the pursuers dropped and the other dived for cover in a recessed doorway. Dan could hear the footsteps of more of the enemy pounding up the pavement, and car motors roaring to life.

"Get off... the street," Wyatt wheezed, vitae seeping from his mouth. "Go between the... buildings. Easier to shake them off our tails."

As his companions began to obey him, the Toreador who'd dropped lurched up and resumed shooting. Leaning out of his doorway, his partner did the same. Startled, Dan and the anarchs scrambled frantically to get out of the line of fire.

And, as Dan realized an instant later, by doing so, they'd inadvertently split up. Because they'd been spread out along the street, in their haste they'd lunged into at least two different gaps between thebuildings. He and Wyatt were in one and the remaining anarchs were somewhere else.

Dan decided it would be suicide to try to link back up with his friends by retracing his steps. He'd run right into the arms of their pursuers. It would be better to keep going forward, hoping that he and the remaining anarchs would spot one another along the way, or, failing that, meet up at the van. So, cradling Wyatt in both arms again, he dashed on, vaulting over the heaps of trash that choked the narrow passage. Wyatt's shotgun slipped from his hand to clank on the broken brick pavement. His eyelids drooped shut, and his head lolled.

Plunging into an alley, Dan peered up and down, looking unsuccessfully for some sign of the other anarchs. All he could detect was the pounding footfalls of Prince Roger's vassals, still racing along behind him.

He wondered fleetingly whether, if he crouched motionless behind some piece of cover, his newfound powers of concealment would keep him safe from discovery. But he wasn't at all confident that they'd shield him from the notoriously keen senses of the Toreador, and even more dubious that the force that masked his own presence would veil Wyatt's as well. And so he hurtled on through a maze of unpredictably twisting passages, always fearful that his sense of direction was playing him false, or that the way would dead-end at some impassable barrier.

Plunging into a small, pentagonal space defined by the grimy back walls of five decaying tenements, where it looked and smelled as if garbage had been accumulating for years, he paused, trying to decide by which passage he should exit. And at that moment, a cold voice said, "Who are you?"

Startled, Dan jumped and then peered wildly about. Though the voice had seemed to come from nearby, he couldn't see the person who had addressed him. But he could still hear the sounds of pursuit echoing through the labyrinth of passages; there was no way to know whether the Toreador had lost his trail or not. Hoping that the speaker lacked the means to detain him until the hunters caught up with him, he said, "We're just passing through." And strode on toward one of the alleyways on the other side of the courtyard.

"Stop!" cried the unseen presence. "Stop, or I'll hurt you!"

"Screw you," muttered Dan, breaking into a run, and then pain ripped through his knee. Losing his balance, he fell heavily, pinning the inert form of Wyatt beneath him. He frantically disentangled his arms from the other Kindred and sat up. Looking at his leg, he gaped in horror.

He'd only scraped his knee when he'd jumped out the window, a minor injury that wouldn't have slowed him down even were he still mortal. But now reeking, suppurating flesh was sloughing away from the injury as if he had an advanced case of gangrene.

"I told you I'd hurt you," said the invisible speaker, a

gloating note in his voice. "Little Haiti belongs to the Samedi. *No one* hunts here without our permission."

Dan had heard rumors of the Samedi. Supposedly they were a vampire clan who'd arisen in the Caribbean: rotting, corpselike creatures as hideous as the Nosferatu, though less diverse in their deformities, with the uncanny ability to inflict a similar decomposition on others by sheer force of will. "We don't want to hunt," said Dan, his senses probing the shadows, still to no avail. "We just want to get out of here."

"Too late," said the Samedi. "You trespassed and killed some of our kine. You showed disrespect, and now you have to pay the price."

Dan imagined that it was a payment neither he nor Wyatt would survive. Then, finally, he heard cloth rustle on a cracked concrete stoop to his left.

Suddenly twisting, praying that his supersensitive hearing really had pinpointed the noise accurately, he fired his automatic. A stooped, leprous, noseless thing clad in filthy rags seemed to materialize out of empty air even as he recoiled against the door at his back.

Unfortunately, the Samedi wasn't badly wounded, and it had an Uzi in its ulcerous hand. It shot back, and a spray of bullets riddled Dan's chest. The world dissolved in a flash of pain.

Dan struggled to focus through the agony, to aim and fire again. His next shot hit the Samedi in the forehead and blew the back of its head out. The deformed vampire collapsed in a heap.

All right, Dan told himself grimly, *so much for that.* He was messed up, but he thought he could still walk. Surely the van couldn't be much farther. All he had to do was stand up, pick up Wyatt, and keeping mov—

Fresh torment blazed through his wounded torso. Skin and muscle softened and oozed off his broken ribs. He thrashed convulsively, and the gun tumbled out of his hand.

A second Samedi, this one wearing a necklace of human finger bones, a top hat and a clawhammer coat with a wilted white carnation boutonniere, shambled out of the shadows. It had a stake in its nearly skeletal hand, and its long, white fangs shone in the moonlight. They were the only part of the creature that didn't look decayed.

Dan tried to grope for the Model 669, but the pain of his wounds and their putrefaction made him too spastic. In a moment perhaps the paralysis would pass, but by that time, he suspected, the Samedi would have the stake in his heart, immobilizing him permanently.

The Haitian undead knelt beside Dan and raised the wooden weapon over its head. Dan managed to lift his hands and fumble at his attacker, only to discover that he still lacked the strength to push him away. And then Wyatt reared up and clutched at the Samedi's shoulder.

The Samedi jerked as if the vampire in white had thrust a blade into it. An instant later Dan felt a fierce heat glowing from inside his attacker's ravaged body. Boiling blood gushed from the Caribbean Kindred's eyes, ears, nose, mouth and sundry lesions, burning trails in its rotten flesh as if it were acid. Wailing, the Samedi lurched to its feet, blundered to one of the tenements, and dragged itself to the door.

"Little trick... my sire taught me," Wyatt whispered. "Guess the bitch was good... for something."

Dan realized that he and his companion *had* to get moving. There might be more Samedi lurking about, or the Toreador might appear at any moment. Trembling with exertion, he dragged himself to his feet. For a moment the world revolved, and a lance of torment stabbed through his injured leg, but somehow he kept himself from falling down again.

He stooped to pick up Wyatt, but the anarch captain shook his head and rose unsteadily. "Can walk now," he wheezed, smiling. "Way you look, I think I'd... better."

Swaying, clinging to one another, they gimped through two more cramped, lightless alleyways. As they emerged from the second, Dan saw the burned convertible, and beyond it their vampire comrades, Cassius and the van, exhaust fuming from its tailpipe, no more than thirty feet away.

Jimmy Ray, Felipe and Laurie dashed forward. "Thank God!" the former hippie cried, her bellbottoms flapping around her legs. "We were afraid—" When she faltered, goggling at him in dismay, Dan realized that she'd seen, or smelled, the pockets of gangrene in his body.

"They're just wounds," he croaked. "They'll heal." At least he assumed they would. In his experience, you could destroy a vampire, but not permanently cripple or even scar one. Their powers of regeneration simply worked too well, even against the occult powers of their fellow undead. "Just get us on the van and get us out of here."

Ten seconds later the panel truck was hurtling through the night. Dan felt weak as a kitten, and every bump jolted pain through his damaged body. Nevertheless, he forced himself to sit up and peer through the rear window until the vehicle reached the interstate, making sure that no one was following it. Afterward, he slumped down on the floor. Laurie took his hand in her cool, soft fingers, and then, though dawn was still hours away, he drifted into slumber.

FIFTEEN: THE TRAITOR

Where we are,
There's daggers in men's smiles:
the near in blood
The nearer bloody.
— William Shakespeare, *Macbeth*

As Elliott opened the front door of Roger Phillips' mansion, he could feel a tingling warmth in his cheeks; when he paused to check his appearance in the mirror, a Venetian antique with an ornate gold wreath for a frame hanging on the right-hand wall of the foyer, he saw that his cheeks were still flushed with freshly stolen blood. He hadn't been lying when he'd told his associates that he was leaving the estate because he needed to hunt. He simply hadn't been telling the *whole* truth.

Lazlo entered the hall while Elliott was twisting his head from side to side, inspecting his silvery hair. Being discovered at such a moment made the Toreador elder feel momentarily foolish, even though he knew the mortal was accustomed to actors and their primping. "It's about time you got back," Lazlo grumbled.

"Why do you say that?" Elliott replied. "Did something happen?"

Lazlo shrugged. "More reports came in."

"I'm sure you were as capable of listening to them as I would have been." Elliott smiled wryly. "We're *all* worried about what's happening, Lazlo, but you have to allow me a *little* down time. Even the Duke of Wellington took a break occasionally. I know, I used to drink with him; or rather, he drank and I pretended to. Now, what's the news?"

"Our people finally located Darrell Burroughs, Roger's novelist friend, but they were too late. The man and his date were already dead. The enemy made it look as if Burroughs brought her back to his house, walked in on a burglary in progress, and the criminal killed them both."

Elliott felt a pang of sadness leavened with a perverse thrill of satisfaction, because Burroughs' murder proved that he'd guessed right. The Toreador's adversaries *did* intend to murder their mortal protégés. Elliott had been correct to take steps to bring the humans to Sarasota for safekeeping.

"Pierre Devereaux, that Haitian painter, was murdered, too, along with his wife and children. Did you know him?"

Elliott shook his head. "Someone must have decided to offer him patronage after I stopped taking an interest in such things." For a second he felt vaguely embarrassed by his ignorance.

"Well, he was eccentric," Lazlo said sourly. "Once his work started selling he had plenty of money, but he insisted on staying in Little Haiti in Miami, living little better than he would have if he'd still been stuck in Port-au-Prince. He didn't even have a phone, so we couldn't just call him and tell him to get himself up here. We had to send people after him, and they caught Dan Murdock and his friends at the scene of the crime."

Elliott's muscles tensed with anticipation until he noticed the reddish brown, a color suggestive of frustration and disgust, flickering in the mortal's aura. The Kindred sighed with his own disappointment. "I take it that when you say 'caught,' you don't mean 'captured,' do you?"

"No," Lazlo replied, "the bastards got away again. They shot their way clear, then lost our people in the streets and alleys. Apparently that part of the city is like a maze."

Elliott clasped Lazlo's shoulder. "Don't fret about it. They can't stay lucky forever. We'll catch them next time, or if not them, *somebody* from the other side." The Toreador smiled crookedly. "Although it would be nice to hear some *good* news."

"There is some," Lazlo admitted, sounding as if he resented having to relate it. Elliott gestured toward Roger's study, and the two men walked in that direction. "A number of the clients are here already, and others are on their way. But there are some, people who don't know their benefactors are Kindred, who said they were sorry but they couldn't just drop everything and rush to Sarasota, not on the strength of one mysterious phone call."

"Then someone persuasive will have to visit them in person," Elliott said as they stepped into the den. A Toreador with the proper charismatic talents could influence a mortal to do all manner of things, a fact of which he'd frequently taken advantage.

"With some of them, that's already arranged," Lazlo said, dropping heavily into one of the green leather chairs. As Elliott perched on the edge of the desk, he noticed that the dresser looked haggard and weary. Attending to Roger's business both by day and through the night, Lazlo had often made do with little sleep; but apparently, in the face of the current crisis, he was resting even less than usual. "I'll make sure that the others are taken care of, too." The mortal rubbed his bloodshot eyes. "Have you thought about what to tell them? Charming as you Toreador are, you can't be vague about the threat forever, or they'll get fed up and go home."

"Every human artist has a Toreador sponsor, who presumably knows him better than the rest of us," Elliott replied. "If the patron thinks his client can be trusted with the secret of the Masquerade, then we'll let him in on it. As for the rest of the mortals… I don't know, we'll tell them that our international investment cartel has run afoul of Muslim fundamentalist terrorists who've threatened to destroy us and everyone we cherish. That might sound plausible enough to satisfy them for a few days, and with luck, by that time the worst of this mess will be over."

Lazlo smiled, his expression a mixture of hope and skepticism. "Do you really think so?"

"We just need one break," Elliott replied. "One prisoner, to rat out the architects of this harassment. And then we'll show the enemy what war really is."

Lazlo nodded thoughtfully and then said, "There's another problem you should be aware of. With all the local kine taking steps to defend themselves from Dracula, some of our people are having trouble hunting."

"We'll have one of the old hands, perhaps one of the Brujah, give stalking lessons. Beyond that, well, we do have human friends who understand our true nature. We can ask them to bleed a bit for the good of the cause. And our neonates can still derive nourishment from animal vitae."

Lazlo raised an eyebrow. "Nobody's going to be very happy about those last two measures. I mean, you Toreador think it's poor form to feed on your friends, and animal blood supposedly tastes vile."

Elliott shrugged. "'Needs must when the devil drives.' Is there anything else you need to tell me? Has anyone found a Kindred answering Dracula's description? Have we received any more anonymous phone calls?"

"No," Lazlo said.

"Then for God's sake, go to bed," Elliott said. "You're exhausted."

Lazlo waved him off. "I'm all right. You might need me."

"I imagine that, working together, we Kindred and ghouls can keep the lid on things for a few hours," Elliott said dryly. "If not, we can always wake you. Go. Grab some liquor or warm milk on the way, if you need it to help you relax. This is the down side of maneuvering me into being a leader. You have to do what I say."

"Yes, *sir*," said the mortal sarcastically, rising from his chair. "Despite this presumptuous treatment, I am glad I pushed you into the job, and not just because the domain needs you. Judy's right: you've come back to us. Roger would be so happy, if only he were well." Lazlo trudged back into the hall.

Elliott stared after him, pondering what the dresser had said. He wondered if he *was* changing, shaking off the pall of despair that had enveloped him for so long. It was true, at certain moments he was too busy, too caught up in the ongoing struggle, to brood over Mary's death. But sooner or later something, like, ironically, Lazlo's remarks just now, would remind him of the tragedy, and then his grief came flooding back. Indeed, he felt horribly guilty for having allowed it to slip away in the first place, even though he was well aware that his wife wouldn't have wanted him to suffer until the end of time.

Sighing, he tried to set his personal problems and perversities aside. He had work to do. Unbuttoning his double-breasted jacket, he moved behind Roger's desk and sat down in the executive chair to look at the notes he'd left on the blotter.

Elliott would have been the first to admit that the scheme he'd concocted was a simple one: select an office in a house where all the suspected traitors come and go at will. Spread important-looking papers across the desk, leave the door unlocked and the room vacant, and see who sneaks in and examines them. But in his experience, simple plans were frequently the best.

First he picked up the documents, held them to his nose, and inhaled deeply. Though Kindred didn't perspire, and were likewise free of most of the other metabolic processes that contributed to a human's body odor, they still sometimes possessed a scent discernible to another vampire with unnaturally keen senses. But all Elliott smelled was paper and ink.

Next, sharpening his vision, he peered at the pages front and back. Undead skin was rarely as oily as that of a mortal, yet it occasionally left traces even so. But the only fingerprints were his own.

Conceivably, there was no traitor. The enemy might be spying on the Toreador electronically, even though they hadn't found a bug, or by occult means. That was one of the many problems with fighting an unknown supernatural opponent. There was no telling what extraordinary capabilities he possessed.

Alternatively, perhaps the spy hadn't gotten around to studying the papers yet, had suspected a trap and avoided them, or was good enough at his job to look them over without leaving any evidence behind. But Elliott had one more examination to conduct before he set the documents aside for another night. He closed his eyes, tried to empty his mind, and held the notes against his face.

Elliott wasn't as psychic as Roger, or as any number of other Toreador and Malkavians he'd known over the centuries, but occasionally he could manage the feat of psychometry, gleaning information about an individual from the psychic signature he'd left behind on some object that he'd handled. And after about thirty seconds, he experienced an instant of vertigo before an image wavered into existence before his inner eye. He saw Schuyller Madison poring over the papers, his pale aura tinged with the murky red and blue of malice and suspicion.

Elliott winced. He'd hoped that the traitor, if indeed he existed, was neither a Toreador, an elder, nor someone he deemed a friend. Sky was all three. Elliott couldn't imagine what inducement could have persuaded the poet to turn on his sire and his clan.

He supposed that he'd better go find out. His feelings

an untidy mixture of anger, excitement and sadness, he rose and marched from the office.

A ghoul directed him to one of the gardens behind the house. Seated on a marble bench, Sky was gazing raptly at the moon, looking so inoffensive, so *himself*, that for a moment Elliott wondered if the incriminating vision might have been merely a product of his imagination. Night-blooming flowers, generally the most common blossoms in a vampire's garden, perfumed the cool evening air, and surf whispered on the beach.

Sky turned and smiled at Elliott. "Over the years," he said, "I've written a dozen poems about gardens in the moonlight. I wonder if I'm good for one more. I saw a shooting star fall into the Gulf a few minutes ago. Perhaps I can work that in."

"We have to talk," Elliott said heavily. "I know that you're the spy."

Sky's soulful eyes blinked in apparent confusion. His wan aura flickered with a rainbow of shifting colors, the signature of startled bewilderment. "What are you talking about?" he said.

Elliott shook his head. "You can drop the act. It's quite convincing, and coming from me, that's a compliment. But I left the notes sitting out in Roger's study as a trap to enable me to determine who crept in and perused them. They don't actually contain any important information; but then, you already know that."

"All right," said Sky, spreading his hands, "you caught me. I confess, I did read them, because I was curious and, to be frank, because some of us are still concerned about your ability to direct the defense. I wanted to gauge the quality of your ideas. But I swear I never passed information to any outsiders."

"Nice try," Elliott said. "But my clairvoyance vouchsafed me quite a vivid vision, one far more informative than those I generally achieve. I even saw your aura. Since you thought you were unobserved, it was clouded with your treachery, not shimmering innocuously as it is now."

A hardness, a bitterness came into Sky's face, twisting it into a countenance Elliott had never seen before: virtually the visage of a stranger. "A particular shade of ethereal light, glimpsed in a dream," the poet said. "Not a superabundance of evidence, to turn you against an old friend. Yet you're convinced, aren't you?"

"Reluctantly," Elliott said. "It should have been Gunter if it had to be anyone at all. Why did you do it? Why would you help destroy art?" It was all but unimaginable that any Toreador, unless his spirit was as damaged as Elliott's, could be a party to such a desecration. "Why betray your clanmates to foes who meant to kill them, and poison poor Roger?"

Sky's lips quirked into a mirthless smirk. "Is that your theory, yours and the sagacious Dr. Potter's? No one poisoned Roger, not in the sense you mean, though I admit to helping others lay him low."

"Why?" Elliott repeated. "Roger loved you and treated you like a son. The rest of our brood esteemed you, too. And you never really cared about wealth or power."

"Can't you guess?" Sky cried, with such unexpected vehemence that Elliott nearly recoiled. "Not even now? I didn't want to do any of it! The memory of doing it, and the knowledge of what I'm supposed to do next, has been driving me mad! He enslaved me with a Blood Bond!" Drops of scarlet vitae seeped from the poet's eyes, mingling their scent with the fragrance of the flowers.

"Who did?" Elliott demanded.

"Drink a Kindred's blood three times and you become his servant," Sky said somberly. "Well, over the years, he must have forced me to drink *thirty* times, and his vitae is more potent than you can imagine. No one could have resisted, not even infinitesimally. Sometimes I think I don't even recall the person I used to be."

"If that's true," Elliott said gently, "then no one will

condemn you for what you've done. Tell me who Bound you, so I can help you win your freedom."

Still crying, Sky laughed bitterly. "Much of the time, I didn't even remember what had happened to me. He had so much control over me that he could erase my memory like a chalkboard. Even when I did remember, I couldn't speak of it, any more than I can reveal anything substantive to you now. But I always prayed that my dear friend Elliott, the man I considered even shrewder than Roger, would discern that something was wrong with me and investigate. Alas, you never did. You were too busy agonizing over Mary's death to spare a thought for the other people who loved you. But now, when it's too late, you want to ride to my rescue! It's rather comical, in its way."

Trying to repress the guilt that Sky's reproach had inspired, drawing on his charismatic powers, Elliott knelt in front of the other Toreador, clasped his hand, and stared him in the eye. "It's not too late," he insisted. "So far, we're holding our own, and you can help us carry the fight to the enemy. *Tell me what you know.*"

Sky smiled mirthlessly. "What I know," he said. "Actually, I know a lot. Once he had me fully in his power, he told me things. I don't suppose he has any true confidants. I wonder if a creature like that can be lonely."

"Who are you talking about?" Elliott said. "The leader of our enemies?"

"Milton's Satan," Sky replied. "At least that's who he reminds me of. Beautiful, arrogant, and very, very cunning. You only *think* you're holding your own. He's been planning the attack for decades. He's anticipated every move you've made, every move you *can* make. Every step you take carries you closer to disaster."

Sky sounded so certain of what he was saying that Elliott felt the hairs on the back of his neck stand on end. "But *why* does he want to destroy us? Did one of us offend him in some way?"

Sky laughed harshly. "Of course not! Could an ant offend *you?* That's what we are compared to him: tiny, crawling insects."

"The hell we are," Elliott said stoutly, as much for the benefit of his own morale as Sky's. "You wouldn't feel that way if he hadn't bewitched you, and I daresay the feeling will pass when we destroy him. If his quarrel with us isn't personal, then what is he trying to accomplish?"

"To draw your master — or mistress rather — his opposite number, into the open."

Elliott frowned in perplexity. "Do you mean Roger?"

Sky sneered through his bloody tears. "No, fool! You see, *this* is why you're doomed. You don't understand anything. You can't even feel the fingers that lift you up and move you from one square to another."

Elliott kept gazing into his fellow Toreador's eyes. "No more talking in riddles. *Tell me the enemy's name.*"

Sky shook his head. "I can't. I wish I could, but your influence is nothing compared to the power of the Bond."

"Please," Elliott said, squeezing the other vampire's hand, "fight it! Don't make us torture your secrets out of you."

"I don't think that would work, either," Sky said, "but I'll spare you the trouble of trying." Suddenly, moving with inhuman speed, he tore his fingers out of Elliott's grip and kicked him in the chest, sprawling the actor on the ground.

Sky thrust his hand inside his coat, evidently reaching for a weapon. But quick as the traitor was, Elliott was faster still. He scrambled to his feet and snatched his Beretta 92F out of its shoulder holster, beating the poet to the draw.

Sky inclined his head in acknowledgment of the other Kindred's superior agility. "I remember when we used to spar and fence," he said wistfully. "I never could beat you in any sort of physical contest, though I fancy I gave you a few bad moments at the whist table. Well, this sorry business is ending better than I thought it would, in that it's ending sooner. Farewell, old friend, and if you can find it in your eart to forgive me, carve some of my verses on my tomb."

"What are you talking about?" Elliott said.

"Behold," Sky said, and then his reedy body burst into rackling blue flame.

Elliott recoiled. Like many vampires, he had an nstinctive dread of sunlight and raging fire, two of the few orces that could actually destroy him. Struggling to vercome his fear, he dropped the Beretta, peeled off his oat, and lunged toward the furious heat and glare, intent n using the garment to smother the blaze.

But it wasn't possible. Even as Elliott reached for Sky, he fire finished devouring the poet and went out in the link of an eye. Shrouded in the folds of the jacket, the urviving vampire's clutching hands encountered only Sky's lousy embroidered shirt and powder-blue silk ascot, in the rocess of tumbling to the ground.

Elliott inspected the traitor's clothing. Though dusted vith the wisps of ash that were all that remained of Sky, hey weren't even singed, nor was the grass around his empty rousers and sandals. Obviously the fire had been upernatural. Sky's mysterious master had provided him with n occult means of suicide, just as a human spymaster might ave equipped an agent with a cyanide capsule.

First Mary, then Roger, then Rosalita, and now you, Elliott hought sadly. *I didn't save you, either. You were right to ondemn me, because I should have been able to.*

He felt a renewed desire to abandon the fight, to retreat o some secure haven and grieve, but the feeling was ounterbalanced and, in a few seconds, drowned by a swell f rage. He realized that he *couldn't* retire from the world, ot yet, because he wanted to avenge his clanmates too adly. He wanted to watch their tormentors burn on a pyre. Ie wanted to cut their leader's head off with his own hands.

He picked up his automatic, returned it to its holster and ut his jacket back on, making sure it hung evenly. Then he gathered Sky's effects and, weeping, trudged toward the house.

Clutching a cellular phone, scurrying along, Karen met him halfway up the path. "What's wrong?" she exclaimed. "Why are you crying?"

"I found out that Sky was the security leak," Elliott answered.

The younger Kindred goggled at him. "I can't believe that!"

"It wasn't his fault," the vampire said somberly. "Someone on the other side" — involuntarily he pictured the malevolent, godlike, bat-winged Lucifer of the Doré illustrations for *Paradise Lost* — "forced him to accept a Blood Bond. If only I'd noticed — but that's water under the bridge. When I confronted the poor fellow, he killed himself." He grimaced. "As usual, I didn't learn a damn thing. But maybe there's a clue to the enemy's identity in these clothes, or in Sky's home. I doubt it, but we'll check. Now, I gather that you wanted me?"

"What?" The dark eyes behind the amber lenses widened. "Oh! Yes! Palmer Guice wants to speak to you." She offered Elliott the phone.

Inwardly, Elliott winced. Guice was a Ventrue Justicar based in Raleigh, North Carolina, and a particularly high-handed and officious magistrate of the Camarilla. Even in the best of times, the Toreador might have received a communication from him with the same enthusiasm that a mortal would have greeted a visit from the police or the IRS. Of course, it was conceivable that Guice was calling to offer the vampires of Sarasota genuine aid in their hour of need, but Elliott's instincts insisted otherwise.

He gave Sky's belongings to the female Toreador, accepted the phone from her and, switching it on, raised it to his ear. "Hello, Palmer," he said with all the unruffled charm he could muster. "It's been what, twenty years?"

"Nearly that," the Ventrue replied. His voice was a

mellifluous bass that always reminded Elliott of Father Christmas and doting uncles in sentimental Victorian novels. The Justicar invariably sounded genial and sympathetic, even when picking some malefactor apart with a scalpel. "Your young friend seemed a bit rattled once I told her who I was. I hope you aren't teaching your childer to be skittish of other clans, or of those humble officials charged with the enforcement of the law."

"Perish the thought," said Elliott, allowing a hint of irony to enter his voice. Guice would expect no less. "We teach them that we're all one big happy family in the Camarilla."

Guice chuckled. "Oh, indeed, indeed! I'm glad you haven't lost that sardonic wit. People told me — but people always gossip, don't they, especially about charismatic entertainers embroiled in some lurid tragedy. Let's not get off on that. How are things going down your way?"

Elliott assumed that Guice knew about Roger's illness. Since the prince had gone mad on stage, in front of an audience of his peers, the entire Camarilla must know. "Roger's resting comfortably. Lionel Potter's treating him, and we anticipate a full recovery."

"That's splendid," Guice said. "And what of your other problems?"

Elliott wondered grimly just how much the Justicar knew about those difficulties, and exactly how he knew it. "Everything's under control."

"Of course it is," said Guice. "With Kindred such as yourself at the helm, how could it be otherwise? Still, I trust you understand that you and your people don't have to shoulder the burden alone. Your brothers and sisters stand ready to assist you."

"We appreciate that," said Elliott, "but —"

"I'm going to convene a Conclave in Sarasota," Guice continued inexorably. "We'll gather Kindred from across the South, perhaps the entire country, and discuss how best to ensure the security of your domain."

SIXTEEN: WYATT

Beware of false prophets, which come to you in sheep's clothing, but inwardly they are ravening wolves.
— Matthew 7:15

Standing in a shadowy doorway, Dan peered up and down the ruined street. Nothing moved, nor did he hear any bipedal footsteps, just vermin scurrying and the dilapidated buildings creaking and groaning their way toward collapse. He waited another moment and then, sacrificing the invisibility his immobility had afforded him, stalked on down the cracked and broken sidewalk.

Dan had discovered that Wyatt and the other anarchs had laid claim to an entire deserted block near the Port of Tampa. Despite overcrowding and the hordes of the homeless that increasingly choked their streets, many cities had such vacant sections: blighted areas where memories of ghastly tragedies, sinister rumors or merely an ominous vibe in the air served to drive the kine away. Sometimes indigenous vampires were the cause of the problem. Sometimes they weren't, but settled in such places after the humans had cleared out, availing themselves of the privacy the isolation afforded.

The anarchs spent much of their time together in the abandoned auto repair shop. Frequently they even slept there. But each one also had a private retreat. By keeping his eyes open, Dan had discovered which crumbling, gargoyle-encrusted, yellow-brick building housed Wyatt's personal refuge, and he meant to search the place tonight while his new friends were supposedly out hunting.

Abruptly, sensing a presence peering down at him from above, he tensed. Reminding himself that he hadn't done anything indisputably illicit yet, though his stealthy advance down the block might well have roused an observer's suspicions, he looked up. A mangy calico cat with a ragged ear and a scabbed-over gash on its shoulder held his gaze for a moment, then spat, wheeled, and vanished through the shattered fourth-floor window of what had once been an office building. Smiling crookedly with relief, the vampire silently wished the other nocturnal predator good hunting, then continued on his way.

Dan still didn't feel right about betraying the anarchs, but after much soul-searching, he'd decided that he was even more disturbed about the pogrom being launched against the Toreador's pet humans. He didn't feel much of an emotional tie to mortals anymore; indeed, he'd drunk a few of them dry and managed to face himself in the mirror afterward. But he still had scruples of a sort, and the thought of such a calculated massacre, in the service of conquest rather than to assuage anyone's Hunger, sickened him. As far as he was concerned, if Kindred wanted a war, they should fight each other and leave defenseless kine alone.

Moreover, he was worried that Wyatt wasn't what he seemed. Dan didn't *want* to suspect the vampire with the mohawk. The guy had saved his life. But the more he'd thought about it, the more convinced he'd become that Wyatt hadn't just happened to possess a key that fit the Haitian painter's door. He'd manufactured one out of thin air. And while it was true that a given vampire's supernatural abilities were sometimes unique and unpredictable, neither the creation of useful objects by sheer force of will nor the ability to boil an enemy's blood with a touch were characteristic talents of the Ventrue.

If Wyatt had lied about his bloodline, what else might he have lied about? It was conceivable that the anarch captain had a secret agenda, something that would appall Laurie, Felipe and Jimmy Ray if they knew about it.

But Dan actually hoped not. He hoped that Wyatt was the friendly, trustworthy idealist he seemed. That he could search the rebel leader's haven and find the name of his contacts in the Movement without anyone ever realizing what he'd done. And that when he relayed his discoveries to Melpomene, who would presumably pass them along to Prince Roger's people, the Kindred of Sarasota would be content to strike at the generals commanding the offensive against them and leave small-fry like his new friends alone.

Dan took a final look around. As far as he could tell, no one was watching him. Pulling on the yellow work gloves he'd purchased in a hardware store, he strode to the front door of a derelict five-story building. Three floors up, a huge pair of spectacles — an optician's sign projecting from the sooty brick wall at a right angle — groaned as it swung in the almost nonexistent breeze. Above that the owl carved on the cornice, which the sculptor had chosen to depict with talons outstretched and wings slightly furled as if it were diving, glared down at its seeming prey on the ground.

Dan twisted the doorknob and found that the entrance was locked. He wasn't surprised. Had he possessed the power to materialize keys at will, he himself would have kept the door to any haven in which he happened to be squatting secured.

Stalking around the building, he checked the windows, whitewashed like cataract-afflicted eyes, and the side and back doors. They were locked, too.

He supposed that somewhere along the line he should have taken the trouble to learn to pick locks. It would be easy enough to break a window, but that would mean abandoning any realistic hope of keeping his intrusion a secret.

Fortunately, a rusty wrought-iron fire escape snaked down the back wall of the building, terminating about ten feet above the alley. He could have jumped that high even before Melpomene permitted him to drink her vitae. He flexed his knees, leaped, and grabbed the guard rail.

The sudden addition of his weight made the fire escape squeal and shudder. For a moment he was afraid that it would tear away from its moorings, dumping him back on the ground and crashing down on top of him, but it didn't. He swarmed over the rail and began to move along the walkways, testing the upper-story doors and windows.

They were all locked, too. Finally, impatient, knowing that he needed to finish his work before Wyatt returned, and reasoning that the rebel captain would be less likely to notice signs of forcible entry above the ground floor, he drew back his fist and punched a window.

The glass shattered. In the midst of all this stillness, the crash was loud enough to make him wince. He hastily swept the remaining shards out of the window frame and clambered through.

He found himself in what had once been a dentist's office. Most of the fixtures and fittings were gone, but the chair with its chipped and discolored attached sink remained. Pale rectangles on the dingy walls indicated the spots where the doctor's diplomas and professional credentials had probably hung.

Dan had always hated going to the dentist, hated the whine and the hot smell of the drilling, the spitting out of the grit, and the Novocain-induced numbness in his mouth hours afterwards. Reflecting wryly that whatever else he disliked about being a vampire, at least his regenerative powers spared him any more of that particular ordeal, he skulked deeper into the building.

Once he moved a few paces away from the painted windows, there was hardly any light. Even his newly sharpened vision was barely sufficient to allow him to grope his way along. The darkness smelled of rats, rot and dampness. Somewhere in the building, the rain had been leaking in.

He'd already thought about where to begin his search. His intuition, and his sense of Wyatt's personality, suggested that the vampire with the mohawk would have chosen to reside on the top floor. Prowling down a corridor, he spotted a pair of elevators which, even if Wyatt had bothered to restore power to the building, might well be unsafe. Across from them was a set of stairs. As he set his foot on the flight leading upward, he thought he heard a faint, indefinable stirring in the gloom above him.

Drawing his new pistol, a Herculean Firearms .38 Paladin — he reflected fleetingly that, since beginning his mission, he'd been running through guns like a kid gobbling M&Ms — he peered up the staircase. He didn't see anything lurking in the shadows, not between his position and the landing. Of course, it was possible that someone had just now slipped around the bend in the ascent.

Dan dashed up the risers, turned, and pointed his automatic up the next flight of steps. There was nothing to shoot; the space was empty.

He supposed that he'd probably heard a rat, or that his nerves were playing tricks on him. He hoped not the latter; after the inexplicable fascination he'd felt for the Haitian painter's pictures, he was already a little worried that he might be cracking up. Scowling, his senses still probing the darkness, he climbed on.

For an instant, just as he emerged onto the top floor, he caught an aromatic whiff of vampire vitae. Startled, gun leveled, he swivelled back and forth.

Once again, there was nothing to see. He supposed that he'd merely smelled a lingering trace of Wyatt's blood, left behind when, his bullet wounds still not completely healed, the anarch had returned here after the trip to Miami. Commanding himself to get over his jitters, he began to examine the various chambers and suites.

Fortunately, the internal doors weren't locked. And behind the sixth one he tried, he found the former office that must now be Wyatt's haven. An air mattress and a sleeping bag sat on a section of floor no sunlight leaking through the painted windows could reach. Ivory-colored candles, glued down with their own wax, lined the built-in bookshelves like a row of severed fingers. Among them reposed an assortment of the anarch's personal belongings, while a white leather backpack and shotgun case leaned in the corner.

As Dan began to enter the room, he heard a tiny, stealthy pattering. This time the noise was coming from behind him. He spun around and peered down the tenebrous corridor.

He didn't see anything.

A rat, he told himself, *it's just a damn rat.* But he wasn't quite sure that he believed it. Since Melpomene's vitae had honed his senses, he'd heard his share of rodents scuttling through walls and heaps of trash, and it seemed to him that the noise he'd just caught had been slightly different. But perhaps that was only his imagination.

He decided he'd better finish his snooping and get out of here before he wigged out completely. He strode on into Wyatt's refuge and over to the shelves. For a moment he was tempted to light some of the candles, but then realized that Wyatt might smell the smoke when he returned. Better to risk a little eyestrain and poke around in the gloom.

Among the tapers lay a disposable plastic lighter, a handful of pennies, nickels and dimes, and Wyatt's battery-powered razor. There was also a dainty single-shot pistol covered with ornate scroll work — the kind of weapon ladies had once concealed in their muffs — the kit to oil and clean it, and two bullets. Dan wondered what the rebel, who carried a combat shotgun everywhere and wielded it one-handed, wanted with such a tiny, antiquated weapon. Perhaps it was a memento from his exploits in the previous century.

Beside the gun sat a long, thin, bone-handled knife, a box of colored sidewalk chalk, several rags and a plastic spray bottle of green all-purpose household cleaner. To Dan, the presence of the chalk seemed even stranger than that of the muff pistol. What the heck did Wyatt need with that? He peered about, but couldn't see any chalk marks anywhere in the room.

Prompted by a sudden hunch, he spritzed a bit of the cleanser into the air. He noted the sharp, astringent smell of the mist, then prowled around, sniffing, searching for another trace of the same odor.

His nose led him to a patch of floor less dirty than the grubby linoleum surrounding it. It was conceivable that Wyatt had been writing or drawing there, then washing away his work when he was through.

For a moment Dan felt a thrill of accomplishment, but the sensation faded when he realized that this particular stab at playing detective had taken him about as far as it could. It was *intriguing* to know that Wyatt had been writing on the floor, and that he'd been scrupulously careful to erase his handiwork afterward, but it wasn't *useful*, not unless one also knew *what* he'd been writing. And Dan couldn't see any way to discover that.

Smiling ruefully, he turned toward the leather pack, a handsome article studded with the same cryptic patterns of rivets that decorated Wyatt's coat. He reached for it, then faltered, his skin crawling. Suddenly he was certain that he felt eyes glaring malevolently at his back.

He whirled. And saw nothing. He *almost* heard a peal of

nasty, mocking laughter, but he knew that that, at least, really was only his imagination.

Even prior to his brush with the Samedi, Dan had had some experience with invisible Kindred. Heck, he was learning how to be invisible himself. But he hadn't seen any indication that any of the anarchs possessed such powers, and he couldn't imagine who else would be lurking in Wyatt's haven. Furthermore, given his superhuman senses of hearing and smell, it was hard to believe that even an invisible man could remain entirely undetectable in the cramped confines of the office. Besides, if an enemy was present, what was he waiting for? Why hadn't he attacked Dan when his back was turned?

You're alone, fool, the vampire told himself firmly. But just in case he wasn't, he meant to finish his search and get out of the building as rapidly as possible.

Reluctantly reholstering the .38 to free up both hands, his fingers trembling slightly, Dan fumbled open the knapsack. It occurred to him that it, the shotgun case, and Wyatt's coat might be custom-made, and that the label might provide a clue to the revolutionary's secrets. But it only bore the name of the manufacturer, Podolak, a name that meant nothing to Dan.

Scowling, he reached into the pack and pulled out four items: a plastic pack of felt-tipped pens, each filled with a different color of ink; an ancient-looking and -smelling leather-bound tome with tarnished brass hinges and ragged-edged parchment pages; a three-ring notebook; and a neatly folded map.

When Dan carefully opened the crackling antique book, half expecting it to fall apart in his hands, he caught a second scent, mingled with the musty odor of the paper. Time had nearly effaced the aroma, but unless he were mistaken, the flaking brown ink on the pages was human vitae.

Unfortunately, he couldn't decipher the crabbed handwriting. He had a hunch that he was looking at some archaic form of Latin, as incomprehensible as Martian to him. But from the complex geometric forms — they were called pentagrams, weren't they? — and the drawings of hideous, demonic creatures, he suspected that he was looking at a sorcerer's journal. For a moment one of the pictures, a portrait of a voluptuous nude woman with eyes where her nipples should have been and a crown made of entwined serpents, threatened to entrance him the way the immigrant's paintings had. Dismayed, snarling, he wrenched his gaze away.

Even edgier now, he closed the ancient volume, then opened the notebook. It was more of the same, except that the text and sketches were in various shades of ordinary ink. They looked like the notes of a modern wizard attempting to build on the secret wisdom of his predecessor, one who probably used the sidewalk chalk to draw pentagrams on the floor.

Unfolding the remaining item, Dan saw that it was a map of Sarasota, spotted with mysterious symbols written in black and red. Some of the icons marked locations that the anarchs had visited just before Judy Morgan's Brujah attacked them.

Behind him, something softly clicked.

Even as he pivoted, Dan thought, *This'll be just like the other times; there won't be anything there*. And at first it didn't appear that there was. Half-disgusted at his own jumpiness and half-relieved at the absence of any threat, he began to return to his inspection of the map. But then he glimpsed a white flicker of motion on one of the shelves where Wyatt's belongings lay.

He squinted and then felt an impulse to blink his eyes in disbelief. A pale creature, no larger than a rat but shaped more like a monkey, had cocked the muff pistol and was endeavoring to point it at him. Except for the disproportionately large eyes and the twin fangs that extended all the way to the bottom of its chin, its face was a dead ringer for Wyatt's. A stray bit of dried blood encrusted the left corner of its mouth. Dan surmised that the creature had been tailing him since he'd entered the building and that he'd missed spotting it because of its tiny stature.

In any case he had no desire to let it take a potshot at him. Dropping the other objects in his hands, he skimmed the ancient book of magic at it.

Fast and nimble as the monkey it somewhat resembled, the diminutive monster abandoned the gun, leaped to the floor and scurried toward the door. The grimoire thumped against the shelf and broke apart, scattering a blizzard of brittle pages. Jarred loose from their moorings, candles toppled.

Dan dived after the fleeing creature, but his clutching fingers missed it by an inch. It raced into the hall, and, lurching up into a crouch, he scrambled after it.

He faltered when he saw Wyatt. The vampire with the mohawk was standing a few paces down the hall, his boyish face grim and his new shotgun leveled. Though he'd tried hard to clean his long white coat, the garment still had a few faint bloodstains around the bullet holes.

The little creature darted to Wyatt, hugged his ankle and then, clutching at his clothing, climbed up his body to his shoulder. Without taking his eyes off Dan the anarch captain used his free hand to tickle the little creature behind the ear. "It's okay," he said soothingly. "The wicked man won't hurt you now."

"How did it call you back?" asked Dan. "Dial a beeper number?"

"He didn't have to *do* anything," Wyatt replied. "We're linked mind to mind. He's my homunculus, blood of my blood and flesh of my flesh." Toying with the hairs of the anarch's goatee — grooming him, Dan decided — the creature chittered in seeming agreement.

"I did notice the family resemblance," said Dan. He wondered if he could ease his hand toward his automatic without Wyatt shooting him instantly. He decided not to chance it, at least not yet. Maybe he could talk his way out of this. "I wasn't going to hurt him, even though he tried to put a bullet in me. I was just curious. I wanted a closer look at him."

"Uh-huh," said Wyatt skeptically. "And what's the idea of going through my stuff?"

"I was curious about you, too," said Dan, trying to sound sheepish. "Something about you didn't add up, and I'm the kind of guy that looks in other people's closets and medicine cabinets. I always have been, and I guess I always will be. For what it's worth, I apologize."

To Dan's surprise, the anarch smiled. "Apology accepted. I've been known to do the same thing. And what do you think you've found out about me?"

"Obviously, that you lied about your lineage," Dan answered. "You're not Ventrue, you're Tremere. Not just an ordinary vampire, but a member of the *wizard* clan. I wondered what you actually expected to find on your 'scouting mission' into Sarasota. Until I saw your map, the whole thing seemed pretty pointless. You were doing something occult, weren't you?"

Wyatt nodded. "I was doing geomancy. Finding pressure points in the web of forces that girdle the earth. I need to know where they are in order to lay a curse on all of Prince Roger's flunkies at once." He hesitated. "Can you understand *why* I lied? The Tremere have a terrible reputation for deceit and intrigue, and they've always been at the forefront of any effort to crush the Movement. I was afraid that if I claimed to have defected from a chantry, no one would trust me."

Dan made a wry face. "Believe me, I do understand. I know what it's like to be on the outside looking in. To be rejected by people you care about. I promise that your secret's safe with me."

"Thank you," said Wyatt. "In that case, I guess everything's all right." The two vampires looked one another in the eye for a moment, and then both smiled ruefully.

"Well, so much for that little tap dance," Dan said. "I don't believe a word you're saying, and I can tell that you don't believe me."

"The problem is that we're two of a kind," said Wyatt. The homunculus began picking at his mohawk. "Both too damn smart for our own good. What gave me away? I'd hate to think that I was losing my talent for lying."

"I don't know anything about magic," Dan replied. "But heck, you make keys out of nothing. You boil the Samedi's blood. You create a living creature, like Baron Frankenstein. It's obvious even to me that you've learned too many Tremere secrets to be a dropout. I wouldn't be surprised if you were some kind of junior vice-president. And I wonder if even a hot-shot magician —"

"Magus," Wyatt interjected.

"Excuse me, *magus*, could put a spell on a whole domain all by himself. I'm guessing that you plan to team up with a bunch of other Warlocks for that particular piece of voodoo."

Wyatt sighed. "Too damn smart," he repeated. "Look, before you hooked up with us, you didn't care about the Movement. What if I tell you that I truly do like Laurie, Felipe and Jimmy Ray? Even though I'm tricking them, using them for my own purposes, convincing them that they're fighting for the anarchs when they're really serving a different cause altogether, I mean to look out for them as well. When the battle's won, they'll be rewarded for their efforts. You can be, too, if you'll play along."

Dan no longer trusted Wyatt enough to be tempted even momentarily by such an offer, but he figured that he had nothing to lose by trying one more lie. "Maybe we can work something out. Rewarded how?"

Wyatt sighed. "Sorry, I can still see through you. What is it they say? 'Never kid a kidder?' You know, I truly like you. Hell, you've saved my life twice. This whole situation stinks."

The Tremere sounded sincere, and to his dismay, Dan felt a keen, reciprocal pang of friendship. "I know what you mean."

"I wonder if you really just wandered up here out of curiosity, or if someone told you to infiltrate our little group. Would you care to enlighten me?"

"It was just curiosity," said Dan.

"Then it was rotten luck for both of us," said Wyatt. "Good-bye."

Dan made a grab for his automatic. Just as it cleared the holster, Wyatt fired. The boom was deafening in the cramped confines of the hall. .33-caliber pellets tore into Dan's belly, staggering him. The pistol tumbled from his suddenly spasming fingers.

Wyatt could blow him apart if he paused to pick up the automatic. Struggling to ignore the pain blazing in his midsection, the wounded vampire lunged at the Tremere, intent on grabbing the scatter-gun and tearing it from his grasp.

Wyatt's eyes bored into his. "*Stop!*" the magus cried.

Dan felt his muscles seizing up like an overheated engine. He managed to keep lurching forward, but now his progress was as slow and clumsy as a paralytic's. Stepping casually back to avoid the injured Kindred's outthrust hands, Wyatt pumped another shell into the breech and shot Dan in the knees.

Dan collapsed on his side. Staring down at his face, Wyatt repeated, "*Stop.*" Dan's treacherous muscles strained, obeying the command, clenching themselves as hard and useless as chunks of stone.

Wyatt shot Dan in the chest. This time the burst of agony was so intense that, for an instant, the spy blacked out. When the world swam back into partial focus, Wyatt, his fangs now extruded, was staring down at him as if trying to determine whether he was truly helpless. Whether he needed any more holes in him to allow precious vitae to run out and go to waste. The homunculus bobbed and chattered in excitement.

Dan didn't know if he was defenseless or not. Between the torment of his wounds and the rigidity in his limbs, it sure felt like it. But he was certain that his only chance of surviving this battle was to make Wyatt *believe* that he was already incapacitated. He tried to make it look as if he were still stunned, staring glassy-eyed and expressionless at nothing.

And Wyatt dropped to his knees beside him, set his smoking, blue-finished weapon on the floor, and bent over his intended prey.

Dan tried to seize the other Kindred. For an instant nothing happened, and then mobility surged back into his body with a sharp, rippling pain that reminded him of a piece of paper tearing in two. Evidently the hypnotically induced paralysis could only freeze a victim for a little while. Grabbing Wyatt by the throat, he scrambled on top of him and started to pound his head against the floor. The homunculus emitted an earsplitting shriek, bounded off its master's shoulder and raced away back toward Wyatt's room.

His wounds notwithstanding, Dan was far stronger than Wyatt. He was certain that he could pound the magus insensible in a matter of seconds, or even tear him limb from limb. And then the bogus anarch's fingers feebly clutched his wrist.

Fiery agony screamed through Dan's flesh. The pain of a gunshot wound was a mere pinprick by comparison. His blood was boiling like the Samedi's, scalding and cooking him from the inside out.

Wyatt broke Dan's grip on his neck and started to squirm out from underneath him. Screaming, forcing his burning arms to move despite the anguish, Dan grabbed the Tremere again and smashed his head down on the linoleum. Wyatt's skull crunched, and he went limp.

Unfortunately, victory in itself did nothing to relieve Dan's pain. His flesh was still ablaze and the Hunger had him in its grip. He felt as if every drop of vitae in his system had changed into blistering steam. He threw himself down on Wyatt and ripped open his throat.

He guzzled frantically, and the Tremere's rich, coppery vitae gradually extinguished the searing torment. The relief was a kind of ecstasy, nearly as sublime in its way as the joy of sucking Melpomene's potent blood. Once lost in its embrace, he kept drinking long past the point of satiety, until Wyatt's lifeless body began to stink and decay in his arms.

Still dazed with the savage pleasure of his gluttony, Dan lifted his head just in time to see the homunculus laboriously dragging the muff gun into the hall. The tiny monster looked at the tableau before it. Its huge eyes widened as it evidently recognized that it had returned to the fray too late, that its creator was already dead. It screamed, abandoned the weapon, and ran in the opposite direction. In a moment it vanished into the shadows.

Now that the Beast, his inner demon, was back in its cage, Dan regretted killing Wyatt. And not merely because, despite everything that had happened, he still liked the Tremere, although that was part of it. Since the anarchs didn't actually know anything about the conspiracy against the Kindred of Sarasota, and since their captain was now unavailable for interrogation, it was quite possible that Dan had just bungled his mission beyond any hope of recovery.

Once again he was tempted simply to abandon his errand. Maybe if he explained to Laurie, Felipe and Jimmy Ray that Wyatt hadn't been what he seemed — but no, that was a bad idea. Though the anarchs had welcomed him into their midst, he'd been rebuffed, told there was something foul and untrustworthy about him, too many times to assume that he could convince them he'd had a valid reason for killing their beloved leader. But he could deny he was the person who'd destroyed the magus. Heck, if he could spirit the rotting corpse away, his new friends wouldn't know that anyone had. They wouldn't know what had happened to Wyatt.

And with their link to the shadow army assailling Sarasota broken, they'd be free, no longer a part of the ongoing struggle. Perhaps Dan could convince them to go away with him to some other part of the country where neither Wyatt's colleagues nor Melpomene could find them. Maybe they could settle in California, where the *real* Anarch Movement was in power.

Dan sighed. It all made for a pleasant fantasy, but he realized that he *wasn't* going to abandon his mission. He still wanted to save the innocent humans targeted for destruction. And, though it might be a perverse way to think, he couldn't see quitting now that he'd come this far. That would mean he'd killed Wyatt for nothing.

He went through the magus' pockets. He found an eelskin wallet, a book of matches, a pack of Camels and an unfamiliar key — probably the one that opened the door to this building. He didn't locate the key to the Haitian artist's loft. He wondered if Wyatt had thrown it away, or if it had evaporated when its work was done.

The wallet contained seven hundred dollars, several credit cards, including Diner's Club and an American Express Platinum, a driver's license with an Orlando address, and a blood-red key card bearing an embossed drawing of a plumed and visored helmet with the similarly elevated word *Camelot* in Gothic script on one side and a magnetic stripe on the other.

Taken all in all, it didn't seem like Dan had discovered very much. But at least he now had some excuse for a lead. Pocketing the wallet, he rose, located his .38 — and then an idea struck him.

The muff gun barely seemed capable of inconveniencing

a mortal. Against a Kindred, such a weapon ought to be a joke. And yet Wyatt had considered it worth leaving with the homunculus, and even though the shot would reveal its presence, the tiny creature had been hell-bent on firing the pistol at Dan. Was it possible that the firearm, or its ammunition, was magical?

Dan decided that he had nothing to lose by taking them with him. He grabbed them and then, his heart heavy, wondering if he'd ever see Laurie, Jimmy Ray and Felipe again, and whether they'd try to kill him if he did, he trudged toward the stairs.

SEVENTEEN: REPORTING IN

I will have this done, so I order it done; let my
will replace reasoned judgment.
        — Juvenal, *Satires*

Now dressed in the new, unperforated, unbloodied jeans,
T-shirt and denim jacket he'd burgled from a second-hand
shop — he hadn't wanted to return to the cache of clothes
in the auto repair shop and risk running into any of the
anarchs — Dan found a pay phone outside a grubby little
bar on the fringes of Ybor City, Tampa's historic Latin
quarter. Living in Sarasota, he'd heard vaguely that the area
was undergoing a revitalization, filling up with trendy
nightclubs, restaurants, boutiques and art galleries; but if so,
the process of renewal hadn't reached this shadowy corner
of the district yet. Most of the streetlights were broken, and
many of the shops were boarded up. Discarded paper cups,
beer cans and the stinking body of a dachshund, its legs stiff
with rigor mortis and its flanks pocked with stab wounds,
filled the gutters. Through the wall of the tavern sounded a
dirgelike death-metal anthem: "Kill, kill, kill the children,
generation *last*—"

Glumly reflecting that the tone, if not the lyrics, of the
song suited his mood, Dan dropped a quarter in the public

phone's coin slot and punched in the digits Melpomene had bade him memorize. The phone whirred and clicked repeatedly, and he imagined his call being routed from one dummy number to the next, making it more difficult to trace.

The phone went dead. Frowning in puzzlement and annoyance, Dan wondered if he should hold on or hang up and dial again. Then a soft white light flowered behind him.

Startled, his hand jerking reflexively toward his .38, he spun around. Melpomene was standing on the cracked, uneven sidewalk behind him. Something about her looked strange, and after a moment he realized what it was. Though the air was still, strands of her dark hair were stirring as if a breeze were blowing, leading him to suspect that she was only present in spirit.

"You didn't tell me you were going to appear to me," he growled, hoping that she hadn't noticed how he'd jumped. "I thought we were just going to talk on the phone."

"So did I," Melpomene said. "But I like to see a person's face when I converse with him. And I can discern that no other Kindred are nearby. So why shouldn't I come to you, particularly when I can sense that you're in distress?" She gave him a sympathetic smile.

Even if she weren't physically present, her charm was no less potent than it had been during their previous encounter. Abruptly he felt grateful for her show of concern, and ashamed that he'd greeted her rudely. Struggling to suppress those responses, he said, "Yeah, I am upset. I'm not cut out for this spy stuff."

She caressed his cheek with her slim white fingers. He couldn't feel the touch, but, remembering the silky smoothness of her skin, he imagined it, and that was enough to wring another outpouring of affection from his soul. "Why do you say that?" she asked gently.

"I just killed someone," he replied heavily. "The guy was a liar, a con artist, but hell, so am I. Maybe all vamps are.

Anyway, even though he wanted to trick me and use me, he was my friend, too. And now I'm turning my back on three other people that I liked." He smiled grimly. "Oh, yeah, and I'm worried that working for you is driving me crazy. After all the hard times I've been through over the past thirty years, I would've thought that I was too tough to go nuts. But *something's* happening to me."

"Tell me everything," Melpomene said.

Dan did tell her most of it. Midway through his recital, a dilapidated, exhaust-belching, zebra-striped Cadillac full of black teenagers roared down the street. He wondered what they'd make of the pale, beautiful woman clad only in a gauzy gown, but they didn't even slow down to ogle her. Maybe they couldn't see her.

When he finished describing his clash with Wyatt, Melpomene said, "The long and the short of it is, you killed in self-defense. The magus was trying to murder you."

Dan smiled crookedly. "When you put it that way, the guilt and the sadness I'm feeling don't make a lot of sense, do they? But I feel them anyway."

"Oh, they make perfect sense to me," Melpomene said. "I remember when my fellow Methuselahs and I were young and still cherished one another. Do you think that our hearts didn't ache when the wills of our sires and our own ambitions and grievances turned us against one another?"

"Evidently they didn't ache enough to keep you from fighting," Dan observed.

The ancient vampire sighed. "No. No, they didn't. Perhaps the greatest devotion a Kindred can experience is a debased and tainted thing compared to the love of mortals. I don't know; after all these centuries, I'm not certain that I remember how it felt to be human. In any event, love is scarcely the force that makes our benighted world go around. The thirsts for blood and power do that."

"Some of us just want to get by and have somebody to hang around with."

"Some of you are very young," Melpomene said, "and must either harden or perish as the centuries creep by. Still, I'm sorry that it grieves you to part from the anarchs. But after I reward you, you won't lack for companionship."

Considering the way that his fellow undead had always shunned him, Dan wondered if even Melpomene could convince other vampires to befriend him the way Wyatt, Laurie and the others had. He guessed that at this point he could only hope so. "I'll hold you to that. Now, what's the deal with the art? Why did it hypnotize me?"

Melpomene hesitated, then said, "I assure you, you aren't going mad. I could tell from your aura if you were."

"Good," Dan said, "but what *is* happening? I can't see *your* aura, but I'm pretty sure you know."

Melpomene's exquisite lips twisted. "I imagine that my vitae is responsible. You know that I belong to the same bloodline as Roger Phillips' Toreador. All those who share that heritage are enthralled by beauty, a fascination that occasionally freezes us dead in our tracks. When I allowed you to drink from me, I only meant to share some of my powers, not one of my weaknesses. I apologize."

After a moment's consideration, Dan shrugged. "Well, I guess the trade-off is worth it. Heck, what I saw in those paintings was pretty wonderful. If I'm going to keep seeing it, it could brighten up my life." He snorted. "If it doesn't get me killed. Anyway, it's nice to know that I'm not any crazier now than I was before I met you."

"I'm glad I could ease your mind," Melpomene said. "Then we're still friends?"

With her unnatural charm tugging at his affections, he wanted to say yes, of course; but he knew that he couldn't fully trust the emotions she inspired in him, and he hadn't completely forgiven her for leading him to betray Wyatt and the anarchs. "I'll keep working for you," he said. "Let's leave it at that."

She smiled sadly, as if he'd wounded her feelings. "If only

for the sake of the poor kine destined for slaughter," she said, a hint of irony in her musical contralto voice. "In that case, we'll talk about the war. Let's think: what do we actually know now that we didn't before?"

"That the Tremere are behind the attack on Sarasota," Dan replied. Somewhere far to the north, someone fired three shots and a child began to wail. "By sending out agents posing as honchos of the Anarch Movement, they've recruited a bunch of stooges to do their dirty work for them."

"I wouldn't assume that *all* of their front-line troops are would-be anarchs," Melpomene said. "Elliott Sinclair clashed with a band of Nosferatu, and Kindred of that lineage join Garcia's Movement about as infrequently as the Tremere themselves. But you've articulated the basic principle. I imagine that many members of their army were recruited under one pretext or another, and have no notion for whom they're actually fighting. A precaution to keep the architects of the assault from being called to account for their actions if the scheme goes awry."

Dan frowned as an idea struck him. "What if the Tremere aren't at the top of the ladder?" he said. "What if we have another bunch of enemies positioned above them, pulling *their* strings? And, as long as we're speculating, why not even *another* gang, controlling the Warlocks' bosses? For all we know, there could be a *hundred* levels of plotters between people like Laurie and the enemy Methuselah."

Then he thought about what he'd just said and snorted in derision at his own paranoia. "Or maybe not. It's a complicated situation, but it couldn't very well be *that* complicated, could it?"

"You'd be surprised," said Melpomene dryly. "But in this case, you're probably right. I believe that, except for my personal rival, a cabal of Tremere *is* at the top of the chain." She frowned. "I'd *prefer* that that weren't so, but my wishes won't change the reality."

Curious, Dan cocked his head. "Why would you prefer

it?" he asked. "Just because you know how powerful they are?"

"No," Melpomene said. "They are powerful, of course, but every clan has its own extraordinary resources. It's just that —" She faltered momentarily, as if uncertain that she truly wished to confide in him. He wondered fleetingly if simple loneliness didn't sometimes loosen her tongue as effectively as her preternatural charisma did his. Then she pressed on. "Do you know that of all the bloodlines, the Tremere are the only ones who don't trace their lineage back to Caine?"

"I've heard stories to that effect. Supposedly the founders of the clan were Transylvanian sorcerers who turned *themselves* into Kindred, using magic, about a thousand years ago."

"The stories are true," Melpomene replied. "And because their bloodline was newly come into the world, because no Methuselah could claim them as his descendants or had done the work necessary to bring them under his influence, for a time they played only a minimal role in the Jyhad."

Lucky them, thought Dan. Two skinheads reeking of cheap gin and greasy onion rings emerged from the bar. One, a pudgy kid with a swastika tattooed on his forehead, sneered in Dan and Melpomene's general direction, and the vampire wondered if he was going to have to beat them up. But then the other guy, pasty-faced and sweaty, swallowing repeatedly as if he were on the brink of throwing up, tugged at his companion's arm, urging him to come away. The flabby teenager grimaced and nodded. Weaving, the two blundered off in the opposite direction.

"Many of us didn't realize just what valuable agents the Tremere could make," Melpomene continued, seemingly oblivious to the skinheads. Maybe, Dan thought, *she* hadn't been able to see *them*. "We were accustomed to thinking of age and lineage as power, and since the magi possessed neither.... But there was one Methuselah who had himself explored the powers of dark sorcery available to Cainites, losing all his humanitas in the process. He *did* recognize the Tremere's potential, and he was the first member of my generation to take control of any of their covens. His name was Tithonys, and it was my misfortune that, of all his peers, he hated me the most profoundly."

"Why?" asked Dan.

"Because once upon a time, in the days of Agamemnon and Achilles, we were lovers," Melpomene said, turning slightly, hiding her face behind a veil of raven hair. "And then later, after he threw me over, I murdered his new mortal leman." She laughed sadly. "The fiery passion of my bloodline isn't always as wonderful as it's made out to be. Of all my sins, I've had cause to regret that one the most."

She sounded so mournful that Dan raised his hand to squeeze her bare white forearm. Then he remembered that his fingers would pass right through her.

Melpomene stood up straighter and shifted her shoulders as if shrugging off her ancient sorrows. "Needless to say, Tithonys used the Tremere against me," she said, her tone now brisk and matter-of-fact. "My minions had never faced anything like that assault. I feared that each and every one would perish before they learned to cope."

"Are you afraid that Tithonys has come after you again now?"

"No," Melpomene said, so firmly that Dan wondered if her insistence wasn't for her own benefit as well his own. "Because I won a total victory in that conflict. I cremated Tithonys' decapitated corpse with my own hands, in a tumble-down little farmhouse in Normandy. Someone else, someone — unless I'm extraordinarily unlucky — less cunning and powerful, is attacking me this time. It's just that his use of the Tremere stirs unpleasant memories."

"I understand. Are you going to warn Prince Roger's brood that the Warlocks are behind the attacks on Sarasota?"

The ancient vampire shook her head. "Not yet, because we don't know *which* Tremere are to blame."

"Does that matter?" Dan asked. According to rumor, the Warlocks were far more organized and homogeneous than the other six principal clans of the Camarilla. That was one of the reasons other vampires feared them, and it implied that, on some level, the entire bloodline was involved in the present conflict.

"Yes, it does matter. Your notions about the Tremere aren't entirely accurate." The observation gave Dan the creepy feeling that Melpomene had just read his mind. "There *are* rivalries and conspiracies within the clan; you just don't hear about them because the magi take care to ensure you won't. It's entirely possible that some regent, lord, or pontifex has undertaken this campaign without the knowledge of his peers, or even of the Inner Council of Seven in Vienna. I don't want my descendants picking fights with innocent Tremere, or flinging wild, unprovable accusations around in Conclave. That could make the present crisis worse than it is already."

"What Conclave are we talking about?" Dan asked.

"The struggle has taken on an overtly political dimension," said Melpomene vaguely. "You don't have to worry about that. Your task is to continue your investigation."

Dan grimaced. "Yeah. I was *hoping* that I'd already uncovered enough to satisfy you, but I actually knew better."

"Do you have an idea of how to proceed?"

"Uh-huh. I went through Wyatt's wallet and found his address. And this." He showed her the scarlet key card.

"'Camelot,'" Melpomene read. "Do you know what that means?"

A little pleased that he knew something she didn't, Dan nodded. "I recognize the logo. Camelot's one of the big new theme parks in Orlando. And you'll notice that this isn't just some kind of season pass or discount card. The park wouldn't give a customer a key that would open anything. This looks like something an employee would have." He grinned. "I'm going to search Wyatt's home, and then I'm going to Disneyland!"

EIGHTEEN: THE CONCLAVE

<hr>

*Laws are like cobwebs, which may catch small flies, but
let wasps and hornets break through.*
> — Jonathan Swift, "A Tribical Essay upon the
> Faculties of the Mind"

Standing in the shadowy wings of the theater of the
Performing Arts Center, awaiting his cue as if the present
situation were a play, Elliott fingered the Windsor knot of
his favorite red silk tie, making sure it was tight and centered
between the points of his well-starched collar. "Stop
fidgeting!" Judy Morgan said. "You're making me nuts!"

Elliott turned toward her. Her black leather halter was
even skimpier than usual, and her skin-tight jeans were
tattered and oil-stained. He suspected that her appearance
was an expression of her rebel's disdain for the whole idea
of a Conclave. "You could have done with a little more
fidgeting yourself," he said dryly.

"Bull," she replied. "Everybody expects me to look like
a rough, tough Brujah, just as they expect you to look like a
sissified Toreador. If I walked out there in a power suit, that
really would make a shitty impression. Speaking of which,

don't you think we might as well schlep our butts out on stage?"

"Absolutely not," Elliott said. Surreptitiously, to avoid annoying Judy anew, he inspected his charcoal-gray trousers for lint. "No one looks more foolish and ineffectual than a person passively waiting in front of an audience for someone else to appear and commence the festivities. Witness Gunter." He nodded at the ruddy-faced Malkavian elder, who'd already taken one of the seats arrayed before the tall, massive teak desk on stage; a spasm of loathing passed through him. "I should have staked the wretch when I had the chance."

"I take it you still think he put Palmer Guice up to convening the Conclave."

"Him, or one of our phantom enemies. Even if he isn't responsible, you can rest assured that everything Gunter says now will be directed to one end: convincing the Assembly that he ought to be proclaimed acting regent of Sarasota, or even prince outright."

"I imagine that's true," said Judy, frowning and massaging one of the old scars on her shoulder. "But... look, I know I haven't done as much of this political crap as you have — I never had the patience for it — but I don't quite understand why you're acting like we're on trial. We haven't done anything wrong. Someone else is doing things to us."

"That's exactly the point," Elliott replied. "Our enemy has made us look vulnerable, and — though you won't find the principle stated in the Six Traditions — weakness is the gravest crime of all among our predatory breed. It arouses people's avarice. If someone can exploit the law to satisfy his rapacity at our expense, you can rest assured he will."

A footfall sounded behind them. They turned to see Palmer Guice bustling toward them, followed by a pair of his black-suited deputies — or Archons, by their proper title. Guice was a long-nosed, lantern-jawed vampire with webs of wrinkles surrounding his steel-gray eyes. He affected an old-time English magistrate's black robe and curled white wig, wearing the outfit with a self-assurance that made it seem appropriate. His pale aura was a confusing smear of constantly shifting colors; Elliott couldn't draw any inferences about his mood.

As usual, Guice *sounded* cordial to the nth degree. "Elliott! Judith! I'm so sorry to have kept you waiting, but our flight was delayed. Damned airplanes! Can't abide 'em. The kine should have stuck with steamships and railroads."

"Welcome to Sarasota," Elliott said with all the warmth he could muster. He extended his hand and the Justicar shook it. "I don't think your visit was necessary, but we're honored to have you, and we'll try to make your stay as pleasant as possible. Before we begin, may I ask you a question?"

"You can certainly *ask*," the Justicar said, clearly implying that he might not feel inclined to answer.

"Why did *you* think you needed to come here?" Elliott asked. "Who's been talking to you?"

Guice chuckled. "Why, Elliott! That actually sounds a little paranoid. Poor Roger's illness is common knowledge, and the 'Dracula' murders have made the national news. Moreover, speaking strictly hypothetically, if anyone *had* been carrying tales, I'm sure you understand that a Justicar can't afford to reveal his sources. Otherwise they'll dry up on him." He gestured toward the stage. "Shall we?" He beamed at Judy. "After you."

Looking sourly bemused that anyone would defer to her on the basis of her gender, the Brujah walked out from behind the curtain, and the other Kindred followed. The drone of conversation filling the hall grew louder. The house lights were burning, and Elliott was surprised to see that the majority of the seats in the spacious auditorium were occupied, by patrician Ventrue in outdated clothes; gorgeous Toreador;hideously deformed Nosferatu; Gangrel marked with the pointed ears, flattened, snout-like noses and other stigmata associated with their shape-changing powers; and other undead whose lineage was less readily apparent. It was one of the largest Assemblies he'd ever attended. No doubt some of the mysterious enemies of Sarasota were in attendance as well. He wondered how many of the vampires in the chamber were present to support Roger Phillips' people — precious few, he suspected — how many in hopes of seeing them come to grief, and how many simply to enjoy the spectacle of the deliberations.

As Elliott sauntered to his chair, he picked out certain faces in the audience, including those of Otis McNamara and Catherine Cobb. The Toreador dared to hope that at least these two old friends were on his side. Perhaps Malachi Jones, the newly crowned Ventrue prince of Tampa Bay, peering alertly from one of the nearest boxes, was also. A thin man with bushy muttonchop whiskers and pince-nez glasses, Malachi was renowned for his sagacity, even temper, and general benevolence; he'd always gotten along well with his Manatee County neighbors. But there were others whose presence was more ominous. Like Gilbert Duane, the Malkavian prince of Miami, a bald, muscular black man with a beard and a perpetual scowl. And Pablo Velasquez, a member of the Tampa Bay primogen, a handsome Latino also of Malkavian blood who was dressed as elegantly as Elliott himself, with a gold tack in the shape of the Moon trump from the Tarot gleaming midway down his tie. Both Duane and Velasquez seemed likely bets to support Gunter, their clanmate, in any bid that he might make for power.

As Judy and Elliott sat down, Gunter glowered at them. Meanwhile Guice climbed onto the high seat behind the lofty bench. Standing at parade rest, the poker-faced Archons took up positions on either side of the massive piece of furniture. The Justicar picked up his gavel and rapped once for order.

To his surprise, despite his apprehensions, Elliott experienced a thrill of anticipation. As he gazed out at the crowd, he felt a desire to perform. And though the business of the Conclave was deadly serious, it was a public entertainment as well — a person had only to notice some of the gawking faces in the seats to appreciate *that* — and one in which he had a stellar role.

It took a few seconds, but the Assembly finally quieted down. Smiling out at the audience, Guice said, "Thank you. I'm Palmer Guice, Justicar of Clan Ventrue and the Camarilla, and this Conclave is convened on my authority to discuss certain recent events in the domain of Sarasota deemed to be of general concern. As at any Conclave, anyone is welcome to speak his mind, but I've taken the liberty of seating certain individuals on stage because I imagine they'll need to speak frequently. They're Prince Roger Phillips' primogen: Judith Morgan of Clan Brujah" — some of Judy's rowdy progeny whistled and clapped — "Gunter Schmidt of Clan Malkavian, and Elliott Sinclair of Clan Toreador." Trying to look confident and competent, invoking his supernatural charisma, the actor nodded to the crowd. With luck, the power would influence *some* of the spectators, even if the more powerful and the more hostile ones proved resistant.

"As many of you are aware," Guice continued, still addressing the house, "this domain has been experiencing a number of problems. I believe I can say without fear of contradiction that the trouble began when Prince Roger went insane." Elliott stood up. "Yes, Elliott?"

"I take exception to the term 'insane,'" the Toreador said. "It sounds so permanent. Roger has fallen ill, as even Kindred sometimes do, but we anticipate a full recovery."

"Speak for yourself," Gunter growled. "I think as highly of the man as you do—"

Liar, Elliott thought.

"—but there's no point in closing our eyes to reality."

"Careful," Elliott said. "Keep talking like that and they'll throw you out of the Malkavians." He was pleased when the quip got a laugh. The more he entertained the crowd, the more likely they were to come down on his side.

Gunter grimaced. "Roger's no better, even though we brought in Lionel Potter to take care of him." He pointed toward the back of the hall. "The doctor's sitting right there. We can ask him."

Guice smiled out at the crowd. "Dr. Potter. Perhaps it would be helpful if you could enlighten us as to the prince's current condition."

Looking reluctant, the physician rose. Elliott surmised that the Caitiff was torn between the desire to sustain his reputation as a miracle worker and a wary unwillingness to make promises he might not be able to keep. "There isn't any improvement as yet," Potter admitted. "But neither is there any deterioration. I certainly remain hopeful."

"Can you tell us precisely what ails the prince?" Guice asked.

Potter hesitated. "Not as yet."

The Justicar frowned, not angrily, but in what Elliott assumed to be a bogus display of concern. "Or when we might expect him to return to his duties?"

"No," Potter said.

"Thank you for your candor," said Guice. Potter quickly sat down, and the Ventrue resumed speaking to the Assembly at large. "Inasmuch as we can't assume that Prince Roger will make a speedy recovery, I'm afraid that we need to consider how Sarasota is likely to fare in his absence. Which is to say, how well it's being led."

"It isn't being led at all," Gunter said. He glowered at Elliott. "This… *popinjay* wants to run things by *committee*. It violates the Second and the Fifth Traditions."

Elliott guessed that he should have officially proclaimed himself acting governor despite his concern about offending the pride of the Brujah and the Malkavians, but he hadn't anticipated Gunter advancing this particular argument in

Conclave. It was too late to declare himself sole commander now; the maneuver would only make him look desperate.

"Actually, the situation doesn't violate anything," said Malachi Jones mildly. Everyone looked up at the prince's box. Malachi struck a match with his thumbnail and lit a cheroot. Elliott admired the other Kindred's oratorical technique. By making the audience wait for the rest of his observations, he was influencing them to weigh his words more seriously. "The Traditions merely direct us to respect those in authority. They don't mandate that a single lord be in control. That's the most common situation, but I can think of several cities governed by council, and I haven't noticed anyone hauling *their* elders up in front of a tribunal."

"Right on!" Otis shouted. It might well have been the first time that the free-spirited, copper-haired Brujah had ever endorsed a political position espoused by a conservative Ventrue prince. Evidently appreciating the incongruity, Malachi arched an eyebrow. Catherine and certain other members of the audience nodded in a more decorous show of support.

Pablo Velasquez stood up. His slicked-back raven hair gleamed. "It seems to me," the handsome Malkavian said, "that the question is, how well is this *particular* council holding things together? How well are they protecting the childer and obeying the laws of the Kindred?"

"They aren't!" Gunter said. "*I've* been trying, but Sinclair invariably opposes me; and for some reason, probably his miserable Toreador charm, Judy always backs him up. Surely you've all heard about Dracula. The kine are starting to believe in vampires. The whole Masquerade is in jeopardy!"

Playing to the crowd, Elliott smiled and shook his head, conveying amused pity at Gunter's hysteria. "That's an exaggeration," the actor said. "We have one rogue feeding indiscreetly. It's happened before, in many other domains. We'll trap the criminal and then, in a week or a month, the humans will forget there was ever anything amiss."

"How close *are* you to catching the outlaw?" asked Guice.

"My brood and I patrol the city every night," Judy said.

"But do you have any *leads?*" the Justicar persisted.

"We have a description of the killer," Judy said. "Someone phoned it to us anonymously."

Guice shook his head doubtfully. "'Anonymously.' I'm afraid that doesn't inspire a lot of confidence."

Glaring at him, her aura flaring red with anger, Judy took a deep breath. Afraid that she was about to explode, and that her outburst would prejudice their case, Elliott directed his charismatic powers at her. With a look, he implored her to hold on to her temper. Through gritted teeth, she merely said, "I promise, we *will* nail her."

"Well, everyone certainly wishes you well in the endeavor," Guice said unctuously. He turned back toward Gunter. "Are there other matters troubling you?"

"You're damn right there are," the flaxen-haired Malkavian said. "Since Roger went mad, Sinclair here has sent several of his clanmates to their deaths." The spectators babbled excitedly. They'd already known about Roger and Dracula, but now they were hearing something that was new to them.

Guice frowned. "That's extremely disturbing."

"No doubt," said Elliott, "you're all aware that recently, around the world but primarily in North America, various works of art have been mysteriously destroyed. Each of those treasures was created by a Toreador of this domain, or by one of our human clients. Some enemy is vandalizing them to injure us." The audience jabbered some more. "When we moved to protect the art, we clashed with our foes and suffered casualties. Unfortunate, but inevitable in war. I can assure you that every one of my clanmates felt the goal was worth the risk—"

"Only after you bewitched them with that voice of yours!" Gunter interjected.

"—and that we've taken measures to ensure our safety in the future."

"With whom are you at war?" asked Guice.

Elliott positioned himself so that he was looking at the bench without turning his back on the audience. "We don't know yet," he said steadily, "but we're going to find out, and God help them when we do."

"That sounds very macho," Gunter sneered, "but so far you're only managing to kill your *own* people, like poor old Schuyller Madison."

The audience babbled even louder. Guice craned forward, peering at Elliott like a vulture on a perch. "You *killed* Sky?"

As if you don't already know, the Toreador thought. "No. When I confronted him, he committed suicide to avoid capture and interrogation. He was a traitor, though it wasn't his fault. One of our enemies forced him to accept a Blood Bond."

"How do we know any of that is true?" Gunter demanded. "No one else was present when he burned to death. No one's seen any kind of evidence of his guilt." The Malkavian's progeny yelled their agreement.

Elliott gave the ruddy-faced vampire what he hoped was an intimidating stare. "You know it because I told you so," he said.

Uncowed, his fangs peeking out from beneath his upper lip, Gunter said, "And why would I take your word for *anything*? You've been crazy with grief since your wife died, and everybody knows it. You've got no business trying to run anything!"

Elliott nearly smiled. Despite the seriousness of his situation, the inherent irony of being accused of lunacy by a Malkavian wasn't lost on him.

"Elliott was together enough to kick *your* sorry ass," Judy said. Her Brujah cheered, and other spectators laughed.

"Let them fight it out!" someone cried. Many vampires shouted in agreement.

Guice pounded with his gavel. When the clamor subsided, he said, "I'm not convinced that it would solve anything to have them fight. As I understand it, Elliott has already demonstrated that he can best Gunter in hand-to-hand combat, but the issue here is one of sound judgment and fitness to command, not physical prowess."

"Clearly," said Elliott, exerting his superhuman powers of persuasion once more, "the weight of the evidence is on my side." Inwardly, considering the failure of his agents and himself to capture Dracula, or even to identify the enemies conspiring against Sarasota, he considered this a dubious proposition at best; but he wasn't about to admit it. "It's true that I went through a period of debilitating grief after Mary's murder, but I've recovered. I believe that Judy, her progeny and the Toreador will vouch for me. That makes it our word against that of Gunter and his offspring, and there are considerably more of us than there are of them."

Gilbert Duane rose from his seat. "But this matter isn't just between you people," the muscular black prince said. His deep voice was mellow and reasonable, a virtually schizophrenic contrast to his menacing glower. "Should you fail to preserve the Masquerade, our entire race will suffer. And as the master of my own domain, I object to your flagrant violations of the Fifth Tradition." The Tradition in question, that of Hospitality, required a vampire visiting another city to present himself to the reigning monarch.

Elliott was glumly certain he knew what Duane was talking about, but he decided to play dumb and thus gain a few more seconds to consider a defense. "What do you mean?" he asked.

"I'll let my vassal François explain," Duane replied. "He and his progeny actually witnessed the crime."

A cadaverous figure dressed in a top hat, a clawhammer coat and a necklace of human finger bones rose from its seat by the left-hand wall. The seats around it were vacant, and when Elliott caught a whiff of its nauseating reek, he understood why. The ghastly apparition smelled as dead as it looked.

Even in his self-imposed exile from the affairs of his people, Elliott had heard that a handful of Samedi, undead of Caribbean origin as physically repulsive as the Nosferatu, had sworn homage to Duane. Evidently François was one of them.

"Many Toreador came to Little Haiti," said François in a heavy Creole accent. "They did not see me, but, watching from the shadows, I saw them. I heard them talk about Sarasota and the crazy prince. I see them here again tonight." Turning, stabbing with a finger that was as much bare bone as flesh, it pointed out several of Roger's offspring. "You, and you, and you."

"I'm not following this," Elliott said. "Unlike many of the rest of you, we Toreador travel frequently, and we make treaties with the princes of various cities for the right to pass through unhindered. And Gilbert, unless I'm as demented as Gunter has alleged, Roger long ago forged such a pact with you."

"These men weren't just visitors," François said. "They were a war party, carrying many big guns. They fought a battle with their enemies in *my streets!*"

Elliott realized that, in essence, the agitated Samedi had just claimed right of domain over Little Haiti. He suspected that such presumption, particularly in a public forum, might well anger Duane. But if it had, the Malkavian didn't allow it to divert him from the main issue. "And the treaty *doesn't* allow you to send heavily armed troops into Miami, or to conduct hostilities there," said the prince. "Just as it *does* require you at least to phone my people and notify us of your presence within our boundaries. Otherwise, you *are* trespassing."

Trying to look a little contrite, Elliott spread his hands. "You have a point, and I apologize. But the situation was an emergency. We had to move quickly in an effort to protect one of our human clients and his paintings."

Gunter snorted. "You broke a Tradition for the sake of a kine and his pretty pictures. If that doesn't prove what I've been saying about your judgment, I don't know what would." Certain members of the audience nodded grimly in agreement.

"I don't give a damn *why* your people were shooting up my city," said Duane. "No excuse is good enough. I'm sitting on the Sabbat down there, trying to keep them from marching north and destroying the rest of you—"

"My hero," said Catherine dryly. Though the blond, statuesque Ventrue only seemed to murmur, her own charismatic powers allowed her voice to carry through the hall and trigger a ripple of mirth.

Duane shot her a glare as he continued. "—And the last thing I need is anyone else importing his personal problems onto my turf." He looked around the auditorium. "Don't you people feel the same way? Do you doubt that you've had gangs of heavily armed Sarasota Toreador sneaking in and out of *your* cities to steal back their precious art, ready to blast the shit out of anyone who got in their way, no matter how that jeopardizes the Masquerade?"

An angry muttering ran through the theater. Guice rapped for order. When the ugly sound subsided, he said, "It seems to me that this matter boils down to a question of confidence. Do we feel that events here in Sarasota are out of control, or not? And given that what happens here has implications for us all, would we prefer to see Mr. Sinclair, Miss Morgan and Mr. Schmidt continue to govern on Prince Roger's behalf, or would we be more comfortable with a different arrangement? I'd like to determine the will of the majority."

"In other words," said Duane, "you want a vote. The present system versus… somebody. One acting monarch, the usual setup, and certainly the most effective in an emergency. I nominate" — he made a show of looking around the hall as, smirking, Gunter preened — "Pablo Velasquez."

"I accept," the Hispanic vampire said.

The situation could scarcely have been more serious. No new overlord was likely to desire Roger's recovery, or to look after the interests of the Toreador as earnestly as Elliott had. A vampire from another clan probably wouldn't allow them to defend their art or the human artists at all. It was even possible that Velasquez was one of their enemies and would use his new position to annihilate them.

Yet Elliott couldn't help feeling a tingle of wicked amusement at the way Gunter's mouth fell open and his eyes bugged out. The actor suspected that his fellow lieutenant had asked Duane to nominate him, and that the prince of Miami had agreed. But now that Gunter had denounced the present government of Sarasota as vehemently as possible, now that his usefulness was over, Duane had stabbed him in the back, passing him over for the candidate he truly favored.

"This — this isn't right!" Gunter stammered. "I told you, I opposed Sinclair's ideas, and I've lived in Sarasota for more than a century. *I* should be the new master!"

"I'm sorry," Duane said. "But if you were any great shakes as a leader, you'd already be in control. Your views would have prevailed over Sinclair's. No, I think we'd be better off with someone altogether new."

"If Sarasota is under siege," drawled Malachi Jones, exhaling a blue plume of smoke, "perhaps I should point out that Pablo scarcely has an unblemished record as a military commander. He and his brood recently lost a battle to a band of Lupines led by a renegade Kindred, sustaining heavy casualties and ultimately losing their haven." Elliott suspected that Malachi didn't like the idea of one of his lieutenants trying to win his own domain without consulting him. Velasquez scowled up at him, and the Ventrue gave him a shrug and a crooked smile.

"That may be," said Palmer Guice, "but I know Mr. Velasquez, and I'm satisfied that he's qualified to lead. You must feel the same, or he wouldn't be a member of your primogen." Malachi waved a hand, tacitly conceding the point. "I realize that others are qualified as well, but considering the crisis facing Sarasota, I want to keep this simple, and not get bogged down in the long nights of politicking that would inevitably result from a large slate of candidates. Therefore, I'm closing the nominations."

"May we each make a statement before you call the vote?" Elliott asked. Guice inclined his head, giving permission, whereupon the actor gestured to Velasquez, inviting him to go first.

"Whatever my prince has to say about me," said Velasquez, shooting another venomous glance at Malachi's box, "I'm a fighter and a seer. I can defend Sarasota and catch Dracula, *without* breaking the Traditions or bringing trouble down on my neighbors' heads."

"Succinctly put," Elliott said. "Since there are three of us representing the current regime, we'll try to be brief as well." He gave Gunter a sunny smile. "You can go first, dear colleague. Would you care to defend our stewardship?"

Still trying to come to terms with Gilbert Duane's betrayal, with the fact that the vote now threatened to *diminish* his authority, Gunter looked both furious and bewildered. His mouth worked, but no sounds emerged. The audience, many of whom comprehended the Malkavian's situation as clearly as Elliott did, roared with laughter.

When the swell of mirth subsided, Elliott said, "Judy?"

The former slave said, "My progeny and I are Brujah. No one tells us where to give our loyalty." Her fangs slightly extended, she sneered at the crowd. "If you're smart, you won't try to stuff a new boss down our throats." She glared at Velasquez. "And if *you're* smart, you'll keep your ass off our turf, no matter how these bozos vote."

Palmer Guice shook his head as if she were a naughty child. Elliott imagined a *tsk, tsk, tsk.* "I sympathize with your pique, my dear, but no matter what the outcome of this Conclave, I recommend that you abide by its decisions. The Camarilla has the will and the might to 'stuff them down your throat' if it needs to."

"My turn to make a statement," said Elliott, striving to project all the supernatural charisma at his disposal. "My fellow Kindred, you've already heard Judy and me describe and explain our recent actions. You've already had a chance to form an impression of our capabilities. I won't speak to those issues anymore.

"But I will say this. All but the youngest and the most fortunate of our company have struggled to survive in desperate circumstances. We've fought Lupines, anarchs, the Sabbat and witch hunters, bending even the Traditions when necessity dictated. Some of us even remember the nightmare of the Inquisition, when the mortals rose against us *en masse*. Before I walked onto this stage tonight, I reflected that the worst thing about such a dark time is that, when trouble threatens to lay a Kindred low, he can always count on his fellow Cainites to rejoice or even to connive at his downfall, either because they hope to profit from it or out of sheer sadism."

Certain members of the Assembly growled as if the Toreador had offended them. He kept talking, gazing at them steadily, willing them to fall silent. They did. "And yet, as I look at you now, marking the faces of a host of friends I've cherished over the years, I can't believe that my grim perspective is true. Surely the Beast doesn't rule in each and every one of our hearts. Surely we aren't quite the devils the humans have always deemed us. Surely the existence of the Camarilla itself, with its covenants and accords to preserve the peace, proves that we're capable of brotherhood, honor and charity, not just greed and blood lust. If so, then I dare to hope that you won't turn against a community of your fellows in their hour of need. You won't force them to accept a new master, an outsider they can't support and behind whom they cannot rally. You'll trust them to manage their affairs as best they can, as you'd wish to be trusted yourselves in the same situation. Even when the stakes are high, when they've carelessly given offense, and the fool Toreador" — he gave the crowd a self-deprecating smile — "giving orders is, as Gunter has attested, a man of distinctly impeachable character and judgment. You'll do it because that's the noble and the generous thing to do."

For a moment the theater was silent. Then Malachi Jones said, "Hear, hear." A number of the assembled vampires began to clap enthusiastically - but not all of them. Elliott had no way of telling whether he'd swayed enough of them for it to matter.

He supposed he'd know in a moment. Turning back toward Guice, he said, "All right, we've all spoken our pieces. Would you care to call the vote?"

"Yes, and I'd like to do it with a simple show of hands, unless someone has an objection," the Justicar said. He looked out at the crowd, none of whom spoke out against the proposed procedure. "Very well, then. How many want to see Pablo Velasquez take over as regent of Sarasota?"

Elliott reflexively held his breath while he looked around the hall. Only about a third of the Assembly had raised their pallid hands. It was encouraging, but he wasn't out of the woods yet. If a large number of those present abstained from the plebiscite, then he, Judy and Gunter might receive even fewer votes.

"And how many wish to see Prince Roger's primogen remain in control?" asked Guice.

About half of the assembled vampires signaled their support.

The Toreador, Brujah, and even some of the Malkavians of Sarasota applauded and cheered. Bounding out of her chair, Judy whooped and threw her arms around Elliott. Lifting him up, she whirled him in a circle, hugging him so tightly that his ribs ached and he was glad that the undead didn't need to breathe.

Guice gavelled insistently for order. Finally the noise subsided and Judy put Elliott down. The Justicar cleared his throat. "This is a little awkward," he said.

Elliott felt a pang of apprehension. "And why is that?"

"I always try to determine the will of the Conclave," said Guice, "and I almost always follow it. But I trust you all do understand that ultimately an Assembly is only an advisory body. It's the Justicar who makes the decisions, and in this case, noting that the majority of our wise elders and princes supported the idea of change, I feel obliged to act on the basis of my own conscience and my own misgivings. I hereby declare Pablo Velasquez the acting sovereign of Sarasota."

"You bastard!" Judy screamed. Faster than any mortal, she hurled herself forward. More agile still, Elliott lunged after her and grabbed her. Using her Herculean strength, she tore herself free instantly. The Archons flanking the bench hastily reached inside their coats.

"Calm down!" Elliott rapped, using his charismatic powers on the Brujah leader. "This isn't helping!" He gripped her chill, bare forearm. Shuddering, fangs bared, Judy allowed him to drag her back a step.

Elliott looked up at the bench. When he beheld Guice's smug, sanctimonious expression, he nearly went berserk himself. He was now certain that either the Ventrue was one of the enemies of Sarasota, or someone had bribed him. Either way, the outcome of the Conclave had been fixed from the start. And he didn't know what to do about it. The Justicar, damn him, was right. Elliott and his friends couldn't fight the entire Camarilla by themselves. "I request that you reconsider," the actor said.

"As do I," said Catherine. Many others shouted the same sentiment.

"I'm sorry," said Guice. "I've made my decision, and no one here is empowered to gainsay me."

"You're wrong," said a deep voice from the back of the auditorium.

NINETEEN: THE ORDEAL

Indescribable, O queen, is the grief you bid me to renew.
— Virgil, *Aeneid*

As Elliott turned to peer out into the audience, a huge Kindred, whose bushy brown beard, wild mane of hair and barbaric gold earring contrasted oddly with his conservative suit and tie, rose from his seat and headed down the aisle.

"Do you know who that is?" Judy whispered excitedly, shrugging off Elliott's grip.

"Of course," murmured the Toreador, half-dazed with astonishment. "Angus, the Gangrel Justicar."

"What's he doing here? Is he on our side?"

"I don't know, but I'll tell you one thing. Now that I've heard him speak, I'm all but certain that it was him giving me Dracula's description on the phone the other night."

The audience murmured. Looking as surprised as Elliott felt, Guice stared at the giant approaching the stage. "This is, ah, unexpected," the Ventrue Justicar said. "I had no idea you'd even returned to your duties, let alone that you were present tonight."

Angus bounded lightly onto the stage. "But I have and I am," he rumbled. "And I dispute your ruling. As far as I'm concerned, the government of Sarasota should stay the way it is."

Much of the crowd cheered. Scowling, Guice pounded with his gavel until the din subsided. The exertion caused his curly white wig to slip slightly askew. "May I point out," the Ventrue magistrate said, "that *I* called this Conclave."

Angus shrugged his immense shoulders. "You may, if I can point out that it doesn't matter. According to the letter of the law, I still wield as much authority as you."

"If you two can't agree," called Otis McNamara, light glinting on the gray iron ring in his septum, "then there's no decision. If there's no decision, then things stay the way they are."

Guice's mouth twisted. "Rest assured, we *will* come to a judgment," he said.

"Considering your deep respect for the opinions of the Assembly," said Malachi Jones dryly, the air in his box now hazy with rum-scented tobacco smoke, "why not let the vote you just conducted break the deadlock?"

"Because I don't consider that appropriate in this situation," Guice replied.

Angus smiled unpleasantly. "Shall we fight it out then, you and I? Provide the gory spectacle so many of them" — he nodded at the audience — "crave?" Though struggling to retain his composure, Guice looked somewhat taken aback.

"Surely," said a male vampire, rising from his seat, "we ought to try to resolve this matter in a more rational manner than that." Elliott recognized the speaker as Sebastian Durrell. Durrell was a Tremere elder from Louisville, a tall, well-dressed, fortyish and somewhat prim-looking vampire with a high, bony forehead, deep-set eyes, and a pronounced widow's peak.

Arching a shaggy eyebrow, Angus said, "I'm guessing that you have a suggestion."

"Not to minimize Ms. Morgan's or Mr. Schmidt's importance to their city," said Durrell, giving the vampires in question an apologetic smile, "but on the basis of what I've heard here tonight, it seems that the heart of this matter is *Mr. Sinclair's* fitness to lead. His mental stability, that is. Well, matters deadlocked in Conclave are occasionally decided by an ordeal, are they not? As it happens, using my magic, I can subject him to high levels of psychological stress."

"How?" Judy demanded.

"You'll see," the Warlock replied. "Rest assured, it does no physical harm, and it will work. If he doesn't crack under the strain, then perhaps we *can* trust him to serve as Roger Phillips' steward."

"Ordinarily," said Angus slowly, "we use ordeal to determine an alleged criminal's guilt or innocence, not to decide questions of praxis."

"What about the invasion of my domain?" said Gilbert Duane. "If breaking the Fifth Tradition isn't a crime, what is?"

Elliott drew a breath to say that he'd submit to the ordeal. Evidently sensing his intent, Judy gripped his forearm with crushing force. "Don't do it," she whispered. "You don't know what Durrell's really talking about. He could be one of our enemies. Maybe the whole point of the Conclave was to set you up for this. To do the same thing to you that they did to Roger!"

"It doesn't matter," the Toreador murmured in reply. "Durrell's right. One way or another, this has all turned out to be about me. Perhaps if I prove myself, Guice will feel obliged to let us alone." He raised his voice. "Ladies and gentlemen, I'll be happy to let Mr. Durrell read to me from the complete works of Bulwer-Lytton, subject me to easy-listening music" — the audience laughed — "or whatever he intends." He gave Guice a level stare. "Provided, of course, that you first guarantee that my performance will settle the issue before the Assembly."

Guice gazed out at Durrell for a moment, then looked back at Elliott. "Agreed."

Angus shrugged. "It's your sanity and your position on the line, Toreador. If you're willing, I won't object. I just hope you know what you're doing."

Elliott grinned at him. "That would be preferable, wouldn't it?"

Durrell hastened toward the stage. Lacking Angus' inhuman strength and grace, he had to clamber up out of the orchestra pit. Elliott derived a bit of pleasure from seeing his would-be torturer's dignity compromised, even if only for a moment.

Rising to his feet, the Warlock looked at the bench. "If I may proceed?" Guice nodded curtly. "Then could we have some room, please?" Angus and Judy stepped back, the latter with manifest reluctance, abandoning center stage to Durrell and his subject.

Elliott felt a twinge of apprehension, which he did his best to mask. "If I remember my vaudeville days," he said to the Tremere, "you're supposed to ask the audience for absolute silence, too."

"I don't think that will be necessary," Durrell said, smiling thinly. He plucked a silver stickpin, its circular head embossed with a cryptic hieroglyph, from his lapel. "However, I will require a drop of your vitae."

Elliott offered his index finger. Durrell pricked the tip, squeezed out a blob of fragrant blood, and smeared it in the palm of his own white hand. The Toreador noticed that the other Kindred had been correct. Even if he did want quiet, it hadn't been necessary to ask for it. The onlookers, most of whom had never had the opportunity to witness any of the legendary Tremere sorcery, were watching in fascinated silence.

Durrell lifted his hand to his face, causing Elliott to wonder if he intended to lick the vitae off. But the Warlock simply inhaled deeply, filling his head with the coppery scent. Then, lowering his arm again, he used his finger to draw a symbol in the crimson liquid. "Please close your eyes and open your mind," he said.

Elliott obeyed. For a moment nothing happened, and then a terrible vertigo seized him. He felt the world spin, and he staggered to stay on his feet.

The dizziness was matched by a comparable feeling inside his brain. His *thoughts* were whirling too, disintegrating into a maelstrom of confusion.

The surface under his shoes abruptly stopped rotating, throwing him off-balance once more. Reeling, he opened his eyes. He had a vague sense that he shouldn't, that he'd told someone that he'd keep them closed, but he longer remembered to whom he'd said it, or why.

He found he was standing in the foyer of his own home. For a moment everything looked strange. The soft lights burning beyond the doorways. The high corners of the hall. The sweet-smelling yellow roses in the delicate white porcelain vase, and the green marble-topped stand on which they sat.

He shook his head, perplexed at his own reaction. Nothing was strange. The house looked the way it usually did. He didn't understand why he was picturing it as it had *never* been — neglected, shrouded in shadow with veils of cobweb hanging in the corners, the vase full of long-withered blooms, dust coating every surface and hanging in the air.

He couldn't remember when, or from whom, he'd last drunk. He wondered if he'd imbibed vitae laced with alcohol or drugs. He supposed it didn't matter; his disorientation was fading. Noticing the sheaf of neatly typed pages in his hand, he remembered that he'd gone away alone to finish his new comedy without distractions. Well, the piece was done now, and it had a wonderfully funny part for Mary. Eager to see her, kiss her and show her the script, he called her name.

His shout echoed through the building. No one replied.

Puzzled — he'd phoned and told her to expect him this evening, hadn't he? — he ranged through the lavishly furnished ground floor of the house. Neither she nor anyone else was there, so he headed for the second story.

Halfway up the staircase the odor hit him, the rich scent of Kindred vitae mingled with a sickening stench of decay. Suddenly terrified, moving with every iota of his superhuman speed, he charged up the steps.

He found his wife, both pieces of her, lying on the bedroom floor, her yellow hair as luxuriant as ever but the flesh already black and rotten on her bones. She was still wearing the gorgeous sky-blue silk kimono she used for a dressing gown, and several of the gold and crystal vials on her vanity — the cosmetics he'd never been able to convince her she didn't need — were open. Evidently the killers had surprised her shortly after sunset, while she was still busy with her toilet.

Elliott couldn't believe what he was seeing. Mary was both the most wonderful, important person in the world and a powerful immortal, a queen of the night. Someone like that couldn't simply be butchered like a beast in her own boudoir. It wouldn't make any sense.

And yet, simultaneously, he *did* believe it. He understood instantly, instinctively, that the center of his life, the fountainhead of all his joys, was gone forever, and that all the best parts of himself had perished with her. He threw back his head and howled like an animal.

The room spun, whirling him into darkness.

When the light returned, he was climbing the stairs, looking for Mary and shaking with fear, though he didn't understand why. Just because she hadn't answered his call and he hadn't found her on the first floor, that didn't mean anything was wrong. Then he smelled blood and decay, and his dread turned to outright horror. He bolted up the steps, into the bedroom, beheld the carnage and shrieked.

The world went dark, then light, like a great eye blinking.

His nose full of the smells of rot and vitae, Elliott raced across the landing, burst into the bedroom and saw his wife's decapitated body. He screamed in anguish.

The universe lurched, and now he'd just this instant blundered into the bedroom doorway. Spying Mary's lifeless and desecrated body, he cried out. Then the moment repeated, over and over again, the bursts of agonizing grief and despair pounding his mind like a hammer.

He couldn't tell how many times he'd relived the instant of discovery. Oblivious to everything but his pain, he didn't know that each time wasn't the first. But finally, wailing, his hands upraised as if he were King Lear raging on the heath, he noticed the red streak of blood on his finger.

Time skipped backward, repeating that one second like a scratched record, scrambling his thoughts. He nearly forgot about his wounded hand.

Nearly, but not quite. Because he couldn't recall how he'd hurt himself, and somehow the blood wasn't right. He had a sense that it didn't belong in this ghastly place and time.

That suspicion did not halt the agony associated with Mary's destruction; nor did it enable him to grasp that he was trapped in a single recurring moment, or otherwise restore his capacity for rational thought. Yet murkily, instinctively, he fumbled after the meaning of the tiny injury, groping in his own head like a drowning man struggling to reach a life line.

A series of images tumbled through his mind. He was standing on stage. But not for a performance, because he had a sense that he was in danger. And then a Kindred with a pinched, sober-looking face that reminded him of Cromwell and his Roundheads climbed up on the platform and stuck his finger with a silver pin. The other vampire's name was Durrell, and he was one of the Tremere!

Though Elliott's thoughts were still fragmented, he now seemed to remember that Durrell had cast a spell on him. And if that were so, perhaps this hideous experience was only a dream. He strained to wake himself up, just as, when mortal, he'd often managed to rouse himself from a nightmare.

It didn't work. The sight of Mary's severed head, with its skeletal grin and eyes dissolving into slime, smashed at him again and again and again, until he began to doubt that his recollection of Durrell was real. Perhaps it was merely a delusion manufactured by his mind in a last-ditch effort to deny the truth of his wife's murder. Certainly, he felt himself going mad.

And perhaps it was that very disintegration of reason, or his Toreador powers of perception, that at last enabled him to grasp intuitively the nature of his situation. This moment, this experience was true. Mary was dead, and he couldn't escape by hysterically insisting otherwise. Yet the moment was a lie, as well, because she was *long* dead, her murder savagely avenged and her bones laid reverently to rest. If there was any justice in the universe, her spirit had found bliss in some paradise for joyous, loving souls. Elliott felt a surge of rage at the cruelty that would force anyone to relive such excruciating grief when the pain should have faded long ago.

Fighting the pull of the spectacle before him and the overwhelming anguish it inspired, he struggled once again to free himself from the illusion. Abruptly, Mary's corpse, and the bedroom around it, evaporated.

TWENTY: THE PROMISE

Better it is that thou shouldest not vow, than that thou shouldest vow and not pay.
— Ecclesiastes 5:5

Elliott saw that he was back in the theater. His body jerked involuntarily: his kinesthetic sense was addled since, although he'd believed he was standing in a doorway, clutching at the jamb, he now perceived that at some point during his torment he'd fallen to his knees. His eyes stung and his cheeks, chin, lapels, shirt collar and the top of his tie were wet with blood. Indeed, he'd wept away so much vitae that he could feel the Hunger stirring. His throat ached severely. Evidently he'd shrieked it raw.

Drawing on his inhuman speed, he scrambled up into a crouch, hurled himself at Durrell and carried him down with a flying tackle. Straddling the Tremere, he raised his fist to pummel him.

But then he remembered why the other Kindred had bewitched him in the first place. It had been an ordeal, sanctioned by the Conclave, and the point had been to see whether he'd emerge from it with his sanity intact. It might give Guice and Angus the wrong impression if he tore Durrell limb from limb. It took willpower, but he managed to lower his arm.

"My apologies," he rasped to the Tremere. "I'm in control now." He blinked as an insight struck him. "And I don't suppose I have any right to be angry with you. All you did to me was what I've been doing to myself for years on end."

Powerful hands gripped him and hauled him off Durrell. Turning his head, he saw that Judy and Angus had taken hold of him. "I really am all right," he said, beginning to hate the froggy croak of his voice. The Brujah and the Gangrel exchanged glances, then released him. "How long was I in the trance?"

"About fifteen minutes," Judy said.

My god, Elliott thought with a kind of awe. *If time skipped back every second or two, that means I relived the discovery of Mary's body at least* — He cringed even from doing the arithmetic.

"What did you think was happening to you?" Judy asked.

"I'll tell you later," Elliott said. Knowing that the effort was futile, he quickly tried to mend his appearance, wiping his face with a handkerchief and straightening his ruined tie and lapels. He reflected ironically that he hoped the audience had enjoyed the geek show he'd provided. Then he turned to Guice and Angus. "Gentlemen, though both my voice and my appearance are rather the worse for wear, I'm as sane as I was at the start of the Conclave. I've passed your test."

"I agree," Angus rumbled. Elliott thought he heard a note of respect in the Gangrel's voice that hadn't been there before.

Frowning, Guice hesitated as if he were unwilling to grant the judgment to Roger Phillips' primogen even now. A hostile murmur ran through the theater. "All *right*," the

Ventrue said, a little petulantly. "With the understanding that the Toreador will respect the Fifth Tradition, even when taking back their art" — Elliott inclined his head in acquiescence — "I'll permit the present situation to stand. For the moment."

Angus stared at him coldly. "For the moment?"

"My esteemed colleague!" said Guice, smiling, some of his accustomed joviality oozing back into his voice. "What a suspicious glare and tone! Whatever do you take me for? I assure you, I would *never* seek to reverse a judgment unilaterally that we two had reached together. But I do feel a responsibility to monitor the situation in this domain. And, if it doesn't stabilize in the near future, to communicate my concerns to our masters of the Inner Circle."

"Fine. But it will stabilize. Do you think I came to Sarasota just to dabble in politics?" he asked contemptuously. "I came to address the one local problem of true concern to the Camarilla as a whole. To hunt down Dracula. And I promise to catch her in seventy-two hours." The Assembly babbled in excitement. "Will that ease your anxieties?"

Guice blinked. "Ah, yes, I suppose so. *If* you truly can."

"Then let's ring down the curtain on this circus." The giant Kindred wheeled and strode toward the wings.

Caught by surprise again, Guice stared after his departing colleague for a moment, then hastily rapped with his gavel. "The Conclave is adjourned," he said. "Thanks to one and all for your participation."

The remaining vampires began to exit the stage. Elliott was eager to catch up with Angus, but when he made it into the shadowy wings and saw Gunter trudging along dispiritedly just a few feet away, he decided to confront the Malkavian without delay, while he was still demoralized. Employing his supernatural speed and agility, the actor suddenly whirled, rushed the ruddy-cheeked Kindred and grabbed him by the throat, thrusting him against the wall.

"All right," Elliott said, "you've played your little game and discovered how it can blow up in your face. This maneuver tonight was your final ploy. From now on, you're going to forget all about seizing praxis and devote yourself to helping Judy and me defend the domain. Otherwise, I'll destroy you. Is that clear?"

Gunter glared. His fangs began to lengthen, and his muscles bunched. For a moment Elliott thought he was going to have to fight him again. But then the Malkavian lowered his eyes. "All right," he grumbled, "you win. For now. But in a year or two, when the threat is past and if Roger is no better...."

Elliott inspected Gunter's aura. The pale envelope of light glowed dull orange and gray, a mix suggestive of anxiety, dejection and resignation, which seemed to indicate that the Malkavian was sincere. The actor released him and then, seized by an impulse he never would have anticipated, grinned and clasped his shoulder. "I understand. Better luck next time. Let's just hope that there's something left for us to wrangle over. Excuse me, please." As he strode away he could sense Gunter's gaze on his back, but it felt more surprised and speculative than hostile.

As the Toreador exited the backstage area, he was suddenly concerned that Angus might have departed as mysteriously as he'd come. When he reached the gleaming, high-ceilinged white marble lobby, however, he saw that he needn't have worried. Most of the vampires who'd attended the Conclave were milling around chattering, and, frowning, the towering Gangrel was standing in the midst of a circle of elders, many of whom were no doubt eager to curry favor with a Justicar.

Elliott made his way forward against a steady stream of well-wishers, all intent on congratulating him on the Conclave's verdict. He gave everyone a cordial smile, some gracious reply and a firm handshake — God knew, he couldn't afford to alienate anyone who was kindly disposed toward the domain — but he didn't allow anyone to detain him for more than a moment. With his Toreador charm, it was easy to extricate himself from conversations without the other party feeling slighted.

Slipping between a stocky, scar-faced Kindred in a hideous lime-green tuxedo and matching eye patch, and a heavily perfumed female Nosferatu cursed with the snout, ears and tusks of a wild boar, Elliott finally arrived at Angus' side. "I'd like to talk to you privately," he said.

The hirsute giant nodded. "Yes," he said, "I thought you would." He nodded to his circle of sycophants. "Pardon us."

Elliott started to lead him toward one of the offices adjoining the foyer. "No," Angus said. "If you don't mind, let's get outdoors into the clean air."

The actor shrugged and conducted his companion to one of the exits. The night was cool and humid; traffic moaned on the nearby highway. The two vampires walked about fifty feet into the darkness, halting beside a royal palm. "Is this all right?" Elliott asked.

"It's fine," Angus said. He inhaled deeply, taking in the scents of the plants around them.

"Thank you for your help," Elliott said. "But why are you giving it?"

Angus chuckled. "I'm a Justicar. Wouldn't you expect me to have a keen commitment to truth, goodness and the welfare of my Kindred brothers?"

Elliott smiled. "Based on my previous experience with the breed, not necessarily."

"Very astute of you," the shapeshifter said. "To be blunt, I'm not going to tell you how I learned of your problems, or why I took an interest. I'm here, and I'm on your side. That will have to be enough."

"Before my friend Sky died," Elliott persisted, "he hinted that the war we're fighting has aspects we haven't even perceived. He implied that my friends and I are being manipulated like pieces on a chessboard, and that the leader of our enemies is some horrible demon the like of which we've never imagined. At the time, I thought he'd gone mad from the strain of resisting the Blood Bond, but his words have been preying on my mind ever since. I don't suppose you could shed any light on them?"

"If you suspect that you're a chessman," Angus said somberly, "rejoice that you don't know for sure. Perhaps pieces that understand their situation are more useful to the player. Perhaps they're deployed in the most hazardous positions in one game after another."

"You're talking about yourself," Elliott said.

Angus snorted. "Of course not. I was merely responding to your bit of whimsy. I'm oath-bound to the Inner Circle and loyal to them alone, and I'd gut any slanderer who insisted otherwise."

Elliott perceived that Angus had said everything on this particular topic that he was going to. Ergo, despite his own frustrated curiosity, it was time to turn the discussion to more immediate concerns. "Why did you phone me anonymously?" the actor asked in his now-laryngitic whisper. "Why didn't you reveal yourself before?"

"I figured that if you Toreador didn't know I was around," Angus replied, "it was a reasonable bet that Dracula and your other enemies wouldn't either. I wouldn't have spoken out tonight if you hadn't needed me, and I certainly wouldn't have put my reputation on the line by promising to catch the rogue in three days. But the way we thwarted Guice and make him look foolish — and deprived him of a bribe, for all I know — I had to say something bold and dramatic to deter him from running to the Inner Circle as soon as he left the Elysium. Trust me, you don't want those seven ancient ogres overseeing your business, not even the overlord of your own clan. They'd begin by destroying Roger Phillips, just to simplify the political situation here."

Elliott felt a pang of trepidation. "But it wasn't an empty

promise, was it? You obtained Dracula's description, so you must know how to apprehend her, mustn't you?"

Angus grinned, a white flash of teeth in the gloom. "So far," he admitted, "I haven't got a clue."

TWENTY-ONE: THE AVENGER

Perish the Universe, provided I have my revenge.
— Cyrano de Bergerac, "La Mort d'Agrippine"

Malagigi skulked through the shadowy corridors of the derelict office building, trembling with fear and weakness, jumping at shadows, his belly cramping with hunger. His mind was a jumble of rage and despair, and stupidity.

Muddled though his thinking was, the pallid homunculus remembered that he hadn't always been in such a wretched, degraded condition. Only a few days ago he'd been strong and well-nourished, the capacity of his tiny brain augmented by its psychic link to a larger one. He'd been confident of his ability to outfight or outwit any threat the crumbling building could throw at him, and even more certain that Wyatt, his beloved father and master, would always be there to succor him should his own capabilities prove wanting.

But then the unimaginable had happened. The Wicked Man, as Malagigi's creator had called him, had *killed* Wyatt, leaving the homunculus to starve and to fend off the rats which, seeming to sense his feebleness, grew ever more aggressive.

Something rustled in the gloom ahead. Malagigi flattened himself against the baseboard. For a moment his mind was full of terror — and then he felt a surge of desire. Because he knew the rodent he'd heard was full of blood.

He also vaguely sensed that that fact didn't matter, that the animal's vitae wouldn't do him any good. But he couldn't remember why he suspected that, and he was far too famished to wrack his brain for the answer. His throat dry and raw and his stomach aching, his thirst an irresistible compulsion, he stalked forward.

He smelled the rank odor of the rat and then glimpsed its hunched form and long, skinny tail. He broke into a charge and tried to hurl himself on top of it.

Squealing, its beady eyes flaming, the rodent spun around and flung itself at him. They slammed together. Malagigi grabbed hold of it, and then they were rolling across the grimy linoleum, the rat winding up on top of him. Its yellow, chisel-like front teeth gouged at his head. Its clawed feet scrabbled at him, slashing long cuts down his torso.

Desperately, clutching at the animal's matted, flea-infested fur, the homunculus grappled with it, trying to drag himself into position to deliver an effective attack. At last he managed to sink his long, curved fangs — sabertooth-tiger teeth, Wyatt had called them — into his opponent's throat.

Blood gushed out from a punctured artery. The rat went into convulsions and then collapsed to lie twitching on the floor. Its bowels and bladder released, filling the air with the reek of urine and excrement, and its fleas began to hop away from it.

Malagigi guzzled vitae from the wound he'd inflicted. The liquid tasted foul, yet for a moment it eased the fire in his gullet and the hollow ache in his midsection. Then a surge of nausea overwhelmed him, and he vomited the blood back up again. The sickness didn't abate until he'd purged himself of every drop.

Clasping his belly, his wounds ablaze with pain, kneeling in the pool of filth he'd created, he remembered why it had been futile to attack the rat. A homunculus could only feed on his master's blood. Which, since Wyatt was dead, meant that Malagigi was doomed.

Whimpering, the homunculus rose and staggered away from the scene of the battle. His system was too depleted for his wounds to close completely, and he left a trail of blood spatters behind. It would have been easier to stay put, but a recurring compulsion kept drawing him back to the scene of his master's demise.

There wasn't much left there to grieve over. Three Kindred, the other ones Wyatt had thought of as both friends and dupes, to the perpetual bewilderment of Malagigi's straightforward mind, had come and carried the Tremere's bones and treasures away while the homunculus hid in fear. Nothing remained but a sticky stain and the faint smells of gun smoke, vitae and rot, still lingering in the air.

Malagigi slumped down beside the discolored patch of floor. *This is where I'll die*, he thought bleakly. He hesitantly, reverently, touched the tacky edge of the discoloration on the floor.

Gradually, so slowly that at first he wasn't truly conscious of it, he began to feel a sense of presence, a sort of muted echo of the psychic bond that he and his master had once shared. When he noticed what was happening, he peered wildly up and down the hallway, but there was nothing to see.

Malagigi… Wyatt moaned, so faintly that the sound was nearly inaudible. Malagigi looked around again, with the same lack of result. The hairs on the back of his neck stood on end. With mingled awe and grief, he decided that Wyatt hadn't miraculously resurrected himself from the layer of scum on the linoleum. Rather, the homunculus was hearing the voice of a spirit.

"Oh, Wyatt," he said in the staccato chitter that only his master could understand. "Oh, father." Crimson tears dripped from his enormous eyes, mingling with the steady flow of vitae from his wounds.

Avenge us, Wyatt said. *Before you join me in death, you have to kill our murderer.*

Malagigi sobbed. "I want to," he said. "I hate the Wicked Man! But I don't know *how* to hurt him. He stole the gun, and I don't know where he went. I don't even know his *name!*"

Yes, you do, the phantasmal voice replied. *You know everything that I know, even if you don't understand the meaning of it. It's all there, packed away in your skull. Dredge the information out and then give it to Laurie, Felip, and Jimmy Ray.*

As Wyatt spoke the names, the anarchs' faces flickered through Malagigi's mind, and he realized whom his creator was talking about. "No," the homunculus said, "I don't want to. They're the same as the Wicked Man!"

No, they're not, Wyatt answered firmly, *and they're our only chance to get even. Please, if you love me, go to them. Do what I can't.*

"All right," Malagigi promised miserably, and then his sense of Wyatt's presence dwindled away to nothing.

Another type of being might have questioned whether he had actually communicated with his master's ghost at all, might have speculated that pain and the imminence of death had both sharpened his ability to reason and transformed some of his thoughts into hallucinations. But even at his most lucid, the homunculus would have been incapable of that kind of abstract speculation. As far as he was concerned, Wyatt had spoken to him, and he had no choice, or indeed no real desire, but to obey. He dragged himself to his feet and stumbled, zigzagging, down the shadowy hall.

For a minute or two he was afraid that, in his enervated condition, he wouldn't be able to get out of the building. But as he neared the stairs he remembered that the Wicked

Man had broken a window to get in. He should be able to use the same breach to get out.

Unfortunately, when he reached the abandoned dentist's office, he realized the flaw in his plan. The windowsill was about two-and-a-half feet above the floor. At his physical peak Malagigi could have leaped that high easily, or pushed some object under the window to use as a makeshift ladder; but now he wasn't at all certain that he had the strength.

He wondered if he should descend to the ground floor. Perhaps Laurie, Felipe and, and — he realized that the anarchs' names were already fading from his memory — and the Kindred with the sunglasses had broken down a door to gain entrance. But what if they hadn't? What if there was no way out below? Malagigi doubted that he'd have the strength to clamber back up the stairs, either.

He picked his way through the dully gleaming shards of glass on the floor, flexed his knees, and leaped. The convulsive effort ripped a fresh burst of pain through his wounds. His fingers missed the sill by several inches, and he fell heavily back onto the linoleum.

He tried again. This time, to his own surprise, he jumped just high enough to grab a precarious hold with his fingertips. Clutching desperately, shaking with pain and effort, he slowly dragged himself up onto the windowsill. Then, dizzy, he immediately tumbled off the other side.

He fell onto the fire escape with a dull clank. Half-stunned, he lay on the cool, rough, rusty iron surface for a time, gazing blearily up at the stars. His blood seeped through the gaps in the grillwork beneath him. He could hear it plopping on the earth below.

Finally, less because he'd recovered much of his strength than because he felt that if he didn't move soon he never would, he struggled to his feet and blundered down the steps. In a minute he reached the end of them: the point where a human's weight would make a ladder drop on down to the ground.

Malagigi peered over the edge. He was still ten feet up. He knew that ordinarily it wouldn't have been much of a fall for a creature as light and nimble as himself, but in his weakened condition it terrified him. Still, there was no other way. Shuddering, reminding himself that he was doing this for his beloved master, he closed his eyes and, with one lurching motion, hurled himself into space.

The world seemed to vanish for a moment. He supposed it was his awareness that had really disappeared, that the shock of the fall had knocked him unconscious. He felt grateful: better temporary oblivion than another burst of agony. Sprawled in a patch of crabgrass and sand spurs, he tested his limbs and was somewhat surprised to find that they still worked. He stood up, then realized that he couldn't recall where he was supposed to go next.

Fighting panic, he closed his eyes and concentrated as hard as he could. Eventually the image of a derelict garage formed inside his mind. Of course, the anarchs' communal haven! It was just down the street!

Its proximity infused him with a final bit of febrile energy. Panting reflexively though he had no need for air, tripping repeatedly over the bumps and declivities in the ground, he tottered out to the desolate street, then onward toward his goal.

Until something hissed at him.

Nearly losing his balance, Malagigi jerked around to see a crouching calico tomcat with a ragged ear and a stinking pustulant gash on its shoulder regarding him from the shadows. Its tail twitched, then it slunk forward.

The homunculus knew he couldn't defeat it in a fight. He couldn't have bested a second rodent. But he also knew that the animal could run him down effortlessly. So he shrieked and lunged at it, gnashing his oversized fangs and waving his gore-encrusted hands.

The cat halted in its advance, backed up a step, then

wheeled and raced away. No doubt the fact that it had never seen a creature like Malagigi before had served to make his aggressive display more intimidating. Perhaps the feline had even belatedly sensed that it was facing a supernatural entity.

In too much distress to feel even a momentary flush of triumph, Malagigi staggered on. Blessedly, the door to one of the garage's service bays hung a few inches above the concrete floor: perhaps someone had left it open for ventilation. When the homunculus slipped under it and skulked on past Wyatt's green van, he saw that the door leading into the office area was ajar as well. Voices murmured from the dimly lit hallway beyond.

He crept down the corridor and peeked through a doorway into what had once been a waiting room. Three glum-looking Kindred — one in sunglasses, one with a thin black mustache and gleaming gold chains around his neck, and a brunette girl in bellbottoms and a fringed buckskin jacket — were seated inside. For a moment, Malagigi knew their faces but not their names, and then those came back to him. Jimmy Ray, Felipe, and Laurie. Still intent on fulfilling Wyatt's last wishes, yet, despite himself, wary of people whom his master had considered a potential threat as well as allies, the homunculus paused to study them.

"I'm not going to spend my whole life hanging around in this dump, waiting for some honcho from the Movement to contact us," Jimmy Ray said. Irritation made the country twang in his voice more pronounced.

"Don't you care about liberation anymore?" Laurie asked, glaring at him. "Don't you care that Wyatt's dead and Dan's disappeared?"

Slumped in a chair in the corner, using a coffee table heaped with old magazines for a footstool, Felipe hefted the object that had been resting in his lap. It was Wyatt's ancient grimoire; the pages that had broken free of the binding had been carelessly stuck back inside. "Wyatt was a Tremere," the Hispanic vampire said.

"You don't know that," Laurie said. "You can't read that book. You don't know what it means."

Felipe rolled his eyes. "Give me a break. Doesn't it look like a book of magic to you?" He set it down and picked up Wyatt's notebook. "And this is more of the same, in our fearless leader's own handwriting."

Laurie grimaced. "All right, maybe he was a Tremere. A Warlock *could* defect to the Movement, couldn't he?"

Jimmy Ray shrugged. "Hell, I don't know. But I do know that he lied to us."

"Because," she replied, "he knew that if he told you the truth, you wouldn't trust him."

"And maybe that would have been pretty smart on my part," said Jimmy Ray. "Look, don't get me wrong. I don't want to think bad stuff about Wyatt. I liked him. I care that he's dead, and if Dan didn't just run out on us, I care that something's happened to him, too. But I'll be damned if I know what to do about any of it."

If, despite their suspicions, the anarchs still cared about Wyatt, then they were indeed his one hope for revenge. Malagigi tried to walk into the room.

Suddenly going numb, his leg gave way beneath him, dumping him on the floor. Though he was now sprawled in the doorway, the three Kindred talked on, oblivious to his presence. In the gloom, he was too small for them to notice.

He tried to drag himself to his feet, but discovered that he lacked the strength. His thoughts and memories were crumbling into confusion again. Black spots swam at the corners of his vision, and he could feel death sucking at him like a whirlpool, relentlessly striving to pull him down.

It mustn't end this way! He had to fulfill his master's last request, and that meant that somehow, he had to fend off annihilation for at least a few more minutes. He had to replenish his strength, and he could only think of one even remotely possible means of doing so.

He tried to chitter to attract the anarchs' attention, but

found that pain and weakness had clogged his throat. And thus he had no recourse but to crawl, leaving a trail of vitae like the track of a snail.

He blacked out twice on his way across the waiting room, terrified each time that he'd never wake up. But he did, and finally he made it to Laurie's foot. Clutching at her sneaker, he hauled his upper body high enough to bite her on the ankle.

As soon as his fangs pricked her, she squealed and kicked. The sudden motion hurled him two feet away. He slammed down on his back and lay inert, now too feeble to stir at all.

The vampires approached and knelt around him, peering down. "Damn," said Felipe, curiosity and loathing mingled in his voice, "what *is* it?"

"I don't know," Jimmy Ray answered, "but it's sure nasty-looking, and torn to shit to boot."

Gingerly, as though afraid Malagigi might try to bite her again, Laurie nudged him with her fingertips. The homunculus' head lolled in her direction, and she gasped. "It has *Wyatt's* face!" she exclaimed.

"You've got to be kidding," said Jimmy Ray.

"Just look at it," she said. "It must have been his what-do-you-call-it, his *familiar*. And I think it needs vitae, just like we do."

Felipe shrugged. "T. S. for it."

"No," said Laurie, "Wyatt wouldn't want us to let it die." She extended her fangs and ripped a gash in the heel of her hand. Aromatic vampire blood welled out.

"I know that you loved Wyatt," said Felipe, "but what you're about to do is just plain nuts. You don't know where that creature has been or what kind of magic cooties it's carrying." Ignoring him, she picked up Malagigi and pressed his face against her self-inflicted wound. Her companions cringed in disgust.

At first the homunculus was too weak even to suck the

flowing blood, but a little trickled into his mouth anyway. And gradually, new strength began to seep into his tortured limbs.

It wasn't like the vitality he'd derived from Wyatt's vitae, nor was it accompanied by any sense of well-being. His flesh felt fiery hot, vibrant, as if he were shaking violently on the inside. Yet despite its toxic qualities, Laurie's blood was far more akin to his master's vitae than that of the rat had been. He was able to keep it down, and, like an overdose of amphetamines, it was giving him a final burst of energy before it killed him.

When he'd gulped his fill, he looked up at his benefactress, and a sudden wave of panic swept over him. Now that he was here, how was he supposed to communicate with her? For a moment he had no idea at all.

Then he recalled that Wyatt had said that everything he'd ever learned had left an echo somewhere in Malagigi's brain. The homunculus just had to tap into it. He concentrated, straining, and after a few seconds the answer came to him.

Gazing beseechingly at Laurie, Malagigi pointed at the floor. She got the idea and set him down. Felipe and Jimmy Ray shifted their feet, evidently poising themselves to stamp on him if he did anything they didn't like.

Malagigi stuck his finger into one of the open wounds on his chest. Ignoring the resultant jab of pain, he crouched and began to scrawl crude block capital letters on the floor with his own blood.

He prayed that he was writing coherently. He'd never tried before. It had never occurred to him that he could. When he finished and Laurie read, "Dan kill," he felt a swell of joy.

"Somebody killed Dan?" asked Felipe, frowning. The homunculus impatiently shook his head.

"Dan killed Wyatt?" asked Laurie. Malagigi nodded

violently, and the petite brown-haired vampire looked stricken. "My God! He was our *friend!* Why would he do that?"

Even if the homunculus had been capable of explaining, a sudden paroxysm of agony alerted him that he didn't have time. When the pain eased, he dipped his finger in his own blood once again and then wrote ten numbers.

As soon as he'd inscribed the final character, he collapsed beside his handiwork. Finally releasing his hold on his little life, he soared into the dark to seek his father.

TWENTY-TWO: MISGIVINGS

Care
Sat on his faded cheek.
— John Milton, *Paradise Lost*

Sebastian Durrell peered up and down the length of nondescript concrete-block corridor and then, seeing no one, reached for the invisible door. As usual, he hesitated just before he touched it.

On occasion, he'd tried to find some humor in the security arrangements of his secret partner, Timothy Baxter. Durrell and his clanmates had a complex tunnel system underlying the amusement park, to which only they and their kine servants were granted access. Concealed in the middle of that was a Tremere communal haven, the chantry in which he was presently standing. And beneath *that* was the hidden lair of whose existence only he and its occupant were aware, a warren created in an instant by sorceries that Durrell didn't pretend to understand. Secrets nested in secrets like a chain of Chinese boxes. It ought to have seemed absurd, a droll comment on the paranoia generated by the Kindred way of life.

Yet try as he might, Durrell couldn't summon even a flicker of amusement. The shadows in the catacombs he was about to enter were too black even for a vampire's liking, the dank air too vibrant with spells and forces that set even a Tremere's teeth on edge, particularly now that the plan seemed to be going awry. And yet, for that very reason, he didn't feel he could put his visit off. Grimacing, he pressed his palm against the surface before him.

What appeared to be and felt like a cold, solid, off-white wall crawled under his hand like the hide of a horse. According to Timothy, the entrance was *tasting* him and so confirming his identity. A thin outline of green light shone around the door, and the Tremere elder pushed it open.

Beyond the threshold, a splintery, rickety wooden staircase descended into a different world: a maze of tunnels so roughly excavated that they looked almost natural, smelling of loam and illuminated by a sourceless viridian phosphorescence. Somewhere in the midst of it water dripped, the echoing *plink* a reminder that the warren shouldn't exist. The water table was too high in the Florida peninsula for anyone to carve out passages underground unless he had access to modern construction techniques or the ancient secrets of the Nosferatu. Durrell occasionally wondered if the place existed in a dream, or on another level of reality. It felt like it.

He hurried down the steps and onward. After ten strides his patent-leather loafers were encrusted with muck. A small creature, something he couldn't see clearly despite his inhumanly keen vision, scuttled out of his path and squirmed through a narrow crevice in the wall.

After Durrell had made the first couple of turns, the nagging suspicion that he'd lost his way began to plague him. He firmly reminded himself that he had felt that way every time he ventured down here, and it had never turned out to be so.

The dripping sound grew louder, and now he could tell

that the source was ahead of him. Suddenly he caught the rich scent of human vitae, and, though he'd fed only last night, for a moment he quivered and his fangs ached in their sockets. Perhaps he wasn't hearing falling *water* after all.

Rounding a final corner, he beheld the cavernous chamber which, as near as he could make out, was the only part of the complex in which Timothy spent any time. Why the Methuselah had bothered to create the rest of it was only one of the many mysteries that surrounded him. In the exact center of the room floated the pudgy, sunburned corpse of a tourist clad in a garish Hawaiian shirt, tan Dockers, brown sandals and black socks, dangling head-down like a slaughtered hog. A few last drops of vitae were seeping from the gash in his throat. No doubt Timothy had seized the kine in the theme park. The manner in which he departed and returned to his catacombs without seeming to traverse the tunnel system above was also an enigma to Durrell.

Timothy was kneeling beside the drying pool of gore beneath his victim. His nude, muscular form looked as inhumanly perfect as ever, with golden skin utterly unlike the alabaster pallor of the average Kindred. Though ordinarily little affected by the glamors spun by his fellow vampires, Durrell had had to learn not to gaze directly at the Methuselah for too long, lest he start to tremble with adoration and terror.

Timothy flowed to his feet. "A waste of time," he grumbled, his bass voice musical despite his irritation.

"What was?" Durrell asked.

"The divination," Timothy said. He nodded at the pool of blood, and Durrell realized he'd been using it to scry. "I didn't learn anything that I really wanted to know." He waved his hand and, behind him, both the vitae and the levitated cadaver vanished in a burst of azure flame. The ancient vampire was standing less than a yard away from the blast, but it didn't appear to bother him, even though

Durrell could feel the flare of heat all the way across the chamber.

Durrell took a deep breath to steady himself. "The Conclave didn't work out," he said, walking nearer. "It wound up confirming Sinclair's right to serve as Phillips' regent, at least for the moment."

Timothy sighed like a father whose child has brought home a bad report card. "I thought you assured me that Guice was in Duane's debt, and that Duane wanted our friend Velasquez to assume the rule of Sarasota."

"And I was right," Durrell replied. The ambient green phosphorescence faded for a moment, then glowed brighter again. "But Angus, that Gangrel Justicar, showed up —"

"Angus!" The Methuselah's mouth curved upward in what an observer with perceptions less acute that Durrell's might have mistaken for an affectionate smile. "Well of course he turned up! How is he?"

"All right, I suppose," Durrell replied warily. He didn't understand Timothy's reaction, and as usual, that made him edgy. "I gather you know him?"

Timothy's smile grew wider. "We had dealings, once upon a time. You were about to tell me that Guice and Angus deadlocked on a verdict."

"Yes," said Durrell, "so I used the alternate plan, the spell you taught me. But Sinclair came through the psychic assault with his mind intact."

"Ah well," said Timothy, waving a dismissive hand, "I'm sure you did your best. It's only a temporary setback." For an instant the smell of lilacs filled the air, and Durrell thought he felt ghostly fingers toying with the hair on the back of his head. Then the sensations ended as abruptly, and as randomly, as they'd begun.

"Guice did make noises about carrying the whole matter of the regency to the Inner Circle," said Durrell, "and to put him off, Angus promised to catch Dracula in seventy-two hours."

"And I think we both know how likely *that* is," the Methuselah said. He reached out to clasp Durrell's shoulder. The younger vampire simultaneously craved the contact and felt an impulse to cringe from it. "From your hangdog demeanor, I had thought the Conclave was an unmitigated disaster. But that isn't so at all. The wolf and his allies will lose a great deal of credibility when he fails, and then we'll oust them in the *next* Assembly."

Durrell shook his head reflectively. "I hope so. Meanwhile, there's more bad news. Wyatt Vandercar is dead. A Caitiff whom he recruited into his supposed circle of anarchs killed him and then disappeared. I know this because, bizarrely enough, Wyatt's homunculus gave our phone number to one of his other pawns, and she called us."

"That is remarkable behavior for a familiar," said Timothy. "It's too bad the little creature is doomed, if it isn't dead already. Dare I hope that whoever picked up the phone managed to preserve the fiction that Wyatt was a *rogue* Tremere, and this citadel is an enclave of his fellow rebels?"

Durrell felt a twinge of anger at the condescension in the older vampire's tone, but he was careful not to let his feelings show. "Yes. We kept up the pretense. Evidently she was quite fond of Wyatt. She very much wants to believe that he dealt with her honestly."

"Does she know *why* the Caitiff killed Wyatt?"

"No. She speculated that he was an 'enemy agent.'"

"And perhaps she was right. Bring her here. Her comrades too, if they're equally trusting. They can keep watch for the assassin, just in case he finds his way to the park."

Durrell blinked. "Do you think that's wise? Won't they catch on to the fact that this is a Tremere enclave?"

Timothy shrugged. "I don't see why they should, if you and your people manage them properly. Have someone with the appropriate talent charm them, the way Wyatt evidently did. If they do tumble to the fact that you're all magi, you might try selling them on the lie that, in reality, the Tremere support the Anarch Movement. All the tales suggesting otherwise are merely a smoke screen."

Durrell shook his head. "They'd never believe that."

"Then bring them down to me. I do have to feed, and it will save me the trouble of hunting."

Durrell felt a chill ooze up his spine, well aware that Kindred of his companion's age could only survive by diablerie. It was one reason among many why he strove to treat Timothy with respect. "I just wonder if this Caitiff is important enough to risk bringing outsiders into the base."

"He could become so," Timothy said. "I can sense it."

Sighing, Durrell gave up the argument. "Then we'll bring them. You realize that Wyatt left the geomantic survey uncompleted. I suppose I can send other scouts into Sarasota —"

Timothy shook his head. "No. The Toreador and their allies are on their guard now. I doubt that we'd achieve anything but the loss of valuable troops."

"*You* could go. Sinclair's people couldn't stop you."

The Methuselah grinned. "Whence comes this egalitarian spirit? Neither of us is going to go. We're too valuable. It's our role to conceive the strategies and our underlings' roles to carry them out. Ultimately it doesn't matter if we can't lay a curse on all of Sarasota. If we don't destroy the Toreador that way, we'll annihilate them through one of our other schemes."

Durrell grimaced. "I hope so."

Timothy lifted an eyebrow. "You sound unconvinced."

"Sinclair was supposed to turn out to be an inept leader, or even to refuse to lead at all. Instead, he's coping rather well. We thought that the Toreador would be thoroughly demoralized by now, yet that hasn't happened either. Perhaps nothing will work out as we planned. Perhaps you should have picked an easier target."

"I chose the only possible target," Timothy replied.

Durrell wished he understood what the older vampire meant by that, but he knew from past experience that Timothy wouldn't explain his goals and motives any further. "I do have faith in you, and in my own people as well. I suppose I worry because I launched this dirty, unprovoked war without my Lord's knowledge or permission. She thinks I'm sitting home in Kentucky — if she finds out otherwise, she'll haul me up in front of a tribunal. And then what will I say, that I turned my back on the policies and chain of command of my clan at the behest of an outsider and a Methuselah? I might as well cut off my own head and be done with it."

"But Lady Wetherill won't find out," said Timothy with such utter conviction that, even understanding the nature of the Methuselah's charismatic powers, Durrell couldn't help feeling a shade less anxious. "Soon, one way or another, long before she misses you, Sarasota will fall. All of our servants, witting or not, will share in the plunder, and I'll instruct you in the mysteries of *Al Azif*."

Durrell nodded somberly. *Al Azif*. That was the carrot Timothy had dangled in front of his nose at their first meeting, to lure him into committing himself and his subordinates to a desperate and illicit venture. In spite of the fact that the conquest of Roger Phillips' domain had begun to look like a protracted and deadly dangerous business, the bribe still seemed just as enticing today.

The volume in question, a legendary grimoire penned by a mad medieval visionary known as Abd al-Azrad, was allegedly the key to a magic more potent than even the greatest secrets of Clan Tremere. Durrell had stumbled on a badly damaged copy nearly a hundred years ago and had been obsessed with it ever since. At times, his mind reeling after hours of intensive study of the paradoxical syllogisms, cryptic ramblings, and apocalyptic prophecies that made up the surviving text, he could *feel* the power blazing from every tattered, worm-eaten vellum page, but he'd never discovered how to command it.

Somehow recognizing the Tremere's fascination with the old book, Timothy had claimed to understand its arcana, and, given the uncanny powers the Methuselah commanded, Durrell believed him. When Timothy had offered to share them in exchange for the younger vampire's aid, Durrell had seized the opportunity with an uncharacteristic recklessness.

"Besides," Timothy continued lightly, "I know you have more honor that to walk out on me now, after you've given me your word. I'd be quite upset with you if you did."

Sighing, Durrell nodded. "Don't worry, you can count on me." If *Al Azif* was the carrot, here was the stick. Though the Tremere was more than a match for most foes, he was realistic enough to comprehend that , he'd have no chance at all against a Kindred as old as Timothy. And that his ally — master, now, really, if the truth were told — wouldn't think twice about slaying him if he ever broke their covenant.

The old proverb was true. Having elected to ride the tiger, he didn't dare dismount.

TWENTY-THREE: DEDUCTION

Logic, n. *The art of thinking and reasoning in strict accordance with the limitations and incapacities of the human understanding.*
— Ambrose Bierce, *The Devil's Dictionary*

Frowning, Gunter circled Roger's desk, glaring down at Judy's marked-up map of Sarasota and its environs. Seated in one of the shabby but comfortable leather chairs, Elliott thought that the Malkavian looked as if he were eager to find fault with the patrol routes and schedules the former slave had made. Judging by Judy's pugnacious scowl, she suspected the same thing.

At last Gunter lifted his ruddy face. "I can't see anything that I would have done any differently," he said grudgingly. Judy's dark eyes widened in momentary surprise. For an instant, the sound of Roger's voice, screaming threats and obscenities, penetrated the study door. Elliott's sire was enduring another bad night without the benefit of sedation. Lionel Potter had decided that the drugs might be doing more harm than good.

"I couldn't improve on the arrangements, either," Elliott said, tugging the end of his shirt cuff beyond the sleeve of his jacket. "So why haven't our people caught up with Dracula?"

"Because she can turn invisible," Judy said, "like a Malkavian."

Gunter glowered at her. "*Or* a Nosferatu," he said. "Or like some others I've known, even one or two of you Rabble."

Afraid that his fellow elders were about to begin a protracted argument, Elliott raised his hand. "Let's not go down this road again," he said. "We don't have time. We all agreed that *none* of our people could be Dracula. Everyone has a solid alibi for one or more of the murders."

"Right," Angus rumbled. The Gangrel was sprawled on the couch beside the model of the Globe Theatre. His huge frame made the office seem cramped and fragile, as if he might knock down a wall simply by shifting his shoulders. Claiming that the release from confinement would help him think, he'd stripped off his suit coat and tie. Shoes and socks had also come off, to reveal a pair of large, callused and extraordinarily hairy feet. Photographs and computer print-outs, copies of the pictures and documents that the police and now the FBI were using in their investigation, lay scattered all around him. "And maybe we shouldn't get too caught up in the idea that we're chasing an invisible Kindred, either."

Puzzled, Elliott cocked his head. "Why do you say that? Isn't that the most plausible explanation for why we've never found her?"

"Not necessarily," Angus replied. The door opened and Lazlo stepped inside, carrying a silver tray loaded with fragrant Cuban cigars and a lighter. Elliott could tell from the human's lack of expression and downcast eyes that he'd reverted to the role of unobtrusive, deferential servant, the face he generally presented to unfamiliar Kindred like the Justicar.

Angus waved Lazlo over and selected a long, almost-black maduro Lonsdale. Nodding his thanks to the mortal, he lit the Havana and took a puff. "Not bad," he said. "You know, smoking's a dirty habit, but, aside from torture, it's the only vice that we can enjoy in precisely the same manner as the kine. I suspect that's why even a lot of old-timers like me, undead centuries before tobacco was imported to the Old World, take up the practice. Of course, it also helps you to convince the mortals you're breathing."

Elliott had noticed that, while Angus might look and often behave like a taciturn barbarian warrior, when discussing the Dracula murders he sometimes slipped into a leisurely, expansive mode of discourse reminiscent of Nero Wolfe and certain other Great Detectives of fiction. The Toreador hadn't been able to make up his mind whether the phenomenon merely reflected another facet of the Justicar's personality or was a conscious affectation. Half-irked and half-amused by his mysterious new ally's latest digression, he said, "You were talking about the killer being invisible."

"So I was," said Angus. Lazlo finished passing out cigars and took up a position by the door. Evidently he meant to listen to the discussion. "A few of Judy's Brujah have keen senses, and several of Gunter's more psychic Malkavians have joined the patrols. The sentries I posted — bats, owls and rats — are similarly perceptive. You'd think that someone would have caught a glimpse of even an invisible Kindred."

Judy grimaced around her cheroot. "Then what's the answer?" she asked.

"I don't know yet," Angus replied.

Elliott realized that, his superhuman vitality notwithstanding, the long, fruitless examination of the evidence had left him feeling immensely weary. *We're not going to make it*, he thought glumly. *Everybody's tried so har, and coped with so many problems, but this Dracula business is going to break us*. Scowling, he tried to push the despairing notion away.

At the front of the room, Lazlo stood studying the map. Gunter in turn regarded him with a slight sneer. "And what do *you* think, human?" he asked mockingly. "See anything that your masters have missed?"

"No," the valet replied. "I was just thinking that it's like Dracula has a hidden path through the city. A way of getting from place to place that our patrols never even check, because it hasn't occurred to us that it exists. If Sarasota had subways, or Nosferatu tunnels, or a sewer system with pipes a person could walk through — but it doesn't."

"Actually," rumbled Angus, "my rats have been checking the sewers just in case, though I can't imagine Dracula crawling and swimming through miles of filth to get around. But I agree with you — what was your name?"

"Lazlo," the dresser said.

"I agree with you, Lazlo. The rogue is evading us by using some secret highway, or, at any rate, one clever trick that we haven't begun to figure out." Abruptly Angus frowned, his eyes narrowing thoughtfully. He grabbed a stack of computer printouts and started flipping through them.

"What?" Judy demanded. "You have an idea. What is it?"

Instead of explaining, the Gangrel tore loose a number of sheets and proffered them to his fellow Kindred. "Look at the estimated times of death," he said.

Though he'd already pored over every page of the files the police had assembled, Elliott took some of the autopsy reports and began glancing through them again. Citing factors such as body temperature, skin discoloration, degree of rigor mortis, flattening of the eyes from loss of fluid, and the presence of green-fly eggs, each document specified a range of time, generally from four to six hours, during which the murder had occurred. Evidently, as the Toreador had always understood, forensic medicine couldn't determine an exact time of death: too many factors influenced the rate at which postmortem changes occurred.

Try as he might, Elliott couldn't see what Angus was driving at. "Dracula kills late at night," he said at last. "We'd realized that already."

"We *assumed* as much," the Justicar replied. "Since the murdered policemen were in radio communication with their dispatcher, we know that the aquarium killings did indeed happen at night. That, of course, was before you started hunting Dracula, when it was safe for her to operate by dark. It was even useful, given that her purpose was to endanger the Masquerade. But more recently, if your local coroner knows his stuff, the killer could just as easily be striking in the wee small hours *of the morning.*"

Perplexed, Elliott cocked his head. "Do you mean, after sunrise?"

Angus nodded. "That would explain why the patrols never run into her, wouldn't it? By the time she ventures forth, your people are already asleep in their havens, and my nocturnal animals have retired to their lairs."

"But that's preposterous!" Gunter exploded. "Dracula needs to sleep during the day also."

"I agree," Judy said. "I've known Kindred to stay awake for a single day, when they had a good enough reason. You can do it if you have a lot of willpower and stamina. But Dracula's been killing steadily for weeks. Nobody could keep it up for that long."

Angus smiled. "That's the *other* assumption we made, without ever really examining it. That Dracula is a Kindred."

"But she must be!" Judy said. "The corpses of her victims are drained of blood. I made Potter look at some of the bite wounds, and he was sure they were made by vampire fangs. Hell, *you* said the same thing. And the way she can pick off any kine she wants, no matter how many locks or alarm systems are in her way, shows that she has supernatural powers." She hesitated. "Doesn't it?"

"We aren't the only creatures in the world with mystical abilities," the Justicar replied. "And human ingenuity can accomplish amazing things, even when it only has natural tools to work with. I think that some non-Kindred ally of your principal enemies is doing a brilliant job of *faking* vampire attacks."

Elliott pondered Angus' ideas. They seemed plausible if not conclusive. He felt an odd mix of hope and frustration. He desperately wanted the bearded giant to figure out Dracula's *modus operandi*. Somebody had to, before the Kindred of Sarasota ran out of time and Palmer Guice presented the domain's failure to the Inner Circle. And yet, if Angus was right about the murderer, Elliott couldn't imagine how he and his allies were going to stop her. To him, the daylight hours seemed scarcely more accessible or endurable than the surface of the planet Mercury. The mere thought of trying to remain active after dawn, of risking exposure to the sun's lethal glare, filled him with an instinctive loathing. "If you're right," he said, "I guess our only chance is to send the ghouls out on patrol."

Angus shook his head. "If the cops can't catch Dracula, they couldn't, either. *I'll* catch her. I've stayed up past dawn a time or two myself. I can do it again. I'll put the birds and beasts of the day on sentry duty, and when they find her, I'll go get her."

"How?" asked Gunter skeptically. "You'll burn as soon as you stick your head out the door."

"I hope not," Angus said. "I'm tough. Tough enough even to bear the bite of the sun, if I take precautions. It's a Gangrel trait."

"It's one of my traits, too," Judy said. Her voice was as brash as usual, though Elliott thought he saw an uncharacteristic hint of disquiet in her eyes. "You won't be anywhere near as powerful by day as you are by night. You're going to need help, so I'll sit up with you."

Angus gave her an approving nod. "So be it. Even though it will mean the sun is brighter, let's hope for blue skies. After centuries of black ones, the spectacle is worth the added discomfort."

Elliott took a deep breath and let it out slowly, trying to dissolve the tension in his muscles. "I'll help, too," he said.

"No, you won't," Angus said. "You *don't* have the kind of hardiness it takes to endure the sun." Feeling a guilty relief at being let off the hook, Elliott wondered how the older vampire could be so sure about his limitations. "Besides, you and the Malkavian will be needed to direct all the other aspects of the defense. Remember, you've got plenty of other problems to keep you occupied."

"I'm not as tough as a Gangrel or a Brujah, either," Lazlo said quietly. "But I can stand the sun, I know how to shoot, and I've been around the Kindred long enough not to lose my head when someone does something dangerous or uncanny. I'll join the hunting party, if I may. I'd like a chance to strike back at the people who hurt Roger."

Gunter snorted, manifestly contemptuous of the notion that the stooped, aging mortal had anything to contribute. But Angus studied Lazlo for a moment, then said, "Very well." He turned to Judy. "Keep the nighttime patrols operating, in case our theory is wrong. And go feed. Gorge yourself. You're going to need the strength."

TWENTY-FOUR: CAMELOT

I'm not frightened of the darkness outside. It's the
darkness inside houses I don't like.
— Shelagh Delaney, *A Taste of Honey*

Even in the crowded, brightly illuminated theme park, one could find pockets of quiet and shadow: odd spaces between the rides, snack kiosks and gift shops where there was nothing to see or buy and mortals strode by without lingering. That was where the entrances to the service corridors were generally located. Trusting in his limited powers of invisibility to keep him hidden, Dan was lurking in one such area. A black wall, the rear of Mordred's Haunted Castle, towered at his back, while an artificial lagoon, apparently supposed to be the Lady of the Lake's lake, gleamed and rippled beyond a low brick wall just a few feet away. With his superhuman hearing, he could hear the squeals and laughter of the tourists inside the glorified spook house as clearly as the roar of the power boats participating in the stunt show on the water. At the moment, the balmy evening air smelled of hot dogs, buttered popcorn, exhaust and human sweat.

Dan hadn't learned anything by searching Wyatt's apartment. The experience had merely triggered another wave of regret, leading him to suspect that, irrational though it might be, the remorse he felt over killing the other Kindred was likely to stick with him for a long time. Afterward, he'd been eager to stake out Camelot. He'd hoped that playing spy in the colossal tourist trap, an amusement park as big as Disney World, Universal, or any of Orlando's other stellar attractions, would take his mind off his troubles.

To some extent it had, but so far that was about the only thing he'd accomplished. Using Wyatt's scarlet key card, he'd penetrated the miles of brightly lit, antiseptic-looking tunnels that underlay the park. There he'd discovered employee offices, cafeterias, restrooms and lounges. Whirring electric golf carts whisking staff and cargo to and fro. Machine shops. Storerooms full of tinned food, carbonated-drink canisters, costumes, half-assembled audioanimatronic robots and dismantled floats from discontinued street parades. He suspected that, unless he was dead wrong about the park being connected to the war against Melpomene and Sarasota, an enemy base lay hidden down there too; but he hadn't been able to find it. The complex was simply too large.

Twice during his explorations aboveground, once near the ten-story Firedrake roller coaster and once while lounging outside the Round Table Burger Bar and Pizzeria, he'd glimpsed other Kindred gliding through the crowd, identifiable by their alabaster pallor and the silence of their hearts. Though they might have come to the park merely to hunt, or for diversion, it seemed far more likely that they were enemies. Fearful of discovery, he'd given them a wide berth. But now, frustrated by his lack of investigative progress, he'd decided that his best hope of completing his mission was to shadow another vampire. With luck, the guy would lead him to enemy headquarters, and if he didn't, well, maybe Dan could jump him and beat some answers out of him.

Around the corner, soft footsteps scuffed along the pavement, unaccompanied by the hiss of respiration or the muffled thud of a heartbeat. Tensing, Dan willed himself to stand absolutely motionless. A moment later, a long-legged, brown-haired Kindred wearing jeans, a white shirt with sleeves rolled to the elbow and a black leather vest strode into view. His pale skin was slightly tinged with pink, as if he'd fed recently, and the faint scent of vitae still clung to him.

He marched past Dan without a glance, pulled a red card like Wyatt's out of his pocket, and dragged it through the electronic lock mounted on the wall. The door clicked and lurched ajar. The Kindred in the vest went through and pulled it shut behind him.

Dan swallowed. It seemed mad to follow the other undead too closely. As soon as he moved, his shroud of invisibility would dissolve, and, down in the bare, well-lit tunnels, he was unlikely to find the cover or patches of shadows necessary to recreate it. Moreover, it was a good bet that the guy in the vest was Tremere, a member of a bloodline as renowned for keen senses as the Toreador and Malkavians. But Dan was all but certain that if he *didn't* follow closely, he'd lose his quarry in the frequently branching service corridors. Feeling like the most reckless fool on earth, he waited only a moment before scuttling to the door and unlocking it himself.

As he'd previously discovered, it opened on a set of concrete stairs not unlike those he'd found in Wyatt's derelict office building. His quarry's footsteps clicked and squeaked from below. Dan paused and listened for an instant to make sure they sounded like they were still going downward, then crept after them.

By the time he reached the bottom of the staircase, the vampire in the vest had passed through another door. Cracking it open, Dan saw him striding down a corridor with doors and openings on the right-hand wall.

Dan kept following, trying to move silently without appearing as if he were sneaking. If the other Kindred did turn around and spot him, he wanted to look as if he had legitimate business in the tunnels. To that end, he kept the scarlet card sticking out of his breast pocket. With luck, it would help convince at least any mortal observer that he belonged down here.

Dan's nerves seemed to thrum with tension. Trying to alleviate the excruciating anxiety, he assured himself that he was going to get away with this idiot plan. The Kindred in the vest obviously *didn't* hear him. Either the guy didn't possess superhuman senses, or he was preoccupied. And at least there were no security cameras in the tunnels. Dan had noticed some topside and made a point of avoiding them, but apparently the builders hadn't considered them necessary for the parts of the facility the public never saw.

Eventually his jitters grew slightly less severe. Then a stocky, balding, middle-aged mortal in grease-stained blue coveralls stepped out of a branching tunnel just in front of him. Smiling, the human opened his mouth to speak.

Judging from his expression, the mechanic only wanted to be friendly, but Dan couldn't afford to let him say anything. The other Kindred would surely hear and probably glance backward. Dan lunged at the human, grabbed him by the throat, hoisted him into the air, and squeezed.

For a moment the mechanic clawed feebly at Dan's forearms, then shuddered and dangled limply. His heart stopped thumping, and he began to smell of feces.

Dan winced. He hadn't wanted to kill the guy, just choke him unconscious. But, still not quite used to the extra strength that Melpomene's blood had given him, he'd evidently crushed the mechanic's windpipe or pulverized the top of his spinal cord.

Scowling, the vampire tried to push his remorse aside. His victim was only a kine — a member of a different species, just as Wyatt had said — and in any case Dan didn't have time for guilt. He couldn't lug the corpse along with him, nor would it be safe to leave it sitting out in the open. He had to stash it somewhere quickly, before the Kindred in the vest — fortunately still unaware of the lightning-fast, silent murder that had occurred just a few yards behind him — got away.

Carrying the dead man in his arms, Dan stalked to the next door along the wall. He couldn't hear anything moving on the other side, so he tested the knob and found it unlocked. Hoping that he wasn't about to walk in on a room full of people, he eased it open.

Beyond the threshold was a shadowy storeroom stacked with cardboard boxes. Some had been opened, revealing bundles of postcards, T-shirts stenciled with the Camelot logo, silvery plastic broadswords and plumed, visored helmets, and other samples of the merchandise sold in the gift shops and souvenir stands overhead.

Dan dumped the mechanic behind a heap of cartons in the far corner, where no one peering in from the doorway could see him. Grateful to have resolved at least this one problem so expeditiously, he hurried back to the door, peeked out, and then cursed under his breath. Because the Kindred in the vest had disappeared.

Fighting panic, Dan reminded himself that his quarry had only been out of his sight for a moment. Surely he could find him again. In all probability the guy had turned down that side passage about fifty feet ahead. Moving faster now, less worried about being quiet than catching up, Dan strode to the opening and around the corner.

The long, straight passage before him was empty.

He scowled. Evidently his quarry had vanished through a door, either one of the few between the storeroom and the intersection of the hallways or one of the several immediately ahead. But by the time Dan peeked through them all, the Kindred in the vest might well have disappeared for good through a second door or around another bend.

Which meant that it was time for a different approach. Time to put his new perceptual powers to work. Closing his eyes, trying to sharpen his sense of smell through sheer force of will, Dan inhaled deeply.

And after a moment, he smiled. Because the sweet scent of vitae, the faint odor that he'd detected emanating from the other Kindred, still hung in the dry, cool, climate-controlled air.

Its presence proved that Dan's quarry had come as far as this intersection. Sniffing like a bloodhound, reflecting fleetingly that he probably looked pretty silly, the spy followed the scent down the branching passage.

But after a few moments he faltered, because the trail ended abruptly amid blank walls. Either his quarry had backtracked, which seemed unlikely, or he'd ducked through a *hidden* door.

Crouching, Dan sniffed the smooth gray concrete floor and then the painted off-white walls, trying to find the exact point where the other vampire had exited the hallway, or the spot where he'd pushed some hidden button. He couldn't: even his nose had its limitations. Staring intently, straining now to sharpen his eyes, he began to give the site a visual inspection.

After a moment, peering at the wall, he began to see countless subtle shadings in what had seemed an even, monochromatic layer of paint. Simultaneously, he became acutely aware of the pockmarks in the surface of the concrete blocks. The bands of grayish white and the tiny cavities combined to form complex patterns, like fractal art generated by a computer.

Viewed properly, the designs were amazingly beautiful. So beautiful, he realized abruptly, that they were hypnotizing him like the murdered painter's jungle scene. Snarling, Dan squinched his eyes shut and wrenched his head to the side.

He simply stood for a few seconds, trembling, imagining what might appen if some of the enemy discovered him standing paralyzed with fascination. Finally, when some indefinable change inside his head told him that he might be out of danger, he peeked at the wall through slitted eyes. Though he continued to see it more clearly than any mortal could, it was once more just a nondescript, indeed a rather homely, piece of masonry.

Monitoring himself, lest he fall under the same spell again, he kept looking around. And finally he spotted a pale gray shadow, five feet up the left-hand wall.

Or at any rate it looked like a shadow and not anything carved or painted on the concrete block beneath, but there was nothing hanging in front of the surface to cast it. It was a square encased in a circle, with a triangle jutting like an arrowhead from the upper right-hand side of the ring. The combination of the circle and triangle made it resemble the astrological symbol for Mars or maleness, but any Kindred, even a clanless, ostracized one like Dan, would have recognized its true significance. It was the emblem of the Tremere.

Even as he wondered why he hadn't seen it earlier, it suddenly blinked out of view. He stared at the space it had occupied, and after a moment it wavered back into existence. Obviously non-Tremere weren't *meant* to see it, but his superhuman vision had finally penetrated the magical screen masking it.

Okay, thought Dan, *I found something. Now what?* The obvious move was to touch the symbol. He gingerly proceeded to do so and then, startled, snatched his hand back instantly. The shadow felt cold as ice.

Steeling himself to bear the chill, he pressed his palm firmly against the sigil. The section of wall behind it evaporated, revealing another hallway.

Except for considerably dimmer lighting, the new corridor didn't appear much different from the one in which he was standing. But it smelled different. The musky scent of incense and a noxious odor that he associated with high-school chemistry hung in the air. And it *felt* different. The air seemed to buzz and crawl against his face, as if it were charged with electricity.

Apprehensive but curious as well — it was a rare Kindred who hadn't wondered about the occult mysteries of the Tremere — he stepped through the opening. It sealed itself behind him like a vampire's wound healing with unnatural speed. He made sure that there was a shadow-symbol on this side as well, that he had a way out, and then skulked deeper into the Warlock haven, resisting the impulse to take out his automatic. Displaying a gun would destroy whatever forlorn hope he might otherwise have of convincing one of the magi that he belonged here.

Most of the doors along the passage were closed. From behind one came a faint, regular rasp, as if someone were honing a knife, and broken sobbing; a strange, arrhythmic chanting in a language Dan didn't recognize droned through another.

Feeling horribly exposed in the open corridor, he nevertheless paused to ponder his next move. He couldn't simply open doors and search rooms at random, not when the Tremere were manifestly all around him. He'd blunder in on somebody; and even if he didn't, it would take too long. He needed to locate a command center, or the boss' office. That was the kind of place where the enemy would store the information he needed. Wishing that the Warlocks had seen fit to supply a building directory complete with a you-are-here marker at the entrance, he stalked on.

Eventually the corridor opened out into a broad, gloomy, high-ceilinged chamber lit only by the wavering light of scattered candelabra. Covering one wall was a bookcase crammed with leather-bound volumes, many of which looked and smelled as ancient as the tome he'd found in Wyatt's haven. The side of the room nearest the shelves was carpeted and furnished with armchairs; it looked like Dan's notion of a Victorian gentlemen's club. The other half of the hall was empty, and its bare concrete floor had a drain in the center. He suspected that the magi used the space when they had to draw large pentagrams for group rituals.

It occurred to him that the information he needed might conceivably be written in one of the books in the library, but he was sure that he didn't have time to examine them all, not even just the modern-looking ones. It seemed smarter to search elsewhere and come back here only as a last resort. He started for one of the doorways in the far wall.

Inside the murky opening something shifted, and cloth rustled. Someone was walking toward him! He hastily stepped away from the doorway and crouched behind a high-backed chair in the shadow of a softly ticking grandfather clock, willing himself to blend with the darkness.

Ponderous footsteps carried the newcomer into the chamber. His heart thudded slowly, like a bass drum beating out the cadence of a funeral march, demonstrating that he wasn't Kindred. Despite his lethargic tread and heartbeat, his flesh threw off heat like an open fire, as if he were burning up with fever. Even shielded by the armchair, Dan could feel the warmth ten feet away.

Cautiously, he risked a peek around the side of the seat, then stiffened in surprise. Superficially, the hulking figure standing in the middle of the room appeared human, but one close look was enough to dispel the impression. Its skin was too smooth, utterly unlined and unwrinkled, and subtly luminous, as if it were a thin-shelled mannequin with a lamp glowing inside it. Multicolored tattoos, cryptic hieroglyphs like the symbols in Wyatt's grimoires, mottled its face and the backs of its hands. Lacking both iris and pupil, its eyes shone fiery orange.

Dan supposed that the creature *had* started out human. He wondered fleetingly if it was a magically transformed ghoul, some sort of zombie, or something stranger still. Then it abruptly turned to stare directly at him.

Dan nearly gave a violent start — nearly hurled himself at the creature, or made a grab for his pistol. But another, cooler part of his mind overrode those impulses, told him to remain motionless until he was absolutely certain that the tattooed figure truly did see him. *I'm not here*, he thought, silently chanting the phrase as if it were a mantra. *I'm not here*.

And after a moment, the creature tilted its head as if it were puzzled. As if it had glimpsed something strange from the corner of its blazing eye but, when it lurched around, the oddity had disappeared. Shuffling, it turned in a circle, looking over the room, and then trudged out the doorway through which Dan had entered.

The vampire shuddered as the tension bled out of his muscles. Then he rose and skulked on, hoping that the library represented some sort of dividing line in the communal haven. Perhaps the rank-and-file Tremere occupied the rooms he'd just passed, while officer country was in the tunnels still ahead. He had no evidence that such a thing was true, but it seemed like a reasonable hunch. In any case, he had to start snooping *somewhere*.

He started down the next hallway, a relatively short one with a black door at the end. For three paces he was all right, and then he felt a sudden jolt of alarm.

Thinking that the creature with the fiery eyes was sneaking up behind him, he spun around. Except for himself, the corridor was empty.

He grimaced. Maybe he was imagining things. God knew, all this cloak-and-dagger crap had scraped his nerves raw. But on the other hand, just because he didn't see a threat didn't mean there was nothing there. He hadn't spotted Wyatt's homunculus at first, either.

Peering about, still seeing nothing, he hesitated for a moment, then decided that he might as well go on. Now glancing backward even more frequently than he had been, he proceeded toward the dully gleaming ebon door.

Without warning, agony throbbed through his chest and knee. He stumbled as his leg nearly gave way underneath him. The magical wounds the Samedi had given him had healed long ago, but now, evidently, they'd burst open again and were as rotten as before. He could smell the decay, feel the deliquescent flesh slipping away from his bones.

Terrified, he fumbled out his .38. He almost started blasting at shadows, for all that he knew the noise might bring every Tremere in the place down on his head. Instead, struggling against the impulse and the fright that had produced it, he blundered back out of the corridor into the library. Perhaps his tormentor was hiding there.

As he exited the hall, the pain and stink of his injuries vanished. At the same moment, panic loosened its grip on him.

Looking around, he failed to see any sign of an attacker. With shaking hands he tore open his denim work shirt, showering blue plastic buttons on the carpet. His chest was unmarked.

Even a Kindred couldn't heal that fast. Dan began to suspect that he hadn't really been injured in the first place. Perhaps someone had woven a kind of illusory magic in the hall that would fill an intruder's mind with terror, to keep unauthorized personnel from passing through the black door. If so, then that was probably exactly where Dan needed to go. Holstering his gun again — the weapon couldn't help him against the intangible — he ran through the doorway, intent on passing through the torture zone as quickly as possible.

Fresh pain ripped through his torso and leg, staggering him. After another stride, a wave of terrible weakness flowed through his muscles and his eyes went dim. He could feel his internal organs swelling and bursting like balloons. He experienced a sensation he'd half-forgotten, the desperate need to gasp in a breath, but he couldn't make his petrified lungs inflate.

And suddenly he understood what it meant. Thirty years ago, drugged and delirious, his veins and arteries emptied and his heart falling silent, he'd cheated death by becoming a vampire. Now Nature was taking its due. The alternate reality of human science and common sense was rending the immortality out of his body, transforming him into the shriveled, decay-ridden corpse that it had always intended he should be.

No! he told himself desperately. *I'm not dying! What I'm feeling isn't real!* Somehow holding total, crippling dread at bay, he lurched on, finally reeling against the black door.

He tried to grip the knob, but he couldn't make his stiff, aching fingers close around it. He stumbled back a step, then hurled himself at the raven panel.

Weak as he felt, perhaps he actually still possessed inhuman strength: when his shoulder hit the door, it flew open and struck the wall with a boom. Now completely off balance, he collapsed across the threshold onto the floor.

After a few seconds his head cleared, and his accustomed strength came flowing back. Profoundly grateful, he sprang to his feet.

Had anyone been alarmed by the sound of the door crashing open? There was no way to know. He'd just have close it again and hope for the best. He hastily proceeded to do so and then turned to examine his surroundings.

He was standing in a living room stuffed with dark, massive furniture, much of it upholstered in red velvet. A white marble statue of a Kindred in medieval clothing touching a kneeling woman's brow — a tableau that reminded Dan of Jesus healing the sick — stood in one corner, while a companion piece, the same vampire with his fangs buried in a struggling man's throat, occupied another.

Musty-smelling tapestries, depicting scenes of knightly battles, a stag hunt and courtly love, adorned the walls. Surrounded by such antiques, the big-screen TV and the stereo system were jarringly out of place.

Dan listened. He didn't hear anyone stirring, so he crept on, into a formal dining room. The places around the long table were set with embroidered linen napkins and a variety of gold and crystal goblets, but no plates or flatware. Beyond that chamber was a hallway, and as he glided into it a faint odor tickled his nose. It was like the smell of old, crumbling paper mixed with exotic spices.

Warily he peeked through the next doorway he came to. On the other side was a spacious office, with a drawerless, glass-topped desk on which sat a PC, a phone, a disk caddie, an open ebony box of Turkish cigarettes, and a jade ashtray. The source of the peculiar odor was in the corner: a table on which lay a child-sized, brown, withered, motionless figure. Someone had stripped the brittle bandages away from its head to reveal the sunken, eyeless, noseless, long-dead countenance beneath.

Dan hesitated, uncertain whether to enter the room. The mummy *looked* inert. Truly dead. But as with the Samedi, such appearances could be deceiving. Finally, losing patience with his own timidity, he slipped inside.

The mummy didn't move. Keeping a wary eye on it, he sat down and booted up the computer. The initial screen asked him to enter a password. Frowning, he tried *Tremere*, *Warlock*, *magic*, *Camelot* and *Merlin*. None of them did the trick.

A dry chuckle, so faint that no human could have heard it, rustled through the air.

Dan jerked around in his swivel chair. The mummy hadn't moved. Nevertheless, he was all but certain it was what he'd heard. Reminding himself that he was also an undead entity and therefore shouldn't feel so spooked, he swallowed and said, "Who are you? *What* are you? Some kind of Kindred?"

The mummy chuckled again. The sound made the small hairs on the back of Dan's neck stand on end. "My name is Sesostris, little spy, and no, I don't share the blood of Caine. Would that I did, to walk free and strong like you! In life, in the Two Kingdoms, I was a mage of sorts and an advisor to kings. I helped Kamose drive out Apophis. Beyond the Shroud, my role has been much the same. I served the Beggar Lord until Durrell bound me inside this husk and so made me his slave."

Much of what the spirit said had gone over Dan's head, but he thought he grasped the essential point. He stood up, strode to Sesostris' bier, and raised his fist over the mummy's head. One blow would surely pulverize the desiccated creature's skull. "If you try to hurt me, or yell for help, I'll kill you."

Sesostris made a spitting sound. "Are you so afraid of me, then, vampire? Surely I don't look as if I can bound off this table and overpower you, and you hear just how loudly I can 'yell.' I'm not a sentinel, I'm a research tool, no different from a reference book or that contraption on the desk. And that's as well for you, because your threat holds no terrors for me. I yearn to be released from this vile existence. I want to return to Stygia."

Dan paused for a moment thinking that over, and then said, "If I tore the mummy apart, would that set your spirit free?"

"It would," Sesostris whispered.

"Then how about a deal," said Dan. "If you help me find out what I need to know, I'll cut you loose before I leave."

"I see by your aura that you're honest, after a fashion," said the mummy, prompting Dan to wonder fleetingly how a thing with no eyes could see anything. "Very well, it's a bargain."

"Then answer some questions for me," said the Kindred.

"Who's Durrell?"

Sesostris didn't laugh, but somehow Dan could sense the ancient creature's amusement. "Don't you even know that? You're standing in his haven. You were sitting in his chair."

Dan grinned. "Just like Goldilocks. I guess it does seem weird, but no, I don't know. Tell me, please."

"Sebastian Durrell is the Tremere Regent — their term for the master magus of a city — of Louisville. He also owns a controlling interest in the garden of earthly delights above our heads."

"Is he masterminding the war against the Kindred of Sarasota?"

"Indeed he is," Sesostris said. "And he's rather worried that either his Lord — his superior in the Order of Tremere — or the prince of Louisville will find out about it before he brings it to a successful conclusion. He's convinced that neither one would appreciate his initiative."

"Why did he start a war in the first place?" asked Dan. "What does he hope to gain?"

Sesostris hesitated. "I'm not entirely sure," the mummy said at last. "He doesn't always confide in me. Not that he anticipated a spy creeping into his lair to interrogate me, but I'm afraid that my attitude isn't as sympathetic as he'd like. I do know that Roger Phillips is influential in the councils of the Camarilla, and generally advocates policies of which Durrell disapproves. And I know that the Toreador of Sarasota have immense wealth. If my master could seize Phillips' throne, or failing that, arrange for a collaborator to do so, he could take much of the treasure for his own. Yet I suspect there's more to it. For some reason, Durrell believes that his triumph will serve to further his quest for greater magical power. Like most magi, he's obsessed with learning new and greater sorceries."

Dan wondered if the other Methuselah, Melpomene's opposite number, had promised to teach Durrell new magic in exchange for his cooperation. Ultimately, he supposed, the Tremere's motives mattered far less than whatever plans he'd made. "Are Durrell and his main assistants all living here in these tunnels?"

"They are."

Dan blinked and shook his head. "Then... hell, I've got them. My job's finished. I can pass along the information, the Toreador will stage a sneak attack —" Suddenly frowning, he faltered. Sure, *he* knew the truth, but could he convince anyone else to believe it? Would the high-and-mighty undead aristocrats of Sarasota assault other members of the Camarilla on the word of a despised Caitiff and a supposed diabolist like himself? Maybe, but he'd rather approach them with some kind of corroborative evidence in hand. "Did Durrell keep any kind of records pertaining to all this?'

"His journal," replied Sesostris. "In the machine." The mummy sighed. "When he first captured me, he used to write it by candlelight with a quill pen."

"Do you know the password?" asked Dan.

"Scorpio," Sesostris said. "The moon sign under which he was reborn a Kindred."

Dan dropped back into the swivel chair and typed in the word. Sure enough, the screen shifted to a list of files, one of which was labeled *Journal*. He opened it, skimmed a section of text near the end, and found it to be all he could have hoped. Durrell not only discussed his designs on Sarasota, he even named the non-Warlock allies, mercenaries and dupes from whom he'd assembled his makeshift army.

The spy grabbed a disk and, having copied the file onto it, ejected it and thrust it into his jacket pocket. Rising, he said, "You're a real friend, Sesostris."

"Not so," the mummy said.

Dan's eyes narrowed. "What do you mean?"

"I told you, Kindred," Sesostris answered, his shivery whisper an odd blend of gloating malice and regret, "that Durrell enslaved me. My will is not my own. I cooperated with you to hold you here until the demon-bound, my fellow servant, could answer my call." At that moment the luminous, fiery-eyed figure that Dan had encountered in the magi's library stepped into the office doorway.

Dan's fingers twitched with the urge to draw his automatic. But he still didn't want to make a lot of noise and attract every Tremere in the place. He suspected that the demon-bound was a formidable hand-to-hand fighter, but then, he was pretty tough himself. Emerging from behind the desk with fists raised to strike or block, he edged toward the creature. Its features slack and expressionless, arms dangling at its sides, it shuffled to meet him.

As soon as Dan got within range, he snapped a kick at the demon-bound's crotch. Suddenly moving fast as lightning, the glowing creature parried the attack. The force of the contact threw the Kindred off balance. Stumbling, he barely managed to avoid a counterpunch to the face.

Okay, Dan thought grimly, *now I know. It might be as strong as I am, and its hands are just as fast as mine. But the way it lumbers around, maybe its feet aren't. It's between me and the door, but if I could get around it, perhaps I could outrun it.* He faked a shift to the left, then dodged right, stomp-kicking the demon-bound in the knee as he darted around it. Bone cracked.

For an instant, lunging toward the doorway, Dan thought the maneuver had worked. Then a hand grabbed him by the shoulder and jerked him backward.

The vampire used a judo throw to tumble the demon-bound over his shoulder and slam it onto the floor. The creature retaliated by seizing his ankles and jerking his legs out from under him. Grappling, tearing at each other, the two combatants rolled back and forth across the carpet.

Dan tried striking at what, on a mortal or even most

Kindred, would be vulnerable areas: the groin, solar plexus, throat and eyes. Such blows neither elicited an involuntary defensive reaction, nor, when they landed, caused the demon-bound incapacitating distress. Evidently it lacked the reflexes that a skillful fighter like Dan could have used to fake it out, and it apparently was incapable of feeling pain. Since the tattooed monster wasn't targeting Dan's pressure points — maybe it didn't know how — that pretty much reduced the wrestling match to a test of raw strength.

As he battered and wrenched at his opponent, a crimson tide of fury swept through Dan's mind. Berserk now, snarling, he extended his fangs and bit at the demon-bound. The creature's blood was too hot and tasted foul, but he kept savaging it anyway.

They wrestled for perhaps two minutes, ripping flesh and breaking bone, neither quite managing to strike a decisive blow. The demon-bound's body grew hotter and hotter, until every touch of it covered Dan with blisters and burns.

And then it burst into flame.

Terrified that the blaze would consume him, Dan struggled to break the demon-bound's grip. Finally the monster's arms loosened. Frantically the vampire wriggled out from underneath it and then saw that the fire had already spread to his clothing. Screaming, he rolled across the floor, smothering the flames. Seemingly indifferent to its immolation, still intent on subduing him, the demon-bound started to crawl after him, but burned to a motionless black stick figure before it could reach him.

Dan knelt on the smoldering carpet, shuddering and reflexively gasping for breath, his broken ribs beginning to knit and his cuts to close. His burns started to heal as well, but more slowly; fortunately they were superficial. Gradually his instinctive dread of fire faded, and he started thinking rationally again. He had to get up and get out of here. Durrell could show up at any time, or Sesostris might be able to summon some other monster. Reminded of the mummy's existence, he glanced over at the table and then gave a start of surprise.

Sesostris was gone. The ancient magician had lied about not being able to walk, too.

Dan leaped up and dashed back through Durrell's apartment. When he yanked open the black door, he saw Sesostris tottering down the corridor to the library. Bits of the mummy's body flaked away with every lurching step.

Steeling himself against another attack of magical fear, Dan ran into the hall. Nothing happened. Maybe the spell only kicked in if a stranger moved *toward* the door. He grabbed the mummy and slammed it against the wall. "You son of a bitch," he growled. "Let's see how far you can go after I tear your arms and legs off."

"Don't stop there," Sesostris said. "I want this prison destroyed. Free me! Please!"

Dan snarled. The ancient creature had betrayed him. Why should he do it any favors? But then he realized that it hadn't really needed to tell him Durrell's password. It could have stalled him until the demon-bound arrived without giving up a thing. Perhaps in a way it *had* tried to help him, as much as its bindings would allow. Feeling like a soft touch, a sucker, he dug his fingers into Sesostris' head and ripped it apart. The mummy's skull crumbled like a stale saltine.

Dan hastily dusted his hands, wiped his gory mouth on his sleeve and checked his pocket to make sure that he still had the disk. Then, the blood thirst that was the inevitable consequence of rapid healing already drying his throat, he skulked back through the Tremere haven toward the exit.

TWENTY-FIVE: MINOR DUTY

*Suspicions amongst thoughts are like bats amongst birds,
they ever fly by twilight.*
— Francis Bacon, "Of Suspicion"

Laurie Tipton sat in the security station — a stark, square, gray room smelling of industrial cleanser — studying the black-and-white TV monitor. Every few seconds the picture changed, bringing her another view of mortals eating corn dogs and cotton candy, standing in line for flume rides, tilt-a-whirls and other attractions, or rushing from place to place, probably eager to experience as much of Camelot as possible before it was time to go home. The anarch reflected sourly that most looked as if they were having a lot more fun than she was.

She supposed that she wouldn't have minded her tedious job so much if this bastion of the Anarch Movement had turned out to be what she'd expected. What Wyatt in his enthusiasm had *led* her to expect, though she shied from thinking about her disappointment in those terms. The implied criticism of her dead friend made her feel disloyal.

But it seemed weird that the vampire resistance would control a zillion-dollar business like Camelot. That was something she'd expect of the elders of the Camarilla, who were generally acknowledged to hold the reins of power in both the kine and Kindred worlds. Nor did she understand why so many of the other undead inhabiting the facility seemed secretive and aloof. Sometimes she almost felt as if they were laughing at her behind her back. By the same token, she didn't comprehend why Durrell, the anarch captain who'd brought her, Felipe and Jimmy Ray to the park, seemed so convinced that Dan was going to show up here.

Dan. Shifting restlessly in her chair, she grimaced. She hated the murdering bastard. How could she not? But there was more to her feelings than that, because she'd liked him so much at first. Like nearly every other vampire — or mortal male — she'd known, he'd tried hard to come across as tough, but she'd sensed a terrible aching loneliness inside him, the same feeling that had tortured her before she met her other friends. It had made her like him instantly, and even now made her flinch from believing him a traitor. She guessed that she really was gullible, loyal to a fault. Even in the Haight in the Summer of Love, when everybody was supposed to love and trust everybody else, people had told her as much.

But she couldn't grasp *why* Dan had done what he had! If he was an agent of the Camarilla, why hadn't he moved to destroy the other members of the anarch cell? Not for the first time, she toyed with the notion that Wyatt's poor, dying familiar had been confused about the identity of its master's slayer; but try as she might, she couldn't buy that either.

She realized that, lost in thought, she'd stopped watching the monitor. Conscientiously she focused her eyes on it again. She just had time to register a familiar silhouette before the picture changed.

Crying out in dismay, she lunged for the control panel on the desk before her. One of Durrell's associates, a snotty guy who usually wore a black leather vest, had taught her how to use it, but after that first night she hadn't had the occasion or the inclination to fool with it. Still, after a moment's fumbling, she managed to flip back to the previous view.

The monitor showed her a rangy figure with light-colored hair striding through a crowd of tourists milling in front of the Sir Lancelot's Tourney equestrian stunt show. By now he'd nearly reached the edge of the picture, but, frantically pushing buttons and flipping toggle switches, she manage to make the security camera pivot after him and then zoom in for a close-up.

She'd been right. The guy *was* Dan. His mouth was set in a grim line, and he kept glancing from side to side. His hair needed combing, and he had dark stains on his jeans and jacket which might be bloodstains, scorch marks, or both.

He looked so tense and harried that for a moment she felt sorry for him, and her doubts about Durrell and his associates loomed large in her mind. Then she pictured Wyatt's affectionate, devil-may-care grin, and the ghastly look and stink of his rotting corpse.

Weeping tears of blood, she grabbed the phone and punched in the three-digit number Durrell had bade her memorize. When someone answered, she said, "I saw Murdock! He's near the Tourney, moving east!"

TWENTY-SIX: THE DELIVERY

To labour and not ask for any reward
Save that of knowing that we do Thy will.
— St. Ignatius Loyola, "Prayer for Generosity"

When Dan shoved his way around the crowd of humans watching the motley-clad band of jugglers and fire-eaters obstructing the cobblestone lane, he saw the gate. Like most of the other architecture in the complex, it was a combination of the sort of structures found in any theme park and of phony medieval gingerbread: a row of cashiers' booths and turnstiles topped with crenellated ramparts, turrets and multicolored heraldic banners. Beyond it lay a fake drawbridge and then the nearest parking lot, still full of cars despite the relative lateness of the hour. Unlike its competitors, Camelot stayed open nearly until dawn.

All right, thought Dan, *just a few more steps and I'm free and clear.* He started across the plaza, a circular area with a fiberglass replica of Excalibur standing tall in its anvil and stone in the center; then two mortals dressed in red surcoats and gray shirts and pants decorated with a pattern intended to look like chainmail emerged from a doorway on his left.

Dan had poked around the park enough to recognize the uniform. The guys were Camelot security guards, and probably ghouls to boot. Reminding himself that they weren't necessarily here to apprehend him, the vampire marched on toward the exit, fighting the urge to quicken his stride.

But after a moment he realized it was no good. The guards were headed right for him. The one in the lead, a chunky Asian who, to Dan's hypersensitive nose, reeked of cigarette smoke and barbecue sauce, shouted, "Sir! Sir! You, the blond man in the dirty jacket! Wait up, please!"

Dan started to run, lunging around tourists, driving between them or, when necessary, knocking them out of his way. They cried out in protest, and the guards pounded after him. After a moment the exclamations from the crowd took on a different note as people realized that a chase was in progress.

Dan vaulted a turnstile, then dashed on across the drawbridge. The planks groaned and thunked beneath his feet. Glancing backward he saw that his pursuers now had pistols in their hands, but they were pointing them at the sky, not at him.

Evidently they weren't willing to start shooting in front of the paying customers, which probably meant that none of the enemy knew that he'd penetrated the tunnels. But that might change at any second. Some Tremere could discover Sesostris' remains and alert his fellows by radio.

A yellow jeep with a line of open carriages in tow sat waiting by the curb to carry tourists to the more remote parking areas. Snatching out his .38, Dan leaped into the seat beside the driver, a slender, twentyish girl with long, chestnut hair pulled back in a ponytail, then jabbed the gun into the side of her neck. "Stonehenge Lot, Row M," he told her. "Fast! Go!" She didn't move, so he prodded her again. "I said go!"

The driver jerked the gearshift into drive and put her foot on the gas. Two tourists scrambled out as the train lurched forward. Looking around, Dan saw that the guards were catching up with the chain of carriages and might well manage to haul themselves aboard before it picked up speed. He fired twice in their direction, not actually trying to hit them, just discourage them. They stopped running and shot back. Some of the passengers screamed.

"Please don't hurt anyone!" said the driver. "Please don't!"

Despite his frequent feelings of alienation from kine in general, Dan felt a pang of sympathy for her. He was sure that she didn't know that her bosses were vampires, or even that such improbable creatures existed. She was just an employee, maybe a college kid working to pay her tuition. But he didn't let his pity show on his face. As long as she was terrified, she wouldn't put up any resistance. "If you don't want to die, go faster," he replied.

The jeep sped on through the darkness. The cool wind riffled his hair. The Hunger smoldered in his throat and belly, and he imagined himself climbing back into the passenger cars and feeding on one of the tourists. Even if it had been a practical notion otherwise, there was no time. He'd just have to tolerate his thirst till he got away.

In another minute the train reached its destination. "Now go back to the gate," Dan said. "Drive just as fast; I'm going to shoot at you." He jumped from the moving jeep.

The string of carriages swept past him, some passengers gaping at him, others averting their eyes. The train turned in a half-circle and raced back the way it had come.

Dan sprinted to his rented green Lexus, clambered inside, set the .38 on the passenger seat, and turned the key. The engine roared to life. He sent the car hurtling out of the lot and onto one of the roads which, running through acres of thus far undeveloped Camelot property, ultimately connected to a public highway. Weaving through traffic, sometimes with scant inches to spare, veering off the pavement when necessary, he passed one departing vehicle after another. Horns blared.

After he'd gone about a mile, a sedan raced out of the darkness ahead. Its headlights were on high-beam, dazzlingly bright. Squinting against the glare, he tried to determine if the driver was out to intercept him.

Someone leaned precariously out of the other car's backseat window. Dan couldn't actually see the gun in the figure's hands, but he was sure it was there. Trying to spoil his attacker's aim, he jerked the steering wheel. Then the Lexus' windshield exploded inward, spraying him with shards of glass. A split second later, the world went black.

As he came to, he cried out at a fierce throb of agony in his head. Slightly lesser pains burned in his legs and right hip. Wiping vitae out of his eyes, blinking in a vain effort to clear his blurry double vision, he peered through the shattered windshield and saw that the Lexus had left the road, hurtled another ten yards and slammed into a live oak. He tried to restart the engine, but the car only made a grinding sound.

He felt his injuries begin to repair themselves, but slowly. This time around he had too little blood in his system to heal efficiently.

If his attackers would only come within reach, maybe he could do something about that. Grunting at the fresh spasm of pain the effort required, he twisted in his seat, peered back in the direction of the road and then growled an obscenity. His two assailants had pulled off the pavement and climbed out of their car, but they were just watching the Lexus with automatic rifles cradled in their hands, not advancing. He suspected that they were ghouls, not Kindred, and, wisely leery of approaching even a wounded vampire by themselves, awaiting the arrival of reinforcements. And he didn't see how he could go to them, not with two broken legs.

His hands shaking with pain and weakness, he grabbed

the Lexus' cellular phone and punched in Melpomene's number.

The whirring and clicking as the call was relayed seemed to take forever. Finally, however, the Methuselah's thrilling contralto voice said, "Dan?"

"I've got the information," the younger vampire replied. "But I'm in trouble. You've got to do something to help me."

"What have you learned?" Melpomene asked intently.

"Are you listening to me?" Dan demanded. "The enemy is closing in on me. I'm hurt and can't get away. I have everything you need, it's on a computer disk, but you're never going to get it unless you help me escape." He had no idea *how* she could help him, but surely, with her godlike powers, she could do *something*. It was his only chance.

A silvery glow flowered in the seat beside him. Dan wondered fleetingly what his attackers made of the light. As long as it didn't provoke them into rushing the Lexus, he supposed it didn't matter.

In a few moments the phosphorescence coalesced into an image of Melpomene. Desperate for aid, and stirred as always by her extraordinary personal magnetism, Dan felt a surge of affection. "Thank you," he said. "Thank you for coming."

"Show me the disk," she said.

Without thinking, he fumbled it out of his pocket.

"I'm going to see if I can bring this to me," she said. "I mean, to the location of my physical body. Sometimes that's possible, if conditions are right. If the disk arrives intact, I'll transport you next."

Despite the devotion her presence inspired, he felt a twinge of alarm. Of suspicion. He jerked the disk back. "Move us both at once. If it's dangerous, I'll risk it."

The Methuselah shook her head. "I can only translate one object at a time. When it's your turn, you'll have to be naked and empty-handed. Now hold out our prize. Before it's too late."

He did as she'd directed. He *wanted* to trust her, and he didn't have any choice anyway.

Her slim ivory fingers closed around the square black disk. Gradually Dan felt the object growing lighter and indefinably less substantial, shadowlike in his hand, until at last he couldn't feel it at all.

Melpomene lifted it, and then her dark eyes widened in dismay. "Oh, no," she whispered.

"What's wrong?" Dan asked. The other vampire's astral projection winked out of existence.

"Melpomene!" Dan screamed. "Come back! Don't leave me!" There was no reply.

The wounded Kindred grabbed the cellular phone out of his lap. The white plastic instrument sparked, crackled, smoked and grew hot in his hands. He could smell the circuits burning.

For the next few moments he merely sat, stunned and aghast at his patron's treachery. His eyes ached, but he had too little vitae left in his system to shed any tears.

Grimly, he struggled to goad himself into action. He had to get past his shock, start thinking again, figure another way out of his predicament. What if he got out of the Lexus and fired at his attackers? If he put them both down, he could crawl to them and drink their blood. Considering his spastic limbs and murky vision, it was a forlorn hope at best, but he couldn't think of a better alternative.

Fumbling the automatic off the floor, he gripped the door handle, jerked it, and sprawled heavily out onto the ground. He rolled, getting himself faced in the right direction, raised the pistol in both hands —

Bullets ripped his throat and hammered his torso. He passed out again.

TWENTY-SEVEN: DRACULA

Murder most foul, as in the best it is;
But this most foul, strange, and unnatural.
— William Shakespeare, *Hamlet*

Angus and Judy sat slumped in Roger Phillips' study, waiting for the call to battle. Rap music pounded from the boom box that the Brujah elder had set on the desk. As far as the Gangrel was concerned, the sound was reminiscent of bursts of automatic-weapons fire, and extraordinarily unmelodious.

And yet, though it hurt his head and set his teeth on edge, he was glad to have it. The vent above his head was blowing a steady stream of cold air, and thick velvet curtains completely covered the French windows, but somehow he could still feel the leaden heat of the sunlight outside, pressing down on his mind, trying to crush out his awareness. The grating chant served as a sort of antidote.

In another hour, if nothing happens, I can go to sleep, he reflected, then scowled, disgusted by the weakness that had prompted the thought. He *wanted* one of his agents to find Dracula. If he and his allies didn't catch the murderer this morning, he'd miss the deadline he'd so vaingloriously set himself; and Palmer Guice, oily, treacherous weasel that he was, would run and tattle to the Inner Circle.

The office door clicked open. Lazlo entered carrying a silver tray laden with two crystal tumblers of warm, fragrant vitae. Angus seized one and guzzled it. It took Judy a moment to bestir herself and do likewise. A stray drop of crimson oozed from the corner of her wide, sensuous mouth and down her chin.

"I gather we haven't had any news," Lazlo said, his tone carefully neutral. Sensing the human servant's inner desperation, the Justicar had to admire his self-control. Of course, potential prey that he was, his mere presence a provocation to any vampire experiencing the Hunger, he probably couldn't have survived for long among the Kindred if he weren't capable of keeping his emotions on a tight rein.

"No," Angus said.

Lazlo hesitated. "Do you think you could have been mistaken about the killer operating after dawn?"

Angus shrugged. "Do I think I could have been? Of course. Do I believe I was? No, and I have an instinct about these things. Look you, mortal, we're taking our best shot, guided by our best reasoning. No one could do more, so it's useless to worry."

"It's easy for you to be philosophical," Judy said sourly. Despite the blood she'd just drunk, her voice sounded a little hoarse, as if the daylight beyond the curtains were drying her out. "It isn't your home and your friends on the line."

That's all the more reason for you to show a proper gratitude for my help, the giant Gangrel thought, annoyed, but he resisted the temptation to say it aloud. He realized that Judy didn't really want to pick a quarrel with him. The suspense of waiting and the stress of their unnatural wakefulness were making them both irritable.

As he tried to think of a less provocative reply, something rapped sharply on the glass behind the drapes.

Lazlo took a step toward the windows. "No!" Angus said. "You'll scare it away." He hastily rose and pulled on his long brown overcoat, tan kid gloves, sunglasses and sacklike hood. Judy donned a similar costume, simultaneously withdrawing to the shadows at the back of the room.

When Angus' towering frame was completely covered, he pulled back the curtain. His first glimpse of the early morning sunlight both dazzled him and drove a lance of weakness and nausea through his body. For an instant his knees went rubbery, and he nearly stumbled. Behind him, Judy gasped in a hissing breath.

Squinting, Angus looked down at the ground. An inky black raven, its eyes bright and its head cocked, stood at the base of the French window peering up at him. He opened the glass door, and the bird flapped into the air and perched on his arm.

He stared at the raven, trying to make contact with its mind. The process was more difficult than it should have been: the sun truly had diminished his powers. But after a moment a parade of images and wordless concepts marched from the avian's head into his own. "The birds have found Dracula," he said, stumbling over the words; sometimes it was hard to speak like a man when he was telepathically linked to an animal. "She just killed three people in a diner near the courthouse."

"But where exactly?" Lazlo asked.

"It's a bird," Angus snapped, releasing the mind link. "It can't give me a street address. But its fellows will lead us to her. Come on!"

Half-running, he led Judy and Lazlo out onto the dewy grass. For a second the light seemed to crash down on him like a torrent of molten lava, and then the pain grew somewhat less intense. The Brujah fell to one knee. Lazlo tried to take her arm and help her up, but she wrenched herself away from his hands, scrambled to her feet, and strode on toward the black Cadillac with the tinted windows.

Lazlo jumped into the driver's seat and the two Kindred into the back, where they'd previously stowed their rifles. The raven, still riding Angus' forearm, peered curiously about at the interior of the car. As the vehicle sped down the driveway, the Justicar turned to Judy and murmured, "Are you going to be all right?"

"Hell, yes!" she said. "I knew I had the power to move around after dawn, but I never actually had to do it before. I just needed to get used to it." Her voice softened. "You were right, it is kind of cool to see a blue sky again, even if the damn thing is making me sick to my stomach."

Ignoring stop signs, red lights and speed limits, yielding to no one, Lazlo reached the downtown area in less than ten minutes. Peering out the window, Angus saw that, as he'd expected, an unusual number of crows, sparrows, pigeons and seagulls were soaring and wheeling above the streets. "Stop the car!" he said.

Lazlo obeyed. When, brakes squealing, the Cadillac lurched to a halt, Angus threw open the door. Judy tensed, possibly straining not to flinch from the unfiltered sunlight that streamed in.

Stepping out of the car, Angus sent up a silent call. A white-winged gull with a hooked yellow beak landed on his free arm, imparted its tidings, and took off again.

Angus swung himself back into the Cadillac. "Dracula's heading east on Wood Street." Lazlo stamped on the gas; the sudden acceleration pressed the Gangrel back against the soft gray leather seat. "In a red car."

When they spotted the serial killer her vehicle, a gleaming vintage Thunderbird with sharklike tail fins, was halfway down a block of upscale storefronts occupying the ground floors of five- and six-story buildings. The early morning traffic was still light, but even if there had been other red cars on that section of road, she would have been easy to spot. A number of birds were flying directly above her, frequently swooping down at her vehicle as if to point it out.

Smiling fiercely, looking more vicious than Angus could have imagined, Lazlo pulled up even with the T-bird and then jerked the steering wheel. With a crash, the Cadillac sideswiped the murderess' car, which then jumped the curb and slammed into a fire hydrant. Sparkling water sprayed into the air.

The vampires' car began to spin. Turning into the skid, Lazlo brought the sedan back under control and then to a stop. A few yards down the block, Dracula scrambled out of the Thunderbird; evidently the valet had succeeded in disabling it. She was still wearing her long, dark coat and beret; indeed, except for the blood now streaking the left side of her pale, oval face, she looked just like the image the manatees had conveyed to Angus.

So far she hadn't reached for a weapon, but the Gangrel didn't find that reassuring. She must have surmised that Lazlo had hit her car because he knew who she was. If she wasn't going for a gun, maybe she *did* have supernatural powers.

Employing their inhuman speed, or as much of it as they could muster in the debilitating daylight, Angus and Judy leaped out of the Cadillac and raised their rifles to their shoulders. Cawing, the raven flew off the Gangrel's arm. The hunters' guns were loaded with tranquilizer darts. They wanted to take Dracula alive, to make her tell who'd sent her to Sarasota.

The murderess gestured with her left hand. Though she was standing in shadow, the large emerald ring on her left hand flashed. The vampires tried to shoot, then Judy cursed when nothing happened. Both rifles had jammed.

"She's a mage," Angus said.

"She's dead meat," Judy snarled. She threw down her gun

and charged Dracula. Wishing fleetingly that the Brujah weren't quite so reckless, Angus pounded after her. Meanwhile, moving at merely mortal speed, Lazlo clambered out of the Cadillac.

A single stride carried Dracula to the entrance of a trendy-looking women's clothing boutique. The green stone on her hand glowed as she opened the door - which, at this hour, should have been locked — lunged through and slammed it behind her.

Running won't help you, Angus thought with the cold satisfaction of a predator closing in for the kill. *We're faster than you, and we can smash down any door you lock behind you. In another minute we'll have you.*

The Thunderbird burst into yellow, crackling flame. The two Kindred instinctively recoiled, then, overcoming their fear, circled around the blaze toward the door through which Dracula had disappeared. Above their heads, something rumbled.

Startled, Angus looked up to see shards of the building's brick facade hurtling down at him and Judy. He threw up his arms to shield his head, and then the rain of rock crashed over him.

Despite his supernatural strength, it hammered him to his knees, bruised flesh and cracked bones and, most terribly of all, tore his protective layers of clothing. Instantly his exposed flesh began to cook, filling the air with an odor of roasting meat. Terror yammered through his mind.

Grimly, exerting every bit of his willpower, he quashed the panic. Lurching to his feet, shedding chunks of brick, he turned to Judy. Her garments were torn like his, and for a moment she slapped frantically at herself as if her body had burst into flame. Then, evidently overcoming her fear as he'd quelled his own, she scrambled over the pile of ruddy broken stone, kicked the door to the boutique off its hinges, and raced on into the shadowy interior. He dashed after her.

The shop smelled faintly of perfume. Smiling

mannequins clad in silk blouses and sequined gowns posed on pedestals. Dracula was nowhere in sight, even though the Kindred were still only seconds behind her.

"Where is she?" Judy snarled.

Angus thought it was a damn good question. Some of the reports of the murderer's crimes suggested that she could become invisible. He didn't intend to walk right past her and so let her get away.

He was no Toreador or Malkavian. In human form, he had merely human senses. But his animal forms had their own keen perceptions, and here, out of the sunlight, he could transform himself. It wouldn't matter that his protective clothing would vanish when he did.

Smiling inside his hood, grateful to get rid of his encumbering garb even if only for a moment, he willed himself to change. Like communing with the birds or simply moving around, the shift was harder than it should have been, particularly now that he was injured and expending vitae to heal. Still, after a moment his garments melted away and a pelt of gray fur spread across his alabaster skin. His jaws extended into a muzzle and a tail sprouted from the base of his spine. Dropping to all fours, he became a wolf.

Suddenly vision was less primary a sense than it had been an instant before. The world was a web of enticing, informative aromas. Sniffing, he caught the smell of his companion, and then the odor of a human female. The scent trail led to a blond mannequin dressed in a loose green floral-print dress, beaming at nothing in the rear of the shop.

Staring intently, head held low, Angus slunk toward the figure and Judy stalked after him. Rippling like the reflection of a moving object in a fun-house mirror, the dummy turned into Dracula. Her eyes wide, her bloody face finally looking rattled, she scrambled toward a doorway in the back wall. The short corridor beyond it appeared to lead to fitting rooms, a store room and an exit.

Angus and Judy charged. The mage gestured, her ring

flared, and a portion of the ceiling groaned and caved in on the vampires. It wasn't as damaging an attack as the avalanche of brick, but by the time they floundered clear of the mass of acoustic tiles, fluorescent-light fixtures and boards that had engulfed them, their quarry had reached the exit. She yanked open the door, admitting an excruciating blaze of sunlight, and dashed outside.

"Dead," Judy rasped, clearly on the brink of frenzy if she wasn't berserk already. "The bitch is dead." Heedless of the daylight now, she charged toward the door.

In large measure, Angus shared her rage. Dracula was making him and his comrades look like fools, and no kine, witch or otherwise, could be allowed to get away with that. He almost scrambled after Judy before he remembered that he needed his clothing back. Snarling, resenting the extra seconds it was taking him to shift, he reverted to human form and then sprinted after the Brujah elder.

Plunging out into the sunlight, enduring another stab of pain, he found himself in an alley. Still visible, Dracula was standing about sixty feet away. Evidently she hadn't had time to camouflage herself again, or was simply unable to do so. Perhaps, now that the vampires had defeated the spell once, it wouldn't work on them anymore. The sorceress had struck a melodramatic pose, hands upraised and the gem in her ring glowing like a green sun as if, unable to shake the Kindred off her trail, she were drawing on every bit of her magic to annihilate them.

Midway between Dracula and Angus, Judy was dodging to and fro, trying to come to grips with the human woman. But every time Dracula clenched her fists, a wall of roaring flame erupted from the cracked gray pavement. Only the Brujah's agility kept her from being caught in one of the blasts. Even so, as more and more barriers sprang into existence, she was gradually being imprisoned in a sort of blazing maze. Soon she'd have no more room to maneuver, and then, no doubt, Dracula would incinerate her in a final conflagration.

Intent on her work, the kine apparently hadn't noticed Angus' emergence into the open yet, but he didn't doubt that that would change if he rushed her. Then she'd trap him between walls of fire, too. And so, instead of charging, he lifted his eyes and silently called for aid.

Birds hurtled down from the sky at Dracula, pecking and slashing with beak and claw. Staggering, caught by surprise, she cried out, ducked her head and threw up her arms to ward the attackers off. A raven, perhaps the same one that had flown to Roger Phillips' house, swooped upward, clutching the mage's beret in its talons.

Taking advantage of Dracula's distraction, Judy managed to extricate herself from the walls of fire. Running at merely human speed now — apparently her wounds and the sunlight were taking their toll — the tail of her black leather trench coat flapping behind her, the Brujah dashed at her tormentor.

Angus charged, too. He felt parched and drained himself, but it shouldn't matter. In another moment he and Judy would get their hands on Dracula, and then the battle would be over. No mere human, not even one who could witch down walls and draw flame from asphalt, could contend with their superhuman strength once they'd had a chance to bring it to bear.

Dracula cried out an incantation in a language that, to Angus' ears, sounded like Hebrew. Her ring pulsed with light, and a whirlwind roared into existence above her head, scattering the attacking birds. And then, when Judy and Angus were only a second away from grabbing her, she thrust out her fists at them.

A blast of air smashed the Gangrel in the face, knocking him off his feet and sweeping him back across the pavement. The magical hurricane twisted his hood, blinding him, but he didn't need to see to know that the wind was ripping the tears in his clothing wider. The fresh bursts of pain as the sunlight seared hitherto shielded patches of flesh were proof of that.

He scrabbled at the blacktop, trying to anchor himself, but he couldn't find anything to grab. Somewhere behind him, Judy screamed, a shriek of agony audible even over the howl of the wind.

Whatever was happening to her was likely to happen to Angus if he couldn't stop his helpless tumbling. Reasoning grimly that a few more holes in his garments scarcely mattered now, he attempted a minor transformation.

After one terrible moment, when nothing happened and he thought that his shapeshifting power had failed him, his nails grew into curved, razor-sharp claws which punched through the fingers of his gloves. Using every bit of his inhuman might, he clutched at the pavement again. His talons ripped into the asphalt like the spikes on a mountaineer's boots, holding him in place.

He yanked at his mask, which was fluttering madly in the wind, but couldn't get the eye holes back in their proper positions. After a moment, more concerned about seeing what was happening than guarding himself from the light, he tore off the hood.

Hot pain flared across his forehead, cheeks and nose. Noting that Judy had stopped screaming, he looked around for her, then snarled with rage at what he saw.

The wind had pressed the Brujah against a Dumpster. Obviously she hadn't been able to anchor herself as he had, and the gale had hurled her through some of the walls of flame. Now she lay motionless, burning, her lithe, lovely, whip-scarred body already blackened and shrivelled beyond recognition. Angus had no doubt that she'd died the true death.

His fangs bared, still using his claws to resist the tempest, he began to crawl toward Dracula. The top of his head felt sizzling hot, and he wondered if his hair was about to ignite.

The wind died abruptly. Perhaps Dracula had realized that it wasn't going to keep him away from her, and had turned it off to create some other effect. Hoping to deny her sufficient time to do so, he leaped up and ran at her.

The emerald ring glowed, and then the world blazed white with glare. Only Angus' dark glasses kept him from being completely blinded. Burning pain stabbed across every inch of his body, as if his clothing had become transparent.

He thought he understood what was happening. Dracula's magic was collecting sunlight and focusing it on him like a magnifying glass. It was a good trick, but, staggering onward, he promised himself that it wasn't going to be good enough.

Blisters swelled and burst on his face and hands, releasing blood that boiled away to steam. His skin blackened, crackled and flaked off. But now Dracula was only ten feet away. Grateful that she apparently couldn't maintain this particular spell and retreat at the same time, he stretched out his arm to grab her. And then all the strength went out of his legs.

Angus collapsed. Sprawled on his belly, he struggled to drag himself forward, only to discover that suddenly his arms wouldn't obey him either. Dracula tittered, a giddy sound that made him think she'd believed he was going to reach her. He wished she'd been right.

Something popped with a noise like a balloon breaking. Dracula gasped and clutched at her shoulder. The dazzling glare surrounding Angus died abruptly, and he saw that someone had shot her with a tranquilizer dart.

Lazlo, of course. Because he'd been slow getting out of the Cadillac, Dracula's first spell hadn't targeted and disabled his rifle. And now Angus and Judy had detained the fleeing mage long enough for the kine to catch up and nail her.

Dracula swayed. The emerald in her ring flickered feebly

for a moment, but no new miracle ensued as a result. Evidently the drugged dart had already muddled her sufficiently to keep her from using any more magic.

The cessation of her last devastating spell, and the sight of her helpless at last, lent Angus a final surge of strength to rear up and plunge his claws into her hip. Yanking her to the ground, he bit her in the throat and began to feed. Lost in the bliss of taking the nourishment he so desperately needed, he didn't realize that Lazlo had come up behind him until the mortal threw a coat over his smoldering head.

TWENTY-EIGHT: INFORMATION

War, war is still the cry. "War even to the knife!"
— Lord Byron, "Childe Harold's
Pilgrimage"

When Elliott awoke, a dark figure was standing over him. In the blink of an eye he bolted upright and grabbed it by the throat, and then realized it was Lazlo. Startled, probably frightened, the mortal quailed.

The Toreador felt the pulse beating in Lazlo's warm flesh. It had been three days since Elliott had fed, and the Beast murmured in the depths of his mind, telling him to rip the human open and drink his fill. Ignoring the impulse, he hastily released the dresser. "I'm sorry," he said. "I was having a nightmare." It had been his usual one about Mary's death, but he didn't see any need to say so. Probably Lazlo could guess as much anyway. "And I didn't remember where I was." He'd moved into one of the lavishly appointed guest rooms in Roger's mansion for the duration of the crisis. After years of keeping to his own dark, silent, dusty home, it was disorienting to awaken anywhere else.

"That's all right," said Lazlo, straightening his tie and shirt. His voice was an odd mixture of excitement and sadness. "I shouldn't have come into your room uninvited.

But I have news, and I didn't want to wait to tell you. We caught Dracula!"

Elliott felt a thrill of elation, alloyed by a certain wariness. "But I gather there's bad news, as well."

Lazlo sighed. "Yes. Dracula's a mage, and she destroyed Judy before we got her."

The actor stared at him in horror. "Oh, God, no. Not Judy, too. I should have been there! I should have insisted on coming along!"

"It wasn't your part of the fight," Lazlo replied. "Even Judy and the Justicar could barely function in the daylight. There wouldn't have been anything you could have done, except possibly lose your own life, too."

"You don't know that."

"Yes, I do," said Lazlo firmly. "I was there."

Elliott decided that he didn't want to talk about it anymore. Looking away, he said, "All right. I'm sure that Gunter, Angus and the others want to confer with me as soon as possible. Just give me one moment alone and then I'll be down."

Frowning, the human cocked his head. "You'll be all right?"

"Yes," said Elliott resisting the impulse to snap at him. "Just go. Please." Eyes narrowed, Lazlo studied him for another moment, then withdrew.

Elliott's face twisted, and red tears ran down his cheeks. He wanted to throw himself back down on the ornately carved bed, pull the covers over his head and hide from the world, sobbing his heart out like some anguished mortal child.

Judy was gone. Since Mary's death, he'd shut the Brujah out, just as he had Sky; now he'd never get a chance to make it up to her, either, to show her just how much he'd treasured her friendship. For a moment his grief and regret were almost insupportable. Somehow emblematic of all his other guilts and sorrows, they started to drag him down into his familiar despair.

But then a flash of realism, of disgust and sheer boredom with the old, crippled Elliott obsessively wallowing in his personal tragedies, cut through his self-flagellation. Judy's death was a calamity. He was certain that he'd never stop missing her, not even if he survived until the end of the world. But it *wasn't* his fault, and the last thing she would have wanted was for him to sit around crying about it. She'd want him to carry on the fight.

Rising, he strode into the bathroom and washed, then dressed and combed his hair with his customary care. Though he'd told Lazlo he'd hurry, he was sure that the evening's business could wait another few minutes. Performer that he was, he understood that the appearance of haste in a leader could arouse his subordinates' anxieties. And in the wake of Judy's demise, no doubt that was the last thing any of his fellow Kindred needed.

When he was certain he looked his best, he sauntered downstairs, sighing when one of Roger's shrieks resounded through the house. As he'd expected, he found Lazlo, Gunter, Angus and the mortal prisoner in one of the cells at the rear of the house.

The huge Gangrel's skin was red and peeling, presumably not quite healed from its exposure to the sun. Elliott noticed with fleeting amusement that, at the moment, the Justicar and the burly, perpetually ruddy-faced Gunter looked a bit alike. Nude, trembling, eyes wide, seemingly unharmed except for a telltale pastiness and scabby puncture wounds on her throat and hip, Dracula lay strapped down on an operating table with an IV drip in her arm.

"Allow me to introduce the terror of Sarasota," Angus said. He gave the prisoner a leer, lengthening his fangs slightly. She flinched.

"Thank you for catching her," Elliott said. "I'm glad that

you two came through all right." He looked at Lazlo. "And I'm sorry I didn't say so before."

The mortal smiled. "That's all right."

Angus raised his raw, flaking, hairy hand. He'd jammed an emerald ring halfway down his little finger, which appeared to be as far as it would go. "She used this bauble to work her sorcery." He gave Dracula another malevolent smile. "She doesn't seem very magical without it, do you, little one? At least not with my special recipe flowing into your veins." He rooted in his pocket and produced a steel apparatus resembling an oversized staple-puller with two long, white, pointed teeth for the upper prongs. "She must have used this to simulate a vampire bite; I wouldn't be surprised if the points are genuine Kindred fangs. And I imagine she employed a spell to evaporate the missing blood."

"How clever," Gunter boomed jovially. "And now let's slice some answers out of her."

"Exactly what I had in mind," said Angus. The nails on his right hand lengthened and thickened into pointed claws. Dracula jerked helplessly in her restraints.

As a general rule Elliott disliked the use of torture. In the case of Judy's killer it wouldn't particularly bother him, but he had a hunch that it might actually be more efficient to conduct the interrogation by other means. He walked to the operating table and gazed down at the helpless mortal. "You see how it is," he said. "What we have in store for you."

Dracula made a visible effort to pull herself together. Though still trembling, she managed to hold his gaze. "It won't work," she said with the slightest quaver in her voice. "I'm a mage, disciplined in mind and body. Neither torture nor drugs can break me."

Gunter chuckled. "You have no idea what a mind *is*, or how fragile the cramped little prison you call sanity is. But I'd enjoy showing you."

"We *can* break you," Elliott said, beginning to draw on

his charismatic powers, making himself appear as intimidating as possible. Nearly as susceptible to the effect as Dracula, Lazlo caught his breath. "If all else fails, by compelling you to drink our blood. No sorcerer's trick will protect you from that. Three nights, three swallows, and you become a helpless slave for the rest of your life."

Veins of orange, the color of fear, writhed through Dracula's aura, a cloud of light flecked with the countless sparks characteristic of magic use. But she still managed to look Elliott in the face. "Maybe you don't have three nights. Maybe you need to know what I can tell you right now."

"You sound," said the Toreador, "as if you think you can make a deal."

"I do," Dracula replied. "My life and freedom in exchange for answers to your questions."

Gunter made a spitting sound. Elliott altered the pitch of the psychic vibration he was projecting. He still wanted the prisoner to perceive him as menacing, but trustworthy now as well, a man of honor who'd keep his word once given. He pretended to ponder Dracula's proposal, then shrugged and said, "All right, it's a bargain."

"*What?*" Gunter exploded. "That's ridicu—"

Elliott wheeled and shot him a glare. The flaxen-haired Malkavian lurched back a step and fell silent.

Dracula studied the Toreador for a moment, obviously trying to judge if he was sincere. Then she said, "How do I know I can trust you?"

"I suppose you don't," Elliott answered. "But I'm through dickering with you. Take the deal, *now*, or my friends will go to work on you."

The mage hesitated, then her mouth tightened with resolution. "Okay. You seem... decent, for a vampire. What do you want to know?"

"May I?" Angus rumbled. Since the Gangrel was presumably a skilled interrogator, Elliott nodded and stepped back, permitting him to take over. The actor would keep scrutinizing Dracula's aura, monitoring it for any indication that she was lying.

Angus approached the table and rested his massive hand on the edge where the mage could see it. His talons were still very much in evidence. "What's your real name?" he asked.

"Ellen Dunn," she said.

"Where's your chantry?" the Justicar said. Elliott knew very little about mages, but he had heard the term Angus had just used. Supposedly it referred to a coven of sorcerers, often consisting of a teacher and his disciples, perhaps the rough equivalent of a Kindred clan elder and his brood.

Dracula — after weeks of thinking of the murderess by that alias, Elliott continued to do so even after hearing her true name — shook her head. "I don't have one anymore," she said. "They kicked me out."

"What was the point of the murders?" Angus asked.

"I sell my services," Dracula said. "For money usually, and occult lore when I can get it. A vampire I know, a guy with wealth to burn and mystical secrets to trade, hired me to make it look like an undead was running amok killing people openly in Sarasota. He warned me that there were real vampires in the city and that I'd need to operate just after dawn to keep out of your way." She shook her head. "I never dreamed you could jump me in the daylight."

"We're full of surprises," said the Gangrel ironically. "Who *is* your client?"

She hesitated for a heartbeat, then said, "Wesley Shue. A Tremere." Elliott reflected that that made sense; the Warlocks seemed far more likely than other Kindred to have ties to mortal sorcerers. "He lives in Calgary."

Angus glanced around at his associates, who all shrugged. Evidently none of them knew Shue. "Why did he want you to do what you did?" the Justicar said, turning back to Dracula.

"I have no idea," the captive said. "He didn't want to tell, and the pay was good enough that I didn't push him."

"No," said Lazlo, scowling, loathing in his voice, "you just butchered forty-seven people without even understanding what it was for."

Dracula curled her lip contemptuously. "They were only sleepers, or as your masters call them, kine. A resource for superior beings to use, and use up, as they see fit. Hell, throughout history the Kindred have slaughtered them by the thousands, often just for fun, and never given it a second thought."

Gunter chuckled. "She's got you there, mortal."

"I'd rather not debate the question of our ethical responsibilities to the human race," Angus said dryly, "fascinating though the discussion might be. We have more immediate concerns." He looked down at the prisoner. "What else can you tell us about the campaign against the Kindred of Sarasota?"

"Like I said," Dracula replied, "nothing. I was hired to fake vampire murders, and I did. End of story." Elliott surmised from the relatively stable patterns in her aura that she was telling the truth.

"Did you also drive our prince mad?" Lazlo asked.

"No," Dracula said. The dresser scowled in frustration.

"What did you mean," Angus asked, "when you said we might not have three nights to break you?"

Dracula swallowed. "It was a bluff," she admitted, "to convince you to make a deal." Turning her head, she looked beseechingly at Elliott. "And we do have a deal, right? I kept my end."

The Toreador felt both a surge of gloating cruelty and a pang of shame. "No," he said. "I'm afraid I lied to you. You killed my friend, you threatened this domain, and now you're going to pay for it. We'll hand you over to Judy's progeny to deal with as they see fit." He glanced around at his allies.

"Shall we continue this discussion in more congenial surroundings?"

For a moment the murderess simply stared at him, too horrified to speak. But as Elliott walked out the door she began to shout, begging him to come back, she had more information to trade, secrets that he desperately needed to hear. The sound of her pleas and curses followed him and his companions down the hall.

Gunter gave Elliott an admiring grin. "After all the years I've known you," the Malkavian said, "I still believed that you meant to let her go."

Feeling guiltier and less vengeful now, the Toreador shrugged. "I'm an actor. One with — how did you put it?— a bewitching voice. I didn't want to make a promise I didn't mean to keep, but I was afraid that, for whatever reason, she *would* resist the torture, and that we *might* need to know what she had to tell us without delay."

Angus gripped his shoulder. "We're at war," he said. "We do what we have to. Don't agonize over it. Unless I read you wrong, you're prone to that kind of masochism. I suppose it's a sign that you still have a fair measure of humanitas, but if a Kindred isn't careful, over the centuries it can eat him alive."

Gunter regarded his fellow undead, then clucked and shook his head. Clearly he had no idea why Elliott felt ashamed. "You did well," he said to the Toreador, "though I have to admit I was looking forward to taking the bitch apart."

Elliott did his best to mask his distaste. Gunter was Gunter, and it would be pointless, if not counterproductive, to annoy him by reproaching him for his sadism. Besides, having just experienced the same impulse in his own heart, the Toreador would have felt hypocritical decrying it in someone else. "The Brujah will probably let you sit in on the execution. I imagine they'll do their best to make her suffer."

The group entered Roger's study. Elliott sat down behind the desk; the other Kindred settled in two of the leather seats in front of it and Lazlo took up his customary position standing by the door. "Are we sure she told us the truth, and that she told us everything?" the mortal asked fretfully.

"I am," Elliott said. He explained how he knew.

"But it's not *enough!*" the dresser exclaimed.

"It certainly isn't everything we'd hoped for," Angus said. Reaching into his navy pinstriped suit coat, he produced a cigar and a box of matches. Despite the claws which he had, perhaps absentmindedly, retained, he lit the long, black Lonsdale dexterously. "Our chief adversary has done a first-rate job of making it difficult for us to trace him through his agents. I imagine that Wesley Shue is at best only a lieutenant himself, and that when we inquire in Calgary we won't find him at home. He may well be lurking here in Sarasota, or somewhere nearby. Still, his identity could ultimately provide the key to this entire situation. You never know just how far a clue will take you."

"Meanwhile," said Elliott wearily, "the vandalism of the art and the assault on our financial holdings will continue." And then a square shadow about three inches across shimmered into existence on the desktop.

Startled, the Toreador jerked his hand away from it, then warily touched it. His fingertip went right through the square — it wasn't solid — but he felt a vibration that somehow suggested it was in the process of *becoming* solid. He pulled back his hand and sure enough, over the course of the next fifteen seconds, the dark form became fully opaque, with sharply defined edges. Now he could see it was a computer disk.

"What the hell is going on?" Gunter growled. The cellular phone in Lazlo's sweater pocket buzzed.

The dresser pulled it out and said, "Hello." After listening briefly, he frowned and handed the instrument to Angus. "It's the woman who called before to tell Judy and me that there were enemies prowling around near the Tropical Gardens. She wants to talk to you, Justicar."

Angus raised the phone to his ear and then, a moment later, gave it back. Elliott heard the drone of a dial tone; the person on the other end had hung up. "She said the password is Scorpio," the bearded vampire said. "The password to open the disk, I assume."

"*Who* says?" Elliott demanded. "You know who she is, don't you?"

"She's on our side," the Gangrel replied. "Let's leave it at that."

"The hell you say!" Gunter snarled. "We want to know what you know, and right now!"

Angus smiled. "You just *think* you want to know. I guarantee that the knowledge would only depress you."

"Vee haff vays of making you talk," said Gunter, his voice a caricature of a movie Nazi's. Leering, fangs extending, he sprang to his feet.

Elliott understood the Malkavian's frustration. He *hated* the feeling of groping in the dark, of being forced to grapple with phantom opponents and to rely on equally elusive allies in a game whose rules he didn't understand; the notion that one of his own comrades was withholding information was particularly galling. Yet he trusted Angus: after the way the Gangrel had helped him in Conclave and tracked down Dracula, how could he not? And so, projecting his Toreador charisma, he shouted, "*Stop!*"

Gunter jerked around to face him. Angus, in the process of rising, slumped back down onto his chair.

"I don't like all the mystery, either," Elliott said to Gunter. "But I daresay that each of us has his own closely guarded secrets, and Angus has proved himself a friend."

Gunter glared at his fellow member of the primogen for a moment, then sighed. "All right, I'll let it go for the moment."

"Thank you for your forbearance," said Angus dryly. He turned to Lazlo. "I assume you have a computer somewhere in this palace."

"Of course," the dresser replied. Though his voice was nearly as steady as usual, Elliott sensed how relieved he was that the Gangrel and the Malkavian hadn't come to blows. "Several, including one in my own office." He tucked the phone back in his pocket. "Shall we go there?"

As the four men strode through the house, Elliott realized that he'd never seen Lazlo's office. It turned out to be a spacious, well-lit room furnished with the eclectic mix of antiques and exquisite modern pieces characteristic of the house as a whole. A faint scent of fine cognac hung in the air — evidently the mortal had had a drink in here within the last day or so — and framed circus posters from the nineteenth and early twentieth centuries adorned the walls.

Lazlo sat down at his desk and turned on his computer, which chimed and began to hum. As the screen lit up, he inserted the disk in a slot in the side of the machine, waited for the image on the monitor to change, and then typed *Scorpio*.

The screen altered again, to display paragraphs of text. Crouching, peering intently, the three Kindred spent the next half-hour reading over Lazlo's shoulder.

Finally, feeling giddy, his body light and vibrant with elation, Elliott said, "We've got it. There are gaps — it's not entirely clear why Durrell picked on us — but still, everything we truly needed to know is here."

"Not quite," Lazlo said. "He doesn't explain how he and his accomplices made Roger sick. He alludes to it, but he doesn't go into details."

"Don't worry," said Elliott, straightening up and gripping the valet's shoulder. "We'll make them tell us."

"Assuming that the information is legitimate," Gunter said.

Cocking his head, Elliott regarded the Malkavian quizzically. "You have doubts?"

Gunter shrugged. "If someone wanted to ruin the Kindred of Sarasota, he might try to trick them into taking hostile action against other, innocent members of the Camarilla. Imagine how that could be made to look in Conclave."

"But obviously, my acquaintance on the phone sent this intelligence," Angus said, "and as I told you, she's on our side."

"I agreed that I wouldn't try to force your secrets out of you," Gunter replied dourly. "But on the other hand, you can't expect Elliott and me to make vital decisions on the basis of your unsupported word."

"But it isn't unsupported," Elliott said reasonably. "By every indication, the journal is the real thing. Look at all the corroborative detail. And remember, it was Durrell who tried to drive me mad in the Assembly — Durrell who just happened to be prepared to work the requisite magic without a moment's delay." He shoved away a tiny, nagging doubt that the Tremere could be the satanic demigod Sky had described. Possessing charismatic powers himself, he understood how a Kindred could cloak himself in a semblance of terrible glory; his friend, after all, had been more or less insane. "I'm as paranoid, as worried about making a wrong move, as you are, Gunter, but if this document isn't proof enough to spur us into action, I despair of ever collecting enough before the enemy ruins us."

Gunter scowled, pondering, and then slowly smiled. "You're nowhere near as paranoid as I am," he said. "I'm a Malkavian. A trained professional. But all right. I admit that, ninety-nine chances out of a hundred, the disk is for real. What are we going to do about it?"

"You can convene another Assembly," said Lazlo, swivelling his chair to face them. "This time, *you* take the offensive and denounce Durrell and his henchmen."

"We could," said Elliott, "but that would give them advance warning that we're on to them, and the chance to flee. Or to mobilize allies like Palmer Guice to subvert the cause of justice."

Lazlo looked up at Angus. "Then you could take the matter directly to the Inner Circle."

The huge Gangrel shook his head. The gold ring in his ear gleamed against his shaggy brown mane. "As I told Elliott, you don't want to involve my masters in your problems. They have their own perspectives, their own rivalries and their own agendas. They might do something that would appall you, for reasons you wouldn't even comprehend."

Elliott sensed that Angus had spoken honestly, but that he also had another, personal reason for not wanting to appeal to the overlords of the seven clans. Perhaps he didn't want them to find out about his affiliation with the woman who'd sent the disk. But since the Justicar was advocating Elliott's own point of view, the Toreador could see no advantage in confronting him about his motives.

"Since we know that Durrell is holed up in Camelot," the actor said, "I propose a sneak attack. *Afterward,* if anyone challenges us about it, we'll present the evidence that the Warlock was our foe. Neither Guice nor anyone else will pursue the matter further, not on behalf of a man and a scheme we've already destroyed."

Gunter nodded. "I like it. Revenge *should* be personal."

Elliott silently agreed with him. He genuinely believed that he had sound tactical reasons for the course he'd recommended, but inwardly he couldn't deny that a yearning for vengeance, for Judy, Sky, Rosalita and all the rest of the fallen, was motivating him as well.

Lazlo grimaced. "If you fight, of course I'll fight with you. A part of me is eager to. But the domain has taken too many losses already. Sneak attack or no, there are bound to be more."

"I know," Elliott said somberly. "But if Durrell disappears, any hope of curing Roger may go with him."

The mortal sighed. "Okay. When you put it like that."

Elliott turned to Angus. "I understand that you came to Sarasota to apprehend Dracula, and you have. You never said that you intended to march into battle against our other enemies —"

The Justicar snorted. "Oh, I'll tag along, Toreador, for various reasons. A Kindred in my lofty position" — his rough bass voice dripped sarcasm — "might overlook Durrell and Shue plotting against Roger Phillips and his subjects, but I can't tolerate them deliberately endangering the Masquerade to do it. Shall we go rally the troops? Maybe your friends Cobb, Jones, McNamara and their broods would like to join the party. McNamara could lead our Brujah...."

TWENTY-NINE: REVELATIONS

But evil men and seducers shall wax worse and worse,
deceiving and being deceived.
— II Timothy 3:13

Dan awoke to the intoxicating scent of mortal vitae, the feel of the warm liquid splashing against his upturned face, and the burning throat and cramped stomach that the Hunger always produced if denied too long. He frantically gulped at the cascade.

Half-delirious with the ecstasy of feeding, he felt the blood begin to wash away a hundred aches and pains. Half-healed injuries — he dimly remembered being shot, although as yet he couldn't summon up the details — resumed the process of regeneration. And then the stream of vitae stopped pouring down.

His eyes flew open. He seemed to be lying on a surface about a yard above the floor, although, strangely, he couldn't exactly feel the solid length of it pressing against his back. The only light was a sourceless green phosphorescence, illuminating the rough dirt walls of a cave or tunnel. Above him towered a nude man, his skin golden, his musculature and face as perfect as those of a masterpiece of classical sculpture, clasping a chubby, unconscious woman with long brown hair in his arms. She had a wound in her throat, and Dan imagined the golden man effortlessly holding her above his prisoner's mouth, squeezing out her blood as if she were a wineskin.

Smiling down at him, the naked man said, "That's enough refreshment for now."

But it wasn't. Dan's system was still depleted. He tried to make a grab for the woman, to drag her bleeding body back to his lips. But something not unlike the coils of a python tightened around his form with crushing force, holding him in place. He peered down the length of his body, but couldn't see what was holding him; his restraints were invisible.

He didn't think he could break the bonds, at least not instantly; yet, half-berserk with blood lust, he almost kept struggling against them anyway. But he didn't want to humiliate himself in front of the golden man; he wanted to appear rational and self-possessed, not like a mindless animal. And so he held himself in check.

"Very good," said his captor, as if commending him on his willpower.

Though he realized that he was in no position to express resentment, Dan bristled at the condescension in the other man's tone. "Who are you?" the prisoner asked. Sharpening his hearing, he discovered that the naked figure had no heartbeat. Evidently, despite his atypical coloring, he was one of the Kindred.

Dumping the unconscious woman casually on the muddy floor, the other vampire smiled. "Durrell knows me as Timothy Baxter, but perhaps you're familiar with my original name. In Hellas, when your mistress" — the matter-of-fact manner in which he alluded to Melpomene convinced Dan that it would be useless to deny he was her agent — "and I were fledglings together, I went by Tithonys."

Dan felt a jolt of fear. Since the beginning of his mission, he'd dreaded the thought of coming face to face with

Melpomene's opposite number. Now it had happened: he was bound and helpless, and the enemy Methuselah had turned out to be the adversary that his faithless patron feared most of all.

Except that he couldn't really be, could he? Eager to discount the other vampire's claim, Dan said, "Bullshit. Tithonys is dead. Melpomene killed him in France, hundreds of years ago."

The golden Kindred's beautiful smile grew wider. Beholding it, Dan was convinced that this godlike creature was telling the truth, that he could have no *reason* to deceive someone as insignificant as his prisoner. The younger Kindred belatedly grasped that he was responding to an unnatural charisma like Melpomene's, but recognition did little to free him from the effect. "You're half right," Tithonys said. "I *was* dead. But after my demise I entered the service of a, well, a god or a fallen angel according to your point of view, known as the Count of the Wasteland. Ultimately, after many achievements on its behalf, it saw fit to restore my earthly existence. Someday, perhaps, I'll tell you the whole story. I can assure you that you've never heard anything like it."

Struggling to mask his fear, trembling slightly anyway, Dan said, "What do you want with me?"

"Relax," Tithonys said. He clasped Dan's shoulder, and the prisoner's fear gave way to a sense of profound relief. Knowing the feeling was artificial, that the ancient vampire was still manipulating his emotions, Dan struggled not to succumb to it. "If I'd wanted you harmed, I could have left you in Durrell's clutches instead of persuading him to turn you over to me. But I'm hoping that we can be friends. You are, after all, quite special."

Puzzled, Dan frowned. "What do you mean?"

Tithonys grinned impishly. "Aha! I didn't think you realized, and yet you might have guessed, if you'd pondered the clues. You never knew your sire, did you?"

Dan instinctively felt leery of giving the Methuselah any information about himself, but he couldn't see the harm in disclosing such a simple fact. "No."

"And how long have you been a vampire?"

"About thirty years."

"And you've discovered you're quite powerful, haven't you?"

Dan grimaced. "I don't feel very powerful strapped down like this."

"Possibly not. But I rummaged through your memories while you were unconscious" — the idea of such a thing made Dan feel sick to his stomach — "and I saw that, even before Melpomene enhanced your abilities with a measure of her blood, you sometimes held your own against vampires far older than you were: undead against whom no one would have predicted you had a chance."

Dan shrugged, causing his bonds to tighten slightly. He still had no idea what Tithonys was driving at. "All right, I guess I'm reasonably tough. So what?"

"So this." Somewhere in the tunnels something thumped four times, a dull sound like a colossal heart beating. For a moment a foul, fecal stench suffused the air. Startled, Dan twitched, but the Methuselah didn't react. "Do you understand that our race has two sources of power: generation, the number of ancestors that separate one from Caine, and sheer longevity?"

"I've heard it said."

"Then you should be able to see," Tithonys replied, "that, lacking the latter, you must be gifted with regard to the former. The creator who embraced and abandoned you was a Methuselah. Specifically, she was Melpomene."

Dan goggled at his captor, so astonished that for a moment he forgot to be afraid. "That's crazy! And even if it were true, how could *you* know it?"

"Various means, some of which you simply wouldn't understand. Suffice it to say, I took the liberty of obtaining a sample of your vitae. It smells and tastes much like hers. And, as I mentioned, I looked into your head. Your conscious mind doesn't recall your transformation, but your unconscious does, albeit murkily. Someday, when time doesn't press, perhaps I can help you recover the memory... if you're interested."

Dan scowled. "I don't understand why you're telling me this —"

Tithonys smiled. "We'll get to that."

"— but I do see that you aren't giving me any proof. I'm just supposed to take your word for it."

"Not so. Be patient, I'm building a case. We've already discussed your unusual strength. Now consider the weakness you've developed since drinking Melpomene's vitae. The tendency to stand helplessly transfixed before beauty. The Achilles' heel of your treacherous mistress' bloodline."

"Like you said, I caught it from drinking her blood."

Tithonys grinned boyishly. Despite himself, Dan felt a pang of affection for his captor. "Take it from an old diabolist. You can't 'catch' other vampires' handicaps that way. Otherwise I'd be as ugly as a Nosferatu, as hairy as a Gangrel, as short-tempered as a Brujah — well, you get the idea. That second drink from your sire's veins merely activated a trait which, like certain of your abilities, has lain dormant inside you since the draft that made you."

Belatedly Dan remembered something Melpomene had told him, a fact that seemed to contradict what Tithonys was saying. "Wait a minute. Melpomene told me that she had spent most of the last hundred years hibernating."

"If so, and I think you've discovered just how far you should trust her word, then she roused herself long enough to create you. Although she evidently had no notion that I'd already returned from the afterlife, perhaps she, psychic that she is, had a premonition that she might need you, a powerful agent with no perceptible ties to her, a seasoned combat veteran who'd grown up in Sarasota and was thus well prepared to act in its defense. An ace in the hole. Or perhaps it was merely a precaution. We ancients concoct safeguards to defend ourselves against the unlikeliest contingencies. It's what keeps us alive."

"Why didn't she tell me this herself?"

Tithonys arched an eyebrow. "Would you have pledged her your allegiance if she had? Haven't you always hated the sire who Embraced and then abandoned you?"

Dan's muscles tightened in rage. He couldn't tell to what extent Tithonys' charismatic powers had evoked the surge of emotion and to what extent it simply flowed from his heart. "Yes," he admitted.

"And you don't even know the full extent of her abuse."

Dan stared at him. "What do you mean by that?"

Tithonys squeezed the prisoner's shoulder as if to comfort him. "She didn't want to teach and nurture you herself. That might have compromised your usefulness. But she couldn't allow you to find affection or a master who would accept your fealty elsewhere, either, for fear that she wouldn't be able to lure you into her service when the time was right. And so she laid two curses on you.

"First, she deprived you of the ability to feel affection for kine. Many Kindred pursue friendships with mortals for centuries after their transformations. A few never lose their fondness and their empathy for humankind. But you felt alienated from your prey immediately, didn't you?"

Dan swallowed. "Yes."

"Second, she put an invisible mark on your brow, a stain that would make you repellent to other vampires. And thus you've always been scorned, and desperately lonely. She removed the symbol the night she met you on the beach. Had she not, Wyatt Vandercar and his anarch tools might not have welcomed you even after you saved them from the Brujah."

Dan remembered how, as he was sucking blood from her, Melpomene's fingertip had traced a symbol on his forehead.

Her touch had left a tingling trail. He decided that everything Tithonys had told him was true: the female Methuselah was responsible for every bit of the misery he'd endured over the past thirty years. The realization made his fangs ache in their sockets. "God damn her," he growled.

Tithonys smiled. "Why should we let the Deity have all the fun? If you'll help me find Melpomene, we can punish her ourselves."

Puzzled, Dan peered up at him. "I don't know how to find her. I'm surprised you didn't get *that* from my memory."

"I did," Tithonys said. "But you're her childe. Her blood. The two of you are linked on the astral plane. If you'll open your mind and soul to me willingly, completely, I believe I can attack her through you."

For a moment, still seething with hate for Melpomene, Dan was tempted to go along with the plan. Then another reflexive flash of repugnance at the notion of having his innermost being invaded cut through the haze of fury.

He had to remember that Tithonys was a Methuselah too, and, beneath his preternatural charm, no doubt as icily intent on controlling him as Melpomene had ever been. If Dan were fool enough to take part in whatever piece of black magic his captor was proposing, there was no telling what terrible harm it might do him.

No, damn it, he was through being anybody's flunky. He just wanted out of this nightmare. But maybe if he pretended to go along with the program, Tithonys would set him free. Trying to control his emotions — a painful tangle of fear, anger and, still, the irrational affection that the golden-skinned vampire had instilled in him — he said, "I'm with you. Let's kill the bitch."

Tithonys studied him for a moment, then sighed and shook his head. "Dan, Dan, Dan. You can't deceive me. I'm too old and wise. I can see your aura too clearly. But *why* won't you help me? Melpomene betrayed and abandoned you *twice*: once when she Embraced you, and once when she left you to perish last night. And my cause is just. She murdered the only person I ever loved. Hell, she's been committing similar atrocities since the dawn of time. Are you concerned about doing something that might endanger her other pawns in this game she and I are playing? If so, I can't imagine why. Roger Phillips and his people certainly never did anything for you. And they're doomed in any case."

Dan's eyes narrowed. "How's that?"

"As I told you, a wary old general like me is prepared for every contingency. Even as one scheme fails, it empowers a *new* strategy. Long ago, I laid plans to curse Prince Roger into madness. Since I needed some of the prince's personal items for the spell — they're buried in this chamber — I enslaved one of his progeny to steal them and to serve as my spy thereafter. I arranged the murder of Mary Sinclair, the wife of Phillips' chief lieutenant, to cripple the grieving husband psychologically. And I recruited Durrell to organize a multifaceted campaign against the Kindred of Sarasota. The goal of it all, of course, was to destroy Melpomene's descendants and the artistic treasures they'd created, gradually and painfully. I knew that such a calamity would devastate her even if it didn't draw her out into the open.

"Alas, the strategy isn't panning out. With the Toreador's beloved Phillips unable to command, Elliott Sinclair was supposed to prove inadequate as a leader; but somehow he's pulled himself together and is holding the line rather well. And now you, unbeknownst to poor Durrell, have provided crucial information about him and his efforts to Melpomene. She in turn has passed it along to her soldiers, who intend to launch a surprise counteroffensive after the park closes, in the final hours before dawn."

Tithonys smiled. "But it doesn't matter a bit. Because, having met you, I have a new plan.

"When Sinclair and his friends invade the fortress above our heads, they'll find to their dismay that the resident

Kindred have had a *little* advance warning of their arrival. The resultant fighting will be chaotic and bloody in the extreme, and because the gore in question will be of supernatural origin, it will generate an energy I can use for occult purposes. Specifically, to strike down every living or undead being — except for you and me, of course — for miles around."

Dan gaped at the ancient vampire. "We're just outside Orlando. You're talking about thousands, probably tens of thousands, of innocent people. Why the hell would you want to do that?"

"As a sacrifice to *my* patron, the Count of the Wasteland," Tithonys said. "In return, he'll grant me the power I need to reach through you and smite your mistress. I'd *like* to believe that I have enough power to destroy her unassisted, but she *is* my peer, and she did kill *me* once, so it would be foolish to take chances." Sighing, he shook his head. "Please believe me, ordinarily I wouldn't be so profligate with the lives of the masses, or betray and squander my servants either. But I'm on the brink of a final victory." As he spoke, his somber expression gradually warped into a savage grin. "*Now*, not in five hundred or a thousand years. You can't imagine the joy I'm feeling!"

What I imagine, Dan thought grimly, *is that Melpomene told me the truth about one thing, anyway. You Methuselahs are all crazy.* "I thought you said I had to cooperate for you to get at her," he said.

"And now that you know everything, aren't you willing to do so? Think it through, my friend. Melpomene forsook you twice over. So far, I haven't harmed you, and you understand something of what manner of being I am. I rose from the final death. I have ties to an entity more powerful than Caine himself. Someday I'll win the Jyhad, the *entire* Jyhad, and reign over this planet. Don't you understand the futility of defying me? Wouldn't you prefer to be on my good side?"

A wave of dread and awe swept through Dan's mind. He cringed, tightening his bonds, and squinched shut his eyes. His courage and pride began to give way to a desperate *need* to capitulate, before his godlike captor squashed him like the gnat he was.

But something, perhaps his innate stubbornness, wouldn't let him give in. *He's using his damn eyes and voice on you*, he reminded himself desperately. *You aren't really this scared, it's just a trick.* And after a few more agonizing moments, his fear loosened its grip.

He decided he had nothing to lose by trying to lie one more time. Shuddering, panting reflexively — manifestations of terror he didn't have to fake — he said, "All right! Please! I *do* want to work for you!"

Tithonys smiled. "That's better." Dan shivered anew, this time with surprised relief. "I *almost* believed you." The prisoner flinched. "I see now how you managed to deceive your late associate Wyatt. But as I told you, you have no hope of fooling me. And since I evidently can't convince you to help me in your present frame of mind, I'm afraid that I'm going to have to undertake renovations in your head."

Dan had to struggle to keep his voice steady. "What do you mean — a Blood Bond?"

"No," the ancient vampire replied. "Would that we could resolve the issue so painlessly. But alas, we don't have three nights. I'm not sure I can hold on to the magic that the Count will grant me that long. And if Melpomene sensed the threat and chose to hide in slumber deep within the earth, we might not be able to find her even by exploiting your link to her. Thus I'm afraid we'll have to change your attitude the hard way."

Dan strained convulsively, struggling again to break his bonds. Tithonys said, "*Stop*," and the prisoner's muscles locked up on him.

Frowning thoughtfully, like someone solving a puzzle, the

Methuselah began to pass his index finger through the space about twelve inches above Dan's eyes. His fingertip left trails of blue and crimson light, as if he were finger-painting on the air.

Dan's intuition warned him to shut his eyes, but when he tried, he couldn't. The luminous structure materializing above him was already too beautiful. Too captivating.

"You won't be able to stop looking," Tithonys said. "No Toreador could. The spectacle is simply too exotic." He added another stroke, and a bolt of agony stabbed through Dan's skull, a pain that was as much psychic as physical.

Tithonys was right. Dan *still* couldn't look away. If anything, the glowing matrix was even lovelier, more fascinating, than before. And yet there was something *wrong* with it, something that tortured the eyes and ripped at the foundations of the mind.

"The design is a hyperspatial construct," Tithonys said. He added another curve of azure sheen, and Dan screamed. "It exists in five dimensions. Unfortunately, the average psyche, kine or Kindred, is only equipped to see in three. If one forces the psyche to exceed that limitation, the result is anguish." He added a final scarlet loop. "That should do it."

"All right," Dan croaked frantically. "I'll help you. Just take the lights away!"

"You don't mean that," said Tithonys. "Even if you believe you do, you'd change your tune if I released you so soon. But by the time I return from conducting the sacrifice, you *will* mean it. You won't care about *anything* except ending the pain."

The Methuselah turned and strode toward an opening in the wall, his bare, filthy feet leaving tracks in the muck. Dan's head throbbed, and he shrieked again.

THIRTY: THE WARNING

Necessity is the plea for every infringement of human freedom. It is the argument of tyrants; it is the creed of slaves.
— William Pitt the Younger, in a speech before the House of Commons

Restless, Durrell prowled through the shadows in the new, uncompleted addition to the theme park. Lattices of girders rose around him, slicing the night sky into squares. To his hypersensitive nose, the balmy air held the smell of freshly poured concrete. Off to the south, in the portion of Camelot that was open to the public, colored lights glowed, rides groaned and clattered, and competing strains of modern pop and medieval music sounded from various pavilions.

Unlike many of his fellow Tremere, Durrell wasn't truly psychic. His great talent was casting spells. But he sometimes suspected that he had a vestige of second sight, because he occasionally got edgy shortly before something went wrong. That was how he felt tonight.

Shaking his head as if to clear it, he reminded himself that his formless premonitions had proved wrong as often as they'd been correct. Perhaps he was simply out of sorts because the campaign against Sarasota was advancing so slowly, or perhaps because he and his associates had had such a close call last night. The mysterious Dan Murdock might easily have gotten away, and God — and presumably Timothy, by now — knew how much the Caitiff had learned sneaking around the chantry, or what he might ultimately have done with the information.

Despite his usual reluctance to visit Timothy's warren, Durrell decided to go and learn the results of the interrogation. Perhaps the intelligence would soothe his jangled nerves. He turned, glancing around for the nearest entrance to the service tunnels, and then a hand tapped him on the shoulder.

Badly startled, the Tremere jerked around to see that somehow Timothy had crept up behind him. "Good evening," said the ancient Kindred. "Can you spare a cigarette?"

His hands shaking slightly as he struggled as usual to conceal the mixture of artificial devotion and largely genuine fear that Timothy inspired in him, Durrell removed a gilt silver cigarette case and matchbox, both gifts from Aleister Crowley, from his pocket. "It's been a while since I've seen you outside your cave," he said.

"I have rather urgent news," said Timothy. Maddeningly, instead of going ahead and relating it he paused to take one of the custom-made Turkish cigarettes. He waved away the matches, however, and when he placed the cigarette between his lips, the tip began to burn of its own accord. "I'm afraid Murdock was working for Elliott Sinclair. During his reconnaissance, he learned your identity and exactly what we're up to. And he managed to relay the information before your people captured him."

For a moment Durrell could only gape in horror. "What are you telling me? I thought you said you were certain that we captured him before he could do any real damage!"

Timothy shrugged. "I didn't see how he could have, considering that the phone in his rental car didn't work. The circuits were fused. And my *instincts* told me no harm had been done. Apparently even I can err occasionally. I've since learned that Sinclair, his subordinates and certain allies are assembling in Orlando even now to raid Camelot as soon as it closes."

Durrell ran his fingers through his hair. His mind felt frozen, paralyzed by the shock of his secret partner's tidings, and he struggled to goad it into motion. "Then we have just enough time to evacuate."

Timothy grimaced as if he were disappointed in the Tremere. "That would be foolish as well as cowardly."

With the force of the Methuselah's supernatural charisma behind it, the insult stung. Exerting his willpower, Durrell tried not to let it influence him. "The plan was to snipe at the Toreador from all sides, wear them down and then, if we had to, finish them off with one lightning stroke. We never figured on permitting *them* to attack *us*."

"Strategies change to fit changing circumstances," the ancient Kindred said. "That's the nature of war, or at least it had better be if one wants to win. My astral sources tell me that thus far, desiring a personal vengeance, Sinclair and his associates haven't revealed your identity to anyone but their troops. Destroy them tonight, win the victory for which we've been striving, and they never will. Disappear, however, and they'll denounce you to the Camarilla."

"It would be my word against theirs."

Timothy snorted, puffing out a burst of pungent smoke. "Do you think they won't be able to find proof to back up their allegations, now that they know where to look? If you flee, I imagine they'll find damning evidence in the very chantry beneath our feet. And once they've made their case against you, the pleasant existence you've known for the past few centuries will end abruptly. You won't be Sebastian Durrell the respected elder and magus anymore, but a wretched fugitive. Neither the Kindred of Sarasota, your prince, your clan, nor, indeed, the Camarilla as a whole, will rest until they've hunted you down. Remember, you willfully threatened the Masquerade."

Durrell swallowed. "I have Guice to protect me."

"Guice is an amoral opportunist who'll abandon you at the first indication that supporting you might undermine his own position. And your enemies have their own Justicar."

The Tremere grimaced. "Very well, we'll stand our ground. I suppose it is the only way. We have troops billeted in the general area. I can summon them to act as reinforcements. The only problem is that many of them — the anarchs, for example — don't know for whom they're actually working."

"You can delude them for an hour or two. After the battle begins it won't matter if they realize they've been duped. With Prince Roger's raging childer at their throats, they'll have to keep fighting or die."

Durrell nodded. "I imagine Sinclair will still have us outnumbered," he said grimly. Many of the Tremere's minions were scattered around the world, destroying art. Others were stationed in the Sarasota area, too far away to reach Orlando in time, because he hadn't anticipated that he might need them to defend his base.

"But you and your people know the battleground," Timothy said encouragingly. "You have your thaumaturgy. And you have me."

Durrell peered at his companion in surprise. Timothy's words inspired a glow of optimism, and yet the ancient vampire had always been so concerned with concealing his existence that the wary part of the Tremere, the part that habitually resisted the Methuselah's charismatic spell, found the promise difficult to credit. "Are you saying that you're going to fight alongside us?"

"Absolutely," said Timothy, gripping the magus' shoulder. Despite his doubts, Durrell felt a surge of affection and gratitude. "Now that we've reached the endgame, it's time for me to emerge from the shadows. So you see, our victory is assured. At least it will be if you get moving. You have preparations to make."

Durrell glanced at his platinum Rolex, then felt a jolt of alarm. It was later than he'd imagined. He'd assumed he'd be able to map out a cunning defensive strategy, identify and fortify key positions, place his troops where they could do the most damage and be least vulnerable to harm. But there simply wasn't time. Camelot would close in about eighty minutes, and no doubt the Kindred of Sarasota would storm the place immediately thereafter. "My god," he exclaimed, "when did you figure all this out?"

"Just a few minutes ago," Timothy replied. "Interrogations and divinations take time."

Durrell had to admit that they did. For the average Kindred. But with his charismatic powers and command over the potent magic of *Al Azif*, shouldn't Timothy have been able to cut the required time significantly? The Tremere's instincts told him that the ancient vampire had been *sitting* on the information, but he couldn't imagine why Timothy would do such a thing. Surely, if he'd decided to betray his partner, he wouldn't have warned him of the forthcoming attack at all. The only reason for waiting until the last possible moment would seem to be to ensure a protracted, savage struggle, one in which neither side began with a clear-cut advantage and both would suffer heavy losses. But what could be the point of that?

None, Durrell supposed. Not unless, as he'd sometimes suspected, his enigmatic collaborator was profoundly sadistic or outright mad.

"You have the oddest expression," the Methuselah said mildly. "If I didn't know better, I'd think you were having misgivings. You *do* trust me, don't you, Sebastian?"

Prompted by Timothy's charm, Durrell felt a twinge of guilt for doubting the Methuselah, but his suspicions lingered in the other, less susceptible part of his psyche. Yet there was no point in acknowledging them. Indeed, he was *afraid* to acknowledge them. "Of course I do," he said.

The handsome Methuselah smiled, his white teeth gleaming in the gloom. It looked as if his fangs were protruding slightly, but perhaps that was only Durrell's imagination. "Good. You can. You should. When the battle is won, your faith will be rewarded with safety, new wealth, enhanced status and all the deepest secrets of Abd al-Azrad."

For the first time, hearing the name of the grimoire Durrell felt not greed, but a pang of loathing. Because *Al Azif* was the lure that had drawn him into this mess.

"If I didn't trust *you*," the ancient vampire continued, his dark eyes shining, "if I suspected that you might consider running out on me, I'd feel obliged to ask you to consider who you were *more* afraid of, Sinclair and his minions, or me. I'm glad our friendship is firm enough to preclude the need for such threats."

Durrell repressed a shiver. "I am, too," he said.

THIRTY-ONE: THE INVASION

It is well that war is so terrible; else we would grow too fond of it.
— Robert E. Lee

Standing on the grass among his restless troops, waiting for the last few minutes to crawl by, Elliott looked at the night sky and thought of Mary.

When he'd confronted Gunter in front of the assembled Kindred in Roger's house, and when he and Rosalita had traveled to Ohio to retrieve the Fouquet painting, he hadn't known for a fact that he was going to wind up in mortal combat. This time he did. He could feel Death's door standing open, inviting him to enter. Promising him surcease from loneliness, sorrow and guilt; and perhaps, if the universe was kinder than it seemed, even reunion with his love.

The prospect of perishing in battle tempted him, but not as much as he might have expected. He realized that, at bottom, he wanted to *win* this war, end the harassment of Sarasota and restore his sire to health. He wanted to stake Sebastian Durrell and his thugs through their treacherous hearts and leave them lying outdoors to burn in the sun. The recognition made him feel vaguely uncomfortable with himself. He supposed he'd grown accustomed to the old, wretched Elliott, sunk in misery and self-pity. He didn't quite know what to make of the angry, iron-willed stranger who'd supplanted him.

Dressed in loose-fitting black, his Herculean chest crisscrossed with bandoliers and his eyes glowing an eerie red, Angus looked at his watch. "The park closed fifteen minutes ago," he said. "The last tourists should be pulling out of the parking lot by now."

"Indeed they should," Elliott said, shifting his grip on his Armalite AR-18 assault rifle. Evoking his charismatic abilities, he turned and regarded his followers. "Ladies and gentlemen, it's time. The enemy we're about to engage poisoned our prince, murdered our friends, destroyed our treasures and tried to drive us from our domain. Let's make the bastards pay!" He pivoted and sprinted into the darkness. Silent and fast as swooping hawks, his companions dashed after him.

Elliott supposed that his companions really hadn't needed his little speech to hearten them. They were, after all, vampires, not mortals. The abuse they'd endured, and the Beast lurking in every one of their souls, would ensure that they were avid for the fight. But he'd felt an urge to address them, so he had.

The vampires crossed one service road after another. Eventually raw Florida scrub land, coarse saw grass and palmetto bushes gave way to landscaping: smooth, verdant lawns; artificial lakes with gushing fountains; flower beds; topiary figures of dragons, damsels in conical hats, and knights on horseback. Then Camelot itself appeared, first as a smudge of glow against the eastern sky, then as a fantastic collection of illuminated turrets and battlements. Perhaps amused by the phony medieval architecture, Angus snorted. As the Kindred approached the outer wall a few of Gunter's Malkavians, who'd moved up earlier, relying on their powers of concealment to avoid detection, slipped out of the shadows to join them.

Elliott raised his hand to halt his onrushing troops, then took out his cellular phone and began making contact with the leaders of the other three advance teams. When he'd verified that everyone had moved up on schedule, that Camelot was surrounded on all four sides, he gave the order to go in.

The Toreador elder and his companions slunk up to the eight-foot wall. It was concrete, but textured and painted to look as if it had been constructed of blocks of rough-hewn granite. Scrambling over it without difficulty, the Kindred found themselves in a lane of obnoxiously quaint wooden structures with shops, including an ice- cream stand and a salon where tourists could be photographed in mock medieval clothing, occupying the ground floors. Evidently the scene was supposed to resemble an English town of King Arthur's mythic age.

The cool air still smelled of sweat and sunscreen and all the greasy and sugary snacks the day's visitors had consumed. Some of the street lights, fashioned to resemble flickering oil lanterns, were still burning, but the majority had been switched off. Elliott neither saw nor heard anything stirring in the shadows ahead.

"Let's press on," he said. "Remember, we're looking for a way into the service tunnels. That's where the Tremere base is."

The vampires glided forward. The street of shops led them into an open square. A double Ferris wheel towered on their right and a row of oaks bordered by a low brick wall — the edge of the Enchanted Forest of Arden, according to a sign — rose before them. A few pieces of litter, Coca-Cola cups and shiny foil hot-dog wrappers, lay on the cobblestones.

Angus stiffened. Looking around, Elliott saw that the

Justicar was staring at the trash. "What's wrong?" the Toreador asked.

"No clean-up crews," Angus replied harshly. "After the tourists go home, workers should come out to get the park ready for the next day. We haven't seen any."

"That doesn't necessarily prove anything." Pausing, Elliott sharpened his hearing to the utmost. "But I don't *hear* them, either. I think their bosses gave them all the night off. Which can only mean that somehow Durrell was expecting us."

He turned, scanning the landscape anew for any sign of hostile activity. Even so, he almost missed it: it wasn't his superhuman vision or hearing but sheer intuition that prompted him to look up at one of the gondolas hanging from the Ferris wheel. Just in time to see the man inside it aiming a rocket launcher in his direction.

Elliott jerked up his rifle and fired. The sniper lurched back against the side of the gondola. His long tube of a weapon flew from his hands and, tumbling end over end, plummeted toward the ground.

Long before it landed, Elliott was pivoting, looking for other attackers. He found them. Suddenly dark figures loomed in windows around the square. Fortunately, the actor's comrades saw them too and were already starting to shoot at them.

Elliott ran. Leaping over the low wall encircling the stand of trees, he hunkered down behind the barrier and grabbed his phone. He had a second contingent of Kindred and ghouls waiting in reserve; those who, lacking both superhuman speed and powers of invisibility, might have had difficulty sneaking up on Camelot. Now that taking the enemy by surprise was no longer a consideration, it was time to call them in. As he dialed, stray bullets streaked over his head.

THIRTY-TWO: THE REUNION

He travels fastest who travels alone.
— Proverb

For a long time, Dan couldn't think. His head was to full of the terrible beauty floating before his eyes. Too fu of pain. As the intolerable spectacle ripped at his mind, h thrashed, and his invisible bonds tightened repeatedly, s suddenly and powerfully that in other circumstances h might have worried about them cutting him or cracking h bones. Now, however, fascinated and tormented by th hyperspatial matrix, he was barely conscious of the coils.

Eventually, however, his anguished psyche groped its wa back toward rational cognition. It wasn't that the uncann spectacle before him had become any easier to bear. Rathe he supposed, his brain was making a last-ditch effort t escape the torture through intellect and ingenuity befor fleeing into howling dementia.

There *had* to be a way out of this. If he could just clos his eyes, or turn his head! He tried for perhaps th thousandth time, once again to no avail. Obsessively, agains his will, his perception fumbled at the lace-work of red an blue light, trying to comprehend its structure. A burst of agony blazed through his skull, and his self-awareness, his fragile hold on sanity, began to crumble.

"No!" he croaked. Exerting the last of his willpower, he fought to hang on. To stay focused on the prospect of escape. And somehow he succeeded, at least for the moment.

Maybe if he could get out of his bonds, he could walk or crawl backward from the matrix, loosening its hold on him with distance. Struggling to ignore his torment, to think beyond it, he considered the invisible coils. And after a while he realized something.

His bonds constricted whenever he shifted more than a fraction of an inch. But then they loosened up again. Their violent resistance prevented him from breaking them or squirming out of them rapidly, but it might not keep him from worming his way out of the end of the coil slowly, one tiny movement at a time.

He flexed his legs and dug his heels into the peculiar, only half-felt surface beneath him, straining to move with infinite care. Another flare of anguish transformed the maneuver into a spastic lurch. The bonds tightened.

No matter how many times he made the attempt, the result was always the same. The pain robbed him of the fine motor control his plan required. Unless he could somehow block out the crippling spectacle burning at the center of his vision, he was, in a real sense, going to die here, crumbling into the psychotic, cringing puppet that Tithonys required for his magical assault on Melpomene.

Alas, there seemed to be way no way to blot out the matrix. But what, he wondered abruptly, if he managed to understand it? To perceive it clearly? Tithonys obviously did, and with the enhanced vision Melpomene's vitae had given him, maybe Dan could do the same. Then, perhaps, the construct would lose its hypnotic fascination, or at least stop hurting him.

Up until now, though he hadn't been able to look away

from it, he'd been straining to do so, flinching away from the torture. If he was to have any hope of seeing it whole, he'd have to do exactly the opposite. Steeling himself, he sharpened his vision to the utmost.

A blast of pain even more devastating than those he'd already experienced wracked him. He fought to ignore it, to keep peering, analyzing, trying to grasp the relationships of the luminous planes and angles hanging in the air. Another spasm wracked him, and then another. He felt as if someone were chopping him with an ax, one that cut his flesh and spirit both.

Despite himself, he felt his resolve beginning to fail. But then something changed inside his mind, like a lamp coming on in a darkened room. The glowing matrix altered without altering, reminding him of the optical illusions that had interested him as a kid, like the drawing that was a pretty young girl or a hook-nosed old woman, depending on how you looked at it.

As he grasped the true shape of the hyperspatial construct, his pain vanished. Now only the matrix's loveliness remained, more compelling than ever because he recognized the five-dimensional symmetry that produced it. He gazed at it raptly, drinking it in, until it finally released him.

His mouth tasted of his own blood, and his lower lip stung. He realized that at some point during his ordeal he'd unconsciously extended his fangs and cut himself. Scowling at the discomfort, petty though it was compared to what he'd just undergone, he tried again to inch his way out of his restraints.

The process seemed to take a long time. Periodically he moved too aggressively, and the coils constricted. Telling himself repeatedly to take it easy, praying that Tithonys wouldn't return for a while yet, he eventually managed to work his upper body free. He dug his fingers into the muddy floor for leverage and yanked his legs out with one convulsive pull. The coil made a metallic clashing sound as it snapped shut on itself.

Sprawled in the muck, Dan lifted his head and looked around. The fine hairs on the back of his neck stood on end. The surface on which he'd been lying was invisible, too. Several feet away, and out of his visual range until this moment, his wallet, keys, .38 and the little antique gun he'd stolen from Wyatt's haven were hanging above the floor as if resting on an unseen shelf. Apparently Tithonys' magic was so potent that he casually hardened empty air to serve as furniture, or else cancelled the force of gravity.

Dan tried to stand, and a wave of dizziness swept over him. A pang of Hunger cramped his belly. His exertions had left him weak and famished again. He scrambled to the chubby woman, still sprawled where Tithonys had dumped her, and pressed his fingers against her carotid artery.

To his surprised delight, he found a pulse. He flung himself on top of her and buried his fangs in her neck.

He meant to spare her life, but *she* was weak, too, from having been bled once already. As he guzzled her vitae, desire and need overwhelmed him. He couldn't stop drinking until she shuddered and an ugly, rattling sound came out of her throat.

Refreshed and slightly ashamed of his murderous gluttony, his torn lip tingling as it healed, he sprang to his feet, grabbed his possessions off the invisible ledge, and slunk toward one of the openings in the wall. There were two sets of footprints on the floor: Tithonys' bare ones and others left by someone wearing shoes. With any luck, one of them would lead him out of the earthen tunnels. From that point, he hoped, he shouldn't have too much trouble getting out of Camelot. He only prayed that the Methuselah's magical H-bomb, or whatever the hell it was going to be, wouldn't go off until he was clear.

And then, much to his surprise, a twinge of, if not guilt,

at least uneasiness, lanced through his resolve. Did he *really* want to run away?

He scowled at his own idiocy. Of *course* he wanted to book. If he tried to interfere with Tithonys' "sacrifice," that would mean that he was still doing Melpomene's dirty work, and the very thought of that enraged him. He didn't care if Durrell's Tremere and Sinclair's Toreador got killed. Both sides had abused him in one way or another. He didn't care about kine getting massacred, either; hell, he'd just drained one himself. Even if he *had* given a damn about stopping Tithonys, he was realistic enough to comprehend that he was nowhere near powerful enough to do it alone, and since every other Kindred and ghoul in the park regarded him as an enemy, who could he get to help him?

And yet....

The man, the human, Dan had once been *would* have cared about the impending slaughter. He suspected that the undead creature he'd become might have also, if Melpomene hadn't tampered with his psyche. If he truly wanted to defy the Methuselah's efforts to control and exploit him, to be his own person again, maybe he needed to try to rekindle the empathy and the principles she'd extinguished in him, by behaving as if he still possessed them. And besides, suicidally reckless though it might be, he yearned to get even with Tithonys for torturing him.

Someone among his fellow vampires would listen to him. He'd *make* them listen. Straining his hearing, trying to make sure he wouldn't unwittingly walk up on his erstwhile captor, he followed the sets of tracks.

His caution was unnecessary. Except for small, strangely blurry creatures hissing and scuttling in the shadows, the cave appeared to be empty. Maybe Tithonys had needed to move closer to the battle to cast his spell.

The Methuselah's footprints simply ended in the middle of a chamber. But the other set led Dan to a rickety-looking wooden staircase ascending to what appeared to be a blank rectangle of concrete blocks set in the dirt wall.

Dan bounded up the steps and examined the surface, looking for another shadow-symbol or some other catch that might open a secret door. For a moment the cold stone seemed to quiver beneath his hand, but nothing else happened.

He guessed he'd have to do it the hard way. Drawing on his superhuman strength, he pressed his palms against the wall, braced himself as best he could, and shoved.

His arms and shoulders quivered with effort. The platform beneath him groaned ominously and he was afraid that it would collapse before the mortar gave. But then several of the blocks broke loose and fell outward, crashing down on the other side of the barrier. Dan sprawled forward into the breach he'd created.

Peering about, he saw that he'd opened a hole into one of the service tunnels he'd visited before. After the dim green phosphorescence of Tithonys' lair, the fluorescent lighting hurt his eyes and made him squint. Fearful that the noise he'd made would draw some potential attacker, he hastily scrambled through the breach and snatched out his .38.

After a moment he decided that, once again, he needn't have worried. He didn't hear anyone rushing toward him, nor did he hear any gunfire or other sounds of commotion echoing through the tunnels. Maybe Durrell and his men hadn't wanted to fight down here, where they might conceivably be cornered. Perhaps they'd preferred to make their stand aboveground, where they'd have more room to maneuver and, if worst came to worst, might find it possible to flee.

It didn't take long to find a stairwell to the surface. As Dan neared the door at the top he heard shooting. When he cracked it open and peeked out, the scents of gun smoke and vitae filled his nose. But no one was fighting on the section of sidewalk before him.

Wishing as he so often had that his powers of invisibility would shield him when he was in motion, he stalked out under the starry sky and toward what sounded as if it were the nearest battle. And then an assault weapon clattered, just to his left.

He reflexively leaped to one side. One of the bullets hit him anyway, shattering his knee. Somehow lurching on despite the burst of agony, he threw himself down behind the nearest available cover — a fish-and-chips stand in the shape of a miniature castle, topped by a sign that read *The Fisher King's Feast*.

"Why did you do it?" cried an anguished female voice. Laurie's voice. "We *cared* about you! We wanted you to be part of our *family!*"

Dan felt a mixture of dismay and hope. He cringed at the prospect of fighting another friend, but with luck, it wouldn't come to that. Surely he could convince Laurie of the peril that Tithonys represented far more easily than he could persuade a stranger. "I'm sorry about Wyatt!" he called. "But you have to listen to me. We're all in terrible danger!"

"Because you brought the enemy here!" she shouted back. "To the anarch *base!*" Dan thought he could see her now, a vague black shape in the dark, but he wasn't positive. At the moment the fierce pain of his wound was clouding even his superhuman senses.

"Durrell and his people aren't anarchs," he said. "They're rogue Tremere. He and Wyatt lied to you about everything. There are these two Methuselahs —"

"Shut up!" she screamed. "I'm not gullible enough for you to con me this time! You murdered my friend, I've caught you escaping, and now I'm going to *get* you!" She charged out of the darkness, her flapping bellbottoms, Yellow-Submarine T-shirt and leather peace-symbol pendant an ironic contrast to her fiery eyes, bared fangs and the AK-47 blazing in her hands.

Dan couldn't run from her: his leg was still healing. Nor would his powers of concealment protect him when she'd already pinpointed his location. All he could do was fire back.

She lurched backward, and the gun flew from her grasp. She collapsed and lay motionless on the asphalt. Clutching the wall of the fast-food stand, Dan dragged himself to his feet and limped painfully forward. After a moment he flinched and averted his eyes.

He hadn't meant to destroy her, just incapacitate her, but his pain, or perhaps simple bad luck, had spoiled his aim. One of his bullets had penetrated the center of her forehead and splashed her brains out of the back of her skull. Some Kindred could recover even from a wound as ghastly as that, but he could see that she wasn't one of them. She hadn't had the necessary stamina.

His eyes stinging, shedding tears of blood, he waited for his knee to finish repairing itself. When the pain in his leg disappeared, he picked up her assault rifle and skulked on.

THIRTY-THREE: FORSAKEN

*And he answered and said, He that dippeth his hand with
me in the dish, the same shall betray me.*
— Matthew 26:23

Driven from their last redoubt, Durrell and his
bodyguards — a Tremere, a Caitiff anarch and a ghoul —
pounded down a cobblestone lane looking for a new refuge.
As they passed beneath a flickering crimson lantern it
dashed their shadows onto the ground.

Actually, the elder magus and his soldiers were racing
by any number of shops and enclosed rides which might have
sheltered them. But Durrell wanted to stay outdoors, where
he could see more of what was going on. It gave him the
feeling of being in control.

In his present straits, he *needed* that feeling, even though
he recognized that it was an illusion. Because he hadn't had
time to position and instruct his forces properly, the battle
had turned out to be every bit as chaotic as he'd feared,
disintegrating into countless small but deadly confrontations
scattered throughout the park. He and his officers had
cellular phones for communication, but as the enemy struck
savagely, repeatedly, unpredictably, and as more and more
of his troops lapsed into frenzy, it had become impossible to

maintain any semblance of overall direction. At this point, the only thing he was certain of was that his army was being gradually overwhelmed by superior numbers.

Where was Tithonys? Where was the awesome sorcery that was supposed to turn the tide? Durrell peered about for any sign that some great work of magic was rising to his aid, but could only see the mundane flashes of guns and explosions flickering in the murky distance.

He wondered if the Methuselah had abandoned him. If he, who'd worked so deviously to ruin Roger Phillips and his minions, had been himself deceived. The suspicion was so excruciating that he struggled to expel it from his mind.

The Caitiff, a coarse-featured, redheaded woman with a perpetually swollen belly — evidently possessed of a perverse sense of humor, her sire had embraced her when she was pregnant — lurched to a halt and pointed. "There!"

Startled, Durrell spun around. "What?" he barked.

"That pen," she replied. "Isn't it what you wanted, a place where we'll have cover and be able to see in all directions?"

He saw she was referring to Elfland. The attraction, intended specifically for small children, featured miniature cottages and giant concrete mushrooms, lawn-jockey-sized statues of butterfly-winged fairies and pipe-smoking leprechauns, all surrounded by a four-foot version of Camelot's usual phony castle wall. "Yes," he said tersely, "it'll do. Come on."

He and his minions ran to the enclosure. The three Kindred vaulted the wall, and the ghoul, a shaven-headed youth with a pentagram tattooed on his cheek, ducked through the child-sized gate. "Spread out," said Durrell. "I want one of you watching north, one east, and one south." His warriors scurried away.

The master magus looked again for some indication that Tithonys was about to reach out and start killing the enemy, soon, while some of Camelot's defenders were left alive. He still couldn't detect any. Fighting to quash a fresh wave of doubt, he jerked his phone off his belt. Maybe this time more of his lieutenants would answer. Maybe he could gather some useful intelligence, something that would actually enable him to organize his forces. Maybe —

A winged shadow with glowing scarlet eyes swooped over his head.

Durrell pivoted, firing his Uzi wildly, but didn't hit anything. The flying creature — the *bat*, he realized, the *shapeshifter* — had already disappeared. Startled by the racket, crying out, the magus' trio of warriors jerked around.

"It's Angus!" Durrell said. He was all but certain he was correct. As far as he knew, the Justicar was the only Gangrel involved in this fiasco, and one of the few members of the enemy army powerful enough to contemplate confronting the Tremere elder and his bodyguards by himself. "I think he landed in the center of the enclosure!"

"How right you are," rumbled Angus' voice, sounding grimly amused. Suddenly, moving as fast as any Toreador or Brujah, the bearded giant popped up from behind a pixie-sized gingerbread mansion with candy-cane trim and fired his automatic rifle at the ghoul. The servant flew off his feet. By the time the remaining defenders brought their own guns to bear, the Justicar had ducked from sight again.

"Move in!" Durrell cried. His minions hesitated, and he repeated the command using the coercive power of his voice and glare. "Do it! Damn it, we've got him surrounded!"

This time they edged forward. Sharpening his senses to the utmost, Durrell studied the whimsical shapes — lollipop trees, thatch-roofed cottages scarcely larger than ostentatious tombstones, dwarves playing baseball, and a hollow stump with spindly minarets rising from its center — that sprouted from the ground before him. Surely a Kindred as huge as Angus couldn't hide among such objects for long.

From the corner of his eye, the magus glimpsed

something gray, something that *was* built low enough to the ground to conceal itself easily, streaking across the gap between two of the huts. Turning, he fired, but the shape was already gone.

The Caitiff screamed. Lurching around again, Durrell saw a huge wolf with shining crimson eyes spring at the woman and carry her down behind a row of vendors' stalls in a goblin market. Her severed head tumbled over the barrier a second later.

Though Durrell couldn't see Angus and didn't have a shot at him, at this moment he knew his approximate location, and thus was able to cast a spell at him. Hastily he gestured and jabbered the three syllables that triggered the effect.

An instant later, despite his anxiety, he felt a rush of pleasure and vitality. The magic had stolen a portion of Angus' blood and transferred it into his own system. He could tell that the spell hadn't siphoned enough to incapacitate his opponent, but at least it had hurt him.

Fangs bared and assault rifle leveled, the other Tremere, a gray-haired, fortyish-looking vampire with a saber sheathed at his hip, charged the fairy marketplace. Reaching a position from which he could see Angus' last known location, he shouted, "He's moved on, Sebastian!"

"Not very far," Angus' bass voice replied. In human form again, or nearly so, he shot up behind the junior magus and grabbed his throat in his taloned hands.

The Tremere dropped his gun and frantically groped over his shoulder. Durrell understood what his clan brother was attempting. If he could grab his attacker, he could blast him with magic. Evidently understanding the same thing, Angus kept knocking away and otherwise avoiding his arm.

Durrell fired. The other Tremere was pretty much shielding Angus, but it would be worth hurting or even destroying the younger magus if he could cripple the attacker. Bullets hammered into the gray-haired vampire's chest, and then the Uzi clicked, its magazine empty.

Angus' claws ripped the younger Tremere's head off. The corpse fell, pungent vitae flowing from the raw stump between its shoulders. Its slayer was bleeding, too, from the bullets that had driven through the magus' body to strike his own, but he didn't seem to feel the wounds. Pulling a stake out of his belt, leering at Durrell, he said, "You, Warlock, I'm taking alive. Sinclair and his people want to talk to you."

For some reason, the smug self-assurance in Angus' tone reminded Durrell of Tithonys. It roused the Beast and swept the fear out of his mind. By God, he was a *sorcerer,* a master of the unseen forces governing the universe. He'd *earned* his powers through centuries of study and perilous experimentation. In contrast, the Gangrel, however much brute strength he commanded, had received his abilities automatically, simply as a result of his transformation. Like most Kindred, he was little better than the undisciplined savage, the *animal,* he so resembled.

Durrell realized he didn't have time to reload the Uzi. With his supernatural speed, Angus would be on top of him before he could ram a new clip into the gun. But that was all right. He wanted to humble the arrogant Gangrel with his wizardry. He should have relied on it from the start. "Come on then," he said, tossing aside the firearm. "Take me if you can!"

Angus hurtled forward. Striving to exert every ounce of psychic might at his disposal, Durrell cast another spell. A statue of a pointy-eared gnome playing an accordion wrenched itself loose from its base, streaked through the air and slammed into the Gangrel's shins, tripping him. Angus fell, but instantly leapt back to his feet.

Still straining, feeling the vitae in his system burn to fuel his magic, Durrell levitated an entire miniature cottage and slammed it down on Angus' head. The Justicar sprawled back onto the path. With a murmured phrase and a flick of his fingers, the Tremere drained another portion of the other vampire's vitae.

He expected that the second theft, combined with the purely physical punishment Angus had taken, would put the giant down for good. It didn't. His gashed scalp streaming blood, the Justicar scrambled to his feet and lunged into striking range. He poised the stake for a thrust at Durrell's heart.

Staring into his opponent's fiery eyes, Durrell said, "*Stop!*" The command *didn't* stop Angus, but he faltered for a split second, affording the magus enough time to sidestep the attack, grab the Gangrel's forearm, and work yet another charm.

Angus stumbled as his blood began to boil. Releasing him, Durrell stepped nimbly backward, certain that this final injury would finish the shapeshifter off. He was looking forward to watching the meddler die.

Recovering his balance, his ivory skin blistering and crisping, Angus whirled. His empty hand shot out and grabbed Durrell's forearm, the talons tearing agonizingly into the Tremere's flesh. Then he yanked the magus forward. Onto the stake.

Durrell felt a terrible stab of pain, and then a wave of weakness flowed through his muscles. He slumped in Angus' arms, utterly paralyzed. The fire raging inside the Gangrel's flesh seared his own body.

Angus swayed, nearly dumping both of them on the ground. "I need blood," the huge man croaked. "In all these centuries I've always shunned diablerie, until tonight. Another offense I lay at your door, you Warlock son of a bitch." He buried his fangs in Durrell's throat.

THIRTY-FOUR: PERSUASION

No more tears now; I will think upon revenge.
— Mary Queen of Scots

His forearm throbbing, Dan prowled through the shadows. Fortunately the last gunman's bullet had only creased him, and after a few more steps, the wound closed and the pain faded. Somewhere in the darkness automatic weapons rattled, and a woman screamed.

Dan reflected sourly that in other circumstances he might have relished the carnage unfolding all around him. After three decades of slights, rebuffs and aching loneliness, he could have enjoyed trading shots with the arrogant Kindred of the Camarilla, or just sitting back and watching as they butchered each other.

But not now, not when he knew that Tithonys was preparing his death magic. Now the martial fervor of Dan's fellow vampires, the rage that prompted them to start blasting away at him as soon as he made his presence known, that kept them from *listening*, filled him with anguished frustration.

Once again he felt the urge simply to run away and save himself, but he knew he wouldn't heed it. He'd made his decision and he was going to stick to it, no matter what the cost.

His mother had always told him he was stubborn. He paused for a moment, wondering when he'd last thought of her, if she was even still alive, and then his hypersensitive hearing caught the sound of soft, stealthy footfalls coming around the next bend in the lane.

Dan stepped into a shadowy doorway between two display windows full of dolls that looked like Medieval Barbie and Ken. A moment later Elliott Sinclair glided around the corner, darting glances this way and that, fangs bared, all alone. Evidently the battle was so fierce and so chaotic that even a general could find himself separated from the rest of his army. Dan noted with a fleeting twinge of amusement that the foppish Toreador's starched and ironed fatigues fit perfectly, as if he'd had them custom-tailored.

Dan was still wondering how best to approach Sinclair when the elder whirled with blinding speed. His senses, which were evidently at least as keen as Dan's, had penetrated the outcast's shield of invisibility. The muzzle of the silver-haired Toreador's AR-18 swung into line.

Dan's instincts screamed for him to lift his own rifle and defend himself — he couldn't help anybody if he let Sinclair blow him apart! Instead he let the weapon fall from his hands.

Sinclair's gun blazed. Two bullets slammed Dan back against the door behind him, rattling the glass. But then, as he'd hoped, Prince Roger's lieutenant stopped firing.

"Don't hurt me," Dan rasped, his voice thick with pain. "I'm on your side."

"The hell you say," Sinclair replied. "Don't you think I remember your face, Murdock? You diabolized one of Gunter Schmidt's people. You fought against Judy and her Brujah by the Gardens. You *killed* one of them."

"It wasn't like you think," Dan replied, struggling

desperately to think of a way to convince the actor that he was telling the truth. His story was too damn complicated, to say nothing of unlikely. "I didn't mean to kill the Brujah. When I worked against your people, it was an act to help me infiltrate Durrell's conspiracy."

Sinclair scowled. "That's ridiculous."

"No, it's not!" Dan said. A bullet slowly slid from his chest, then fell, as his clenching, regenerating flesh expelled it. But even though he was healing, he knew it would be a while longer before he'd have a snowball's chance in hell against Sinclair, even if the older vampire were fool enough to turn his gun aside. "There are other people involved in this war, people you don't know about! I was working for one of them!"

Sinclair frowned. Dan realized that his words had hit home. However he had come by the knowledge, the Toreador *did* know that there was more to the campaign against Sarasota than was apparent on the surface. "Keep talking," the actor said.

"There are these two Methuselahs," said Dan. "You and Roger Phillips are descended from one of them, named Melpomene, and she cares about you and your art. The other one, Tithonys, hates her, and he sicced Durrell on you to hurt her."

His brow furrowed, Sinclair hesitated, evidently mulling over what Dan had told him. After a moment he said, "That's… interesting. I want to hear all about it. But first I have a battle to fight."

"You don't understand!" said Dan. His chest throbbed as the other bullet slid out of it. "Tithonys doesn't care who wins your little war anymore, as long as it's as bloody as possible. He's a magician, like the Warlocks only better, and when enough Kindred have been destroyed, he's going to tap into some kind of energy the deaths will create and use it to slaughter everyone for miles around as a sacrifice to the devil. So Satan will give him the power he needs to kill Melpomene.

"You've got to order your people to stop fighting. That'll derail his ritual."

Sinclair laughed. "Do you know, you actually had me going for a moment there. You're good at managing your face and aura both; you should have gone on the stage. But no, I'm not going to pull back my troops on the basis of a lie as preposterous as that. I'm not sure, but I believe we're winning. Apparently you think so, too. Goodbye, Mr. Murdock." He shouldered his rifle and sighted down the barrel.

Dan's arm shuddered with the desperate impulse to make a grab for the .38 hidden under his tattered, blood-encrusted jacket. Instead he cried, "Tithonys killed your *wife!*"

Sinclair gaped at him. "*What?*"

"The guy murdered your wife," Dan repeated. "These Methuselahs set up schemes that take years to come together. Tithonys decided to make war on Sarasota a long time ago. Part of the idea was that if he drove Prince Roger nuts, and his second-in-command was crippled with grief, there wouldn't be any effective leadership: the domain would fall apart in nothing flat. And so he had somebody whack her."

"That *would* explain why the witch hunters picked on Mary," Sinclair murmured, more to himself than to Dan. "I could never understand, why *her*, out of all the Kindred in the region?" His tone, and his gaze, hardened once again. "But I only have your word for this."

"Do you think I'd try to sell you such a weird story if it *weren't* true?" Dan replied. "Do you think it would even occur to me to mention your wife? Why would a social reject like me know anything about your personal problems? Look, if you don't believe me, fine, gun me down and get on with your war. But you'll be letting Mary's *real* murderer walk away. You'll be letting him kill you, too, and all your buddies. You'll be letting him *win!*"

Sinclair glared at him for another moment, then turned the muzzle of his assault rifle to the side. "If you've lied to me, you're going to suffer for a very long time before you meet the true death."

"Whatever," Dan said. "Just pull your people back."

The Toreador shook his head. "I can't. They're scattered over the entire park. Most of them don't have phones, some are no doubt in frenzy, and others would probably have difficulty disengaging themselves from their current situations even if they knew they should. Besides, for all we know, enough of us have *already* died to fuel Tithonys' conjuration. He may be reciting it even as we speak. Our only hope is to find him and stop him."

Dan felt a cold pang of terror even though, deep down, he'd known the situation would come to this. "You have no idea how tough this guy is."

Sinclair shrugged. "Perhaps I do. I've heard stories about Methuselahs. But I don't see that we have any option but to go after him." He smiled savagely. "Not that I truly want another option, of course. We don't have time to round up many reinforcements, but we'd be fools if we didn't try to link up with Angus the Justicar. He's almost certainly the most powerful fighter on my side." The actor took out his cellular phone and punched in a number.

After a moment a deep voice rumbled out of the instrument. With his superhuman hearing, Dan could hear it clearly: "Yes?"

"It's Elliott," said the Toreador tersely. "We've—"

"Well, hello," the Justicar boomed. "I just staked our friend Durrell. It looks to me as if we're winning this—"

"Listen to me!" Sinclair rapped, exerting his supernatural powers of influence. The effect rocked Dan back a step even though he wasn't the target. "I've met someone who tells me we're in trouble. Supposedly Durrell was working for an ancient Kindred, who's also in the park—"

"Oh, *shit!*" Angus exclaimed.

Sinclair grimaced. "I take it that you knew all along that there were Methuselahs involved in this affair."

"Where are you?" Angus said.

Sinclair looked around. "On Tennyson Lane. One of the streets of gift shops that run off—"

"I remember where it is from the map. I'm not far away. Stay put until I get there." The phone clicked, then droned a dial tone.

Sinclair gave Dan a sour smile. "All right, *now* I believe you," he said.

THIRTY-FIVE: END GAME

*And if any mischief follow, then thou shalt give life
for life, eye for eye, tooth for tooth, hand for hand, foot
for foot, burning for burning, wound for wound, stripe for
stripe.*

— Exodus 21:23-25

Elliott strode through the dark, his senses honed, peering
for any sign of the Methuselah. Beside him his two
companions, both clad in bloody, pungent, perforated
clothing, were presumably doing the same. Angus' eyes
glowed crimson.

The Toreador kept thinking that he ought to be
frightened if he was about to battle a primordial vampire
powerful enough to snuff out thousands of lives at once. Yet
he wasn't. The sight and smell of Mary's rotting body and
severed head filled his mind. The knowledge that there was
still something to be done about it, a retribution to be
exacted, filled him with a kind of feverish joy.

But he could tell that Angus and Murdock — or Dan, as
the Caitiff had asked his comrades to call him — *were* afraid.

Their faces and voices concealed the fact well enough, but Elliott could see the telltale wisps of orange in their auras.

"I never heard of a Kindred rising from the true death," the giant Gangrel rumbled to Dan, who'd just told him his story. "I'd *like* to think that the man you met is some other Methuselah who has assumed Tithonys' identity to rattle Melpomene. The problem with that notion is that, as far as we know, he never tried to *tell* her he was Tithonys; besides which, the description you give fits the vampire I knew. If he *has* come back, then God help us."

Seeking to hearten his allies, allowing a touch of his preternatural charisma to enrich his voice, Elliott said, "If he is Tithonys, I find that encouraging. If you destroyed him once, we can kill him again."

"When we fought him in Normandy," Angus replied glumly, "he was starving and had just been maimed in a brawl with a pack of Lupines. There was one of him and seven of us, including Melpomene herself. Even so, our side lost two Kindred before the fight was over." A shadowy figure with a rapid heartbeat and a shotgun in its hands scurried through the darkness ahead. The Gangrel lifted his assault rifle, but the ghoul strode on across the mouth of the lane and out of sight without so much as glancing in the vampires' direction. Elliott wondered fleetingly which side this particular servant was on.

"Maybe Melpomene will show up to help us now," the Toreador said, aware that it didn't seem likely. He'd already tried to contact the female Methuselah using the phone number she'd given Dan, only to discover that it was no longer in service.

Dan laughed bitterly. "I told you how she abandoned me. I guarantee you, she won't risk her own neck."

"I agree," Angus said. "In France, with Tithonys crippled, her safety was all but assured. Even so she hung back until my friends and I wore him down, letting us bear the brunt of his attacks. No, we won't see her here tonight." He gave Elliott an ironic smile. "Sound pretty scared, don't we? Well, we have a right to be, as you'll find out soon enough. But don't worry, we'll stick. The three of us will nail the bastard somehow." He squeezed Elliott's shoulder with one huge, taloned, blood-encrusted hand.

Elliott repressed a reflexive wince at the thought of what the claws and the filth could do to his shirt. He smiled back at Angus. "I know we will," he said. "I just wish we knew where to look for him. The park is too damn big."

"I think he might be somewhere high and centrally located," Angus replied thoughtfully, "where he can see what's going on. That would help him judge when enough Kindred have died to power up his magic. And sometimes sorcerers like to perform their rituals under the open sky. You two keep searching down here, and I'll hunt from the air." He lifted his arms and they melted into dark, membranous wings. Transformed into a huge black bat, he soared up into the night, vanishing behind the gabled roof of a mock medieval tavern an instant later.

Elliott and Dan stalked on. Guns barked and rattled in the distance. After another minute, the Toreador glimpsed smears of green and silver light hanging in the sky above the flat roof of a white stone structure resembling the Tower of London.

The smudges of glow were so faint that Elliott had to squint for a moment to be certain he was actually seeing them. He doubted that any being with vision less keen than his own would perceive them at all. After a few seconds a twinge of pain, like the beginnings of the headaches from which he'd sometimes suffered when he was breathing, jabbed between his eyes. There was something indefinably *wrong* with the masses of phosphorescence, something that made it painful to look at them too closely.

Elliott pointed. "See that?" he asked.

Dan peered in the direction he was indicating. "No. What are you talking — wait. Yeah, I do see it, sort of. It's more hyperdimensional stuff!"

"Does that mean you think Tithonys is on that rooftop?" Elliott asked.

"Yeah."

"So do I. Let's hope that Angus spots him, too. Come on!" Sprinting, they raced toward the lights. Elliott kept drawing ahead of Dan, then having to force himself to slow down and let the Caitiff catch up. Frantic as the actor was to come to grips with Tithonys, he realized that he couldn't destroy the Methuselah by himself.

As the two Kindred neared their destination, Elliott saw that the pale, boxlike tower rose in the center of an open plaza. There was no structure of comparable height, from which he and Dan might have sniped at Tithonys, anywhere nearby. Even if the actor *hadn't* yearned to confront the architect of Mary's murder face to face, he wouldn't have had another choice.

Elliott reached the entrance several strides ahead of his companion, only to discover it locked. He knew from Judy's account just how strong Dan was. It would have made sense to let him break the door down. But the Toreador was too impatient; the Beast was snarling and pacing in his soul. He whirled, lashing out with a spinning back kick, and the panel burst open with a crash.

Beyond the threshold was a large, dimly lit chamber hung with heraldic banners and filled with steel railings which defined a path running back and forth and ultimately through an arch in the far wall. A sign posted halfway along the twisting aisle read, *Forty-five Minute Wait from this Point*. The air had a distinctive hot-metal smell that Elliott associated with trains and other vehicles that ran on tracks.

Across the room, separated from the path by one of the railings, was an unobtrusive door. Elliott dashed to it and pushed it. It wouldn't move. He kicked it, but failed to break the bolt.

Dan pounded up behind him. "Let me," the younger Kindred said. He punched the door with the heel of his hand and it flew open. The boom echoed hollowly through the spaces beyond.

The service hallway on the other side of the doorway led to a stairwell. In all likelihood there was an elevator somewhere as well, but Elliott didn't feel inclined to take the time to search for it. As the two Kindred hurried up the steps, he began to hear a faint, discordant chanting in an ugly language he didn't recognize. Or perhaps *hear* wasn't the right word. The sound had a peculiar quality which made him wonder if it wasn't somehow entering his mind directly, without passing through his ears. It also incorporated lengthy periods of silence, reminding him of plainsong, of some vile choir croaking and gibbering responses to the inaudible recitation of a priest.

The resemblance jolted him. "Can you hear that?" he said, instinctively lowering his voice.

"I think so," Dan replied. He hesitated. "Is it demons?"

"I suspect it's demons chanting ritual responses to Tithonys' incantation," Elliott replied grimly. "He's already working the spell. Come on!" No longer concerned about leaving his ally behind, only about interrupting the magic before it reached its conclusion, the Toreador charged on up the steps.

Above him, wavering luminous figures and faces, even dimmer than the masses of light he'd seen floating against the sky, began to shimmer in and out of view. They hurt his eyes, too, for reasons that had nothing to do with their gross deformities, and the stench of rotten flesh and brimstone hung in the air around them. He readied his AR-18, but soon realized that the shapes couldn't harm him, though some tried: snapping at him, lashing their tentacles at him, or scrabbling at his face with three-inch claws. It was as if they hadn't quite emerged into the mundane world from whatever hell they normally inhabited. But the Toreador had a nasty suspicion that, if Tithonys concluded his ritual, they would. Doing his best to ignore the horrors, he quickened his pace yet again.

The stairs terminated in another corridor, which led in turn to a ladder. Now Elliott could hear both the infernal chorus and, murmuring down through the ceiling, the masculine voice, beautiful even when framing the grating syllables of the unknown language to which the spirits were responding. He scrambled up the steel rungs and tested the trapdoor above them. It was unlocked.

Despite the urgency of his mission, Elliott paused for one more instant to think of Mary, thus fanning his rage to a white-hot blaze. Then, drawing on every bit of his supernatural speed and agility, he surged out onto the roof and started shooting.

The naked, golden-skinned Adonis in the center of the structure of light was facing away from Elliott. He stood with his arms upraised, chanting to the ranks of phantasmal faces and shapes now blemishing the sky. The Toreador's bullets neither knocked him off balance nor marked his shoulders and back.

Tithonys completed the phrase he was intoning, then turned without apparent haste. He gave Elliott a radiant smile, half-pitying and half-amused, the kind of smile a god might give a petty sinner. A pang of trepidation stabbed through the actor's rage. He hadn't wanted to believe that the Methuselah was as powerful as Dan and Angus claimed, but now, despite his fury, he was discerning the reality firsthand.

"I'm afraid that ordinary bullets and blades don't inconvenience me anymore," Tithonys said gently. "I've grown beyond that."

Elliott dropped the AR-18 and snatched out the wooden stake sheathed at his belt. He meant to stalk forward, but the Methuselah laughed when he brandished his new weapon, and despite himself, he faltered. At that moment Dan scrambled through the trapdoor.

"Well, well," Tithonys said, "the gang's all here, all of my former darling's principal slaves. Even Angus, fluttering round and round the tower, no doubt hoping to take me by surprise. You might as well come join the party, old friend."

Angus swooped over the crenellated rampart, changing form while still in the air. By the time his paws touched the roof, he'd become an immense gray wolf with crimson eyes.

"Give it up," said Dan to Tithonys, a subtle tremor in his voice. "Since you didn't break me, you can't use me to get at Melpomene. So there's no point in killing all those people."

Elliott felt a surge of impatience. He didn't want Dan to *persuade* Tithonys to halt his sorcery. He wanted to destroy the Methuselah! And yet, for a moment, unnerved despite his hatred, he wondered if the situation *could* be resolved without a battle.

Tithonys grinned at Dan. "It's obvious you're no magus. I've rung the dinner bell, and all these spirits" — he waved a perfectly formed golden hand at the specters massing in the sky — "to say nothing of their master, my patron, would be quite upset with me if I didn't put food on the table. Besides which, you *haven't* spoiled my plans. I know *countless* ways to break you, fledgling. Nor, now that I've tasted your vitae, would I have any difficulty locating you, even if your companions managed to detain me while you fled."

Without warning, moving faster than Elliott had ever seen a Kindred move, Angus charged. Drawing on his own inhuman speed, the Toreador elder plunged after him.

The Methuselah snapped his fingers, and his handsome countenance became a gruesome mask of ridged, decaying flesh sporting a leprous snout, a lopsided slash of a mouth full of stained, jagged tusks, and the bulbous, faceted eyes of an insect. Most horribly of all, it was *on fire:* surrounded by a corona of crackling blue and yellow flame.

It was, quite simply, the most terrifying sight Elliott had ever seen. The fear he'd already been experiencing exploding into outright panic, he floundered to a halt and then recoiled. Angus did the same. They wound up cringing beside the equally frightened Dan, next to one of the ramparts. Obviously convinced that he'd rendered his would-be attackers harmless, Tithonys turned away. Lifting his arms, he resumed his incantations.

Shuddering, eyes averted from the ancient vampire, Dan tried repeatedly to edge toward the trapdoor. But he couldn't proceed in that direction without moving toward Tithonys, too, and he couldn't bring himself to do it. He'd shift his foot an inch, then snatch it back. Meanwhile, the flesh beneath Angus' gray fur flowed and bulged. It looked as if he were trying to change shape, perhaps to become a bat and fly away, but was so frightened that it was interfering with his powers.

Elliott was equally terrified, but somehow he found the strength to fight it. *The bastard murdered Mary!* he told himself. *As a ploy to get at somebody neither of us had ever even heard of! He has to pay! And the fear isn't real, just a souped-up version of a trick I can do myself.* And gradually his trembling, and his panic, abated.

Peering about, he saw that Dan was now staring at the rampart as if nerving himself for a leap over the side. Angus was flopping and writhing on the rooftop, his ears batlike and his forelegs transformed into misshapen wings, but otherwise still trapped in the body of a wolf.

Elliott grabbed Dan and jerked him off his feet; then, crouching, he seized Angus by the neck. Forcing both of his comrades to look him in the face, straining to exert every bit of his charismatic powers, he said, "You don't have to be afraid. Tithonys is playing with your minds. *Snap out of it!*"

For a moment, as they stared back at him, wild-eyed and

shivering, he was certain it hadn't worked, that his own influence wasn't potent enough to counteract the Methuselah's. Then the dread in Dan's face gave way to a furious, fang-baring snarl. Angus' useless wings began to turn back into serviceable legs. Elliott released his companions, sprang up and ran at Tithonys.

Turning swiftly, the Methuselah waved his hand.

Some instinct warned Elliott that he was in immediate peril. He dodged to one side, and a dazzling burst of azure flame exploded in the space through which he'd been about to run.

Clamping down on his reflexive dread of fire, he charged Tithonys again. With a flick of his fingers, the Methuselah conjured another blast. As before, only Elliott's superhuman agility saved him from incineration. At the same instant, Angus rushed the ancient vampire, who, whirling, gestured with his other hand. The Gangrel sprang to the side, but not far enough. The new explosion caught him in midair, turning into his leap into a helpless tumble and setting his coat ablaze.

From the corner of his eye, Elliott saw Dan pointing a tiny antique pistol, and felt a surge of disgust. Evidently the clanless idiot hadn't heard Tithonys say that metal weapons couldn't hurt him. Elliott wished he could shout the information, but there was no time for that or anything but trying to dart into striking range of his foe.

The Toreador lunged. Moving almost as quickly, Tithonys wheeled back in his attacker's direction. Now that Angus was out of the fight, *both* of the Methuselah's hands were poised to hurl fire at Elliott, who realized to his horror that it would likely be nearly impossible to dodge two blasts at once.

Dan's pistol coughed. Tithonys staggered and clasped his shoulder. Waves of darkness like concentric ripples created by a stone tossed into inky water pulsed from the wound through the rest of his body. Exulting, taking full advantage of the Methuselah's distraction, Elliott sprang at him and thrust the stake at his heart.

Despite his distress, Tithonys managed to twist his body aside. Instead of plunging deep into his chest, Elliott's weapon gouged a long, shallow furrow. He started to yank it back for another try, but the vampire in the illusory mask — up this close, Elliott could feel that the flames shrouding his enemy's head shed no heat — slapped it out of his hand. The stake rolled clattering across the roof.

No problem, Elliott thought savagely. *My teeth and hands will do just as well.* Kicking and striking, he threw himself at Tithonys. Behind the Methuselah he glimpsed Angus rolling over and over in an effort to extinguish his burning pelt, and Dan fumbling with the pistol, trying to reload it.

Tithonys blocked Elliott's first punch with one arm and gestured at Dan with the other. Fortunately, either because of the dark energy streaming through his flesh or because the Toreador was distracting him, his aim was off. The blue fireball exploded six feet to the side of Dan, not right on top of him. Nevertheless it staggered him, and two bullets flew from his hands.

Elliott kicked Tithonys in the knee without so much as knocking him off balance, then thrust his stiffened fingers at the Methuselah's eyes, or rather at where he believed the true eyes behind the fiery mask should be. He was high by perhaps an inch, feeling his fingertips glance along the ancient Kindred's brow. Then Tithonys grabbed him by the wrist.

The shadowy ripples now fading from his flesh, the Methuselah squeezed Elliott's arm with bone-crushing force. An excruciating pain burned into the Toreador's flesh as if Tithonys' fingers were white hot, or sweating nitric acid.

Screaming, Elliott tried to twist his arm free, but he couldn't break Tithonys' grip. And so, lapsing at last into utter frenzy, his agony fueling his rage, he grappled with the other vampire, biting madly at his golden skin.

Tithonys snapped at him, too, shredding Elliott's shirt and the pale throat and shoulder beneath. At the same time his hands clutched at the Toreador's body, searing and dissolving whatever flesh they touched. Abruptly he bulled Elliott backward. Feeling one of the crenellations slam into his back, the maddened actor realized dimly that his opponent was about to throw him off the roof. He struggled again to break the Methuselah's grip, but to no avail.

Then Tithonys fell onto the rooftop, dragging Elliott down with him. Reeking of charred flesh and hair, his hide a patchwork of burn marks, Angus savaged the Methuselah; evidently he'd charged up behind his ancient enemy and torn his legs out from under him.

Elliott and the Justicar ripped at Tithonys for another second and then, with one convulsive, blindingly fast movement, the Methuselah grabbed each of them by the throat. The Toreador struggled frantically, but couldn't break his opponent's grip; he could see that Angus wasn't faring any better. As Tithonys' fingers ate their way into his flesh, he realized that in less than a minute they were going to burn his head off.

Unable to match the primordial vampire's strength, Elliott glared at him, exerting his charismatic powers, trying to jolt Tithonys with a spasm of fear, praying that it would startle him into loosening his grip. That didn't work either.

Dan appeared above the thrashing combatants. Perhaps he hadn't been able to find the bullets he'd dropped, because the little gun was nowhere in sight. Instead, he had Elliott's stake, and now, grasping it in both hands, moving in slow motion compared to the other three preternaturally agile Kindred, he swung it over his head.

Elliott felt Tithonys tense, preparing to wrench himself from beneath the attack. *No!* the Toreador thought. Now ignoring both his agony and the prospect of his imminent destruction, he clutched at the Methuselah, struggling to immobilize him.

The stake hurtled down and punched into the center of Tithonys' chest. Dan's gargantuan strength buried nearly the entire length of the shaft in the ancient vampire's body. Elliott suspected that it had nailed its target to the roof.

Tithonys screamed, and his magical mask dissolved. His hands jerked away from Angus' and Elliott's ravaged necks. But impossibly, in defiance of everything the Toreador believed he knew about his own undead race, even a piece of wood through the heart didn't paralyze the Methuselah. Instead, he gripped it and began to pull it out.

Elliott grabbed Tithonys' arms and strained to wrestle his hands away from the stake. An instant later Dan did the same. Meanwhile, Angus' lupine jaws ripped at the ancient Kindred's neck.

Despite all that Elliott and Dan could do, the stake lurched upward, an inch at a time. Then Angus flowed back into the form of a bearded giant with talons and flaming eyes. On one knee, he sank his claws into the sides of Tithonys' head, then wrenched at it. Already weakened by the wounds the Gangrel had inflicted in wolf form, Tithonys' neck and spinal column simply couldn't take the punishment. Showering vitae, his head tore away from his shoulders.

Elliott glimpsed movement overhead and looked upward frantically, fearing some new threat. He beheld a gauzy form resembling Tithonys hanging in the darkness. It was only visible for a second. Then the phantoms summoned by the ritual streaked at it, swarmed over it hissing, cackling, clawing and biting, those who were unable to reach it mauling their fellows to clear a path. The Methuselah's spirit screamed, and then he, his tormentors and the structure of light his magic had erected all blinked out of sight at once.

"I've got a hunch," said Dan, an icy satisfaction in his voice, "that the son of a bitch won't come back *this* time."

Angus and Elliott slumped down on the roof and willed themselves to heal. Because their injuries were of supernatural origin, the process was slow and grueling. The Toreador's wounds were more agonizing than ever now that he didn't have the desperate fury of battle to counteract the pain, but his heart was full of the savage joy of vengeance. He wondered vaguely why he hadn't felt this exhilaration years ago, when he'd butchered the witch hunters. Perhaps, somehow, he'd sensed even then that the mortal fanatics were only pawns.

Even as the vampires' flesh repaired itself, Tithonys' perfect body decayed, more rapidly than any Kindred corpse Elliott had ever seen. After a few moments the stake slumped sideways, because there was no material in the Methuselah's crumbling chest sufficiently solid to hold it upright. Soon nothing remained but a shapeless mound of dust, sifting away in the cool night breeze.

Moving stiffly, his eyes no longer red, Angus retracted his claws. Reaching under the singed and bloody remnants of his beard, he gingerly fingered his neck. Evidently deciding that it had healed sufficiently for speech, he looked at Dan and rasped, "You should've told us that you had magic bullets. It might have helped our morale."

"I didn't know they were magic," the Caitiff replied. "I just hoped they were. There are a lot of things I didn't have time to tell you."

Angus grinned. "I'll bet."

Elliott heard shots in the distance, a reminder that the war wasn't over even now. He wished he could simply lie on the rooftop and rest, recover, revel in the fact of his revenge, but it was out of the question. He had to tend to his command. His throat raw and aching, partly from his burns and partly from renewed Hunger, his own voice a broken whisper like Angus', he said, "We should go feed. And then wrap this operation up."

"I'm not going to help you kill any more Kindred," Dan said somberly. "I'm sick of it. But I can tell you where Tithonys buried his voodoo doll or whatever it is he used to make Prince Roger crazy. Maybe if you destroy it he'll get well."

EPILOGUE: PARTINGS

Life's too short for chess.
— Henry James Byron, *Our Boys*

The moon and stars shone brightly from a black, cloudless sky. The hissing waves gleamed as they crumbled into foam. Nature was beautiful tonight, more beautiful than Dan could have imagined before Melpomene's vitae had opened his eyes. Yet he found his gaze drawn, not to the heavens or the Gulf, but to the mortals on the beach: to the round-shouldered, shuffling old man walking a runny-eyed dachshund; the pair of giggling teenagers necking on a blanket; the three big-bellied anglers lumbering toward the end of the fishing pier.

After their victory over the rogue Tremere, the Kindred of Sarasota had forged and planted evidence implicating one of Durrell's captured ghouls in the Dracula murders. Forcing the unfortunate prisoner to write a confession in the form of a suicide note, they had hanged him in his apartment. Now the local humans were venturing out at night again, and ridiculing anyone who'd dared to suggest that there were any such things as vampires. Dan rather wished he had the luxury of sharing their disbelief.

He wondered if Melpomene truly had summoned him here tonight. Shortly after sunset he'd *thought* he sensed a psychic call, but he supposed it could have been his imagination. At any rate, he'd know soon enough. He walked on down the beach, away from the mortals and toward the unfinished condominium and the spot where he and the Methuselah had consummated their bargain.

Her pale figure emerged from the darkness abruptly, as if she'd stepped through a doorway in the air, but he could tell that she was present in body as well as spirit. He could smell the sweet, exotic scent of her flesh, and her long, black hair and gauzy gown stirred with the salty breeze gusting in from the sea.

As usual Dan felt the tug of her supernatural grace and charm, but tonight the sensation was superficial; it didn't reach into his heart. He was acutely conscious of the cold, hard weight of Wyatt's little gun weighing down his pocket. After the fight with Tithonys he'd recovered the two remaining magic bullets, but now that the opportunity to use them was at hand, he realized he wasn't going to do it. Not merely because he knew that, without Elliott and Angus to back him up, his chances of destroying a second Methuselah were pretty close to zip. Angry as he was, he was sick of fighting.

"I suppose you'd like an apology," Melpomene said softly, "and an explanation."

He snorted. "For when you Embraced, cursed and abandoned me thirty years ago, or for when you took the disk and left me to die the other night?"

"Both, I suppose," she replied, "but let's begin with the latter. It would have taken me several minutes to transport an object as large as you into my presence if, indeed, it could have been managed at all, and during that time my spirit would have been vulnerable to an enemy's magic. When I touched your prize, my clairvoyance revealed that Durrell was working for Tithonys, and that my ancient foe was nearby. After that, I was simply too terrified to take the risk. I'm sorry. I can see that you despise me now, and I don't blame you." Her lower lip trembled, and a crimson tear slid from her lustrous eye.

She looked so ashamed, so wretched, that Dan felt an urge to forgive her, but the impulse withered in an instant. "I don't believe you," he said. "I mean, I think that even if you *hadn't* sensed Tithonys' presence, you still would have left me behind."

Melpomene sighed, and her face assumed a more genuine expression. She still looked regretful, but composed now as well. "You're right," she admitted. "Either I'm not as adept a liar as I believed, or you've inherited my intuition. I never had any intention of bringing you to me. I was never willing to linger in enemy territory for as long as the operation would take. Besides which, if I *had* summoned you, you would have found yourself in my most secret haven. No one but me will ever enter there." Out in the water, a fish jumped.

Dan shook his head. "You're a real piece of work, *Mom.*"

Melpomene's lovely mouth twisted. "Have you judged me, then? Have you ever considered how you'd answer if someone presumed to do the same to you? How would you justify yourself if an unsympathetic soul reproached you for all the mortal lives you've taken?"

"I wouldn't," the younger vampire replied. "Sometimes I can't help killing, because, thanks to you, I need blood to survive. But I don't try to con myself into believing that it isn't wrong."

"But it *isn't*," Melpomene said earnestly. "You're free to use humans as you see fit, because you're more *real* than they are. Your immortality makes you so. Mortals are born, live and die so quickly that they can hardly be considered to exist at all. But creatures like you *endure.*"

"Oh, I get it," he said dryly. "And since you Methuselahs are so much older than the average Kindred, *we're* not real compared to *you.* You're as free to jerk us around as we are to mistreat the kine."

"Ultimately," Melpomene replied, the wind spilling a lock of her raven hair across her alabaster brow, "in a certain sense, yes, that *is* what I mean. It's not that I'm cruel, or incapable of compassion, or that I think anyone should be. You know that I cherish my Toreador. But not because they're the same manner of being as myself. My *peers* are the ocean, the mountains and the first-growth forests, the great tales, songs and paintings that live forever. Manifestly, my desires, my happiness, my survival, are more important than those of more ephemeral creatures." She peered at Dan appraisingly, then sighed once more. "You just can't comprehend, can you?"

"No. I guess the problem is that I feel pretty damn real to myself. Maybe you should check back with me when I turn five thousand."

"I'd like to," she said.

"Come again?"

"If I care for Roger Phillips and Elliott Sinclair," Melpomene said, "think how much more I must love you, who are not merely my descendant but my progeny, the only childe I've made in hundreds of years. With the threat of Tithonys hanging over my head, I had no choice but to use you harshly. But now I've decided to make it up to you. Abide with me, Dan. Let me share my secrets with you. Most Kindred never *become* real. They never fathom the deepest mysteries of the world or of their own natures either, and in consequence, eventually, they perish. But *you* can live forever."

"I guess it gets lonely, being the only honest-to-God person in a world of mayflies."

"It does indeed," Melpomene said.

"Well, get used to the feeling," Dan said coldly, "just like I had to. I *would* like to learn what you have to teach, but how could I ever trust you? I'd never be anything more to you than a tool, a toy, or a pet. You just told me as much yourself." He grinned mirthlessly. "Hell, if I *did* get to five thousand, I'll bet you'd tell me that only *ten*-thousand-year-old vamps are *really* real."

The ancient Kindred studied his face for a moment and then murmured, "So be it. And if you wished to revenge yourself, know that you've grieved me." Her lips quirked upward in a sad little smile. "Despite your scorn, I'm glad that you'll part from me possessing the reward you coveted. True friends, and a place of honor in the Camarilla. Prince Roger and his followers dote on you now."

"I kind of got used to them, too," Dan said, "but I'm not staying in Sarasota. I'm going to wander for a while and see where I end up. I'll hit the road tomorrow night."

"But why?" Melpomene asked, sounding genuinely bewildered.

"For one reason: if I stuck around and got to be Roger's asshole buddy, it would mean that I took payment for killing Wyatt and Laurie, to help you win your stupid feud. And I don't want to do that. Now that I don't have magic B.O. anymore, maybe I can make friends someplace else, the way normal people do."

"You're being foolish and quixotic."

Dan shrugged.

"You must want *some* reward," Melpomene insisted. "At least let me purge the effects of my tampering from your mind. You want to recover your empathy for the humans, don't you? I can see from your aura that you do."

"Yeah," Dan said, "but I don't want you messing around in my head anymore, for any reason. Now that I know you screwed me up, I'm hoping my attitude will get better by itself. If it doesn't, I'll live with it.

"Look, here's how it is. As long as you haven't paid me anything, you still owe me. And as long as you do, maybe you won't feel like it's okay to use me in any more of your dirty little Jyhad plots and games, even if I *don't* quite exist. Maybe you'll leave me alone. And that's what I *really* want."

He wheeled and marched back up the beach. For a few strides he was glad he'd vented his resentment, and then the feeling gave way to a twinge of guilt. Perhaps he'd been lonely and frightened too often not to feel a certain pity for anyone, even a goddess, whose existence seemed dominated by the same emotions. Maybe he ought to make it clear that he didn't actually *hate* her. Finally he glanced back over his shoulder; but by that time, Melpomene was gone.

◆

Looking idly about, Elliott decided that the victory celebration was the most lavish party Roger had ever given. A horde of elders from across the continent and even Europe had turned out to partake of the festivities. Some of the lean, pallid guests were admiring the treasure trove of stolen art on display all around the grand saloon. Others were contemplating the skulls of Dracula and Durrell, exhibited with equal prominence in a display case by the main entrance. Many were murmuring together, gossiping, conspiring, exchanging witty barbs and sizing each other up. Quite a few were clustered around the prince himself, congratulating him on his recovery. Though Roger undoubtedly discerned the malice and hypocrisy that underlay many of their felicitations, he acknowledged each with impeccable grace and only the subtlest irony.

Loitering unobtrusively by the kitchen door with his arm, wounded during the raid on Camelot, in a sling, Lazlo kept a watchful eye on Roger as if expecting someone else to try to lay a curse on him, right here, tonight. Over by the bar Gunter was haranguing Walter, the hawk-faced, long-haired

Brujah whom the prince had chosen to replace Judy among the primogen. No doubt the Malkavian was attempting to forge an alliance. Beside them stood Lionel Potter, sullenly sipping vitae from a goblet, glowering as if he resented the fact that his ministrations had ultimately played no role in his illustrious patient's cure. And near the gleaming black grand piano, where a Toreador was performing a Cole Porter medley, Otis and Catherine were chatting once again. Elliott wondered if they actually *had* made peace. Maybe animosity between vampires *could* end somewhere short of the grave; though God knew, you couldn't prove it by the Methuselahs.

For his own part the actor was pleased to see the domain restored to its customary splendor. Yet he felt edgy and vaguely alienated as well, from himself as much as from the throng around him. The demands of the crisis he'd just weathered had forced him from his lethargy and despair, and even led him to a cathartic vengeance. Yet now that the emergency was over, he felt somehow hollow and incomplete, a stranger to himself, uncertain to what extent his spirit had truly healed, or whether he'd actually be able to pick up the threads of his former existence.

Across the room, Angus disengaged himself from a circle of sycophants and made his way over. Though the giant Gangrel's tuxedo was well-tailored, somehow it still looked about as natural on him as it would on a gorilla. He stuck out a hairy hand. "Good-bye, my friend."

Elliott clasped the other Kindred's powerful, callused fingers. "You're leaving?"

"Why not?" Angus replied. "Everything's back to normal, isn't it?"

Elliott nodded; with Durrell's notes in their possession, it had been easy to dismantle the last remnants of his organization and thus bring an end to the destruction of art and the legal and financial chicanery. "And a party like this is way too refined for a crude Outlander like me."

"Where are you headed?" Elliott asked.

"I haven't decided," Angus said, the gold ring in his ear gleaming in the soft glow of the sweet-smelling white candles and the crystal chandeliers. "Maybe I'll take up my Justicar duties again, or check in with my own clan, or go back to the wilderness. The only thing I'm sure of is that I'm not going down into the ground, not yet. I'm not ready to be like her."

Elliott wondered what Angus meant, but he sensed that the shapeshifter wouldn't want him to inquire. "Well, good luck, and thank you from the bottom of my heart. You saved us all."

"You're welcome," said Angus, grinning. "It was a grand hunt. It was fun."

Elliott lifted an eyebrow. "That's not the description that would have sprung to my mind." Angus laughed, gripped his shoulder and then strode out the door.

The actor lingered in the hall for another few minutes, chatting when someone spoke to him, but approaching no one himself. Gradually he came to the realization that he'd rather be alone with his thoughts. He caught Roger's eye, smiled and waved, then slipped through the exit.

Outside the Performing Arts Center the night was cool, and the breeze bore the scents of verdure and the sea. Elliott could still hear the bright melody tinkling from the piano, now muted by the building's marble facade. As he removed his car keys from his pocket the full moon caught his eye.

It was perfectly round, its radiance sublimely pure, its surface mottled with exquisite shadings, altogether more beautiful than anyone but a Toreador could appreciate. Dimly, through the haze of his rapture, he realized that now he *had* finished healing. He had his birthright back. He continued gazing skyward until one of the parking attendants hesitantly shook him out of his trance half-an-hour later. Only then did the actor realize that his cheeks were streaked with bloody tears, his shirtfront sodden with it — but for once, he didn't mind being disheveled.

THE END

RICHARD LEE BYERS BIOGRAPHY

Richard Lee Byers holds an MA in Psychology, and worked in an emergency inpatient psychiatric facility for more than ten years before he left the mental health field to become a writer.

Since then, he has written over ten novels, three of which are Young Adult titles, including *Dead Time*, *Dark Fortune*, *The Vampire's Apprentice*, and *Netherworld*.

His short fiction has appeared in numerous magazines and story collections, including four White Wolf Publishing World of Darkness Anthologies: *Dark Destiny I*, *Elric: Tales of the White Wolf*, *Death and Damnation*, and most recently, *Truth Until Paradox*.

A resident of the Tampa Bay area, the setting he uses for much of his fiction, Byers has taught Writing Horror and Dark Fantasy at the University of Tampa, and currently teaches Fiction Writing at Hillsborough Community College.

FREE VAMPIRE: THE ETERNAL STRUGGLE
CARD REDEMPTION COUPON.

THIS COUPON ENTITLES YOU TO A FREE VAMPIRE: THE ETERNAL STRUGGLE PROMOTIONAL CARD BASED UPON THIS NOVEL, **ON A DARKLING PLAIN**. HOW TO GET YOUR CARD: FILL OUT THE ORDER FORM BELOW. ENCLOSE IT WITH A S.A.S.E. (THAT'S A SELF-ADDRESSED STAMPED ENVELOPE) AND SEND IT TO:

**ON A DARKLING PLAIN CARD
WHITE WOLF, INC.
SUITE 100
780 PARK PARK NORTH BLVD.
CLARKSTON, GA 30021**

ALLOW 6-8 WEEKS FOR DELIVERY. THIS CARD IS A FREE PROMOTIONAL OFFER AND IS SUBJECT TO AVAILABILITY. REQUESTS WHICH DO NOT INCLUDE A SELF-ADDRESSED STAMPED ENVELOPE WILL NOT BE FILLED.

- - - - - - - - - - - - - -

FIRST NAME: _____ LAST NAME: _____

ADDRESS: _____

STREET: _____

CITY: _____ STATE: _____ ZIP CODE: _____

PHONE NUMBER: _____ AGE: _____

ARE YOU FAMILIAR WITH WHITE WOLF PRODUCTS? _____

HAVE YOU EVER PLAYED A WHITE WOLF GAME BEFORE? _____

IF YES, WHICH ONES? _____

_____